THE BOUNDLESS

Also by Anna Bright

The Beholder

THE BOUNDLESS

ANNA BRIGHT

An imprint of HarperCollins Publishers

Readers should be advised that this novel includes subject
matter related to forced marriage and grooming, violence
against children and child soldiers, and content that may be
triggering to readers with emetophobia. For fuller details, see
www.annabrightbooks.com/novels.

HarperTeen is an imprint of HarperCollins Publishers.

The Boundless
Copyright © 2020 by Anna Shafer
All rights reserved. Printed in the United States of America.
No part of this book may be used or reproduced in any manner whatsoever
without written permission except in the case of brief quotations embodied
in critical articles and reviews. For information address HarperCollins
Children's Books, a division of HarperCollins Publishers, 195 Broadway,
New York, NY 10007.
www.epicreads.com

Library of Congress Control Number: 2020933589
ISBN 978-0-06-284545-0

20 21 22 23 24 PC/LSCH 10 9 8 7 6 5 4 3 2 1
❖
First Edition

To Momma and Daddy, who taught me how to be kind,
and how to fight hard

SUNSET

Wie nun Rotkäppchen in den Wald kam,
begegnete ihm der Wolf.
Rotkäppchen aber wußte nicht, was das für ein böses Tier war,
und fürchtete sich nicht vor ihm.
—Rotkäppchen

. . . Just as Little Red Cap entered the wood,
a wolf met her.
Red Cap did not know what a wicked creature he was,
and was not at all afraid of him.
—*Little Red Cap*

1

THE *BEHOLDER*

A storm was building. Dark birds circled the crow's nest. Cold salt water surged around us, crashing against the *Beholder's* hull and the rocky Norsk coast at our back.

They were ill omens, all.

My stomach lurched as the ship rolled, the deck dozens of feet below me, little but mist and trembling ropes between us. Clouds hung low in the sky, gray as pewter, heavy as lead. They threatened to smother me.

Everything looked different from the crow's nest. Everything looked different in the aftermath of their deception.

When we'd left England, after everything that happened at court in Winchester, I'd been relieved to find myself aboard ship again. I'd felt safe out on the ocean, my path ahead clear, the *Beholder* my home away from home.

1

But I'd been wrong about everything. Lang was a liar, and the *Beholder* was no haven for lost girls.

I knew the truth now. With every gust of wind, every wash of water over the *Beholder*'s sides, our route would carry us farther away from my father and my home and the stepmother who had wanted me gone and toward Shvartsval'd and its tsarytsya. Toward the rebellion Lang and the rest had been seeking since before we left Potomac.

But now we traveled east on my orders. Alessandra would never have dreamed of such success when she expelled me from Potomac to search for a husband.

From this height, too, the crew looked different. It wasn't just that I'd never seen the top of Basile's head and broad shoulders before, or noticed quite how gracefully Jeanne loped across the deck; from the towering height of the crow's nest, I could keep eyes on all of them at once.

I hadn't felt I'd needed to in weeks, since I'd come to trust them.

I'd been unwise.

I leaned back against the mainmast and tried to let the salt wind soothe the betrayal that still burned in my gut. The fear that ran cold up my spine when I thought of how far I was from home. How far I had yet to go. How every moment, Asgard and Torden slipped farther behind me.

Lang stood outside Homer's quarters, hands in his pockets, chin lifted as he listened to Andersen. The older sailor was arguing with him about something, his hands waving dramatically as he tried to make his point, his gray-gold hair drifting around his thin face in the breeze. Lang settled his hands in his pockets, arching his brows at Andersen as he rattled on.

But his dark eyes darted up to me, as if they couldn't help seeking me out.

Talk to me, they seemed to plead. *Let me explain.*

Lang was my captain. My friend. The boy with the sensitive face and the wry laugh and lean, ink-covered hands, who I'd come to trust so easily. But I wasn't interested in his explanations.

He'd talked on and on after we'd left Norge the night before, justified himself and his choice to smuggle the *zǒngtǒng's* weapons to those resisting the Imperiya Yotne and waited for me to say that I understood.

On and on he'd talked. I'd said nothing.

I refused to set him at ease. I wasn't happy or comfortable; why should he be?

The crow's nest shifted beneath me. I sat up straight, tensing, then slumped again. "Cobie, you scared me."

"Well, you're scaring a lot of people. You really shouldn't be up here." Cobie glanced at me sidelong, pushing a lock of shiny, dark hair out of her eyes. "Not that I care."

"I don't care, either," I said, staring straight ahead. "What are you doing up here, anyway?" Cobie Grimm was our rigger; the maze above deck was her rightful place, and I was an interloper. But I didn't care about that now.

Cobie squinted at me. "You're aware there's a purpose to the crow's nest beyond your need for a spot to brood, right?"

"I'm not brooding," I mumbled.

"Well, you're not keeping an eye on the horizon for obstacles, either," Cobie said wryly. She arched an eyebrow. "Are you all right?"

I stared down at my hands clasped in my lap, at the ring Torden had given me. It felt heavy on my finger, but that was nothing to the weight of my heart inside my chest.

I missed Torden. I felt every mile between us, stretching taut and painful.

I was brooding.

Fury bubbled in my veins when I thought of Lang and Homer and Yu and the way they'd treated me like a bit of porcelain. Breakable, easily set on the shelf and out of the way. Entirely ornamental to their true purposes.

Torden had never treated me that way. I'd felt strong and free when he looked at me, his eyes steady as the flow of the Bilröst.

Lang hadn't so much acknowledged my fury as tried to smooth it over, tried with explanations and excuses and repeated protests to convince me I wasn't really angry with him.

"You have to understand—" Lang had begun again as I'd walked away from the helm.

"Who knew?" I'd demanded, whirling on him.

Lang had swallowed hard but lacked the good grace to look guilty. He'd eyed me carefully, long lashes shadowing his dark eyes. "Some did, some didn't."

"That's not a straight answer," I'd spat. My gaze had darted between the faces of the crew, uncertain where to land. Uncertain which of them were safe.

They stared at me, expressions strained, nothing like the

family who'd sat with me at dinners in the galley, telling stories by lamplight. Homer, who'd felt like my guardian. Vishnu and Basile and Will, who'd been so kind to me. Skop, whom I'd defended to Konge Alfödr of Norge, when he'd fallen for his ward Anya.

I'd thought he was my friend. I'd thought they all were.

And yet, there I'd stood on the deck again, feeling just as I had on the day I'd left Potomac, the water choppy enough to throw me off-balance, friendless and alone and an utter fool.

Except this time was worse. Because my place beside Torden and my place aboard the *Beholder* were homes I had chosen for myself.

They were all in ruins now.

"Say something," Lang had said, voice low and soft as moonlight. He'd drawn near to me, as if he had any right to lay a hand on my arm, to touch me like a friend.

I'd pulled away.

"I don't know what I can say to you right now that I won't regret," I'd answered tightly. I'd hardly recognized the tone of my own voice.

Out of the corner of my eye, I'd noticed a rope ladder swinging loose and uncertain from the mainmast, leading to the crow's nest. I'd stomped across the deck and taken the rope between my hands, gulping down my fear.

"Selah!" Lang had dashed after me and wrapped a hand around the rope, just higher than my shaking grip. "Selah, stop. What are you doing?"

"I need to clear my head." I'd suddenly been dying to get

away from him, dying to find a quiet space above all the noise, though my palms were growing clammy at the prospect of the climb. The crow's nest was a dizzying height above deck.

"Selah, don't be silly." Lang's cheeks had been pale as the clouds overhead, his bowed mouth shadowed by his upturned nose, his eyes dark, dark, dark.

"Silly?" I'd demanded, my anger rising. "Is that what I am? A silly girl, too occupied with falling in love at court to notice you lying and lying—"

"No!" Lang had burst out. "No, it's just not safe for you to be up there."

"Not safe?" My words had been bitter as bile. "Not safe— like sailing a powder keg across the Atlantic? Like not knowing who my crew members are really working for?" Another step toward him had put us mere inches apart. "Like navigating the English court blind while you hunted for rebels, or passing Asgard's gates not knowing my crew are smugglers?" I'd studied him, desperate for some hint of remorse in his face, but I'd found none. "I'll do a better job looking after myself, if that's the best you can do."

With that, I'd turned away from him, grasping the ladder again in my hands, and begun to climb.

"Selah!" Cobie had called from the deck. "What are you doing?"

I hadn't been able to answer her *and* climb *and* keep breathing. So I'd chosen climbing, and breathing. I'd concentrated on the rough feel of the rope between my fingers and not on the way the ladder twisted and swung in the wind blowing straight through my clothes, sharp as my own anger.

My ears had told me that all movement on deck below me had stopped. I hadn't paused to look down.

The landing at the top of the mainmast was about six feet by six feet, a square with a small lip at its edge. I'd hoisted myself up onto it, out of sight of the crew, feeling it pitch beneath me like the mist swirling in the fjord.

But the roll of the sea and the fog had been nothing to the rage churning in my stomach. To the angry tears dripping sideways across the bridge of my nose and pooling beneath my cheek as I huddled on my side.

I lay that way now, curled up toward Cobie, studying the ring on my finger. Its cluster of stones was as blue as the Bilröst and the Asgard boys' eyes, its rose-gold band the color of Torden's lashes.

I'd left him behind. Torden. The only thing I'd been sure of in months.

How I loved him. How I longed to feel his hands in mine, to feel him at my side, close as breathing.

But Asgard was at our stern, not our prow. And Torden had promises to keep. To Asgard. To his father, whose only concern was defending their home against the Imperiya Yotne. To his stepmother, who had lost one child to death and another to exile.

I had promises to keep, as well—to my crew, as they searched for the resistance, but also to Potomac and my father, whose sadness and sickness weighed constantly on my mind. I'd marked the days as they passed in the back of the book my godmother had given me before I'd left; the marching army of tick marks never failed to make my chest grow tight with worry.

Time loomed vast and substantial behind and before me. So many days, so many miles, and my father's fate still unknown.

I thought of the bones that pressed at Daddy's skin, of the tremors that ran through his limbs. Of the heaviness that had seemed to weigh on his heart for so long.

I believed he would want me to help others defend themselves. I hoped I would get home in time for him to tell me so.

Always seems to be so much noise, he'd said to me the night of the Arbor Day ball.

Only the crow's nest seemed to be above all the clamor.

"No." I shook my head. "No, I'm not all right."

Cobie wet her lips. "It won't kill you," she said. She crossed her arms and leaned against the mast, black shirt flapping in the breeze.

My head knew she was right. The fear and the pain and the emptiness: they would not be the death of me.

But the depth and the breadth and the height of my loss felt as boundless as the ocean I'd crossed to reach this place. And my heart found it hard to believe her.

2

Fat drops of rain began to fall as I climbed down from the crow's nest. My movements were clumsy as I crept toward deck, my palms still sweating a little over the rope.

I couldn't stay up top forever. But I wasn't ready to talk to the crew. I made for the galley instead and found Will soaking dried beans and kneading bread.

"Can you take this over?" he asked with no preamble as the galley door swung shut behind me. "I need to go to the store-room below." He laughed. "*Need. Knead.* Get it?"

Did Will know? I wondered.

My mind rejected the idea. Will was too comfortable, too kind. Too focused on working hard and feeding the crew, surely, to occupy himself with scheming.

But Yu was a doctor; he'd cared for me when I felt unwell. Andersen had made me paper ships and dragons, just to make me smile. They'd lied so easily. Could Will?

I huffed a laugh at him, but it sounded tense and unnatural. "You're silly. Go."

Will left me alone in the galley. Lanterns creaked from the low-beamed ceiling overhead, and dishes shifted gently in the copper sink. The smells of yeast and fat drifted on the air. I closed my eyes and tried to let them comfort me. But I couldn't help thinking of the guns and gunpowder stashed right near the flour and the salt and everything else we needed to survive.

I tied an apron around my waist, shook out my hands, and began to work the bread. As rain pattered on the galley roof, I pushed the heels of my hands into the dough, trying to stretch out the anxious knots in my neck and shoulders. I let my muscles lead, let my mind wander, drifting across the sea and across time. From my godmother to Bear to Torden to Daddy; from Fritz, my waiting suitor at Katz Castle, to the Waldleute rebels we were on our way to aid.

The galley door swung open again, feet crossing the floor in time with the thump of the dough as I worked. But it wasn't Will I saw standing over me when I looked up.

"Should I expect an end to the aerial performances anytime soon?" Lang asked.

I stiffened. Stilled.

Always more talking. He was so clever with words. I should've known he wasn't going to give me space to think.

I shook my head and resumed my work. "I'm not playing games with you, Lang."

"You're still angry at me," he said quietly. "And I don't like it."

He leaned against the counter, hands tucked in his pockets. Golden lamplight slanted across his cheeks and his upturned nose; his hair and his shoulders were spattered with rain.

I bent back toward my bread, pounding the last of the unincorporated flour and salt into the dough, wincing as the salt stung a shallow scrape on my wrist.

Lang passed me a damp cloth. I didn't look at him as I took it.

"You have to accept the consequences of your choices, Lang," I said, wiping my smarting skin. "I'm angry at you, and I don't trust you, and it's because of your own decisions."

He made a noise of frustration. "Come on, Selah."

"No, *you* come on," I snapped. I thought of Daddy, all patience, all gentle listening. Of Torden, of the night he'd told me he couldn't follow me back to Potomac. Of how he'd presented me the truth and then waited quietly while I decided what to do with it. "You think the answer to everything is words and words and more words. You can't wait even a day while I figure out how to cope with this, you're so obsessed with your own agenda."

"Everyone has their own agenda," Lang shot back. "Even you."

"Me?" I demanded, tossing down the cloth.

"Yes, you! As far as your suitors know, you're walking into your courtships with the aim of marriage. None of these poor saps know they don't have a chance. That you're just passing the time with them until you can turn tail and race home."

"I'm trying to protect my father and my country. You know what's at stake."

Lang held up his hands. "And I'm trying to protect millions of innocent people. You're lying for a good reason, just like I did. Are we really that different?"

I stepped close to him, jutting a finger at his chest. "My plan didn't put anyone's safety at risk."

"Selah, you were never in danger." Lang bent his head, casting both of us in shadow. A few droplets of rain trembled in his hair. "I had everything under control before y— Well, before." His face was close to mine, earnest enough to infuriate me.

My breath left me in a rush. Red burned my neck and cheeks.

"Do not treat me like a child," I said through gritted teeth. "I'm not a fool, and you are not all-knowing. Anything could've happened while I was stumbling around blind."

"I would've kept you safe." He swallowed, and his throat bobbed. "I *would* have."

I turned back to the bread, too angry to look at him anymore. Angry at his lies. Angry at my own weakness.

Lang came closer to me, two steps in the silent kitchen. I paused, wrist-deep in my work. When he put his hands on my shoulders, heat spread over my skin, furious and faltering.

"I don't mind if you're angry." Lang's thumbs stretched and tensed against my shoulder blades. He was close enough I could feel the words against the back of my neck. "I can take your anger. I just can't take you shutting me out."

"You were guilty of that long before I was, Lang." I closed

my eyes tightly. "I trusted you from the beginning. You were the one who wouldn't let me in." I looked over my shoulder and met his gaze. "And now you're going to have to wait while I come to terms with this."

My skin was colder when his hands fell away from it.

3

At dinner, the crew members were cheerful, warmed by their food and one another's company. By this, only her second night aboard, Anya had already charmed them all; her sunshine-bright beauty had drawn their attention, but it was her genuine kindness that had everyone eager to make room for her as they'd once done for me. J.J. was attached to her side, his hazel eyes downcast and shy but lighting up every time Anya spoke to him.

Even Perrault, my protocol officer, seemed won over by her. I caught him glancing between Anya and me and the folder beside his plate, his expression almost wistful. Presumably, he'd brought the folder to discuss my next suitor—Fritz, of Katz Castle. I couldn't imagine a topic I'd less rather discuss.

Did Perrault wish Anya were his charge? Was he thinking of how much easier his job would have been had he been tasked with marrying her off, instead of me?

I had sat where Anya sat, once. The crew's shiny new toy, welcomed and admired. But I couldn't be her tonight. I couldn't be that girl anymore.

Skop stood behind her now, hands instinctively protective on her shoulders, laughing at some joke Basile had made. Safe, with Skop at her back, Anya had gotten her happy ending. Mine had slipped through my fingers. I tried not to let myself dwell on the ways that was Anya's fault.

But if Anya had taken my place tonight, it seemed only fair that I be allowed to choose a new one.

The galley was one space divided in two by a low wall. I could still see everyone sitting at the two long tables from the kitchen side of the galley. But it was all the retreat I could make without looking like a spoiled child. With chores and the dividing wall between us, I felt less smothered by their happiness.

"I can take care of it, Selah," Will protested, hands hovering uncertain before him as I shooed him toward where the others sat, smiling the falsest smile I'd ever worn.

I caught Vishnu's eye over Will's shoulder as I turned back to work. The ocean waves tattooed across the handsome sailor's forearm swelled and receded as he pushed a hand through his dark hair, and he dropped his eyes away.

He felt guilty.

Good, I thought. They all should.

Cobie always ate slightly apart from the others, standing sentry against the galley's low dividing wall. Tonight, I mimicked her, eating as I worked.

I felt Lang's eyes heavy on me, frustrated, impatient,

curious. I refused to look at him.

When the dishes were finally clean, I slipped out of the galley, casting a glance over my shoulder at the crew huddled close together. Silver-haired Yasumaro and J.J. with his cap low over his head and Basile with his laugh a mile wide. They were a perfect circle beneath the lamplight, their happiness a golden halo above their heads.

I would ruin their evening if I stayed.

The part of me full of smug, self-righteous anger wanted to remain and force them to confront what they'd done. They deserved to have their comfort spoiled.

The other half of me—the miserable half, the guilty half, the betrayed half—just wanted to hide.

For the first time in weeks, I didn't feel like one of them.

Lang met my gaze, a question in his eyes. Both he and Perrault half rose, Lang's lips parting as if to speak, Perrault's pretty face confused. He lifted the folder in his hands, as if in summons.

I shook my head at both of them, my breath leaving me in a rush, and pushed out into the night and the still-falling rain.

With my cabin door shut tight behind me, I heaved Godmother Althea's book out of my trunk and retrieved the radio she'd smuggled me from where it lay hidden beneath the back endpaper.

My godmother had been my mother's best friend, the angel watching over me for as long as I could remember. Missing her was like an ache in my bones.

I wouldn't be able to speak to her out here on the sea; my little radio and I were too far from a tower to transmit a signal. But it could receive one, if Godmother was speaking into the radio on her end.

I hoped she would be. I longed for the comfort of her voice. I hadn't heard from her since we'd spoken in Norge a few days earlier.

Torden had proposed to me that day. It might as well have been a hundred years ago.

I sat back against my headboard, swallowed hard, and switched on the radio.

Empty air filled the silence. I was still alone.

One tear and then another spilled down my cheeks as I sat on my bed, my weary limbs splayed out like a broken doll's.

I'd cried too much lately. I wiped my eyes and nose fiercely, swallowed the lump in my throat, and replaced the radio inside the endpaper. I added another tick mark to the rows of marching lines that numbered the days since I'd left home and my father behind.

I closed my eyes and tried to envision how the marks would multiply as the days passed, weighing the time apart from my father against the choice I had made to help the Waldleute resist the Imperiya.

Daddy would never want me to turn my back on those I had the power to help. I had to believe this, had to believe my godmother would agree that the danger the Imperiya's subjects faced outweighed my duty to race back to Potomac and stand against my stepmother.

I opened the storybook over my lap and tried to read, to dwell on things that would give me comfort. On my father, on starlit nights on his balcony with him and my mother.

But *happily ever after* felt as far away now as *once upon a time*.

How I longed for the strength and safety I'd felt when Torden held me. How I missed the sense of possibility I'd felt with Daddy at my side, before I'd known I'd be forced to leave him.

No matter how much I told my heart that it was the right choice to venture east, I still felt lost. Adrift, here on the Frisian Sea, making for the Canal Route that would carry us to Katz Castle, where more things than another would-be suitor waited.

Lang and Yu had intelligence that said the Waldleute—the Shvartsval'd branch of the rebels working against the Imperiya—were active in the region near the castle. They were the reason we were adhering to my stepmother's schedule: we were going to arm them with the weapons the *zŏngtŏng*, the president of Yu's home country of Zhōng Guó, had given Yu and Lang to smuggle inside the Imperiya.

I had my own intelligence, too.

I'd been listening to my godmother one day on her radio when I'd accidentally stumbled on another frequency—on another conversation altogether.

Hansel and Gretel, they'd called themselves. They'd been making plans.

"Burg Cats?" he'd asked. His voice had been cool and sharp, his accent almost English, with *v*'s like *z*'s. "Or Burg Rhein—"

She'd asked him if he was crazy. Told him anyone could be listening in.

She'd been right.

I had thought more than once to tell Lang and the others what I'd heard. But something had stopped my mouth before, had kept me from telling the others that they were right, and that the Waldleute were perhaps even working with someone inside the castle. Now there was no mystery to what had kept me quiet: I was too angry to share my secrets. They'd certainly taken their time sharing theirs.

Even having overheard Hansel and Gretel, I faced a great unknown on the map. *Hic sunt dracones. Hic sunt lupi.*

Here be dragons. Here be wolves.

Not only monsters awaited us in Shvartsval'd, inside the gray boundaries of the Imperiya Yotne. We would meet plots already in motion, characters in masks designed to deceive.

The courts I had survived thus far would be nothing compared to what lay ahead. Danger awaited us, and the days loomed long and fearsome as the teeth of the wolves the Imperiya's tsarytsya loved so much.

Looking at my marks scratched out in pencil, wobbling from one edge of the endpaper to the other, I felt doubt creeping cold up my spine and wondered if I had chosen wrong.

Swallowing hard, I set my godmother's book aside and dug deeper into my trunk.

I sat back on my bed and ruffled the pages of the folder in my hand—the folder Alessandra had thrown in my face the day we'd left Potomac so many weeks ago, my father weary and sick, most likely poisoned at her hand, my position as Potomac's seneschal-elect teetering on the edge of a knife. But it was more than a dossier on the suitors ahead of and behind me; it was the story of where I'd come from and how far I had still to go.

Bertilak, prince of England, Duke of Exeter. Firstborn son of the king of England was first inside the file. He was England's crown prince, Oxford-educated, thoughtful and wise, and I'd been horrified to find him close to Daddy's age.

The folder didn't contain details on my real suitor—Prince Bertilak's son, Bear. He had gotten to know me disguised as a guard, and I'd fallen for him. I'd discovered their deception in front of the entire court and left completely humiliated.

I wasn't angry at Bear anymore. He'd done what he had to do, just as I had. But my sigh rustled the pages as I turned past his profile.

Torden's eyes stared up at mine.

When Perrault had first related Torden's profile information—his height and hair color and his rank among Konge Alfödr's sons—I'd asked if Norge was proposing courtship or selling horses. I didn't feel any of that cynicism or anger now as I looked at Torden's portrait. Sparse though it was, the artist had somehow captured the determined square corners of his jaw, the earnest set of his mouth and furrow of his brows.

With Torden at my side I had felt broad as the sky and solid as the earth. Utterly invincible, the future clear before me.

I knew where I was headed now. But thoughts of the future filled me with an uncertainty that shook my bones.

I thumbed the illustration, my throat tight, and turned to the next profile.

Reichsfürst Fritz of the Neukatzenelnbogen. Brown hair, brown eyes, medium height. Age: twenty-seven. Oldest son of Hertsoh Maximilian of the Imperiya Yotne, Reichsfürst of Terytoriya Shvartsval'd.

Then Perrault's note: *Clever.*

"Twenty-seven." I shook my head again—though, at least this time, I'd been informed of my suitor's age.

Lang and I had exclaimed over it together, a lifetime ago, when I thought he cared about what happened to me. Not that it mattered. I wasn't headed for the Shvartsval'd in search of love or a husband. I was going there to honor a mission, to help people defend themselves against a tyrant whose cruelty I'd heard of in whispers and stories since I was a child.

I bit my lip, thinking of everything Homer and Lang and Yu had told me about the tsarytsya and her Imperiya. Of the mosques and churches and temples shuttered and left to ruin, the books burned, the punishment for those who dared flee the villages she controlled. Of spies, and children taken from their families.

I swallowed hard and turned the page again, my forehead pinching as I scanned the remaining profiles. *Prínkipas Theodore, only child of Déspoina Áphros and Despótis Hephaistios of Páfos,* a smiling young man with dark curls; Perrault had scribbled *philanderer* below his description. *Baltazaru Turchinu,* a young prince in Corse searching for a seventh wife after the first six had mysteriously perished or disappeared, to whose profile Perrault had added only the word *terrifying.* And dukes and barons and other nobles besides.

So many men to visit. So many men appointed to ensure I did so. So many who had lied to me and used the cause of my pain for their own purposes.

I had been lonely before; the feeling was an old friend. But I had never been so angry.

It burned.

4

It was late when a knock came at my door. "Selah?" Anya's voice was soft, but I tensed.

"It's not locked," I called, not moving.

The door creaked open, and Anya came and crouched at my side, moonlight from the porthole washing her fair hair pale as silver.

"I can't sleep," she whispered.

I swallowed, searching her face for questions about why I'd left dinner early—questions that would mean uncomfortable answers and truths about how bitter I felt. But I found none.

Maybe Anya was too content to wonder.

"Hammock no good?" I asked.

She shook her head. "Their room's crowded already. And Jeanne's lovely, but . . ." She paused. "I don't think Cobie likes me. She's never nice to me."

"Well, Cobie isn't nice to anybody."

"She's nice to you."

"She isn't, really," I said, my brow furrowing. Though I was still angry at the crew, my ire burned a little cooler at Cobie, and I finally understood why: she had never pretended to be friendly to me. She hadn't smiled and acted like she cared about me while plotting behind my back, as the rest of them had. Cobie's behavior had never changed, and I found comfort in that consistency.

"They pay her not to be mean to me, though," I told Anya with a wan smile. She laughed softly, eyes roving over my wardrobe, my trunks, the bed too large for me alone.

I knew what she wanted me to ask.

I *wanted* to want company. I wanted to feel like myself again.

But the crew's quarters were already cramped. Whether I wanted to share my room or wallow in private, it didn't matter.

"Do you want to sleep here?" I forced myself to ask.

"Yes, *please*," Anya exclaimed, nodding vigorously. She wriggled across the quilt and under the covers, curling up with her back to the wall. She gave a sigh, eyes sinking closed.

"Better?" I smiled tightly.

Her voice was soft. "It's like being at home again."

A lump grew in my throat.

We were a snug fit in the little bed, though hardly a tighter squeeze than we'd been back in her room at Asgard.

But this was nothing like being in Anya's home.

I didn't miss Alfödr, or his rules. But Anya had left her adoptive father of her own volition, had run away with Skop's hand in hers. Torden wouldn't be waiting for me in the galley when

I got up tomorrow, and she had complicated what chance I had of getting back to the father I'd been forced to leave behind.

Even in the dark, Anya must have read my thoughts on my face.

She bit her lip. "I wanted you to be my sister."

"I wanted to be your sister," I said. I meant it. But the words hurt.

"I'm glad I'm here anyway." She squeezed my hand. "I can't believe I get to stay with Skop. For as long as we want." Joy radiated from her face.

I was glad to have Anya here, too. Safe, with us. But as much as it shamed me, her happiness was like salt on a wound still raw.

It wasn't quite fair or true that Anya had gotten her happy ending at the expense of my own. That was her father's fault.

But it also wasn't fair that Anya's happiness took up so much air while I could hardly breathe for mourning what I'd lost. It wasn't fair that Torden had been taken from me so quickly after I'd found him.

I felt myself avoiding Anya and the others, finding places to hide myself as we crossed the cold sea and, on the fourth day after we left Norge, sailed into the mouth of the Canal Route, a bay called the Jade Bight. It was a bleak place, mud flats and gray beaches rendered stark and barren in too-harsh sunlight, but my jealousy was uglier still. It hurt, and I felt Anya's hurt every time I hurried away from her and Skop at the table or in our room.

Anya had endured so much; I wanted not to begrudge her joy. I knew she wouldn't have resented mine, if our places had been reversed. But that only made me feel worse.

I couldn't help that I wasn't the person she was. I was no shield-maiden.

My own weakness disappointed me. But avoidance was my only strategy, so my days aboard the *Beholder* found me every-where but still. I washed dishes during meals instead of eating with the others, busied myself in my little garden of pots and half barrels instead of joining their circle when we were all on deck. When I let myself rest during the day, I didn't take to the room I now shared with Anya; I climbed to the crow's nest with Cobie, taking comfort in her reliable, unvarnished sharp-ness.

When I had first set sail, first begun to visit courts, first begun to contemplate the role that Alessandra had assigned me, I had felt like our figurehead. I had been the belle in search of her prince, the grand symbol at the fore of our journey with stars in her eyes and slippers on her feet.

But I had left my handsome prince behind me, and the stars in my eyes had been put out.

I felt too damaged to be a symbol anymore. But it didn't matter. I wanted to be something more than that.

Until I sorted out what that meant—precisely who and what I wanted to be—I kept to the crow's nest, and kept only Cobie's company.

We watched the banks along the canals, and then the banks of the Reyn when we passed into it from the Canal Route. The river threaded the bottom of a valley whose walls Cobie once said had been wooded. I tried to imagine it as it must have been—deep green forest shrouding the hills, full of secrets and safe places to hide.

But the banks we sailed past now were lined with outposts for gray-uniformed soldiers and with timberlands ravaged to stumps. Villages carefully contained inside walls were scattered across absolute emptiness; we passed no lonely huts, no stragglers making camp on their own.

We encountered none of the horrors for which the tsarytsya was infamous as we sliced along the edge of her territory. But in the bleak little hamlets and the disenchanted forests we passed, it was impossible to miss what had been lost to this land.

It was impossible to see it all and not think of what lay in wait for us deeper within the Imperiya.

"Will and I weren't involved. I want you to know that," Cobie suddenly said to me, about a week after we'd fled Asgard. "We knew, but we didn't help. All I did was watch for the *Beholder*'s return from Odense."

I nodded.

"We needed the work. That's why when Lang told the crew we were making a cargo run as well, I didn't leave." A gust of wind lifted her dark hair from her shoulders, and she pushed a tangle behind her ear. "He said the only rule was we all had to keep our mouths shut around Perrault and J.J. And you, of course."

"Of course," I echoed hollowly, swallowing hard. "And everyone else knew?"

Cobie nodded. "Yasumaro and Jeanne were like me and Will, though. They knew, but they mostly stayed out of it." She paused. "'*Cela ne me concerne pas,*' Jeanne kept saying."

It's none of my business.

I nodded, reviewing the rest of them in my mind. Lang. Yu. Homer. Andersen. Vishnu. Basile. Skop. They had all done this behind my back.

I gnawed my lip. "Why didn't he just tell me?" I asked.

"We didn't know you," Cobie said. "And once we did—I think Lang thought you were safest not knowing. You were already walking into so much uncertainty. He wanted to protect you."

That's our place, Lang had told me. *That's where we belong. Between you and everyone else.*

I envied his surety.

We sailed on, the riverbanks slipping past us. The sky above was unlike Norge's bright blue or England's soft pearl-colored light; it was a sulfurous yellow-gray, the sun shining high and harsh on the earth left bare between the hacked-down stumps. "Why is so much of this forest cut down?" I asked.

"I think the tsarytsya's soldiers did it," Cobie said, squinting against the unforgiving light. "She and her wolves laid claim to the timber after they conquered Deutschland."

Again, I imagined the forests as they must have been— quiet, a home for animals and for those who preferred their own company. "And they left no place to hide."

Cobie cocked an eyebrow at me. "There's always someplace to hide, Selah." She nodded significantly at the two of us, sitting high above deck in the crow's nest.

"I'm not hiding," I bit out.

"Prove it."

"Fine," I snapped.

Cobie was right. It was time to face the others.

I clambered down the rope, bypassing Yasumaro and his searching gaze at the helm as I made my way to Homer's cabin, where I'd seen him convened with Andersen, Yu, and Lang earlier. Lang's quarters would have done, as well, but our navigator inspired confidence—a cast-iron belief the others seemed to lean on, as well.

I could hardly admit it to myself, but I missed Homer. I missed all of them. I wanted to move past my anger and hurt and tell them what I knew: that games were already afoot at Katz Castle, and they might involve the resistance.

They had told me the truth; I would do the same. The ground beneath our feet would be level. We could make a fresh start.

Still, I paused outside the navigator's door for a long breath before I walked inside.

Homer, Lang, Yu, and Andersen were standing over the map at Homer's table, looking grave.

Lang straightened when I walked in, dark eyes searching me as if they were picking my pockets, his expression strangely unguarded. It struck me afresh how much younger he was than Yu and Homer. How unprepared he might feel, compared to others who had seen more and done more.

My fingers wound the sinuous route from England to Norge, from Norge across the sea to the Canal Route to the Reyn. If our map were magic, perhaps it would show us there, one ship along its blue length, a dozen or so interlopers ready to invade the gray mass at its core.

"Selah." Homer's voice was like gravel. "What do you need?" If the older man felt uncertain, his face gave no hint of it.

I swallowed. "Anything?" I asked. "Any fresh leads?"

Yu shook his head. "We have no new information." His voice was even, but there was disappointment at the back of it.

I felt a sudden wash of sympathy; it was no surprise, how tired and drawn they looked. They were trying to help the Waldleute, but they had so little to go on.

I hoped I could be the one to change that.

I drew close to the table. "I had an idea." Andersen brightened.

"We'd welcome your suggestions, Seneschal-elect," Lang said, nodding amicably. He hardly took his eyes off the map as he spoke, barely even looked at me.

Big of you, I wanted to grumble. But acting like a child wouldn't inspire them to listen.

"What if we used my radio to contact the Waldleute?" I asked. "If we could reach out to them before we arrived in Shvartsval'd, it might save us time. We could even leave before my appointed two weeks are up—make up an excuse to go home early."

No one spoke for a long moment. They exchanged glances,

30

all seeming to choose their words carefully. Yu's face was even harder than usual, and Andersen looked wilted, his shoulders slumped uncomfortably, his hair seeming to droop.

Had I spoken too eagerly? Had I come across as a child anyway?

"What is it?" I finally asked.

"We don't have a channel for speaking to the Waldleute," Yu said, pragmatic as ever.

"Well," I began, then paused, uncertain how to explain what I'd overheard.

But Homer spoke first. "What Yu is trying to say is that we've already tried." He watched me with clear eyes, grizzled arms crossed over his chest. "Just a day or two ago."

"You've already—" I glanced around the cabin, frowning. "You have a radio here?" My gaze jumped around, confused. Andersen ducked his head, looking more than a little like J.J.

Lang walked to Homer's bookcase and retrieved a small black object and held it out to me. "Our intelligence said we'd be passing a radio tower a few days ago, so we borrowed yours then," he said, tone careful. "We tried to hail the Waldleute. Couldn't raise them."

My radio was in Lang's hand.

"You—" I shook my head. "You went into my room?"

Lang didn't answer.

"Did you search my things?" My voice rose.

"Your book was on your bed." He bit his lip. "I didn't think you would object."

31

"Obviously I don't object, as I'm here, offering it." My anger mounted. "But what right do you have to take my things?"

"Requisitioning of resources is common in wartime," Homer said mildly.

"Except I don't answer to you!" I shot back.

Andersen pinched the bridge of his nose. "I told you we should've told her," he mumbled, speaking for the first time.

"Yes, you should have." I snatched the radio from Lang's hand and pushed toward the door.

"It's probably best you don't use it for now," Homer said to my back.

I turned, staring at him. My radio was my only means of hearing from my godmother—of obtaining information about Daddy. "Why?"

"It's possible the Imperiya could use any signal your radio emits or receives to determine our location."

"But you used it," I said.

Yu shrugged. "A calculated risk."

"*Your* calculations," I spat. "Not mine."

"We—" Lang began again, then broke off. His eyes were guilty, but he said nothing more.

It was too much. My blood had been boiling, simmering, seething for days. It ran thick now, and hot with anger.

I'd come to them in good faith, with valuable information. And again, they'd treated me like a child. Like a figurehead. Like nothing more than cover for them while they did the real work behind the scenes.

I would tell them nothing. They would regret not having

trusted me. And for once, I didn't care what it cost.

Homer's door gave off a report like a shot when I threw it open against the opposing wall, then another when I slammed it behind me.

"Selah!" Lang called after me. He chased me down the stairs to the hold. "Selah, wait!"

He caught me by my empty hand, and I wrenched my fingers from his. "Never again, Lang. You are never, ever to invade my privacy again." My heart raced. What if he had seen something I hadn't wanted him to see? What if I had done something more personal with the back of my godmother's book than mark passing time?

"You're right. I'm sorry." Lang shook his head, so earnest. "I'm sorry, Selah. I'll never do it again."

If they had come to me, I would have helped them. I would have told them how to contact the Waldleute while we were still within range of a tower.

I would keep my information to myself now. I would do with it what I thought best.

My jaw worked. "You're right. You won't. I'm going to start locking my door."

"I never will." There was a catch in Lang's voice.

I paused. "What?"

"I will never lock my door to you," he said quietly. He took one, two steps closer to me—not so close that I felt pinned between him and the wall, but close enough that I could feel him as well as hear the uncertain rhythm of his breath. Smell the salt on his skin, like sweat, like the ocean. "I had no right to invade your privacy, but you can lay claim to mine. If you ever decide you'd like to."

I forced my chin up. His eyes fixed, dark, on mine.

"Does that mean you're going to start including me?" I asked, voice shaking. "Tell me things? Let me in on your plans?"

"It's—" Lang broke off, stepping back, shaking his head. It broke the spell between us. "Selah, I don't want you any more involved in this than you have to be. It's just not safe."

I bit my lip, holding his gaze.

Nothing had changed. I was still a child to him. Still a prize to be guarded.

I turned and walked away.

5

I passed Lang's closed cabin door a dozen times in the next two days. I stomped resolutely past it, refusing to see if it would open beneath my touch, as Lang had said it would.

I was angry. I didn't trust him. I didn't want his guilt offering, whatever it meant, so I stayed away. But as we drew nearer the court at Shvartsval'd, Perrault was unavoidable.

"Have you reviewed the contents of your third suitor's profile?" he demanded one day during dinner.

"Yes." I set down the pot of soup I'd been carrying.

Perrault smiled with relief; then, seeming to notice my flat expression, tried a different tack. "They haven't given us much to go on regarding the *fürst*'s personality or interests," he said, almost conspiratorially, dogging me back to the kitchen. "I'll have to develop ideas for the two of you once we've arrived at Katz Castle and I've had an opportunity to assess the court. We'll see if inspiration strikes."

It was the height of foolishness to talk this way. Torden was behind me. And surely, so was the part of my trip where we pretended among ourselves that I cared whom I courted.

"Whatever you think is best, Perrault," I said wearily, and turned back to the sink.

"Selah." His tone was abruptly sober. "Stop. Sit. We are nearly at Katz Castle's door, and I need to speak with you."

His voice and the worried lines on his face gave me pause. I swallowed and wiped my hands on my apron. "All right."

The crew quieted a little as I took a seat at the table across from Perrault. It had been days—weeks—since I'd sat with them. My gaze snagged on Skop's, but only for a moment before I looked away.

Perrault's rosebud mouth and dark eyes were serious. He knitted his hands together. "We're sailing into the Imperiya, Selah. You need to be prepared."

I nearly fired back a retort—*Oh, I thought I'd just try being myself!* I wanted to spit at him.

I've been spending too much time with Cobie, I thought.

But it wasn't Cobie's influence that had sharpened my tongue. My anger was my own, a gift from the ones who'd lied to my face and worked behind my back. But Cobie wasn't guilty of that deception, and neither, I realized for the first time, was Perrault.

Many as his sins were, he'd always been forthright about what he wanted from me.

I sighed. "Tell me," I said, soft and serious as I'd ever been

36

for the nuns who taught me growing up. "Tell me what I need to know."

The crew seemed to retreat to the edges of the galley, outside the halo of lamplight that surrounded Perrault and me, as he spoke.

"You must understand," Perrault said as he began, "that Imperiya law impedes the open flow of information. The happenings in one corner of the tsarytsya's land are as mysterious to the rest of it as they are to us outside; there are no writers or newspapers documenting what happens inside her borders. This," he said, fingers tightening around one another, "is the best information I have."

"I understand."

"Good." Perrault leaned slightly forward. "The first rule you already know: no books. Though the tsarytsya circulates her own propaganda, there are—as I've said—no independent publishers operating openly inside the Imperiya. Not even in Shvartsval'd, at its borders, where I suspect the rules may be more relaxed. Promise me you will leave your storybook behind," Perrault said.

"I promise," I said without hesitating.

It stung, the idea of abandoning the book. But if I'd learned anything from fairy-tale heroines, it was to trust wisdom when I heard it.

"The second rule follows from the first: no unapproved art," Perrault said. "The tsarytsya commissions art for the glory of the Imperiya, but art that subverts her worldview is prohibited—and what constitutes subversion is not always clear," he said carefully, pale forehead creasing in thought. "I would suggest you avoid creating or discussing art altogether. No painting, no sketching, no singing, no playing instruments. The tsarytsya's followers even dress all in gray in support of her leadership. Again, standards may be more relaxed at the border, but I cannot say how much."

"I'm not an artist," I said, faltering a little. "I can't sing or draw or play anything."

"I never thought I'd find lack of accomplishment such a relief," Perrault said with a touch of his former pomposity. He rubbed his temples. "The third rule prohibits any and all religious practice." He paused. "I doubt it would be effective for me to ask you to cease to practice entirely, and indeed I suppose there's no need for you to. But I ask you to restrict it to the privacy of your thoughts, for your own safety and that of those traveling with you."

Again, I didn't hesitate. "I will."

Perrault must have heard the sincerity in my voice, because his pallor lessened a little, and his fingers unclenched just a bit. "The final rule," he said, "is linguistic unity. The tsarytsya seeks a unified culture, and to her mind, the exclusive use of Yotne is essential to that goal. You know that when she conquers countries, she breaks them up on unnatural fault lines, intentionally disregarding historic and cultural boundary lines. She renames these, her *terytoriy*, toward the end of reshaping their identity. The court will speak Yotne, in accordance with this thinking, and you will do your best, speaking English, with me as your translator."

I nodded. "So I'm not to refer to Deutschland as Deutschland," I said lightly, staring at my hands.

"No." Perrault spoke so forcefully I drew back. "It is Shvartsval'd for the purposes of our trip, which are limited, in my opinion, to keeping you safe." When I looked up, his eyes were dark with worry, concern etched again into his brow. "Please, Seneschal-elect. Have a care."

Where, I wondered, was the supercilious friend of my stepmother I'd met in Potomac the night before we left? Where was the protocol officer appalled by my table manners, who'd cornered me and criticized me in Winchester when he thought I'd upend his plans for a quick engagement?

I wondered if he'd come to care for me by accident.

I wondered if he'd come to regret it.

"Be unremarkable," he finally said, "and perhaps this visit will go unremarked. Abide by the rules for two weeks, gracefully receive any proposal Fritz may issue, and my counterpart in Shvartsval'd—whatever low-ranked hanger-on issued this invitation on the duke's behalf—may forget you as soon as you pass from his sight."

I bit my lip. "And you think if I play my cards carefully, the tsarytsya may never even know we were there?"

"Gambling metaphors are unsuitable for ladies," Perrault said automatically, then shook himself. "But yes. Her Imperiya is wide and the *hertsoh* is a minor nobleman. I don't believe she'll notice you if you do not draw her eye."

"I'll be careful," I promised.

I suddenly wished for a cup of tea or something to do with my hands—anything to distract me from the truth I was keeping from Perrault. That I would flout all his warnings and break my promise if our mission required I do so. It almost made me feel guilty.

The crew began to shift to life slowly after that—the fold of paper in Andersen's hands, the wash of water over a pot as Will tended to what I'd left back in the kitchen, a yawn escaping J.J. as he slumped on his bench.

"Thank you, Perrault." I rose quickly and made for the door. "I'll keep all this in mind."

But I knew better. I would not keep the knowledge. The dread of what lay in wait would keep me.

Perrault had tried to soothe me. But I could not help imagining the tsarytsya's eyes on me as we neared the edge of her world.

I sensed her watching as I listened out for Godmother Althea at night on my radio; it was enough to still me when Perrault took me aside during the day because he'd remembered a Yotne phrase he wanted to teach me, or a minor point of etiquette I might find helpful.

I wondered what color the tsarytsya's eyes were. Would they be amber, the color of a wolf's? Gray, the color of her Imperiya?

They were every color, I knew, of as many shades as she had spies. A fearful spectrum of blue to black, watching from riverbanks and castle corners.

The fear of them kept sleep from me the night before we reached Shvartsval'd. Anya rested beside me, her expression serene in the moonlight, but I couldn't follow her.

Something about the calm of her mouth and her breathing gnawed at me. Anya's peace aggravated the itch beneath my skin.

Careful not to wake her, I rolled out of our bed and slunk upstairs to the deck, barefoot and bare-armed in defiance of the night's chill. It was black as pitch out on deck. Even with the thumbnail of moon overhead, nights like tonight made me understand the word *Shvartsval'd*—Black Forest.

The trees here stood tall; the tsarytsya's woodcutters had not ventured this far into the *terytoriya*. I wondered what they'd been afraid of.

I'd expected to find Homer or Yasumaro on deck. But it was him. I froze, hand on the stair rail, toes digging into the rough wood grain.

Lang was at the helm.

I backed down the forecastle stairs on tiptoe, silent as the night, and went back the way I came.

I should sleep. I would go back to my room and crawl into bed next to Anya and stare at the ceiling for six hours if I had to.

But I stopped at Lang's door.

I had never been in his room before. And I'd had no intention of accepting his guilty-conscience offer to repay his offense by invading his privacy whenever I liked.

Captain's quarters, he'd said that first day, shaking his head, as if he couldn't believe it, either.

I tried the knob, and found it unlocked.

I crossed the threshold.

Slowly, I took in Lang's bedroom. The bedclothes were drawn up but not tucked in tidily; on impulse, I yanked them down, exposing the fitted sheet over the mattress. Then I crossed to his wardrobe door and flung it open.

Shirts and trousers were hung inside—the plain things he wore on deck and the richer clothes he'd worn at court. My fingers traced a finely woven shirt and a rough-spun pair of pants and the jacket he'd worn to every ball we'd attended in England and at Asgard.

They all smelled of him—salt. Sweat. The ocean.

I took them off the rack, one by one, and flung them on the bed.

Opposite the closet was a beat-up wooden desk with a hutch above. The desktop was clear, so I reached for the clasp on the hutch's cabinet doors.

I wasn't looking for anything. I was merely determined to sack the room, to lay it bare, to leave him feeling as stripped and raw as he'd left me.

I ignored the voice that said Lang's taking the radio wasn't what had left me feeling so exposed, that retribution wasn't what had finally drawn me over his threshold.

The release of the catch sent a flood of papers spilling out of the cabinet, onto the floor. I jumped back, startled, then crouched to collect them.

But I stopped short when I saw myself.

I'd come searching for Lang's secrets. Instead, I saw myself mapped in paper and ink and charcoal on his floor; myself in profile, my face up close, my figure from afar. My nose and mouth and freckles and lashes as I bent over the sink in the kitchen; my hair tangled down my back and the muscles gathered in my arms as I gardened; the elegant slip of my shoulder into the gown I'd worn to the first tournament ball in England.

My fingers left dirt smudges on the papers. I stared at them, unmoving, for how long I didn't know.

When I looked up, Lang stood at the threshold. I had not heard the change at the helm; I had not heard anything but my own racing thoughts.

His chest rose and fell, rapid and vulnerable, as he took in the upended room and me on the floor. I gripped the papers artlessly in my fingers, held them up, a helpless gesture.

"What—?" I began.

"Don't." Lang's eyes were desperate. "Don't ask me what they are."

I swallowed, thinking of Anya and all the rest of the crew in bed. Of the weapons in the hold, of Asgard behind us and Katz Castle ahead and my father at home, of the radio that had spoken little but silence since I left Torden behind. Of his ring on my left hand, heavy as a hammer.

With Lang's eyes on me, I felt the weight of the night in my very bones.

Lang's throat bobbed. He rubbed at his eyes and two fine, dark lashes fell onto his cheek.

That night we'd stood talking late in Asgard's darkened halls, I'd taken his fallen lashes and made a wish on them.

Here, in the dark, having breached the Imperiya's gray shadow, wishing for Torden felt foolish. Like the childish daydream of a girl who had read too many fairy tales.

Either way, I didn't dare draw close enough to touch Lang's face. Not here, with the two of us feeling as if we were standing at the edge of the world.

The darkest, loneliest part of my heart was certain Torden was lost to me forever.

Was it wrong to find myself in someone else's room? Or was it wise to accept that what was behind me was past, and take what comfort came my way?

I stared down at the sketches of me on the floor and in my grip, at the longing in every line, and wondered how I would draw Lang, if the pen were in my hands, if I had his talent. I took in his rumpled dark hair, the fine bones of his cheeks and jaw and hands, the elegant bow of his lips and the upturned tip of his nose.

I would sketch him like midnight, alluring and unknown. He was every question I was afraid to ask, every curiosity that had been forbidden to me from the outset of my journey.

My heart was a field planted with so many wants it was difficult to know what needed uprooting and what I should allow to remain.

Nothing was clear. Not my desires. Not the future. Not the difference between wish and hope and expectation.

Lang wet his lips and took a step nearer, then knelt a foot or two away, the sketches a puddle of paper as wide as an ocean between us.

Trembling, I drew back. When my spine collided with his bed, I rose just high enough to sit on the mattress I'd exposed.

Lang's ink-smudged fingers traced the drawings' edges, touching each page as gently as if he were skimming his hands over my skin.

When he looked up at me, his eyes were pleading.

They told me he didn't want to hide anymore.

I bit my lip as he shifted toward me, moving on his knees, kneeling before me where I sat on the bed.

"Selah," he breathed.

I couldn't look at him. Fear and anger and endless wanting clenched in my stomach.

"I'm angry at you," I whispered. "I'm supposed to be angry at you."

But when I avoided his gaze, there I was, seen through his eyes in his drawings—beautiful, the object of such longing.

I was everywhere in this room. And everywhere I was, there was Lang.

My chest rose and fell as Lang crawled nearer, heedless of the drawings on the floor. I bit my lip.

Slowly, Lang wrapped his arms around my waist, and dropped his head into my lap.

"I'm mad at you," I said again, my voice breaking, even as my hands fisted themselves in the shoulders of his shirt, even as the fabric caught on the stones of Torden's ring. "I'm furious. You've done everything wrong."

"I'll take it," Lang said. "I'll take all your anger. All your burning. All your fire." He looked up at me.

I swallowed, guilt and fear and hunger and dread fighting for control.

"Maybe I'll be smart, and when I burn myself, I'll learn to stay away," Lang said, swallowing, and shook his head. "Or maybe you'll be all I want to keep me warm."

He then devisde himselfe how to disguise; . . .
Sometime a fowle, sometime a fish in lake,
Now like a foxe, now like a dragon fell,
That of himselfe he ofte for feare would quake . . .
—*The Faerie Queene*

6

TERYTORIYA SHVARTSVAL'D, IMPERIYA YOT'NE:
KATZ CASTLE

It was raining when we reached Katz Castle the next day around dusk.

An angry sky wrung itself out on the deck and the lines and the sails and the moss-gray trees on the banks. Water dripped through my hair and down the back of my neck and into my shoes, but at least my trunks were dry, wrapped in oiled cloth to protect their contents.

My radio was safe aboard, where Yu and Homer and Lang had demanded I leave it. It was inside my storybook, which I'd also left behind, per Perrault's advice.

And the precious guns and powder in our hold were cozy and perilously dry while I stood soaked to the bone on deck.

I shook with anxiety and cold, refusing to let the sparks that Lang had struck the night before warm me.

I didn't trust him. I didn't trust myself. I would keep my distance, and keep us focused. Lang himself had warned me what could happen if fire caught, that night we argued over a candle.

You wouldn't mean to do anything. But a single stray spark could burn us alive.

We were a skeleton crew going ashore, Perrault, Lang, Cobie, and me. The others would remain with the ship, though. Skop and Anya had both pressed to come ashore.

"I'm the first mate!" Skop had insisted. "I should—"

"Be guarding our cache," Lang had said in a voice that brooked no dispute. "As first mate, your duty is to the *Beholder*. You stay aboard. Anya, too."

I hadn't argued. Neither had I missed the hurt in Anya's eyes.

I'd welcomed the prospect of a brief respite from her presence with more relief than I cared to admit.

I hadn't known how to explain how much space I needed to heal. To forgive her for something she'd never meant to do.

Cobie and Lang reached for the oars once we were all in the rowboat. The scent of rain and river water filled my nose. Perrault huddled beneath a massive raincoat, looking forlorn. "The Neukatzenelnbogen directly overlooks the Reyn," he said, retreating deeper beneath his coat. "At least our journey will be short."

The protocol officer studied me, his dark eyes unsettled, white teeth gnawing on his lip. When he glanced at my hands, his brows shot up.

"Not the right hand," he said softly, nodding at Torden's ring on my fourth finger.

"But I thought—" I broke off, swallowing hard. I'd taken my engagement ring from my left hand and put it on my right as I dressed that morning.

Torden and I had left one another with no promises—at least, none I believed we could keep. But it felt like a betrayal nonetheless.

"Many in this part of the world wear wedding and engagement bands on their right hands," Perrault corrected me. "I'd advise wearing it on your first or middle finger."

"Very well." A lump grew in my throat as I tugged the band off and slid it onto the index finger of my right hand. It fit well enough.

"There," Perrault sighed. His eyes were troubled. "You're officially unpromised once more."

His words left me aching.

As Perrault nodded at me with grim satisfaction and began again to advise me in low, cautious tones, I couldn't avoid Lang's eyes.

He glanced down at my hand, expression unreadable, and arched an eyebrow in my direction. Guilty heat swept from my collarbone to my hairline, and I shifted and looked away.

I wondered how many more small missteps I would make before the day was out, and how much each would cost us.

I would have to be careful every minute of my stay.

When we finally docked the rowboat at a small wooden pier and heaved our things across its wet planks, I glanced around for our escort up to the castle, remembering suddenly—vividly, with a pang in my heart—the roll of a carriage over cobblestones and the English countryside, the slow trot of golden horses past Norskmen and their fields.

We stared around for a few long moments, squinting into the dripping trees. Rain pattered over the sodden fallen leaves at our feet. The path into the forest was dark, damp, and entirely silent.

The nerves that had been slowly ballooning in my chest deflated. No one was waiting for us.

Cobie sighed and seized the handle of my trunk. "Well, we'd better get going."

The four of us tramped up the hillside, sweating and huffing and wiping rain out of our eyes as we negotiated the wooded hill and its switchbacks, its sludge, its fallen trees. Night had well fallen by the time we reached Katz Castle's great wooden doors; Perrault was pale and clammy. Even Cobie and Lang were panting from carrying our things.

Perrault's voice was breathless with effort. "This is not how I had hoped to present you."

"This is not how I hoped to arrive," I replied, for once in agreement with him. My boots and skirt were covered in mud, and my legs shook with more than exhaustion as I stared up at the high castle walls.

A wolf howled from the iron door knocker, its maw stretched wide.

I shuddered, but I grit my teeth and did not let myself be deterred.

I lifted the knocker three times, each time letting it drop so its echo could announce us.

Lang bent his head down to my ear. His breath was warm against my cold, prickling skin.

"Please," he said. "Please let me do my job here. Please keep to yours, so I can keep you safe."

Cover us, he was asking. *Court Fürst Fritz, and don't cause trouble.*

Stand still somewhere and look pretty, he might as well have ordered me.

We waited in the rain. Water squelched in my shoes. But as before, when we'd waited beside the Reyn, no one came.

Finally, Cobie shoved on the door, and it gave. No one was standing guard. There was no one in sight at all.

I exchanged a glance with Lang. He shook his head; water coursed down his high cheekbones and his nose.

"On we go," Perrault said, giving me a bracing nod. But the confidence was a thin facade.

We drifted forward, down darkened halls, past empty, unlit rooms, searching for signs of life. As we wandered over cracked tiles and damp carpets, I saw dusty walls marked with slightly lighter squares, as though portraits had been removed, and rooms lined with empty bookshelves. We caught voices in the distance and hurried toward them.

And then, as we rounded a corner, we found ourselves where we always did, eventually: at court.

7

The hall smelled of damp, of crumbling things.

Crowds lined the walls dressed in worn, fusty-looking clothes, their colors muted with age but not gray; apparently, customs had been relaxed this far out in the empire, as Perrault had predicted they might be. They stood three and four bodies deep in front of peeling gilt and cream wallpaper. Across the scratched mosaic floor, a dais was raised a foot off the ground. And there he was. The *hertsoh*, the incarnation of the tsarytsya herself here in Terytoriya Shvartsval'd.

Ten girls and a boy stood behind him.

The *hertsoh* was thin but handsome, probably in his mid-fifties. His golden-brown hair was streaked with gray, his forehead lined, his nose aristocratically arched. Clad in a wrinkled suit, he sprawled across a faded brocade chair.

Everything in this room must once have been beautiful, from the chipped mosaic underfoot to the water-damaged ceiling overhead. I imagined it as it must have been before: a cloud of color, of soft-eyed shepherdesses and sweet-faced cherubs, green trees and blue skies, their edges bright and gilded. As it was now, black mold crept across the faces of the girls and the angels alike, dimming the paint and the gold, and a third of the mosaic tiles were missing. Mildewed mortar filled the spaces where they had lain.

The whole room smelled of decay.

It was nothing like Arbor Hall, with its gentle scents of earth and life and growing things. I was so far from home.

I hoped Daddy wouldn't blame me for the time I spent away from his side. I hoped he would understand I hadn't wished to spend it in places like this.

I waited for someone to greet us, but no one had noticed our arrival. When a break came in the chatter between the duke and the courtiers, Perrault steadied himself, and stepped forward. "Hertsoh Maximilian," he began.

I didn't understand the rest of Perrault's address to him or their conference in Yotne, but the duke's blank look of irritation filled me with dread.

When Perrault finally turned back to us, his words were low-pitched and stilted. "He has no idea who we are."

For a long moment, I struggled to speak. Were we early? Late? Who had failed to inform him of our coming? Lang and Cobie exchanged a frowning glance, and the court shifted around us, murmuring, restive. Maximilian was still speaking—barking at Perrault in Yotne, seeming to bombard him with questions.

Perrault had not quailed in Norge before the stern looks of

its Konge Alfödr, but he dropped his gaze now, fiddling with a frill on his jacket. The sight of my protocol officer looking small and withdrawn as the duke berated him made me angry.

In my dread of today, I'd imagined a hundred wicked welcomes; but this, I'd not foreseen.

I stepped forward, moving around Perrault, lifting my chin even as my hands shook. "Do you speak English?" I asked.

"Of course I speak English. Why does a trespasser in the Imperiya come not speaking Yotne?" He shifted in his seat, sitting forward.

"*Batyuskha*," one of the girls broke in gently.

Perrault had taught me the Yotne word for father—*bat'ka*.

So these were Maximilian's children.

But the *hertsoh* only smirked at the girl, reaching up to pat her on the hand she'd set on the back of his throne. She stiffened and drew back slightly, pressing closer to the sister at her side.

"I didn't have much time to study your language," I said, flushing. "I wish I had. But Hertsoh Maximilian, we're not trespassers. I believe I'm here at your invitation—I'm Seneschal-Elect Selah of Potomac. I'm here to court Fürst Fritz."

The hall was silent but for the drip of water somewhere in a corner.

Annoyance flashed again across the duke's face. He nodded to two or three men on the edge of the dais, questioning them in Yotne.

"No," Perrault groaned under his breath.

"What is it?" Cobie asked, shouldering between Perrault and me.

56

"*Nasha tsarytsya*," one of the men exclaimed, a dark look on his face.

It required no translation. Alarm bells shrilled through my brain.

"You are not here at my invitation," the duke finally said, righting himself in his chair. He scowled. "You are here at *hers*."

No.

The duke shrugged. "It's merely a shame the tsarytsya is not here to greet you herself."

No.

Goose bumps rose over my skin, and my limbs shook.

Lang's hand met my lower back, obscured by Cobie and Perrault at my side. I felt its warmth through my wet clothes. And still I trembled.

Perrault and I had warred over traveling to Shvartsval'd, whether my arrival or my avoidance would send my name rising more quickly through the ranks of her administration and into her notice.

We had not known that my invitation had not come from some adviser of the duke's. I was here at the tsarytsya's behest.

I thought of every fairy tale that warned against giving a witch or a spirit or the fae one's true name, and tried not to dwell on how easily Alessandra had offered mine up to Baba Yaga herself.

"Her soldiers may avoid our woods, but Grandmother Wolf never ceases her attempts to meddle," the *hertsoh* said, expression ugly. "As it happens, I'm busy with my own marriage preparations, and not interested in playing host. What say you, Fritz?"

I lifted my gaze beyond the duke and took my first proper look at the *hertsoh's* son and daughters standing behind him.

Fritz was unremarkably good-looking; attractive, but a face I would have forgotten the minute I passed it by. His features were symmetrical, his face pale, his trim figure clad in neutral colors. Tidy, light brown hair was cropped an inch or so short; the eyes beneath his thick brows were nearly the same cool shade.

Fürst Fritz took in my sopping shoes, my bedraggled hair, and shrugged. He rolled his eyes with an annoyance uncomfortably like his father's.

My stomach clenched and dipped again. If Fürst Fritz dismissed me, we would have no excuse to remain, and Lang would never be able to pass the *zŏngtŏng's* weapons on to the Waldleute.

I pressed my lips together and kept my eyes on Fritz, hoping to move him to sympathy without knowing anything about him.

"She can stay, I suppose," Fritz finally said. "She doesn't *look* like a spy from Stupka-Zamok. Though, if she is not, I don't know what the tsarytsya could have been thinking to choose her. What a mess she is." My crew members stiffened beside me—though whether at the cruelty of the comment or how close Fritz hit to the mark, I couldn't say.

Fritz's face was forgettable. But I knew then, as my face burned before the whole of the Shvartsval'd court, that I would never forget the way he'd made me feel in this moment.

I wanted Cobie to step forward for me again, as she had in

Winchester. I wanted to hide behind Lang, to let his warmth burn off some of the cold I felt in this ruined hall.

Instead, I said, "Thank you," as if any of this pleased me.

The duke rubbed his forehead. "We have already supped, and no arrangements have been made for your stay. Your men can bunk where they will—just find a room. You and your lady's maid will stay with the *freinnen*, my daughters." He gestured at the girls standing behind him.

Cobie cleared her throat but had the restraint not to react to the duke's assumption that she was a maid.

"Thank you," I said again.

The words tasted sour. I smiled politely anyway.

"Seneschal-elect," Perrault began, uncertain; but he didn't finish his sentence.

Perrault was my protocol officer. My New York–polished, experience-sharpened etiquette expert and perception manipulator. He had played the chameleon at Asgard and rescued Skop from its king's wrath.

My dismay grew chillier at the fear in his eyes.

I shook myself, straightening and nodding at Perrault. "We'll bunk with the *freinnen* and talk tomorrow." Then I turned to Lang. His canvas jacket was heavy with rain, his dark hair streaming, like mine, into his eyes. "We'll do whatever needs to be done to make this visit a success."

8

Cobie and I followed the *freinnen* out of the hall. If I didn't want Fritz to change his mind and send us away, there didn't seem to be anything else to do.

The girls chattered like a flock of birds, darting irritated glances back at Cobie and me as an attendant led us through damp-wallpapered halls. My trunks scraped over the pitted stone and rough wood floors as we scrambled to keep up.

The castle seemed full of empty spaces: portraits lifted from walls, leaving their pale shadows behind; shelves filled with nothing but dust; crucifixes and relics swept away from what once must have been a chapel. My mind reeled as the queue followed turn after turn, past darkened, barred windows and over mildewed stairs.

The only direction we seemed reliably to be heading was down, down, deep into the bowels of the castle.

Finally, the line paused at a door. The girls at its tail—a

pair of twins who looked about fourteen—pointedly ignored Cobie and me as we followed them over the room's threshold, sweating under the weight of my possessions.

The door slammed as soon as we were inside.

None of the sisters said anything at the sound of bolts flipping shut behind us. Ten locks, one for each girl.

Cobie's jaw was as tight as a steel trap as she stared like a caged animal between the locked door and the ten *freinnen*. I felt my face pale.

I dropped my bag on the floor and crouched, head between my knees. My heart beat hard against my chest, as loud as the echoes of the falling dead bolts, as weighty as the gaze of the tsarytsya, present though she was absent.

I wished for the press of my father's kiss on my forehead. I wished for Torden's arms around me. But the tsarytsya knew my name. No one could hide me now.

"Excuse me," snapped one of the girls—in English, to my surprise. She nodded sharply at my trunk, blocking her path.

"Oh—I'm sorry." I picked it up by its handle, my sweaty palms slipping as I heaved it out of her way, and she sailed past me.

We were in a long room, its dimensions more like a corridor than a normal bedchamber. A dozen or so beds lined the walls, nearly all covered in stockings and hairbrushes and jewelry; four vanities between them were heaped with beauty products.

The girls scattered about the room eyed us with suspicion.

Cobie and I dragged our things toward two beds not strewn with possessions or haloed by the fashion plates and sketches that papered the walls. "We're locked in here," I said in a low, tense voice. I'd never been behind a locked door in my life.

Cobie's hands shook as she set down her carpetbag. "We'll figure it out."

I sank onto the bed I'd chosen. Dust on its blue counterpane hinted at its long disuse, and its sheets were stiff. This room, at least, smelled clean, not like the mold of the upper halls. But it was nothing like my rooms at home in Potomac or on the *Beholder*, nothing like Anya's treehouse-like quarters in Asgard.

How could I help Lang from behind a locked door? How would I ever find Hansel and Gretel if I couldn't search for them?

And how would I survive, knowing the tsarytsya knew my name and where I would lay my head at night? It had been bad enough risking her attention when I was merely courting suitors; now I was transporting contraband.

I clenched my fists tight against the anxiety that crept over my skin.

The *freinnen* busied themselves picking over cosmetics and pawing through wardrobes full to bursting. Dress forms, too, loitered about like half-clothed guests at a party. One fireplace warmed the room, flames crackling beneath the girls' whispers.

No one approached us.

"I wish I'd studied more Yotne," I said, suddenly desperate. I was drowning in a sea of mutterings I didn't understand.

"They're not speaking Yotne," Cobie said quietly, her eyes lit, despite everything. "That's old Deutsch."

I turned my head sharply. "What?"

"Will's and my people are all from Lancaster, up in Deutsch migrant country." Cobie smirked dangerously. "I'm fluent."

I wanted to ask her what they were saying. But suddenly one of the *freinnen* was standing at the foot of my bed.

"I'm sorry no one welcomed you properly." Her hair was black and her skin was fair, her figure soft and her blue eyes kind. "I'm Leirauh."

She was the one who'd tried to break in while her father spoke. I tried for a smile with little success. "It's not your fault. I'm Selah, and this is Cobie," I added. Cobie nodded, mouth frowning, eyes alert.

"Still." Another of the *freinnen* crossed the room, settling her lithe figure gracefully on the tiny bed next to Leirauh. "What an upsetting mix-up." Though her brown eyes seemed to take in everything about us, she appeared not to notice Leirauh's sudden tension at her side. "I'm Margarethe," she said, brushing a strand of waist-length brown hair out of her face with long, deft fingers.

"Pleasure," Cobie said coolly. "We'll survive."

"Of course you will," Leirauh jumped in quickly. Her pale cheeks flushed like feverish roses.

Margarethe tipped her head to one side, showing the elegant length of her neck. "Can I get you anything? Tea? Wine? The castle makes its own Riesling."

I became aware again of how cold I was. "Tea, please," I said, scrubbing a hand over the goose bumps on my arms.

"Wine for me." Suspicion lingered beneath Cobie's polite tone.

Locked in, drenched, and unwelcome.

I ached with the memory of our arrival at Asgard. Of meeting Torden for the first time, of Anya's immediate embrace, of Valaskjálf's blazing fires.

I crouched over my trunk, peeled off my wet clothes, and changed into pajamas, twisting my hair into a knot. A moment later, Margarethe and another girl—light brown–haired and brown-eyed, like Fritz, like Margarethe—crossed the room with our drinks. "I'm Ursula," she said, passing me a cup of tea. Her arms were long and pale, delicate from shoulder to elbow to wristbone to fingertip. "I hope you like milk and sugar."

Grateful despite myself, I nodded, sipping at the warm drink and leaning against my pillow. I wished I could read, or speak to my godmother. But my storybook and my radio were aboard our ship, and the eyes of the *freinnen* were on me. Watching me, like they were waiting for something.

Their expectant faces were the last thing I saw before I fell asleep.

9

When I woke, my head was pounding, and the castle was quiet as death. I felt like I'd slept for a hundred years.

I sat up too quickly. The room spun, and I sank back, easing myself down onto my pillow, pressing my fingers into my face. My skull throbbed like a bruise.

Slowly, slowly, moving only my eyes, I risked a glance at Cobie. She was sprawled out on top of her covers, breathing a sleeper's heavy breath. The other girls seemed to be asleep as well, though they'd at least made it under the covers.

Nausea rocked me, my gut pitching like the deck of the *Beholder*. I scrambled out of bed, searching desperately for chamber pots.

My stomach was empty, since we'd missed supper. When I finished heaving bile, I rinsed my mouth from a jug of water in the privy. Then I crept to Cobie's side.

"Cobie." Nothing.

"Cobie," I whispered more loudly, shaking her by the shoulder.

She flailed suddenly, hand flying from beneath her pillow, clutching a knife. I flung myself backward to avoid her slashing arm, putting a finger to my lips in the universal gesture for *be quiet*.

She blinked at me, bleary-eyed, then pressed a hand to her temple.

"What happened?" I breathed.

Cobie shook her head—rapidly at first, then slowly, with a wince. "Don't know. Could be the wine . . . ?"

"But I didn't—" My volume rose, and Cobie shushed me. "But I didn't have the wine!" I finished in a whisper.

Cobie turned onto her side and nodded grimly at her goblet, still nearly full of pale Riesling. "I didn't have much, either, from the looks of it. Not enough to feel like this."

I rose too quickly and had to clutch the bed for balance. "We need to talk to the *freinnen*. They—"

"Selah, no." Cobie seized my arm and pulled me back down again.

My voice was urgent. "Cobie, we have to make sure they're all right!"

"Selah." Her hazel eyes were sharp despite their weary cast. "Who do you think did this to us?"

I sat back, frowning.

Cobie watched my face. She saw the moment I realized what had happened.

I'd heard those ten locks fall closed behind us. We'd been

entirely alone, and Cobie and I had felt awake and aware, until Margarethe and Ursula had prepared our drinks and put them in our hands.

I rose again, anger pumping through my blood, and faced the ten sleeping girls. But Cobie dragged me back once more. "We have to pretend like we don't know what happened," she whispered fiercely.

"Why?" I gritted my teeth. "I want them to know that I know. I'm sick of games. I'm sick of tiptoeing around the people who hurt me."

It was a thousand times worse than Lang invading my room; these girls had done something to my body. Had stolen time from me—a whole night. I felt sick, fearful, violated.

"I know they all lied to you. I know you're angry at Lang and the rest of them." Cobie narrowed her eyes, sitting forward, only wincing a little at the pain in her head. "But lashing out at these girls won't even the score for what the crew did behind your back. Besides, don't you want to know *why* they did this?"

"What do you mean *why*?" I bit out.

"If they drugged us, they did it for a reason." Cobie's tone was logical, her words slow but not condescending. "But if they think we're onto them, they'll be more careful. They'll close ranks. And we'll never find out why." She paused.

"But?" I prompted her.

"But if we say nothing," she said, "they'll assume we're fools. It'll be easier for us to learn what they're up to."

I rubbed my head. "I'm tired of people thinking I'm stupid," I muttered.

"Who cares what people think?" Cobie said, incredulous. "Lean into it, if that facade helps you along. Let them think you're stupid, if foolishness paves your way forward." She leaned toward me, eyes intent. "You know the truth. We'll stick together, and we'll figure this out."

It rankled. But she was right. I flopped back on my bed and shut my eyes, and waited.

Before long, the girls began to stir. I watched them carefully through my lashes.

Margarethe got up first, yawning and wiping at her eyes. They were smeared with dark makeup, though I hadn't remembered her wearing kohl the night before. She jumped onto Ursula's bed, white nightgown fluttering as she bounced and greeted her sister in a singsong voice. Margarethe laughed as Ursula swatted at her.

The others were slower to wake. One of the twins who'd ignored us yesterday shuffled out of bed and went to rouse the sister whose wide mouth and narrow shoulders were identical to hers.

"*Nein*," the other girl grumbled, burrowing farther beneath her covers. Her twin prodded her only a moment longer before giving up and crawling in beside her. Margarethe laughed.

Their casual intimacy charmed me against my will, which only made me angrier. What right did they have to be kind to one another when they'd done such an awful thing to me? What had I ever done to them?

Once I'd gotten my frustration in hand, I sat up, stretching and blinking. I caught Leirauh watching me, blue eyes anxious, and forced myself to smile at her.

I know what you did, I wanted to spit at all of them.

I made for the privy again, instead; my mouth felt like sandpaper. "We're dressing for breakfast," Margarethe called to me in English. "Are you hungry?"

"A little sick to my stomach, actually."

Ursula clucked and Margarethe frowned, apologetic, high cheekbones standing out sharp.

"Don't worry." I kept my tone sociable. "I'm sure I'll be fine soon."

I know your secret, I told Margarethe with my polite smile. *And I'm going to find out all the rest of them.*

10

I followed the *freinnen* through the castle's silent corridors to another once-grand room lined with peeling wallpaper. Its chandelier was covered in dust.

Hertsoh Maximilian sat at the head of a large table. Leirauh took the chair at his left side without considering any other, as if it were her place and no one else's. He greeted her warmly but merely nodded at the others.

Though Cobie, Lang, Perrault, and I were alone with their family this morning, the *freinnen* had dressed with great care, in elaborate makeup and clothing chosen to flatter their figures—all but Leirauh. She was barefaced, in a high-collared dress that fit like a flour sack, and her black hair was in one long, plain braid. Above all, her blue eyes were lifeless, devoid of the spark that would have rendered her beautiful, regardless of what she was wearing.

She was a lovely girl, but she looked incredibly plain. It was hard to believe she wasn't doing it on purpose.

Perrault and Cobie took seats together among the *freinnen*, looking—for once—not to mind one another's company. Lang sat beside Margarethe, who eyed him like the cat that got the cream. And in the center of the room sat Fritz, at a table for two. The *fürst* waved a hand at the chair opposite him.

It was impossible not to compare the whole arrangement to Asgard, to its noisy hall, to the high table with Torden and his brothers. It was impossible not to compare Fritz to the boy I loved.

Lang's gaze dragged at me as I drew out my chair opposite the *fürst*.

I barely stifled a scream when a rat ran out from beneath the table. It ran along the nearest wall and into the corridor, claws clicking against the scratched marble floors.

Fritz eyed me sharply as I sat, shaking. It took all I had not to look back in horror at Cobie and Lang and Perrault.

I dropped my gaze instead to the setting on the stained tablecloth before me. A bowl of some sort of grain sat at my place; a few slices of toast and a pot of tea sat between us. I tried a spoonful of the porridge, then choked, feeling like I'd tried to swallow a mouthful of cold plaster.

"Millet not to your liking?" Fritz asked lightly. His inflection was cool and elevated, vaguely reminiscent of English I'd heard spoken in Winchester, but somehow squared off at the edges.

I worked down the bite of cereal and reached for a piece of toast. "It's fine," I said, hoping I sounded gracious. "How is yours?"

Fritz put his spoon down. "I don't like small talk," he said bluntly. "And I don't know what you think you're doing here."

We both jumped, this time, as a third chair was dragged to our table.

It was with only slightly less than his usual finesse that Perrault arranged himself perpendicular to Fritz and me. "Her duty, given your tsarytsya's invitation," Perrault answered for me. "Now, we ought to begin."

Fritz frowned. "*Begin?*"

"I've assembled a suggested list of activities for your courtship," Perrault said, extending a few papers, the set of his mouth intent. He had faltered before Hertsoh Maximilian the day before. He seemed determined not to do it again.

Fritz whipped the documents from Perrault's hands, skimming them. "No," he said flatly. "No, no, and no."

Perrault frowned. "May I ask why not?"

"I cannot offer the seneschal-elect a tour of the castle, as much of it is in disrepair and not fit to be seen." Fritz's cheeks pinkened slightly. Then he leveled his chin. "I have no interest in spending an afternoon on the river; I am occupied with my own pursuits. And a tour of Sankt Goarshausen, outside the castle, is impossible. The tsarytsya rejects the image of us as the town's benefactors."

The mention of her sent anxiety jolting sharp as iron in my teeth. "Does she?"

"Yes," Fritz said, sounding as if he were reciting a lesson. "The common are common because they lack the imagination or ambition to make more of themselves."

I gaped at him, ready to deliver an invective full of the curse words Skop had taught me or St. Francis's teachings on poverty or both. Fritz continued before I could.

"Furthermore, the *freinnen* do not leave the Neukatzenelnbogen," he said to Perrault. "As Selah will inform you, they only leave their room for meals with our family and to work in their sewing room for a little while every day. The door is locked otherwise."

"Locked?" Perrault's head whipped, horrified, between Fritz and me. "The door is—surely you don't mean from the outside!"

Fritz spoke without inflection. "For their own safety."

"Perrault," I said quickly, quietly, leaning forward. "It's fine." *Please don't make a fuss*, I begged him silently.

Much as I wanted to be free of the *freinnen* and their quarters, I wanted more to find out their secrets. I wanted more to find the Waldleute and to give them the weapons they needed. I wanted more for my courtship with Fritz to proceed smoothly, and to escape the tsarytsya's borders without reminding her of my existence.

Perrault sat back, looking utterly defeated. And again, the sight of my protocol officer stymied filled me with anger.

"What are these pursuits that keep you so busy?" I asked Fritz. Irritation seeped into my tone. "Do you have a previous"—I paused, measuring my words—"attachment the tsarytsya knew nothing about?"

"No." Fritz took another spoonful of millet. "I don't have time to waste courting. I'm an inventor."

I cocked my head. "An inventor?"

"Yes, an inventor. I build things," Fritz said, long-suffering.

"I'm not an idiot. I know what the word means." My mind was racing. I thought of my radio, abandoned on my bed aboard ship, and the beginnings of an idea formed in my brain. "You said your sisters go to their sewing room every day. Do you have a studio, a workshop . . . ?" I asked.

"Yes." Fritz's tone was guarded. "I'm there most afternoons."

"I'll visit you there," I said, not a question. "I won't touch anything. I won't get in your way." I turned to Perrault, nodding firmly. "Perrault will make the arrangements."

"Yes," Perrault agreed quickly. I didn't think I imagined the flash of gratitude on his face, pleased to have some of his position restored. Across the room, the *freinnen* began to rise, and I made to follow them, trying to look more confident than I felt.

The day continued in much the same fashion. The *freinnen* slept between breakfast and lunch, where I ate in silence as Perrault and Fritz argued over when, exactly, I would intrude on the *fürst's* workshop.

That afternoon, Cobie and I accompanied the girls to their sewing room, a dilapidated salon full of moth-eaten chaises and frayed carpets, where they spent the afternoon adjusting hemlines, pleating skirts and sleeves, beading bodices, and mending tears. It explained, at least, why their attire was as worn as the rest of the court's but cut to more current fashions. Cobie and I sat a little ways off to talk privately.

"I've never been much of a seamstress," I said idly, trying badly to patch the rip in a pair of my trousers.

Cobie shrugged. "I've never held a needle in my life. Except one time when I had to sew a gash on Will's leg."

"That's disgusting."

Cobie shrugged. "He didn't care how pretty the stitches were, so long as he didn't bleed out." She paused, frowning, as Margarethe and Ursula examined the delicate beading on a lilac-colored gown. "It's funny," she said.

"What?"

She shook her head. "They keep so little company. Why do they bother about the way they look?"

I shrugged. "There's little to occupy them here. No books. No music. No society. No opportunity that I can see. Maybe it's just something to do."

Still. I compared the jagged line of my stitches to the delicate work in Margarethe's fair hands, evidence of long practice and skill, and wondered if there wasn't more to the story.

Negotiations continued between Fritz and Perrault at dinner.

I tried to catch Lang's eye through the meal, searching for any confirmation that his plan was going well, that he had some sort of lead. I expected his gaze to roam the crowds as it had in Winchester, to study the lords and ladies sitting at chipped marble-topped tables greater and lesser distances from the duke and his daughters. Were the ones conspiring with the Waldleute dining with us even now?

But Lang wasn't watching the crowd, and he didn't notice my attempts to get his attention, either; he was talking to Margarethe beside him. She was playing with her hair and smiling.

Only the *hertsoh* was watching me. His eyes were full of a dull and sluggish anger, dark and foul as rot. Leirauh sat at his side, her shoulders hunched.

The tsarytsya who had issued my invitation was far away. But the *hertsoh's* scrutiny reminded me of the fear of watching eyes I'd felt aboard ship. Beneath his gaze, I found myself longing for the relative safety of the *freinnen's* room or even the prickly discomfort of Fritz's society.

I felt, more than ever, how convincing my courtship needed to be in order to keep us safe.

Perrault and Fritz finally agreed that I would visit Fritz's workshop the next day, the third day of our visit. Thereafter, I would visit him every third day until our departure. The prospect of structure—of support for our mimicry of a courtship—filled me with relief.

I only hoped it would be enough time outside the *freinnen's* room to help Lang find the Waldleute.

Perrault paused hopefully as we all rose at the meal's end. "Perhaps you might also—"

"No." Fritz turned for the door. Perrault stood at my side, quiet and pale.

I hated that I felt sorry for him, but I did. For all Perrault's trespasses against me, he had never lied about his intentions.

"You aren't normally like this, Perrault," I said softly as I watched Fritz's retreating back. "Usually, nothing breaks your stride."

"This is Shvartsval'd," Perrault said simply.

"Yes, but you stood up against Konge Alfödr. Surely Hertsoh Maximilian isn't any more frightening than he is."

I wasn't sure what I was needling him for. Perhaps it was just that I felt useless and trapped, and I saw that he did, too, and I wanted a little honest company.

"Alfödr is a hard man but a virtuous one," Perrault said, fingering a curl that had fallen in his eyes. He shook his head. "Asgard is a hard place, even a cold one, but not an evil one."

"And here?"

"Katz Castle is a ruin." Perrault's eyes wandered the mildewed ceiling, the dusty chandelier, the picked-apart floors. "It is rotting from the inside out."

11

"Tea? Wine?" Margarethe offered, clasping her perfectly manicured hands. I had returned with Cobie to the *freinnen*'s room, trying to shake off Perrault's grim pronouncement.

"Tea for both of us, please," I said, nodding at Cobie. We'd agreed on tea.

Margarethe's eyes brightened in her thin face. I wouldn't have known her first smile was false if this one wasn't so genuinely relieved.

When the tea came, I was already in my pajamas, curled beneath my covers. I didn't want to spend another night on top of a dusty bedspread, and they'd notice if I moved later. I thanked the girl who passed me my cup and saucer—one of the twins, Hannelore, they'd called her—and pretended to take a long drink. Pretended I didn't feel them watching me like a pack of wolves.

We'd chosen tea over wine partly because the teacups were

opaque, the better to fool them.

After that first sip, the sisters seemed to relax. They drifted around the room, talking to one another, rummaging through their wardrobes. When I was sure none of them were watching me, I poured a little of the tea out onto a black shift I'd left on the floor beside my bed.

We'd also chosen tea because it wouldn't leave behind a telltale smell, as alcohol would.

After that, I pretended to get sleepy. I yawned, wriggling beneath my covers.

"Tired already?" Leirauh asked, drawing up her legs beneath her ugly, oversized dress. Her blue eyes were reluctant, almost guilty.

She *ought* to feel guilty. I wanted to smack the look off her face.

Instead, I nodded, and let my eyes sink closed.

I could have sworn I heard the exact moment Cobie followed me in feigning sleep. The whole room seemed to still, then burst into a flurry of excited whispers.

The *freinnen* kept quiet awhile, but their voices soon rose, careless and eager alongside the rattle of hangers in their wardrobes, the clank of hair tongs on the fire. I wondered at their bravery—or foolhardiness—at speaking old Deutsch when the tsarytsya's language was meant to reign supreme within her Imperiya. I wondered what it could possibly mean.

I peered at them through my lashes, beneath my arm.

Hannelore stood behind her twin sister, Ingrid—or maybe

Hannelore was the one sitting?—wrapping her hair around a curling iron and chattering relentlessly. Two other sisters, Greta and Johanna, daubed cream on their faces before one of the mirrors, debating the merits of a pink satin evening dress. Both girls were soft-figured and pretty, with light brown hair like Margarethe's and high cheekbones like Ursula's; the gown would have suited either of them.

Nearest me, Margarethe and Ursula had cornered Leirauh in front of a mirror. Margarethe seemed to be threatening Leirauh with a pair of sashes, one indigo, one violet, as Ursula rattled jewelry around in a box.

I watched on tenterhooks. I fought to keep my breathing even as the *freinnen* finished dressing, then walked toward my end of the room, past the foot of my bed, and beyond the edge of my vision.

What were they doing? I tried furiously to remember what lay behind me—a few broken-down dress forms, I thought, and the privy, but nothing more. I couldn't see the girls, but I could feel them, clustered together just out of view. My heart raced, fearful, anticipating what they might do next.

There was the scrape of wood against wood, and the click of keys and tumblers in a lock, and the creak of hinges. And then, with a soft *clack* of high-heeled shoes against flagstones, the room went silent.

I kept still for ten long breaths, ten shuddering heartbeats, afraid to move. And then Cobie sat up, swearing. "Where did they go?"

12

"I have no idea," I said, giving Cobie a significant look. "I don't speak Deutsch, remember?"

"Let's not mention it to the *freinnen*. Element of surprise and all." Cobie grinned and climbed from underneath the covers.

I cast my gaze about the room, baffled. They hadn't gone out the door; I'd heard one bolt falling open, not ten. Besides, they'd moved the wrong way, beyond the end of my bed. I stared in the direction they'd gone: there was nothing there besides the door to the privy and another wardrobe.

The privy was a few chamber pots, basins, and two bathtubs; it seemed an unlikely point of exit. But that wardrobe—none of the *freinnen* ever used it.

I drew near, and a humid draft swirled against my skin, warm and damp in the stale bedroom's air. The doors were cracked open. And beyond were the beginnings of a corridor in the same gray stone as the rest of the castle.

The girls obsessed with clothing had sneaked out through a wardrobe. I gave a disbelieving laugh. "Their room has a secret passage."

"That's impossible," Cobie said at my back. "The duke would never have given them this room. He would have known—"

"Not necessarily." I opened the doors a bit wider. "This castle is old—Fritz said parts are in ruins. I'm sure there are things about it the *hertsoh* doesn't know. Or the passage could have been blocked, but the girls cleared it. In a place with this many secrets . . ." I trailed off, my eyes meeting Cobie's.

She shook her head slowly and withdrew to poke around the room, stopping to fiddle with a black gown on a dress form.

I sighed exaggeratedly. "Cobie, why does everything have to be black with you?"

"Black is easy," she said absently. "Black doesn't stain. And black always matches."

"Matches what?"

"Other black things."

"This." I plucked up the pink satin dress Greta and Johanna had been debating and held it up to her. "This would be perfect on you."

Cobie cringed. "Why pink?"

"Why not pink?" I exclaimed. "Wear what you want to wear, but surely you can afford to be impractical about color when the garment's this impractical already."

Cobie reached out to touch the dress, its smooth fabric filmy over her calloused fingers. "They were going to a party," she said after a moment. "Their accent is different from what I grew up hearing. But I don't think I got it wrong."

I set the dress aside and leaned against the wall, thinking. "How could it possibly be worth it, sneaking out at night to go to a party? What would the tsarytsya do if she found out?"

Cobie shrugged. "I don't think the tsarytsya pays much attention to what's happening out here on the edge of the Imperiya."

I wanted to believe that, but I feared it was wishful thinking. "What about their father? Wouldn't he punish them?" Cobie gave a single, short laugh. "What?" I demanded.

She put down the makeup brush she'd been examining. "Selah, sometimes you make it easy to forget you're eighteen and not a hundred and eight."

I put my hands on my hips. "What does that mean?"

"You've never sneaked out of your house?" Cobie asked, arms outstretched. "Never gone out past bedtime to see friends or someone you had a crush on? Never done anything you weren't supposed to do?"

I pursed my lips, thinking. "I forgot to tell Daddy one Easter I was going to the vigil at Saint Christopher's. He nearly had the guard out for me, he was so worried."

Cobie squinted at me. "No, I was wrong. You really are a century old."

I swallowed hard, staring at my pajama pants. "Well." I hesitated. "There was England."

She stilled and sat on her bed, across from me. "England,"

she sighed. "Feels like a lifetime ago."

"It does," I agreed. "I've kissed a lot of boys in the last month, Cobie."

"Two isn't a lot," she countered. "Two is a perfectly reasonable number of people to kiss when you're essentially on an expedition to find your lifetime kissing partner."

"Well, when you put it that way." Slowly, as if against my will, I walked back to the wardrobe door. Cobie came to my side, and we exchanged a silent glance and crept into the hallway.

The stone corridor was damp and echoing, lined with flickering lamps like those in the rest of the castle. But this one sloped downhill.

I watched for guards, for one of the *freinnen* left to stand sentry. For any sign as to where the hallway might lead. But there was nothing.

We hadn't been walking long, though, when we came to another door. I slipped through it, heart beating fast.

It was lucky for me that Cobie had quick reflexes. The dock was so narrow, I nearly fell right into the water.

"Holy—" She broke off, still gripping the back of my shirt.

The ceiling of the little underground canal dripped stalactites and cold water, ringing with the echo of her voice. Just ahead, the waterway opened up into the night outside.

"Where on earth does this go?" I breathed.

Cobie peered out across the water. "We'll have to swim for it if we want to find out."

"I don't know how, remember?" Torden had held me when we swam in Norge. My chest grew tight at the memory.

Cobie made a face, then dropped to her stomach, staring down into the water. Then she jumped up, brushed off her pants, and nodded. "I can see the bottom. It's shallow, and there's barely any current. Besides, it's time you learned to swim," she added rationally, tugging off her boots. "We're traveling by ship."

"I suppose." But I was still backed against the door, my arms crossed over my chest.

Cobie laughed, her arms and shoulders going loose. "Come on, Selah," she urged. "Live a little."

I thought of why I'd come to Shvartsval'd—of those I'd hoped to help. I thought of Lang, sitting next to Margarethe at breakfast, and again at lunch and dinner, apparently in no hurry to share his plans with me.

I thought of Torden, of kissing him in the water. Of what he'd said to me the night I left Asgard.

Be free, elskede.

"Let's do it," I said. Cobie's whoop echoed off the cavern walls.

"Stop thrashing around." Cobie drew back from my splashes, squinting. "Steady strokes."

I felt like a child as she braced my torso while I kicked and paddled, but it wasn't as if I had any pride anymore, anyway. "Maybe we can hang them over chairbacks," I said. We were trying to decide where we'd dry our wet clothes later.

"We're supposed to have been asleep," Cobie argued. "We have to put them somewhere the *freinnen* won't notice."

I worked my arms, turning my head side to side experimentally. "Good point."

"If there are frames underneath our beds, we can hang them there," she mused.

What *was* under our beds? I tried to envision what I'd seen as I crouched beside my trunks.

It was only when I was four or five feet away from Cobie that I noticed I had swum out of her arms on my own.

"You let me go!" I blurted, turning back to her, accusatory.

"But you're swimming!"

"Oh. I am!" I realized abruptly, my arms still paddling at the water. "I did it!"

Cobie laughed and swam toward me, planting her hands on my shoulders. "You're muscular, Selah. You're strong." Her hazel eyes were keen and kind, and in that moment, I was glad to have her with me. "Honestly, you didn't need Torden holding you up all those times in Norge."

Torden. My eyes burned. "It wasn't as though I minded," I said, managing a laugh.

"Still," Cobie insisted. "This is just to say: You can float on your own."

I missed Torden like I'd miss a limb or a lung. But what she said was true.

"Shall we?" Cobie nodded questioningly at the mouth in the castle wall—where the little canal flowed toward the outside world. I nodded and swam after her.

The stream beyond drifted downhill and through the woods. The night air was crisp, more like fall than summer, and goose bumps skated across my skin. But the stars were bright and clear overhead, and the woods were alive with the songs of nightingales and the hoots of owls.

I felt hidden from the tsarytsya, here in the woods. Beyond the notice of the *hertsoh* and anyone else who might wish to harm me.

"We should go back before you tire out." Cobie glanced up through the trees. "It's getting late."

I still wanted to follow the girls. But I nodded, knowing these few gulps of fresh night air would sustain me through the day to come. I swam back toward Katz Castle after Cobie.

We hid our wet things under our beds and crawled beneath our covers. And I wondered until I fell asleep what lay at the far end of the river.

13

The escort came to fetch us not long after lunch. I studied her matron's uniform, her blond braids, her gait—all I could see of her as we tailed her down the hall.

I saw fewer than twenty people a day, apart from distant courtiers at meals. Confined as I was, I didn't know how I'd ever find the Waldleute.

Our chaperone didn't behave suspiciously, and Hansel, speaking on the radio of Katz Castle, had had a man's voice; but what was I even looking for? Yellow cowslips had been the symbol of the Sidhe, the English resistance, but I'd only known that because Bear told me.

Too soon, the escort and the queue of *freinnen* abandoned me outside Fritz's workshop. I watched Cobie walk away at the line's tail, and my palms began to sweat.

His door was peeling white paint, its lower corners sickly pink with mildew. Hints of gilt clung to its edges, as if someone had scraped most of it off.

"Be charming, but not too charming," Perrault had said, taking me aside after breakfast. His voice was nearly a whisper, just a breath above the silence of the corridor we'd stood in. "I know Fritz is hardly as hospitable as either of your two previous hosts, but"—Perrault had paused, looking grim and pale—"I just want your visit to be a success. A bland, forgettable success."

"Understood." I'd nodded, pushing aside sudden fear and nausea. "Thank you for arranging these meetings."

"I wish I could have done more." Perrault had grimaced, looking away from me. "But you will be able to pass two weeks easily enough this way. Just—do your best."

I felt a sudden twinge of guilt now at how starkly I would defy his advice, given the opportunity, and a sharper stab of fear at what attention my maneuvering might attract.

The sound of smashing glass and a string of what could only have been curses burst from behind the door, shattering the quiet and bringing me back to myself. Chewing my lip, I twisted the knob and poked my head inside.

Fritz was sucking on his fingers, shielding his face with his free hand against a gas lamp that appeared to have exploded. The remains of a shredded canvas tube snaked across a cracked marble floor.

"What happened?" I blurted.

"What are— Oh, it's you." Fritz made a face.

The slight stung, and I winced; but I thought of Perrault. Of how he'd stood straight and tall in Valaskjálf and faced down its king, because that was how the king had to be spoken to.

I'd never expected to learn so much from my protocol officer.

I pretended it didn't hurt to be forgotten, dismissed. I smiled at Fritz like I had secrets, too. "I said I'd be here," I said. "And I am."

"Well." Fritz glanced around the room, at the ruin of his lamp, at various half-built mysteries and projects of indeterminate completeness looming under sheets.

I stepped toward one of these lumps, eyeing the white cloth shrouding it. "Don't touch that!" Fritz blurted. I turned to him, making myself smile again despite his blunt tone.

"Why?" I asked, light as a breeze. "Is it a secret?"

"No." He spoke too quickly, and seemed to realize it. "The sheets are only to keep the dust off the machinery." Fritz gave a rictus smile. *No mysteries here!* it seemed to shout.

I took a step back and clasped my hands behind my back, as if to promise I wouldn't touch anything as I wandered. Silvered mirrors caught the light from lamps and more sheet-draped inventions and bookcases filled with nothing but dust; and in the mirrors' reflection, though Fritz had retrieved a broom to sweep up the smashed glass, I caught him tracking my every step.

I studied the ten gilded shelves looming hollow against the damask-covered walls, wondering how Fritz worked without books to help him. How did he learn about what other inventors and mechanics were doing? His fretful hovering over me made sense, in light of what must often be aimless tinkering punctuated with occasional hard-won success.

Perrault had been right to caution me. Even here, at the edge of her Imperiya, the tsarytsya made herself known. Some rules were unbending, even for nobility.

"You can continue working. I'm not a child," I said, finally turning to the *fürst*. "You don't have to worry over me."

Fritz crossed his arms. "Are you quite certain?"

"Yes," I said. "I may not be an inventor, but I know how not to break things. I'm not stupid." I laughed.

"Aren't you, though?" Fritz asked, brow furrowed. "Can you be so unaware that you're not wanted here? Why should I trust you not to damage my things if you can't see that?"

I drew back, stunned.

If I'd been speaking to Lang, he would have immediately yanked back the words with an apology. Torden would never have spoken to me so in the first place. But Fritz's face didn't change.

"You agreed to have me here," I said. Anger and uncertainty rose in me.

"You invited yourself," Fritz said flatly. "And your protocol officer wouldn't let me decline. And while we're on this subject, you *are* a child," he finished. "I'm nearly ten years your senior."

I was winded, hardly sure what to say. I wanted so badly to help the Waldleute, but I had so little to work with, such small windows of opportunity. I needed an ally in Fritz the inventor. Most of all, I needed this visit to proceed unremarkably to the eyes of the court.

"You're an interruption when I can't afford one," Fritz said, stepping toward the door and holding it open. "I think it's best you just go." Only the barest hint of guilt showed in his eyes as I stepped into the corridor.

When the *freinnen* returned, their long line snaking down the hall toward me, Cobie offered me a hand up from where I sat on the scratched gray marble. We didn't speak on the way back to our room.

The knock came just before dinner.

A man's voice outside the door invaded the sleep that had come after my disastrous visit with Fritz. I sat bolt upright, staring wildly around at the *freinnen* beautifying themselves. "What's going on?" I asked Cobie.

"—the seneschal-elect. I'd like to be let in at once, please."

I chewed my lip. Were we being thrown out? Had Fritz tired of me so thoroughly?

Only when I came fully awake did I recognize the voice. Cobie cracked a weary grin. "Lang to the rescue."

The locks began to turn, one at a time. And when Lang stepped into the *freinnen's* doorway, he was no bearer of bad news. He had the breathless look of a hero come to save the damsel from her dragons.

"Come with me, Selah—Seneschal-elect," he said, holding out his hand. Margarethe eyed him with interest; I brushed past her, dragging Cobie with me.

"Please convey my regrets to Fritz at dinner," I said to Leirauh, and nearly raced into the hall.

Lang walked rapidly ahead of us, up the stairs and around

two or three corners before we followed him into a ragged salon not unlike the *freinnen*'s studio. He shut the door smartly, took two steps toward me, and wrapped me in his arms. I let myself relax into his embrace for one long breath of salt, of ocean—of Lang.

The long muscles of his back shifted beneath my hands, and I shut my eyes and tried not to let myself remember the last time he had held me, or the rustle of sketchbook paper against floorboards in the quiet.

"Thank goodness you're all right," he said.

I stepped back to find Cobie's brows arched in surprise. She looked away, studying the faded gilt and mustard wallpaper, the frayed curtains fluttering limply around the window.

"You've seen me since we arrived." I tried to keep the reproach out of my voice, feeling shy and all too conscious of Cobie's presence. "It's not as though you've lacked proof of life. Why haven't you spoken to me at meals if you've been worried?"

"I have a mission to carry out here. I'm trying not to create disturbances." Lang pushed a hand through his hair, his long fingers tense with frustration. "I've had other concerns, and you seemed fine remaining with the *freinnen* when Maximilian ordered it."

"I thought *you two* had a mission to carry out." Cobie smiled darkly, gesturing between Lang and me. "You are, presumably, hunting for the Waldleute, and Selah is providing cover for you to do so. I assume she'd at least like to know what's happening while she's stranded with the duke's ten daughters."

Cobie assumed—but Lang *knew* I hated being kept in the dark. I'd asked him to include me, to give me what details he could; I would ask again. "Do you have any theories? Any word of where they are?"

Lang shook his head. "I scouted out a few taverns in town, bought drinks for a few strangers. Nothing so far."

A strange, jealous feeling flowered in the pit of my stomach. Lang had been outside the castle; Lang had seen the town; Lang was seeking out the Waldleute alone. *He* was the instigator of all this, and he could move freely, the tsarytsya paying him no mind.

"But it's early days, and I'm hopeful yet," Lang continued cheerfully. "Margarethe may offer helpful information. She's been friendly."

Lang's sanguine smile may have been just a smile. But it set my teeth on edge, this talk of helpful Margarethe who'd smiled and played with her hair and who'd so helpfully drugged my tea the night we first arrived. My catastrophic visit with Fritz suddenly felt that much more humiliating.

Somehow, the embarrassment and the anger made me competitive.

"I've been pursuing my own leads," I suddenly said. "I have plans for Fritz."

"Really?" Lang asked, frowning abruptly. Cobie cast me a sharp glance. Clearly, this was not the sense she'd gotten when she hauled me off the corridor floor on the way back to the *freinnen*'s dungeon that afternoon.

I nodded, uncertain at first, and then more decisive.

"And those plans are . . . ?" Lang prompted.

I swallowed, thinking of Margarethe's beautiful smile and how freely she'd shared it with Lang.

"He'll trust me." I shot Lang a grin. "They all come around eventually."

The words felt foolish as soon as I'd spoken them aloud, but their effect on Lang was immediate. He drew back, dark brows raised, mouth working.

Jealous.

I lifted my chin. Cobie turned away to hide a smirk.

I knew I was playing a game with Lang, and it tangled my insides. I fidgeted with Torden's engagement ring on my finger.

But Torden was far away, perhaps lost to me forever. As Perrault had said, I was officially unpromised.

And if Lang and I were going to play this game, feeding the tension between us while freezing one another out, then I was going to win.

Perrault burst just then into the room. "That guard was wrong, Lang. I still don't know where the seneschal-elect— Oh." The protocol officer looked rapidly between Cobie and me.

"I found them," Lang said simply. I sensed he'd done this deliberately—thrown Perrault off our location so he could speak to us first. It irritated me.

"How are you, Seneschal-elect? How was your visit with the *fürst*? How are things proceeding?" Perrault's dark curls clung a little to his forehead, as if he'd been sweating. As if he'd been hurrying around, trying to find us. I felt another flash of gratitude to Perrault. For all his failings, he actually seemed to care about me. With less than his usual grace, he flopped onto one of the worn chaises where his and Lang's things were scattered.

I didn't spare Lang another glance.

I smiled at Perrault with all the cool and competence I could manage.

"Apace," I said.

14

The *freinnen* found me a restless sleeper after I'd taken my tea that evening.

When the wardrobe door shut behind them, I sat up, flinging myself back against the headboard and breathing sharply out of my nose.

"Bee in your bonnet?" Cobie asked mildly.

I leveled a stare at her. "Why do you ask that?"

"You seem agitated." She crossed her arms. "Lang gets under your skin. And I know things didn't go well with Fritz today."

"No, he doesn't," I sputtered. "Lang, I mean."

"No, you're right. You're entirely unaffected," Cobie agreed.

I stood and began to pace, surveying the *freinnen*'s room. "And no, things with Fritz didn't. But they will," I added. Cobie made another wry assent.

I ran my hand over the edge of Margarethe's vanity, piled in jewels and makeup and clothes, flanked by fashion plates. It was all so beautiful, and it irritated me.

I'd left Lang and Perrault's quarters earlier that evening feeling frustrated. But my anger had mounted the more I dwelled on Lang wasting time with Margarethe and pursuing leads in town with no apparent urgency while I had to pretend to be stupid, pretend to sleep, pretend not to care that the *freinnen* were lying and Lang was using me.

Perhaps I'd agreed to this. But I was tired of licking my wounds in the shadow of the rotting house above me, sick of being left behind while Lang kept his own counsel and made his own rules.

Torden had talked to me. Had trusted me. He would never have excluded me like this.

Lang thought I was only good enough to provide cover for his operation—to be a set piece in the larger drama of his tactics.

I might not have my radio. I might not speak the language. But I was going to show him I was more than a curtain for him to pull while he executed his schemes.

I wasn't sure yet how to convince Fritz to lend me the help I needed. But wherever the *freinnen* were going, it was a secret, and secrets tended to travel in packs. I might find Hansel and Gretel if we followed the girls. We might even find the Waldleute. We could help them. We could go home and take care of my father.

And if we were careful, the tsarytsya and the *hertsoh* would never be the wiser.

I rounded on Cobie. "Let's follow them. Let's find out where they're going and who they're meeting out there."

She got up, grinning, and sheathed a knife at her hip. "I thought you'd never ask."

This time, when we reached the dock, I didn't pause before I dove into the water.

We hadn't swum far before we spotted the *freinnen* in their boats. There were five of them, two girls to each vessel. Even at a distance, I could make out their beautiful gowns, their glimmering jewels.

The sisters were quiet, for once, as the boats bobbed downstream in a little parade. We kept well back from them, letting the current carry us, taking care not to splash. My heart stampeded in my chest, nerves running high.

But I was breathing clear air and staring up at a night sky full of stars, alive, alive, even as my lungs began to ache and my shoulders burned.

They rowed down the little canal that led from the castle straight to the Reyn. Cobie watched the current uncertainly, then reached for my hand.

"You said I didn't need help."

Cobie seized my fingers and began to tow me across the broad river. "Everybody needs help sometimes," she said over her shoulder. "We stick together."

"We stick together," I agreed.

I clung to Cobie's hand as we crossed the Reyn, as its waters beat against my side. When we reached the far bank, we clambered up among the mud and the rocks and the weeds, panting and waiting.

Before long, the *freinnen* were tying up their boats at another little dock, and we followed them up the hill, into the forest. I wrapped my arms around myself against the night air and kept close to Cobie, trying to be as quiet as the owls and bats swooping overhead. Moonlight silvered a stand of birches alongside the path.

"Selah," Cobie whispered. "Do you see that?"

Candles clung to the branches of a massive alder, gleaming golden in the dark ahead, so like Arbor Hall I couldn't help but think it was an omen. The sounds of laughter and music were coming from just beyond the candle tree, from a ruined castle hidden in the wood.

Many of its walls were crumbling, half its roof was collapsed, and green lichen spotted its old gray stone; but its every window glimmered with candle flame, and the stars were diamond-bright overhead. And more than all that—the music.

Tears built in my throat. Cobie's brow furrowed. "What's wrong?"

"Nothing." My voice cracked.

I was overreacting. But the music pouring out of the ruins was the first I'd heard in days.

I'd taken it for granted, before—had hardly noticed Andersen humming as he folded his paper figurines or Will singing to himself in the galley. The music at the balls I'd attended in Asgard and England had been background noise to other pursuits.

But after days and nights of decay and silence, the music

and the sparkling hidden castle in the woods had undone me. I swallowed hard and smiled at Cobie.

A path led clearly from the candle tree to the castle door, but we clambered up through the woods to a window instead. Cobie blew out the candle on its ledge, as if to show what she thought of our not being properly invited.

Then we leaned over the window ledge and peered inside.

15

Beauty, beauty, sparkling and bright, lay before us.

I had never longed for an invitation so badly in my life.

The ruined palace was a fairy glen, a cave of wonders. Candles everywhere glimmered on bright jewels and polished leather, on a table piled with food and wine—but above all, on the crowd.

They were girls with elegant hands and boys with broad shoulders, boys with soft eyes and girls with sharp smiles. Glittering skirts and loose sleeves and slim trousers swirled through the room, some fine, some rough-spun. Many guests were masked; others were not; and their hair and skin were of every shade.

Musicians played in one corner as the crowd danced. I counted eight of the *freinnen* among them, wearing a fairy ring into the earth in their high-heeled shoes. Other guests lined the stone walls—some along the very wall beside our window.

Cobie saw them the same moment I did. A girl with black hair, a goblet in her hand, talking to a boy and to a second girl, who was tall and thin and wearing a dress the color of lilacs.

Even in the half-light, I recognized them at once.

I lurched down, pulling Cobie with me. "Leirauh," I gasped.

"And Margarethe." Her eyes were wide.

We'd found them.

"Did they see us?" I panted.

"I—don't think so," Cobie said, uncertain.

I had seen something shift in Leirauh's blue eyes, but it might have been only the flicker of a candle. We crouched beneath the window, backs flat against the castle wall. I grasped at the forest floor, my heart pounding.

A shadow stretched past the window ledge above us, and then the candle was lit again.

Cobie's eyes met mine. We ran into the woods, not daring to look behind us.

"We'll go back tomorrow," Cobie said. Her eyes were intent. "We'll dress up, and go inside, and find out what they're doing out here."

"What if they are just going to a party?" I asked, sliding into the river. The water was cold. "What if that's all that's going on?"

Cobie's smile was feral. "Then we'll go to a party."

My heart beat hard all the way back to our room, my mind sharp with fear and starlight and freezing water, the images of the night still vivid in my mind. The *freinnen* dancing, happy and beautiful beneath the candlelight, so like the ball I'd had to flee in Arbor Hall. They had looked as free as I had felt dancing with Torden in his father's house, surrounded by the Asgard boys. Aleksei and Hermódr and Bragi and Fredrik, all as close as blood.

Turning over, I shut my eyes. Then a thought struck me.

"Have you noticed how similar all the *freinnen* look?" I asked Cobie.

She bit back a yawn. "Siblings tend to."

"Yes," I said slowly. "Margarethe and Ursula and Hannelore and Ingrid. And most of the others. Light brown hair and eyes and thin features. Fritz, too."

Cobie's eyes were drifting closed. I poked at her across the gap between our beds, and she pulled away, yawning. "What's your point?" she grumbled.

"I don't have one." I shook my head. "It's just odd, to me. Leirauh. She doesn't look anything like the rest of them."

16

Our midnight adventure left me weary. I was nearly swaying as Cobie and I followed the *freinnen* to their studio the next day, dreading the long, terrible hours of stitching ahead.

Fritz's mention of the *freinnen* spending *a little time* in their sewing room each day had been a massive understatement. Remaking their clothes was all they seemed to do—though, now, I understood why.

As we passed his workshop, the door swung abruptly open.

"Seneschal-elect." Fritz's voice was relieved.

I curtsied slightly, avoiding his eyes. "Your Highness."

I'd probably gotten the honorific wrong; perhaps I should've addressed him as *Your Grace* or *Your Majesty* or *Your Serene Beneficence*. Neither Torden nor Bear had made much of titles, we never used them aboard the *Beholder*, and Perrault wasn't here to correct me. More important, I wouldn't be standing in front of Fritz long enough for him to comment. I carried on after the quickly disappearing queue, but the *fürst* stopped me. "Your Grace—"

I turned. My smile felt tight. "I'm not due to return to irritate you for another two days."

"Selah, please come in," Fritz said, and the apology in his tone took me aback.

I paused. "Cobie," I called after her retreating form. She turned, and I pointed to Fritz's open workshop door.

Cobie looked surprised, but nodded significantly. "I'll let the others know."

They wouldn't notice my absence, and Cobie wouldn't say a word to them. But she would be watching and listening.

Fritz ushered me inside and closed the door behind us.

The workshop looked a bit tidier than it had the previous day. I wove through the maze of tables and sheets before turning to face him.

"Why did you invite me back?" I asked. "You don't want me here. You said so."

Fritz put his hands in his pockets, shoulders hunched. "I felt bad."

My face burned. "Flattering." I started toward the door. "I'll go join your sisters."

"No—stay. Please," Fritz managed. "Why don't you sit down?" He gestured to a single chair along the wall, sitting by itself. Despite myself, I laughed.

"What?" Fritz sounded affronted.

He had made an effort in the awkwardest manner possible.

"Now I really feel like a child," I said, thinking of our last conversation and beginning to laugh in earnest. "You might as well have me stand in the corner."

"That wasn't my intention." His brow furrowed. "What would make it a more inviting space?"

Books. Fire. Rain. A kiss.

The thought of an attic study above a library suddenly sprang, unbidden, into my mind, followed immediately by a fjord at sunrise.

I swallowed and pushed the memories from my mind. Fritz wasn't trying to romance me, and I didn't want him to. Both realizations eased me a bit.

"A table?" I twisted Torden's ring on my index finger. "Something to eat or drink?"

I regretted my last suggestion as soon as I'd made it, in light of the fare I'd been served at meals, but Fritz immediately straightened. "Yes! Of course." He bustled over to a copper contraption in the corner and poured coffee into a mug, pausing first to set what looked like a piece of paper over its mouth.

He passed me the cup. I peered inside, curious. "What was the paper for?"

Fritz's face brightened. "It's a filter. A woman named Melitta Bentz developed them, to keep the grounds out of the coffee."

"Any sugar?" I asked hopefully.

Fritz repaired to the coffee maker and returned with a small bowl. "Don't ask where I got it." He smiled slightly.

I took the sugar bowl with shaking fingers.

It was nothing. A throwaway comment. A joke.

But it meant Fritz had secrets. Sources. Ways of getting

things from beyond the court. And that was a start.

I would have bet it was a bigger lead than Lang had; reticent though he'd been, I doubted he could have resisted boasting about it.

I sat in my lone chair and sipped my coffee, reveling in the sweetness and my own little victory. Fritz settled down next to one of his machines, slid on a pair of spectacles, and began to tinker with a fitting at the end of a hose.

"So what are you doing in here?" I asked, curious. "Building the perfect woman?"

"I told you, I don't have time for romance."

"So what, then?" I pressed.

Fritz took off his glasses again and looked at me. "Important things."

I laughed. "Goodness, Fritz." Could he really not hear himself?

He passed a hand over his eyes. "I'm sorry. I'm being rude again. I'm hardly the charming host you expected."

What would Fritz make of Bear's initial biting sarcasm and his eventual efforts to win me over? Of Torden, and his brothers ribbing him and upending half his attempts at romance? Fritz was certainly nothing like either of them.

In fact, Fritz reminded me a bit of me.

I tipped my head to one side, startled by a sudden sense of kinship with him. In Fritz's frustrated expression, I recognized every time Alessandra had interfered with my work, every budget of mine that she'd flouted in her extravagance.

"Back home, I'm responsible for about three thousand acres,

not to mention the cattle, the gardens, and other sundries." I swallowed, missing my father even as I spoke the words. "My stepmother arranged to send me here without consulting me. I understand having your pursuits interrupted by someone with no regard for what they mean to you."

Fritz blinked at me, stymied. "I don't know how large an acre is, to be quite honest with you."

I gave him half a smile. "Use your imagination."

After a long moment, he spoke. "A stylist in Rouen invented a way to dry women's hair quickly." He nodded at the hose before him, then gestured to a row of gas lamps on a table nearby, each smashed, each connected to an identical hose.

I stood and shifted closer. "So you want to . . . dry your hair?"

"No, I want to dry out the castle." Fritz pinched the bridge of his nose. "The rot and mildew are everywhere. The carpets, the wood, the tapestries and upholstery. And . . ." He gestured at the machine. "I hoped the stylist's machine might work for my purposes."

"Wouldn't it be better to repair the roof?" I mused. "Or patch the leaking walls?"

"Only my father can authorize improvements on such a scale." He sighed, looking dissatisfied. "Only he can stop things from growing worse."

I thought of my father. Of his body's slow slide toward ruin, of the sadness that had seemed to weigh on him since my mother had passed, of Alessandra's relentless emptying of our coffers. Of my own powerlessness to deal with the source of my problems, rather than address their symptoms.

Fritz did not speak of the tsarytsya, of her thoughts on his castle and his court, and I wondered if he believed what I only hoped was true: that, if not beyond her reach, we were beyond Baba Yaga's notice in a moldering house at the edge of her world.

"You're just trying to make the best of the situation he created," I finished for him. Fritz nodded glumly. With a rush of sympathy, I raised my mug in his direction and drained it.

"I should go," I said after a long moment, heading for the door. "Your sisters will be wondering where I am."

They would not. But I wanted to leave Fritz thinking fondly of me, and to do that, I needed to actually leave him.

"It was nice talking to you," Fritz said. He seemed to mean it.

"We're not so different, you and I." I gave him a wan smile. "You should let yourself trust, sometimes, that someone might understand."

17

I left my watery expression and my platitudes to do their work with Fritz and hurried to the studio.

"What have I missed?" I asked Cobie as I sat beside her. She was holding a needle in her hand like a dart. "Are they talking about the ball?" I assumed they would be, as I assumed the gowns in their laps were the ones they would wear that night.

"No, they're talking about a wedding— Ow." Cobie popped a bleeding finger into her mouth, glaring at the tear she was trying to patch. "Will's so much better at this than I am."

I glanced around at the *freinnen*, all of them immersed in their work. They reminded me of Imani, the brilliant designer and seamstress I'd commissioned my Arbor Day dress from in Potomac. As Imani had, the girls worked with an artist's intention, their fingers moving as delicately as any sculptor's, their eyes roving as keenly over color and texture as any painter's would do. Old garments became new gowns in their hands.

Art was strictly regulated within the Imperiya. It seemed incalculable foolishness to count clothing out of that reckoning.

Suddenly, I straightened. "A wedding?" Certainly, it was a normal enough subject of gossip; but the *freinnen* didn't seem excited. Their voices were quiet—almost grim. "What about it?"

Cobie frowned, concentrating on the torn black trousers in her lap. "Something, something, months to prepare, something, a year and a day . . ." She tugged a stitch through, needle high, wrapping the thread around her fingers so tightly it nearly snapped. "Oh. Their father's wedding." Something cold and slimy squirmed in my stomach.

Hertsoh Maximilian had warned us he was busy with marriage preparations, and indeed, I'd engaged little with him directly. He was a gray presence in my periphery at meals, the incarnation of the unseen tsarytsya, the living image of the castle decaying around me. I had furiously avoided his gaze; the few times I'd looked his way, he'd been laughing at a rat scampering, terrified, across the table, or cajoling Leirauh into letting him feed her off his plate. He was merely a shade of the tsarytsya, possessed only of a shadow of her power, but his presence sent me eagerly scrabbling back to the *freinnen*'s dungeon room. Even Fritz's prickly company was far superior by comparison.

I wanted most of all to flee entirely. I had to remind myself constantly that we were here to help the Waldleute so they could be free of the tsarytsya and the duke and all his ilk.

"Do we know who his bride is?" I asked quietly, wincing as I stabbed my own finger, whipping my hand away so as not to bleed on the gown I was hemming. "I haven't even heard whether she's at court."

"Maybe Perrault knows something," Cobie said. I made a note to ask him after dinner. "Do you think—" But before Cobie could finish her thought, the door to the studio burst open.

As if we had summoned him, Hertsoh Maximilian himself stood in the doorway, clad in gray and flanked by two guards.

Hands in his pockets, he moved across the circle of his daughters, now risen from their threadbare brocaded chairs and faded velvet settees. Each of them curtsied, murmuring their greetings to him in Yotne.

Batyushka. Batyushka.

Ingrid and Hannelore. Johanna and Greta. Ursula and Margarethe and all the rest of them. Their light brown heads bobbed, their hands clasped. Leirauh shook her black hair in front of her face and stared at the floor.

Maximilian ignored Cobie and me. I could not say I took offense at the slight.

The duke turned instead to the dress forms scattered about the room, like dancers frozen in place. The sisters clustered a little closer together when their father's back was turned.

He was a bizarre sight, loping amid the brightly clad gowns like a visitor to a menagerie. His brown eyes were fever-bright, the nostrils of his high-bridged nose flared as if scenting out a prize.

Maximilian was a handsome man, fit and lithe for his age. But the hunger in his gaze frightened me.

Suddenly, he paused before the gown Margarethe had been making over. It hung on a dress form, light fawn brown and fluffy as a cloud, its skirts grazing the floor, with extra tulle wreathing the shoulders. Gold embroidery around the hem and bodice winked in the light like turning autumn leaves, and though the fabric was worn from being worked over and over again, its thinness only added to its ethereal quality.

I recognized it at once: Ursula had worn it the night before.

The duke stood close to the dress, studying it, before putting his hands on its bodice. He skimmed his palms over the gown's waist, tracing the embroidery.

Nausea roiled hot and vile in my stomach at the lechery on his face.

He shook his head. "*Ni*," he said to Margarethe, waving at the full skirts and rubbing a bit of the soft brown fabric between his fingers. She clasped her thin hands tightly and nodded.

The door closed heavily behind the duke as he left.

Margarethe and Ursula instantly hurried to each other, pale foreheads bent close together, long brown locks shielding their expressions from us.

I sat heavily on my chaise, feeling boneless. "Have you ever seen him here before? Did he come when I was with Fritz yesterday?" I asked Cobie.

"No," she said vehemently, then glanced up, distracted as the girls switched again to Deutsch.

"What?" I glanced around. "What are they saying?"

"Apparently the duke has rejected another wedding dress," she said under her breath. I started to ask another question, but Cobie put a hand on my arm, listening hard for another moment.

"That's why they're here," she finally said. "They're sewing gowns for the duke's bride. Ostensibly."

"What do you mean?"

"The duke is a difficult man to satisfy." Cobie met my eyes. "They're taking their time over the clothes, it seems, and putting them to other uses when their father rejects them."

Johanna and Greta began taking the beautiful dress off its form, poking pins into their aprons as they went. One of Greta's curls fell into her eyes as she bent at the dress's waist, but she blew it out of her face and kept working.

It was like the story Homer had told me so many months ago, before I'd become angry with him. Penelope wove her shroud all day and pulled it apart at night as she put off her aggressive suitors, buying herself one day at a time with her sparse resources and her own ingenuity.

I didn't trust the *freinnen*. But it didn't hurt anyone to admit, in the privacy of my own mind, that this ruse impressed me.

Margarethe curled up onto her settee, gathered the gown that had served its purpose onto her lap, and began to unpick some of the embroidery around its hem. The smug little smile that curved her lips appeared and disappeared so quickly I might have imagined it.

"Try to eat through your teeth, instead of over your tongue," Fritz said, nodding at my bowl. Dinner was millet again, mixed this time with potatoes. Unsalted, unpeppered, utterly flavorless, and room temperature. It wasn't spoiled, but that was the most that could be said for it.

I grinned. "Is that how you do it?" He nodded, wincing as he worked down a bite. "Innovative."

Fritz laughed softly, but the sound filled the dining room, silent but for the scrape of spoons on porcelain. A few courtiers looked up from their plates; from the high table, Perrault gave me an encouraging nod.

Well done! I could almost hear him say, as if this were a tennis match and I'd scored a point.

Fritz and I had barely established a rapport, compared to my easy relationship with Torden. Perrault's reaction would have been offensively patronizing if it hadn't been so obviously sincere.

Beside him, Lang's long fingers were clenched tight around his fork, candlelight in his eyes and shadows in his lashes as he glanced back and forth quickly between Fritz and me. Margarethe sat at his side, still talking, unaware Lang was distracted.

I am pursuing our goal, I wanted to snarl at him. *I am trying to find the Waldleute, and I am keeping all of us safe, should the tsarytsya be watching this courtship.* But my satisfaction ran deeper and less selfless than that, and I knew it.

Lang's jealousy was forbidden and indulgent, and I reveled in it, just a little.

I needed to focus. Furrowing my brow, I faced Fritz again. "Why bother enduring meals like this when you can get things like sugar?" I whispered.

There had been food at the party the night before—meat,

cheese, fresh fruit, fresh bread. And here we sat, a whole court eating cold starch in a rotting hall.

It was an empire away from dinners at Winchester, with children playing beneath the table—from nights in Asgard, with Ragnvald telling stories over the crackle of the fire.

"Because I can't," Fritz hissed, glancing at his father. "Not usually."

But he could sometimes. I wondered if Fritz knew his sisters were sneaking out at night. I wondered if they shared the same sources.

I had to press him a little further. "Where did you get it last time?" I made a face at my meal. But Fritz's mood didn't lighten with my attempt at levity.

"I can't talk about this." His whisper grew sharper. "Do not ask me again."

He set down his spoon with a loud *clank* and sat back from the table, arms crossed, expression closed off as it had been the first night I met him.

Unbidden, my gaze strayed back to Lang. He cocked a brow, eyeing Fritz and me. I could read his challenge from all the way across the room.

Do they really all come around, Seneschal-elect?

And when he smiled at Margarethe, and she smiled back, it stoked the fire under my resolve.

Cobie and I would track the *freinnen* into the woods once more. Like the foxes I'd watched the court hunt in England, I would run their secrets to ground.

18

The night before, we'd swum up the river dressed in black. We'd crept through the trees outside the castle wall and watched the *freinnen* through the windows.

Tonight, Cobie had swum out ahead and brought back a dinghy tied up on the riverbank. Tonight, we'd dressed in gowns and masks borrowed from the *freinnen*'s closets. Tonight, we wore shoes for dancing.

I took Cobie's hand as we stood beneath the arch, and her fingers tightened around mine. "Ready?" I asked, breathless.

"No use waiting for an invitation," she said.

Tonight, we walked up the path and stepped inside.

It seemed impossible that they couldn't hear the party at Katz Castle. Where the home of the *hertsoh* was deadly quiet, the ruined castle rang with music and with dancing—a minuet.

Minuets were supposed to be tiptoeing, courtly things. They were set longways, with two lines opposite one another.

The dance we were watching was sequenced, set between two lines of dancers. Feet knew where they were meant to go; hands knew whom they were meant to touch. But there ended the resemblance to anything I'd seen before.

This was bright, fevered, unapologetic. This was a riot.

Cobie and I hovered just inside the doorway, just on the edge of the dance. We grinned at each other, the stars in our eyes no less bright for the masks around them.

We let ourselves draw just a breath nearer, and in an instant, the dance swept us away.

A tall girl with gold hair seized Cobie's arm; a boy in a crimson mask took me by the hand. Lines of dancers surged to circle one another with fingers twisted together. Arms flung freely skyward, hips and elbows swung joyfully, and dancers called out to friends across the floor. I did my best to mimic them.

I glanced around as I circled my partner, suddenly worried about Cobie. But I should've known she'd be fine. Whatever made her brave and sharp enough to clamber through the rigging of our ship rendered her more than equal to the task before her. Quick as the knots she tied, Cobie learned the steps from her partner and threw herself into the music.

So I did the same.

I'd never had such fun at a party.

We didn't try to talk. I let the boy—a little shorter than me, brown-haired and broad as a wall—lead me through the steps until I figured them out.

The music bore me away, blazing through my fingers and my feet and the hair that whipped around my face. When the song changed, we changed partners, and I lost him in the crowd that spun and wove around me.

My new partner, a beautiful boy with black skin and elegant hands, smiled at me. I smiled back, even as my damp hair clung to the back of my neck and sweat clouded beneath my mask and dirt ground into the lining of my slippers. The very stones rang with the stamp of our feet.

I danced until my shoes were near to breaking. And then I came back to myself, and remembered what I had come for. A table in the corner heaped with wine and food was the perfect excuse to step away.

Most of the partygoers were part of the dance, but, as the night before, a fair number lined the walls. If there were any secrets to be heard or gossip to be gotten, it would be from the watchers and wallflowers. Pretending to be focused on the cup of water in my hands, I meandered among them and attempted to eavesdrop.

But it was to no avail. Whether they were speaking in Yotne or old Deutsch or ancient Greek, it made no sense to me, and Cobie was somewhere in the crowd. I sighed, frustrated. Torn.

I looked longingly back at the dance.

I had not understood, at first, why the sisters were sneaking out night after night. The risk had seemed unfathomable to me.

But I understood now. Here in the woods, I felt both hidden and free. Shielded and liberated, all at once. As if, search though it might, the gray shadow could not find me here.

The tsarytsya could try to control everyone—could outlaw

music and belief and books and hem her people in on every side. The *hertsoh* could lock his daughters in their room and control the company they kept.

But like the trees that grew beneath Arbor Hall's marble floors, pressing against stone and creeping through gaps, life could not be stamped out. It could be deterred, hindered, stalled.

But we were young. Our life would out. *Fun* would out.

It was wisest, perhaps, not to fight it.

The first seneschal's people had chosen to make room for life, to fill our halls with the trees that grew in, with their whispers and fresh scent. The *hertsoh* had chosen another way—to deny his children their youth, to press down their energy and believe it had evaporated. And the result was decay in his hall—and this mad, boundless joy, of which he would enjoy no part.

Nights like this were magic, and everyone deserved them. Everyone deserved space and freedom and the wild, just as the Waldleute said.

My mind warned me of the hours that passed, reminded me of the reasons I'd come. But I joined the dance again, jumping in and catching the tail of a line. The girl in front of me took my hand, silver bangles and string bracelets glimmering on her wrist. We pivoted around another pair across from us.

Then I stopped cold.

The music played on. My partner and the girl she'd circled kept dancing. The stones beneath my feet trembled with the steps that carried on without me.

Lang was staring at me from the opposing line, breathing heavily from exertion, eyes wide beneath his thick lashes and a dark blue mask. He looked oddly undressed in just a shirt, without his jacket.

I took his hand and pulled him back into the dance.

"What are you doing here?" he demanded.

"What are *you* doing here?" I countered, glancing around. "Is Perrault—?"

"Of course not." Lang scowled and lowered his voice, following the steps. "I'm chasing down the Waldleute."

"Me too," I bit out. His frown grew. "I didn't see you making any progress, so I took matters into my own hands."

Lang blinked, staring at me like he'd never seen me before.

He shook himself, turning away just long enough to circle the girl at his side, scanning the crowd but seeming distracted. My eyes tracked him as I rounded my neighbor.

And then he came back to me. Lang's shoulders were loose, his body easy; he shook the hair out of his eyes, watching me, seeming not even to notice that his long legs and feet were keeping up with the dance while he was preoccupied. I barely touched his hand, but as we wound around one another, his fingers curled over mine.

He smelled like the sea.

Lang's touch brought back the night he had wrapped his arms around my waist and asked me not to make him tell the truth. The drawings of me scattered across his bedroom floor, smudged in ink and charcoal, utterly perfect, breathtaking in their intimacy.

"Wait." I paused, putting a hand to his chest. His Adam's apple bobbed, and I drew back. "How did you know—how did you get here?"

Lang glanced over my shoulder. I followed his gaze and caught a glimpse of long brown hair and a violet gown and a smile aimed at him from the edge of the crowd.

Fear spiked through me. I whipped around to face Lang. "Are you here with Margarethe?" I demanded.

He flushed beneath his mask. "She didn't say you were coming."

"She doesn't know I'm here!" I snapped, my hand flying to the back of my head to check my mask was secure, my fingers trembling. "The *freinnen* drugged Cobie and me that first night so they could sneak out. And then we wised up and followed them."

"They what?" Lang gaped, then shook his head. "No, you've misunderstood. Surely—"

I stepped closer to him, still following the dance. My pulse rose. "Don't tell me what I've misunderstood!"

"Then don't make hysterical claims!" Lang's eyes flashed as he circled me, and he tugged his mask off, pulling it down his cheeks to hang around his neck by its ribbon. His chest rose and fell, and I could hear him breathing hard.

We promenaded side by side, my grip iron around his fingers. "You're here with Margarethe," I said again, dragging her name out, as if Lang would know what I meant if I repeated it enough times.

"You came here with Margarethe?" Cobie demanded,

incredulous, appearing at my side.

"Enough." The word was heavy as a stone in his mouth. "Take her home," he said to Cobie.

"Excuse me?" Now it was my turn to gape at him.

Seeing Margarethe had set me on edge. But I hadn't done yet what I'd come to do.

Still—though the music rang louder than our argument, partygoers close by were beginning to stare; Cobie and I had little chance of eavesdropping successfully tonight. And if Margarethe saw us, everything would be ruined—tomorrow night and every night after, this opportunity to find the Waldleute and help them gone.

What was more, I didn't trust Margarethe. She was all warmth toward Lang, and she left me more or less in peace by day; but by night, she wanted me ignorant of these parties so badly she'd been willing to drug me. I feared she'd find some way to punish me if she found me here.

I turned to leave the lines of dancers. "I can't believe you're here with her," I spat. Anger and fear roiled in me.

Worst of all was that even those feelings bubbled a little less hot than my jealousy. I shoved them all aside, taking Cobie's hand and turning toward the door.

But before I could walk away, Lang leaned close, his damp curls brushing my temple, his cheek hot against mine. "You aren't the only one who can make friends."

19

I couldn't focus the next day, either at meals or in Fritz's workshop, where he'd invited me to visit again. Perrault looked worried when he approached me after breakfast, asking if the food or sleeping in the *freinnen*'s room disagreed with me.

"Seneschal-elect, you must tell me if you require this visit curtailed," he'd said carefully. His dark eyes were tentative, and the worry and kindness in them almost made me cry.

I had reassured him that of course I didn't need to leave, that everything was fine.

Everything was not fine. My mind kept drifting, my memory running over snatches of songs I'd heard the night before, wondering if Margarethe had recognized me standing with Lang. And if she had—could she report us to her father, or the tsarytsya? I turned the idea over and over, wondering if she could get us in trouble without getting in trouble herself, until I was nearly crawling out of my skin.

I almost wondered if returning to the ball would be wise.

And over and over again, I heard Lang taunting me. *You aren't the only one who can make friends.*

I felt jealous, and the jealousy made me feel guilty. I twisted Torden's ring on my finger, turning the stones face-down, as though they could see the emotions tangled in my expression.

It wasn't fair. I hadn't left Torden of my own accord; we'd been forced apart. And I hadn't fired the shot that had started this race between Lang and me.

During meals, I watched him and Margarethe out of the corner of my eye. I had hoped that Lang was perhaps only humoring her attention; but that clearly wasn't true. Margarethe was beautiful, but with Lang, she was also frank and funny. Even at a distance, I could see Lang found her intriguing.

I hated it. I tried not to think of the marvelous time they'd probably had at the ball after I'd left. When I'd leaned across the breakfast table, laughing flirtatiously and trying to appear interested in my conversation with Fritz, he had merely looked baffled. Lang hadn't noticed, anyway.

He was winning.

"—Seneschal-elect?"

I blinked up at Fritz's voice. He sat before the pieces of his dryer, hands on the knees of his trousers, frowning.

"Yes?" I asked.

"You seem rather trapped in reverie," he said stiffly. "You were humming."

"Was I?" I stalled. Fritz nodded, bemused.

I had been, I realized. One of the songs from the party. The one I'd danced to with Lang.

I wet my lips. "Forgive me. The tsarytsya's rules about music are still not quite intuitive."

Fritz raised his eyebrows, working the end of a hose around the chimney of the lantern. "Indeed."

"I'm sorry if I pushed you too far last night at dinner," I blurted out suddenly. "I'm out of place here and didn't mean to make you uncomfortable asking too many questions."

Fritz leaned back again, propping his ankle on his knee, brow furrowed. "I accept your apology, but that's not all that's happening," he said. "You want something. You pretend not to see things, but you see them. I want to know what you're searching for."

Fritz studied me, and, taken aback, I studied him in return.

Twenty-seven wasn't old. But taking Fritz in where he sat now, I could see the full twenty-seven years he'd lived. Subtle lines had begun to insinuate their way across his pale brow, and his light brown hair was shot with early gray.

Fritz was tired. And Fritz was wise—wiser than Torden, and more perceptive by far than Bear.

Most important, perhaps, he was not enamored with me. He would not be so easily deceived.

I laced my fingers together, nodding at the lamp sitting before him. "Is that working yet?"

He brightened. "It did, a little. I tested it in my suite earlier. The carpet seems much drier than before. The plaster, too."

"That's wonderful!"

Fritz nodded, raising an eyebrow. "It is. But you're also avoiding my question."

I ran my mental calculations as quickly as I could.

Fritz liked me well enough, but he did not trust me. Not when it came to his sources, and not, I suspected, when it came to his sisters.

But if I confided in him, perhaps he might do the same with me. I lifted my chin.

"I want a favor," I said.

"A radio." Fritz's voice was even, but his eyes were incredulous. "You want to borrow a radio." I nodded. He laughed as he blew out a breath, shaking his head. "What makes you think the tsarytsya permits us to keep such things? What makes you think I have one?"

There had to be a tower nearby. Hansel and Gretel must have used it to communicate. I'd told Fritz about the radio I'd had to leave aboard ship, hoping the expression of trust would inspire the same in him.

I waved a hand around the studio. "You're an inventor," I said, putting all my feeling into the word. "I know this isn't romantic, between us. But I've come to think of you as a friend, and I need help."

"A friend," Fritz repeated.

I nodded. "And I'm counting on you not to tell anyone the truth about this." Ordinarily I would have fought the tremor in my voice. I didn't hide it now. I bit my lip, letting all my fears and feelings show.

Perrault would have been delighted to see the show I was putting on. To see how well I'd learned from his expertise. Until, of course, he learned why.

"Why?" Fritz asked, squinting up at me from his chair. "Why would you tell me this?"

Because I want you to tell me your secrets, too, I wanted to say. *I want you to trust me, so I can help the people I came here to help, and get out.* But that wouldn't do.

So I told a different truth.

"Because my radio is how I've been speaking to my godmother," I said. "She and my father are the only real family I have; my mother is deceased. But my godmother and I have been using the radio to speak since I left, and it gives me comfort. But Lang said it was too dangerous to bring ashore." I looked up at Fritz, letting my heart show in my eyes. "My family matters more to me than anything."

Fritz paused. He passed a hand over his forehead, sitting back. "My grandfather was the first *hertsoh* of Shvartsval'd. Did you know? The tsarytsya appointed him herself after she deposed the ruling family." He swallowed, gaze growing troubled. "Sometimes I can't believe what this place has become. What my family has done to this place in barely two generations, when we shouldn't have been—" Fritz broke off, discontented. "I don't know what will be left for the future." He nodded unhappily at the wall opposite us, its plaster crumbling, its wallpaper peeling away.

"That's what all this is about for you, isn't it?" I asked suddenly. "You aren't just an inventor. This is about your family."

"Yes," Fritz said quietly. "The future of Shvartsval'd, and my family. What's left of us."

"Left of you?" I asked, drawing back a little. "Did you have *more* sisters?" I winced as soon as I heard my own words. "I'm sorry, that was insensitive."

But Fritz laughed. "No, no more sisters."

"Leirauh's the last of you, isn't she?" I asked. "That's why your father babies her."

Fritz sobered and shook his head. "Leirauh is seventeen. Hannelore and Ingrid are younger. Both fourteen. And besides," he continued, "Leirauh isn't technically my sister."

My gaze snapped up to his. "She's not?"

"No. My—" His eyes softened, a little sad. "My sisters' and my mother was an actress. She was famous—one of the most sought after in Europe. When I was little, she worked a good deal in Italy." Fritz paused. "She used to write to us about the theaters there, about the brilliant machines that brought the stages to life."

"I'm sure you miss her," I said. "I miss mine, too."

Fritz gave me a pinched smile. In this, we understood each other.

"The tsarytsya was lenient for a time, permitting travel outside the Imperiya for certain elite. But she eventually demanded all expatriates return home. When my mother returned, she brought Leirauh home with her. Her mother, another actress, had died en route. My mother died only a few years later."

"I see," I said quietly.

She looked so different from the rest of them—I'd said as much to Cobie. Leirauh, with her thick black hair and anxious blue eyes, soft-hipped and pink-cheeked. When I pictured her in my mind's eye, beside Margarethe and Hannelore and Ursula and the rest of them, all honey-brown hair and high cheekbones, I knew Fritz was telling the truth.

Leirauh's circumstances reminded me of Anya. She had lost her country and her family and had been adopted into a new home. And she had been charged a high price for her good fortune.

Despite my frustration with Anya, all at once I missed her terribly.

Fritz rubbed at the lines in his forehead. "I worry for them. My father's treatment of my sisters is archaic. It does not bode well for my family, or for the future of our court and *terytoriya*."

I feared for my country's future, as well. But I couldn't imagine fearing the actions of my own father.

Daddy might have failed me. But he was tired, and sad, and sick, and his only sin had been to trust his wife. Duke Maximilian had fallen far, far short of what he owed his children.

My stomach quaked at the prospect of returning to the ball and facing Margarethe. But Fritz's tale made me want, more than ever, to find the Waldleute. It made me believe as much as ever that I'd done the right thing to leave Torden behind, to defer returning to my father, in hopes that we could help old Deutschland shake off the Imperiya and its shadow.

Fritz studied me. "I'm sorry if I've been cold. Distant.

Unkind, at times. I assure you, it's not any fault of yours. I'm overwhelmed with the foulness spreading through this castle, and the corruption I fear it will spread."

"I misunderstood you," I said quietly. "I thought you were cruel, when we first met."

"No." Fritz smiled faintly. "Just a bit inept, and entirely pre-occupied."

"And far more comfortable in your laboratory than you are at court." I paused. "Also, my clothes were wet, and no one was expecting me."

"It was not an auspicious beginning," Fritz agreed. We sat in silence for a long while after that. He fiddled idly with a screwdriver.

"So," I asked. "A radio?"

Fritz hesitated, as if considering, then stood. "A confidence for a confidence, I suppose."

20

He walked to a corner and pulled the sheet off one of his secrets. It was a radio, a little larger than mine. My breath flew out of my chest.

It had been right here, all this time.

"You built this?" I asked.

Fritz nodded. "For the same reason I built everything in here."

For his home. For his sisters.

"The parts are from all over—there are places in Masr and Bharat and Zhōng Guó where they make thousands of pieces at a time. Radios are not uncommon there." A faint grin stretched across his anonymous, handsome face. "Do you want to try to reach out to her?"

I held Fritz's eyes a long moment before turning on the radio and seeking out my godmother's frequency.

It was empty, silent as a night on the sea.

"Godmother?" I asked softly of the quiet.

"Selah?"

It wasn't my godmother's voice. Still, I knew it. I frowned, racking my memory. "Sister—Elisabeth?"

"Yes, it's me." Sister Elisabeth had been my math teacher, and a strict one. "When your godmother has to be away, she has a few of us keeping watch here." She paused, her tone growing curious. "I was led to believe you and your betrothed were on your way home, Seneschal-elect?"

The words ached. For a long moment, I couldn't reply.

I thumbed my engagement ring, shutting my eyes tight, as if refusing to look at the world could make our story any less true—Anya's flight from Asgard. Alfödr's negation of Torden's proposal. Our escape. The duty I had shouldered.

But I couldn't bear to tell her the truth about Torden. About the boy I had loved and lost in barely a fortnight. And even if I could, it wasn't safe to tell her the truth over the air. As Gretel had told Hansel, anyone could be listening.

"We were delayed," I finally said. "I don't have a fiancé anymore."

"I will inform your godmother," Sister Elisabeth answered quietly.

I asked a few other rapid questions after that—my father's condition had improved, ever so slightly, and the baby hadn't come yet. Alessandra was bound to her bed, waiting for her little one to arrive. By my calculations, she had about another month. I wondered if her confinement had anything to do with my father's condition improving, but said nothing.

"We await your return eagerly," said Sister Elisabeth.

I could admit to nothing in front of Fritz. "Take care," I finally said, and switched the radio off. Fritz hid it again under its sheet with a glance toward the hallway.

He'd taken a risk for me. I wouldn't forget it.

I left Fritz not long after. Lang was waiting for me in the corridor, looking like a ruin himself. Shadows circled his eyes, deeper still than the ones he'd worn in Asgard, and his hair was tousled, stiff and salty with the sweat of the night before.

He put his hands on his hips, jaw tight. "I have been looking for you everywhere."

"Did you ask Perrault?" My tone was acerbic. "Our protocol officer? Because I'm exactly where I was supposed to be."

"I assumed you were with the *freinnen*."

"You assumed." I spread my hands, struggling to contain my frustration. "In case you'd forgotten, my courtship is the reason we're allowed to be here."

"As if I could forget." Lang scoffed. "With the way you flirt with him? Laughing at things that aren't even funny and leaning across the table to stare into his eyes?" He turned away but I dogged him, my anger rising, making me forget to leave space between us, making me forget we were in a public corridor and anyone might find us.

"I'm flirting?" I hissed, striding after his back. "You're nose-to-nose with Margarethe at dinner, and *I'm* the one who's flirting?"

Lang whirled on me. "*They all come around eventually. Those* were your words!" he bit out. "Because you're beautiful and you're charming and you know they're all going to fall for it. My congratulations to you." He bowed sarcastically, one lean-fingered hand pressed to his chest. "But two can play that game."

You aren't the only one who can make friends.

A flush surged over my skin. "What happened after I left the ball last night, Lang? With Margarethe? Did she see Cobie and me?"

"Nothing happened." Lang smirked. "I made inquiries."

"What, as to how many buttons were on Margarethe's dress?" I shot back.

I wanted to swallow the words as soon as I'd spoken them.

Lang's grin spread slowly. He crossed his arms and stepped nearer to me. I backed away until I hit the corridor wall.

"You're jealous." Lang's eyes were dark on mine. "You really are jealous."

I was losing, and Lang was winning.

"*You're* jealous." My voice was faint.

"You know I am." He wet his lips, swallowing. "But you've known that all along."

The words felt like a shout in the silent corridor. I couldn't speak.

"You let Torden take care of you. You let Bear fight for you," Lang said. With every word, he drew nearer, until he was leaning over me, looking down at me through thick lashes. "Let me take care of this for us, Selah. Don't go tonight."

His eyes were dark in the shadowed corridor, and his tanned

skin smelled like salt, and my mind suddenly began to race in circles around how strange and different it felt to kiss a new person and what it would be like to try with Lang.

He was so close, and I was tempted to give in to him, to remain in the castle. Margarethe was dogged, and cruel, and I didn't doubt she'd do worse than drug Cobie and me if she thought we knew her secret.

But I couldn't forget what Fritz had confided in me. I shook my head.

"I need to see this through, Lang," I said. "This is larger than us."

Lang ground out a sigh, shifting away. "I was afraid you'd say that. I wish you could just trust me, Selah." He met my eyes. "Please don't make me turn the request into an order."

Warmth heated into anger and volatility in my chest. "An order?" I drew up slightly, closing the space he had created between us.

"I'm the captain of this mission," Lang said, reluctant. "I will order you to stay inside if it will keep you safe and help us reach our goal more quickly."

"And *you* know what will keep me safe?" I asked sharply. "When you didn't even know your friend Margarethe was drugging me?" Frustrated, I bit my lip. Lang's gaze shifted to my mouth. But I shook my head. "I think you're forgetting something, Lang."

His Adam's apple bobbed, and he reached out to touch a lock of my hair, wrapping its length around his fingers. "What's that?" His voice was uneven.

I remembered Yasumaro's eyes on mine, serious and sincere. *What are my orders, Seneschal-elect?*

I shifted forward, eyeing him fiercely. "I outrank you. We're here at my word, and I don't answer to you."

Lang released my hair and put his palm to my cheek, his eyes confused, reflecting all my frustration. "Selah, if something happens to you out there, I can't protect you." He was close enough that I could feel his breath on my cheek.

That's our place. That's where we belong. Between you and everyone else.

"The thing is, Lang?" I said. "Protecting me? I never asked you to." I turned and made for the *freinnen's* room to prepare for the night.

Lang had told me once he wanted all my anger, all my heat.

But I had other plans for the fire burning beneath my skin.

21

Lang's words chafed at me all through dinner. Perrault watched me nervously as I sat across from Fritz, my teeth on edge, sawing at my flavorless supper.

Don't make me turn the request into an order.

I wanted to laugh. As if Lang could tell me what to do. As if *who* was leading our mission was more important than the people we'd come all this way to help.

An argument this sharp would once have paralyzed me—would have kept me safe in the *freinnen's* room, out of trouble, out of range of all the mistakes I could make. But now, it only pushed me forward. Set me in motion.

It made me more reckless.

Cobie swam for the rowboat again as soon as the *freinnen* had left that night, and we shoved off with no hesitation after she'd returned and dressed.

"They're lucky to have a place close by to play," Cobie said as we scrambled up the hill toward the ruin. "Burg Rheinfels is perfect. Abandoned. Distant enough to hide the noise."

I froze. "What?"

"Burg Rheinfels. That's what the castle's called. I heard the sisters say while they were getting dressed earlier."

Burg Rheinfels. I'd heard the name before.

My mind raced.

The witch's cottage, or the woodcutter's? Tell me quickly.

The woodcutter's cottage. My people won't be going anywhere near your father.

In the conversation I'd overheard, a boy named Hansel had asked a girl named Gretel where they should meet. She'd cut him off, but not before he'd named two places—Katz Castle, and Burg Rhein . . . something. I'd analyzed the conversation, had heard their words over and over in my head.

My hands shook at my own foolishness. It had been so many days.

Hadn't I noticed how familiar his voice was?

I knew the speaker. I'd used his radio.

Little Hansel in the woods had never been so inventive as Fürst Fritz of Terytoriya Shvartsval'd.

Back in England, I'd spent weeks watching Lang watch a room. It had irritated me, to see him so distant—always somewhere other than present, with me. He and Yu had hovered in doorways, lingered over their cups long after they were empty.

But though I'd questioned whether I'd know what I was

looking for as I sought out the resistance, observing Lang had taught me. And now, I could do it better than him.

I kept watch over Burg Rheinfels. But I didn't do it from a spot along the wall, looking obvious. I joined the party.

As we spun and stomped and the line of dancers chased its tail, I kept my eyes open, taking in the whole room. The party swirled with a few hundred people in a fantastic array of fashions—jackets and tunics and trousers, boots and slippers. And gowns, in every color, every fabric. Drop waists and empire waists, ballerina skirts and mermaid hems. Some new, some worn, some fine, some cobbled together from scraps.

I'd put on a cornflower-blue gown of my own and dressed Cobie in navy silk dug from the back of Margarethe's closet. Pretty clothes, but unremarkable.

I'd intended us to be forgettable. Fritz's face—his perfect, nondescript features—had given me the idea.

We danced and we watched. The Waldleute were here. They had to be.

My eyes roved the room, waiting for a sign. And suddenly, I spotted Lang, dancing with Margarethe.

He was wearing a mask, so it wasn't his face I recognized first. Not the depth of his eyes or the dark of his lashes or the curve of his brows and his nose. It was his hands.

As he reached for Margarethe, I recognized at once the length of Lang's fingers against hers, the shape of the perpetual charcoal smear around his middle finger and across the back of his hand. He'd been drawing again.

An odd ache spread through my stomach. And when the

dance ended and Margarethe moved away, I surged forward, pushed past the girl who would have taken her place.

Lang shoved his mask up over his forehead. "Again?" he demanded.

"Keep dancing," I hissed. I seized the hand some other girl had been about to take and circled him, rejoining the line.

"I told you not to come."

"And I ignored you." I spoke close to his ear. "I'm here to get some answers and to enjoy myself, and you're not going to spoil it."

"I'm enjoying *myself*, for once—" Lang grumbled, pulling his mask back into place. But Margarethe was gone, and his eyes weren't seeking her out at the edge of the crowd.

I shook my head, taking his hand as we promenaded together. "No, you weren't."

"You're right." Lang's fingers slid between mine, pressing the band Torden had given me against my fingers. "I wasn't."

I felt a flood of guilt, a wicked rush of power.

Lang was a good dancer; he sauntered, loose and bold, every step, every shift of his shoulders and torso in time with the music. He exuded confidence, and it attracted more appreciative glances than mine alone.

Wanting burned in me.

Eyes locked on one another, we circled once more. The music was loud, but not as loud as my heartbeat in my ears.

Lang bent his head, and his nose grazed mine, and the rest of the party suddenly seemed very far away.

142

I took a breath, drew back slightly. "Lang, I need to tell you something."

Beneath the music and between our passes with other partners, I told him how I'd overheard the conversation between Hansel and Gretel. "And I realized tonight that one of them was Fritz," I added, breathless. "And Lang, this is Burg Rheinfels. They talked about meeting here."

"We could find them," Lang murmured. "We might actually find them." He gripped my waist and circled me again.

Potomac. My father. They were close enough to touch.

"And then," I said, "we can go home."

I found another partner after that dance, and Margarethe returned to Lang. We all watched the room from our places, seeking out secretive behavior, Cobie and I avoiding the *freinnen*.

I had lost track of the hours when Cobie appeared at my side later, her eyes wide and panicked. "Selah, the *freinnen* are leaving."

"What do you mean?" I shook my head, trying to clear it of music and sparkle, trying to focus.

"We need to go," she said, urgent. "If they beat us back to Katz Castle—"

"No!" I gasped. "They can't!"

Cobie disappeared and reappeared in half a moment, Lang at her side. He seized my hand. "Come back with me, both of you. I'll make up an excuse, say that we've been together."

My stomach jolted at Lang's touch; I ignored it. "Lang, you

can't make this go away. Margarethe knows you've been here."

Lang cursed under his breath. "Hurry." He pulled me through the crowd, pushed me toward the door, his calluses rough against my palms and my bare shoulders. "Hurry, hurry, and don't get caught."

We tore down through the woods and up the river, abandoning the rowboat Cobie had borrowed somewhere on the banks and swimming up the tributary beneath the castle. Cobie pulled herself onto the dock, the muscles in her arms straining, her navy dress black with water. I hauled myself up after her, slipping over the fabric of my gown.

We hurried down the corridor, hurried toward the chair propping the door open, hurried inside, ready to sneak into bed and put an end to this evening.

But the *freinnen* were already waiting.

Fritz was with them.

22

My heart plummeted, sick and heavy, into my stomach.

Cobie's face paled.

"I knew it," Margarethe said, low and deadly. She nodded at Cobie, whose navy gown was dripping. "I saw my dress across the room. Ruined now, of course."

I didn't know how they'd beaten us back. My mind raced.

Fritz stood beside Margarethe, his eyes on me baffled and hurt.

"You must think we're fools." Leirauh watched us from her bed, arms wrapped around her knees, white silk splayed about her.

I fought the guilt I felt beneath Fritz's gaze. "It's a dress, Margarethe. I'll make amends. But while we're settling accounts, I'll make sure to add every night you thought you were drugging us to your bill. Besides"—I gestured expansively at the mountains of magazines, the dress forms, the fashion plates, the wardrobes—"it's not as though you have nothing else to wear."

"The gown is not the point." Margarethe crossed her fine-boned arms. Her voice was as sharp as a seam ripper. "Though, for the record, we keep the magazines because Papa doesn't think they count as books. He doesn't fear what our delicate feminine minds will do with fashion, as he doesn't consider it art."

"The more fool he. He has no idea what your *delicate feminine minds* are capable of," I snapped. I paused, studying their faces—Leirauh, Margarethe, Fritz. All alike but one. "I would ask if the risk of defying him was worth it, but I've been to your parties."

"The parties are not the point." Fritz shook his head, frustrated. "You can't even see how much you don't understand."

"I understand that being trapped in this room would drive anyone to distraction." Cobie's teeth were chattering. "That anyone would go to secret parties if their only respite was a sewing room." She turned toward the wall and began to strip out of her gown.

"This isn't about release," Fritz burst out, turning on me. "I told you when you arrived that I had too much on my mind to tangle with women. I should've trusted my first impulse." The words were cruel, but his expression was pained.

I held up my palms. "I would've been happy to mind my own business. But I think my curiosity about being *drugged* was understandable!"

Cobie stood, clad now in black pajamas. "I suggest you

start explaining before we go to our crew and instigate an early departure."

"No, please!" Leirauh blurted, sitting up. "Don't."

Cobie and I exchanged a glance. "Why not?" I asked.

"Because." Leirauh's expression tightened, her eyes sad and worried. "They've done this for me."

I was already wearing a dripping gown, already standing in a chilly stone room. Who would have thought I could have gotten any colder?

"What do you mean?" I asked.

"Tell her nothing, Leirauh," Margarethe bit out. Ursula stepped to her side. "She is not to be trusted."

"You did," I said to Fritz. "You were beginning to trust me."

"And much good it did me," he said soberly.

"I meant it when I said we understood each other, Fritz. I understand your desire to protect your family and your home, and if I can, I want to help." I sank in front of Leirauh, my dress puddling around me on the flagstones. "Tell me what's going on," I said, glancing between her and Fritz.

"And if we don't?" Margarethe fired back. Fritz crossed his arms.

Cobie's dark hair was soaked, water running in rivulets down her back. She sat beside Leirauh on her bed. "And if you don't," she said quietly, "we'll leave it alone."

Fritz raised his eyebrows.

"This is clearly important," I said to him. "Your sisters hurt us, but we can let it go. You took a risk to help me. So trust us or don't, but we won't endanger your plan. Although," I added, "you should know we're here to help."

The *fürst's* light brown hair was tousled with sweat, his perfect, nondescript features a painter's nightmare and a con artist's dream. I couldn't read the expression on his face until he opened his mouth and spoke.

"I've told you, Selah, that Leirauh has different parents from the rest of us," Fritz said. I nodded.

Leirauh cleared her throat. "What he didn't tell you was that the *hertsoh* wanted to marry my mother before he married theirs."

I blinked at her. "Did he know your mother first?"

Leirauh shrugged. "The *hertsoh* met Mama the way he met their mother. The way anyone knows an actress. From gossip and from his box seats at theaters abroad. But when they finally, really met, my mother wasn't interested. So he married the woman who became theirs."

Cobie cracked her knuckles. "And now . . . ?"

"And now," Fritz finished tightly, "Leirauh looks like her mother, and my father believes he has a second chance."

I swallowed. "What do you mean?"

I was sure I didn't want to hear the answer.

"He's declared he'll marry Leirauh when she's come of age," Margarethe said falteringly. She pressed her hands together, and the bones in her fingers stood out, pale and worried. Ursula and Ingrid stepped close to her, their desire to comfort their sister intuitive. "He announced three months ago, on her seventeenth birthday, that their wedding would be a year and a day from then."

Staring up at Leirauh from the foot of her bed, I thought I might be sick. "You're the duke's bride?" I finally managed to say. "You've been sewing wedding gowns and sitting with him at dinner and just—enduring this?"

It turned my stomach. Suddenly, Leirauh's deliberate plainness made sense. She made no effort with her appearance until she was set free by night, until her beauty was no longer a dangerous gift she was forced to hide.

It was disgusting.

"That's when Fritz had the idea to host the balls." Leirauh's blue eyes were bottomless. "We'd played at Burg Rheinfels when we were children. And Fritz thought if someone else fell in love with me and married me, that he could get me safely away."

"Have you?" I asked. "Met anyone, I mean?"

Leirauh shook her head, smile wan. "Not yet. I've met lots of nice people, just—no one I'd want to marry yet." She shrugged. "It's marriage, isn't it? I—I want to get out, but I want to be careful, too."

I only wished I didn't understand so well what she meant.

Leirauh's story reminded me of Anya's. For that matter, it wasn't unlike mine.

I knew it by heart, and I hated every line of it.

"Why didn't you just run away?" Cobie finally asked, shaking her head. "Anywhere would be better than here. Anything would be better than marrying a pervert who can't decide whether he's your father or your fiancé."

"Run away where?" Margarethe demanded. "With what

money? Under whose protection?" Her voice was acid. "This is the tsarytsya's territory. It isn't safe outside the towns. It isn't legal."

"Is that why you've been cozying up to Lang?" I asked. "Hoping he'll get Leirauh out?"

Cobie held up a finger. "No. No more wayward princesses. Soon they'll be showing up at the gangplank like stray pups."

Margarethe gave a Cheshire cat smile. "Perhaps. Or perhaps I just think he's handsome."

I gritted my teeth and turned back to Fritz. "But you've been meeting with the Waldleute. Why didn't you appeal to them?" He colored and dropped his gaze.

Margarethe laughed. "So you've figured it all out, have you?" I shrugged, not wanting to give myself away just yet. "You've heard some awfully generous rumors about them, if you think they'll just rush to our aid."

I drew back. "Are they—dangerous?"

"No," Margarethe said. "But they're not a charity. They have an aim, and that is to resist the tsarytsya and the Imperiya. Gretel and her Waldleute can't concern themselves with private worries like ours."

"Then why come to the balls in the first place?" I asked. "Why would they even agree to meet you?"

Fritz shrugged. "To recruit new members. To show their people a good time. Who can say? Gretel's not the most forthcoming of contacts. When she accepted the invitation, I didn't press her as to why."

Leirauh said nothing. As if words were useless, because nothing could be done.

I shook my head, frustrated. "But you're the *freinnen*," I protested. I threw a hand at Fritz. "And you're the *reichsfürst*!"

"And I am doing my best!" Fritz fired back. His voice and his eyes were strained. "I'm failing to protect my family and failing to repair a crumbling castle and failing to forestall the ruin of a dukedom my family has only held for forty years, and should never have had to begin with!" Fritz shook his head, smiling grimly. "Selah, haven't you realized yet how little power I actually possess?"

The defeat in his tone was painful. "So bargain with her."

"We don't have money." Fritz seemed to slump. "Not the kind of money that would change Gretel's mind. And we own very little outright."

"Access, then," Cobie urged. "Surely. To secrets, to power, the kind of thing she wants."

"What kind of access do you think we have?" Fritz returned. "Our court is a ruin. The Shvartsval'd lies on the edge of the Imperiya. The tsarytsya clings to it by her fingernails. And now, if you were seen or followed—who knows if the Waldleute will even meet with us again."

"She doesn't care about you—owing her a favor?" I suggested.

"We don't have anything she wants," Leirauh said softly. "Fritz and Margarethe have already tried."

My stomach clenched. They *had* tried. Their expressions were the evidence of how hard they'd fought for one another, of how hard Fritz had fought to redeem the court and country whose ruin weighed so heavily on his mind.

Leirauh wasn't a child—I was only a year or so older. But the *hertsoh* was raising her among his children. With the intent of making her his bride. It was repulsive.

The very idea of their marriage filled me with cold fury.

Anya's adoptive father had been ready to pawn her off on the first likely ally for the sake of protecting Norge. I'd been furious at Konge Alfödr for not seeing what she and Skop meant to one another. For treating her like a resource instead of a person.

He looked positively reasonable in comparison to Duke Maximilian.

The night I'd been expelled from Potomac, my fear had poured through me like water. And my anger had run hot that night in Valaskjálf, toward Norge's king, burning fiery enough to make me speak up for Anya, as no one had defended me in my own home. But here, in the bowels of the Neukatzenelnbogen, my fury froze cold as ice.

This time, I wasn't going to speak up in Leirauh's defense.

This time, I was going to act. I was going to end this, once and for all, and go home to my father.

"I have an idea," I said slowly. "Give me some time to think. Let me go back with you tomorrow."

Fritz crossed his arms. "Why should we?"

"Because I can fix this." Desperation rang through my every word. "I may have complicated your plans, but I can fix this. I told you—I came here to help."

"And why should we trust you?" Fritz asked.

"Because she's known the truth for days," Leirauh said carefully, "and she hasn't said a word to your father."

I met Margarethe's gaze. She lifted her chin, pugnacious, and crossed her thin arms.

"No, that isn't why," Margarethe said finally. "We can trust her because she's tired of the same *verdammt* story—the one where a man in power makes a decision and a girl's fate is sealed."

Cobie looked up at Margarethe and smiled her feral smile.

Margarethe grinned back at us.

"Because she's fighting the same battle you are, Leirauh," she went on, "and she thinks she can help you win."

23

The sisters didn't offer us tea the following evening. And Cobie and I didn't have to pretend to go to sleep.

We dressed with the *freinnen* after dinner, but this evening, there was no giddy scramble through the wardrobes. Tonight, we all wore Cobie's signature color.

The twelve of us—Leirauh and the *hertsoh's* nine daughters, Cobie, and me—wore gowns in a multiplicity of shapes, cuts, and lengths. But every last one of them was black.

Leirauh's was stunning, off-the-shoulder, worked with silver beads that shone like stars. Cobie's gown was simple, its jet silk loose around her lean frame, with thin shoulder straps.

The gown Margarethe lent me from Greta's closet would not have suited Potomac. With its long sleeves and full skirts, I would have sweltered in our summer humidity. It would not have suited *me* in Potomac, either—at least, not as the girl I was. Its skirts were heavy with feathers, its waist and bodice paneled in black leather. Black pearls buttoned up the back, and the shoulders were ornamented with epaulettes made of obsidian beads. My rosary fit into a small pocket in the skirt.

It was a gown. But it looked—it *felt*—like armor.

I had never been fond of black. But I'd never loved anything more for a night like tonight.

Sitting in front of one of their dressing tables, wearing Greta's gown and Hannelore's shoes, I lined my eyes with kohl and painted my lips red, the only spot of color on me besides Torden's engagement ring on my index finger. I rubbed the back of the band, wishing he weren't a sea away, an empire apart from me.

What would he think of me, in this gown, with this plan spooling out before me? Would he be proud of what I was about to do? Or would he condemn me as his father had, a traitor and a spy?

When Margarethe pressed a circlet of black pearls onto my head, I didn't protest.

I'd once thought to myself that I hadn't been born to wear a crown. But the mirror reflected a girl I believed could walk into a room of resistance fighters and negotiate. A girl who could sit down with Gretel and her Waldleute and hold her weight on the other side of the table.

I looked powerful.

"You look like Midnight herself," Margarethe said, smiling grimly.

"Midnight is a woman?" I asked with a laugh.

She shook her head. "Hope that you never meet her."

"I'll take that as a compliment."

"You should," Cobie said with a laugh. "I'm impressed. But not surprised." She squeezed my elbow, grinning tightly, looking tired. "Remember—you float just fine on your own."

Tonight, Cobie and I did not slip out after the *freinnen*. We did not swim across the river in silence or borrow a boat under cover of dark, did not slip into the ball quiet as secrets.

The twelve of us left together, rowed out of the belly of the Neukatzenelnbogen and up the Reyn together, docked together. We disembarked and stalked through the woods in one long, silent line, an unkindness of ravens in our black gowns, Leirauh on my left, Ursula on Cobie's right.

The revelry didn't exactly cease when we entered, but the musicians seemed to hesitate; the partygoers startled as we strode inside, an assemblage of beautiful wraiths.

The *freinnen* dispersed through the room, Margarethe pushing back her long hair and murmuring something about looking for Fritz, and turned me loose to work my magic.

Now, we simply had to wait.

The dance soon reassembled, and the party carried on around us. Lang came out of the crowd, straight for me.

"They found you out," he blurted, looking around at the *freinnen*. Lang planted his hands full on my shoulders, broad palms and lean-boned fingers splaying across their breadth. "You didn't say anything at dinner—"

"No—I mean, well, yes," I said quickly. "But it's all right."

I hadn't said anything to Lang, hadn't let on that anything had changed.

I told myself it was for fear of giving anything away to Perrault, who was ignorant and needed to remain so for his own safety. Or, worse yet, to Duke Maximilian, who still eyed me with suspicion, the foulness in his expression running as deep as the rot in the castle walls. But I couldn't tell Lang my entire plan, either.

I wasn't angry at Lang, exactly—not anymore. But we had butted heads since we'd set out for Shvartsval'd, striking out at one another again and again. I'd learned caution. And I couldn't risk him interfering.

He stepped back and studied me, eyes narrowing. "You're terrifying."

"That's what Margarethe said."

"You and Margarethe are friends now?"

I smiled at Lang and he raised an eyebrow, drawing back a little as if surprised, as if to take me all in. I lifted my chin and let him.

We danced, and I watched the room, waiting for my time to move. The *freinnen* were scattered, but it was impossible to miss Leirauh. Admiring eyes watched her wherever she went, black gown floating around her soft figure.

Above, finer than all the jewels and clothes in the room, the stars wheeled through the sky, crows circling beneath them. I watched them as I spun, my stomach reeling as we moved in opposition to one another, kaleidoscopic and dizzying.

"Selah?" Lang's voice was quiet, barely a breath on my skin. I returned my eyes to earth and found his brows arched over his stubborn upturned nose and his delicate mouth.

"What is it?" We switched partners briefly, and my pulse quickened as we came together again. I glanced around, wondering if he'd seen something. Or some*one*.

"You just look so—serious." His dark eyes skated over me, as if he were trying to sketch me out. "Older."

"It's all the black." I grinned.

"No, it's not that." Lang's feet followed the dance, but he seemed to hover over me, too close. "I wish you weren't here," he blurted.

My heart kicked painfully against my ribs. "What do you mean?"

"I mean, you distract me." Lang's fingers curled around mine. My pulse jumped as he brought my knuckles to his mouth, his sweet-bowed upper lip parting ever so slightly from the lower.

I ached, remembering once again the night I'd gone to his room to search out his secrets. Remembering the pictures of me spread across the floor.

"This was all easier when I could pretend you were a child." Lang's voice was quiet but so heavy. "Just a job. It was so much simpler before."

"Before I knew the truth?" I asked. "Before I made this my problem, too? I'm not a child, Lang," I said as evenly as I could.

His throat bobbed. "Manifestly not." Lang eyed Torden's ring on my index finger. I squeezed my fist shut.

Perrault had insisted I was unpromised. Regardless of what Torden and I felt, we were not engaged, and I clung to that distinction. My place on this side of that fine line made me not a traitor to Torden, whatever of him still belonged to me.

Guilt stung me at the sight of the ring. Guilt, and frustration.

But was I only an adult—a worthy participant in this mission, in Lang's eyes—because Torden had made me so?

I pushed my anger aside and let anticipation fill me instead. Lang would see, soon enough.

Some part of me had wished for this since the day I had met him. To prove to him—the handsome young captain who'd traveled everywhere—that I could handle myself.

There was something sweeter about earning admiration from those reluctant to grant it.

Then, over his shoulder, I saw her.

Gretel was exactly as Margarethe and Fritz had described her.

The *freinnen* had not told Lang who she was. But seeing her now, it was impossible not to notice the deference the other partygoers paid her. Lang might notice, too, if he was looking.

I had to get to her first.

"Margarethe will be looking for you," I said to him.

"Forget about Margarethe."

"We can't. Not yet." I cut a glance over to where the oldest of the *freinnen* waited with Ursula and Hannelore. "Go to her for now." I stretched up, whispering in his ear. "You and I have time."

Lang bent his temple to mine. His skin was warm. "That's all I've ever wanted with you," he whispered. "Time, and a chance."

And a little part of me wished for it, too.

Guilt and want pinched me near to bruising.

I lifted my chin and kissed Lang softly on the cheek. "We'll have it." I nodded at Margarethe. "Now go."

His midnight eyes watched me for a beat before he left me. And as he walked away, I shoved all my feelings aside.

This was the moment I'd prepared for. My one chance to make all my pain, all the days and miles, worthwhile.

When I was sure Lang wasn't looking, I nodded at Fritz—at Hansel. It was time.

The night air swept over me, clearing my head as Fritz strode my way. "Are you ready to begin? Or do you need more time?" He glanced at Lang, crisp tone belying his evident curiosity.

"No," I said. "I'm ready."

This was my quest. It always had been.

I straightened my shoulders and met Gretel's gaze.

"Well, now." Her voice was high and sweet as it had been on the radio all those weeks ago. "What have we here?"

24

We left the hall and the dancers behind, slipping through a corridor near one of the drinks tables into a tiny room beyond. The three of us sat in a small grotto, our faces lit and shadowed by the half-dozen candles set amid its stones, the stars winking overhead.

Across from me sat Gretel.

The leader of the Waldleute was a beautiful girl, tall and black-skinned with an ethereal cloud of black hair around her temples. The sable chiffon of her gown complemented her skin perfectly, and its swoop and drape emphasized her elegant neck and lean, strong arms.

I knew immediately I didn't weight my side of the table as she weighted hers, but I had to try.

"I'd heard you were courting a young lady, Hansel, but I must say, I'm impressed." Gretel crossed her arms. "I'd figured you were one for a submissive little wife, given the way your father treats his daughters. I wasn't expecting the type of woman who'd seek me out."

"I think by now you ought to know that I'm not my father," Fritz said. His even tone impressed me; the comment would've made me angry—though, once upon a time, I almost never got angry. Bolder emotions had tended to escape me then.

But anger was becoming a familiar friend to me, in the way many strange new things were growing comfortable. Black dresses and forbidden places and meetings arranged without a protocol officer in sight.

Poor Perrault. He'd be so worried if he knew. Yu and Homer would be proud.

"It's a pleasure to meet you, Gretel," I said carefully. "Though I'm sure that's not your real name, any more than his is Hansel or this is a woodcutter's cottage."

"It's all the name you're going to get." Her tone was light. "I'm sure you know what Baba Yaga does to the families of those who dare defy her."

"I wouldn't ask for more than you wish to offer." I shook my head, glancing between her and Fritz. "Most of us want nothing more than to protect our families."

I had practiced that line in my head as I'd buttoned my gown, as I'd pressed paint into my lips and kohl against my eyes.

It still brought with it a surge of memories and worries.

But I forced away thoughts of my father, of my stepmother,

of my new little sibling, of home. There was no time now.

Gretel shoved back from the table. "Not this again." She frowned. "Hansel, we've discussed this. I feel for little Leirauh, I do. But we're fighting a war. Can you imagine what my people would say if they heard we'd diverted our efforts to rescue a princess?"

"How can you justify ignoring her situation?" I countered. "You have resources. The worth of the gems and the gowns on your people in that room *alone*—"

"You can't eat jewels," she said keenly. "You can't fight wars with them, either."

"You can purchase food with them," I said, baffled. "You can purchase arms."

Gretel shrugged. "If there are any arms to be had," she said. "If anyone will risk getting them to you. Transporting contraband—damsels in distress included—is a dangerous business."

"Danger is everywhere here. You can run into danger on a stroll through town or a walk in the woods," I snapped. "And speaking of risk, you're taking one by throwing parties with deafening music every night. You could help her, and you're choosing not to."

Gretel planted her hands on the table. "Music is resistance in the Imperiya's world of silence. And we aren't responsible for these parties. We're invited guests."

"Fair enough," I said. "But I've got more concrete rebellion in mind."

She and Fritz watched me, not speaking. I felt the pressure of the weight I had taken onto my shoulders. I tried to let it steady me and not crush me.

"I didn't come here to ask for favors," I said. "I came here to make you an offer."

This was it. This was my shot to rescue Leirauh. To show Lang and the rest of them I was not to be trifled with. To make everything—leaving Torden behind, abandoning my father to Alessandra's manipulation, crossing into the Imperiya, all of it—worth it.

I straightened and readied my fire.

"My ship is carrying a large quantity of guns and gunpowder," I said. "I'm offering it to the Waldleute, in exchange for your assuring Leirauh safe passage to a court outside the Imperiya. Or to another place of her choosing. Swear to set her up safely and the arms are yours."

Fritz drew in a quiet breath.

I hadn't told Fritz or his sisters my plan. Perhaps the cards in my hand were higher than even I'd hoped.

Gretel's beautiful face had gone sharp. "Details."

I racked my brain, thinking again over the memory of the day I'd seen the crates in the hold, not knowing what they were. I'd never asked Homer what kind of guns the zŏngtŏng had provided, or how many. I hadn't thought to ask how much gunpowder we were ferrying.

The arms weren't mine to bargain with. And I didn't want to hurt Yu, or any of the rest of them, because the crew had never meant to hurt me. They'd agreed to their mission before they'd ever met me—before they could've cared what smuggling could mean for my safety, or for Potomac's politics.

But this voyage was mine. It had been coopted. And I was taking it back.

I was taking it all back.

"Six crates of guns," I said, praying I remembered right. I tried on a grin, felt its wry stretch over my red lips. "And enough gunpowder to blow my ship to the skies."

Gretel gave a dry laugh. "Those are hardly *details*." She paused. "Still, that's more weaponry than we have on hand at the moment."

I let out a tiny, tiny breath. "Do you need to confer with anyone else? Are you in charge of all the resistance—the Sidhe and the Rusalki and all the rest?"

"No. We're too spread out to have a single leader. But the Waldleute will accept my judgment." Gretel's gaze narrowed on me again. "How do I know you won't betray me? How do I know you're not with *her*?"

"My ship's on the Reyn. I can take you there tonight, show you the goods, and you can do with them what you will—as long as you take Leirauh with you. I don't want her coming back to the castle; Margarethe packed her a bag, and she's ready to go."

Fritz glanced at me, startled. But I had taken no chances tonight.

"Fascinating." Gretel's deep brown eyes were inscrutable.

I watched her weigh my offer, praying fervently, thumbing the rosary beads in my pocket.

Finally, Gretel smiled.

"Agreed." She raised her eyes to the heavens, looking like a queen. "We move now. I want it done before sunrise."

25

Gretel led Fritz and me back into the ballroom, nodding at the *fürst*. "Three minutes. Get your sisters out of here."

As Fritz hurried after Margarethe, Lang raced to my side. "Where have you been?"

I tipped my chin toward Gretel. "I found them."

Lang stared at us, dumbstruck. "You found—"

"No time to waste," Gretel cut him off. She slipped away, too, weaving through the crowd of dancers and tapping people on the shoulder. One by one, they slid away from the revel and out Burg Rheinfels's door. Fritz and the *freinnen* followed.

Lang pushed through the crowd again, asserting himself at Gretel's side. "If you're who I think you are, I need to speak with you," he tried again. "I'm prepared to make a deal, on behalf of—"

"The deal has been negotiated," Gretel said shortly. "Your princess handled herself well."

Lang's gaze snapped to me. I didn't acknowledge the betrayal in his eyes.

I told myself there was no time. Perhaps I was just a coward.

"Come on," I said, my throat tightening. "We need to get to the ship."

Lang didn't speak, but his eyes darted to me again and again as we threaded the mile and a half through the woods to the *Beholder*. Trained as my ears were on the crunch of grass and leaves beneath my shoes and Leirauh's quiet talk with Gretel, I couldn't miss the tension radiating through his body.

Part of me wanted to crow over him. *See? I'm not a child.*

Part of me wanted to beg his forgiveness.

But I wouldn't. I wouldn't be petty, and I wouldn't ask him not to be angry for what I'd done. I had more to worry about. I would accept the consequences of my choice.

I forgot about it all when the prow of my ship emerged from the mist.

The *Beholder*'s figurehead still stood at its fore, arms as open as ever, eyes still wide with wonder despite all she had seen. Though her fine polish had faded from salt water and miles at sea, she was still beautiful. The stuff she was made of, it seemed, was stronger than the stuff she'd been gilded with.

I wanted to cry with relief. I wanted to fling myself on her mercy and beg her to carry me home.

Almost. Almost. Just a bit longer.

Jeanne and J. J. and Andersen and Homer raced to the deck rail as we approached, and I raised a hand in greeting. Homer smiled when he recognized me. For the first time since we'd left Norge, I let myself bask in his pride.

"Here we are," I said to our navigator. Lang stood beside me, not speaking. Andersen and Yu came to join us.

Homer put a hand to my epauletted shoulder, bracing warmth in his fingers and in his gray eyes. "Here you are," he agreed.

I nodded at Gretel and her people, looking like ghosts in their finery in the early-morning dark. "And here they are."

"You did it," Andersen said, relieved, to Lang.

"No." Lang jerked his chin at me. "*She* did it." A beat of silence reverberated between us.

Yu went very still. "What did you do?"

Vishnu and Basile and the rest had helped the Waldleute into the hold below. They began now to emerge with barrels and crates in their arms, carrying them down to the bank where Leirauh waited. Her blue eyes watched the woods, black gown standing out beneath the lightening sky.

Guilt and victory warred in my stomach. Finally, I met Yu's gaze and forced myself not to flinch. "I made a deal. The safe passage of one of the *hertsoh's* daughters for the arms." I set my jaw. "Her circumstances were dire, the weapons went where they were intended to go, and I'm not sorry for what I did."

One by one, the Waldleute continued out the stern door with crates of arms, with barrels of gunpowder, their Zhōngwén labels bobbing along above the deck to remind me of what I'd done and whom I'd betrayed.

Something like shame washed over me. But I wanted to

169

shout at all of them—Andersen and Homer and Lang and Yu. *Do you still think I'm a child? Would you trust me with your confidences now, if you had to do it over again?*

A shoulder bumped against mine, and I started. "Well, look who's looking pleased with herself," Skop crowed.

I gave an uncomfortable laugh. But when I met Skop's eyes, they were as uncertain as I felt. He opened his arms, as if asking permission. Asking if we were all right.

I *was* pleased. And better still, I was home. I walked into Skop's arms and wrapped him in the tightest hug I could manage.

Over his shoulder, I saw Anya approaching. My heart rose at the sight of her.

"Does this mean you're finished?" She gave a tentative smile.

"Yes." I took her hand, hoping she'd read how much I missed her in my squeeze of her fingers. How much I was ready to fix things between us and rejoice in all that had gone right for her. "Yes. We can go home now."

But I spoke too soon.

I took my last happy breath as I glanced out over the bank and saw a soldier clap his hand over Leirauh's mouth.

26

They swarmed the banks of the Reyn like a cloud of gray smoke.

The deck felt insubstantial beneath my feet. It was only the roll of the ship on the water. But I knew that all was lost.

I had told myself that out in the woods, the wild itself shielded me from Baba Yaga's view. How wrong I had been.

Before I could stop myself, I raced down the gangplank, hurtling toward the riverbank. "No!"

Shouts and cries broke out behind me as the Waldleute scattered; it looked like some of them managed to escape. I prayed it was so. I prayed that Fritz and the other girls had made it back to the castle from the ball already, that the resistance would make it away with their weapons.

I prayed that all of this—my months lost and my misery and my father left alone—had not been for nothing.

"No!" I screamed again. I dove for the soldier restraining Leirauh.

I caught him off guard. It was the only reason he stumbled back, releasing her. I pinned the soldier to the ground, awkward in my dress, my hands scrabbling at his wrists.

"GO!" I shouted at Leirauh. "Run!"

She hesitated a moment. Her eyes were terrified.

"Please," I begged her.

Something good had to come from this nightmare. All this lying, all this betrayal, had to mean *something*.

Leirauh took the arm of a rebel and ran.

The soldier twisted beneath my limbs and jerked free. When he seized me, his grip was iron, cruel and tight.

I'd only managed to free Leirauh because I'd surprised him so thoroughly. There would be no getting away from him now. But I kept fighting, twisting and snarling when he didn't let go.

A few feet off, Gretel threw a punch at a thin, gray-clad soldier. He reeled, and she backed away, shouting at one of the Waldleute, who seized the last of the gunpowder barrels and took off. I kept struggling in my soldier's grip, throwing my elbows into his ribs, kicking.

Gretel turned to look back at me just once.

"Remember what you promised to do!" I screamed at her. "Don't you dare forget!"

She nodded. And then she ran.

I had fled Asgard in the dark of night, with Aleksei's aid and Torden's kiss on my lips and Anya safe at my side. It did not look as though we would be so lucky this time.

Perhaps one daring escape was all anyone could ask for.

The last of the Waldleute had disappeared through the trees. We were alone in the Black Forest.

It would have to be enough that I had been able to help Leirauh. That we had armed the Waldleute, done what we came here to do.

I tried to remember that as the soldiers boarded my ship, seized my crew, and hauled us away.

27

Hertsoh Maximilian was waiting for us in the early light of dawn.

The castle looked just as it had the first day we'd arrived in the Shvartsval'd. As we were hauled down the narrow corridor to the throne room, watery light streamed in through the few windows that weren't shuttered. In the throne room, courtiers wearing robes and weary expressions huddled against the cold and damp and the eerie silence, quieter still to my ears after the light and music of the ball. Perrault resembled nothing so much as the dismayed rosy-cheeked angels frescoed on the ceiling.

And there, again, sat the *hertsoh* on a dais, looking surprised and displeased to see me.

"Your Grace," I panted as a guard forced me near the dais. "You're up awfully early."

"And you're looking overdressed for bed," he snapped,

taking in my black dress, my dark crown. His face was flushed, his eyes glassy with anger. "I've been up late, counting my children."

My eyes darted to the side of the room where nine of the ten *freinnen* and Fritz waited, all in their pajamas.

I didn't know how they'd gotten back and changed so quickly. The girls had even wiped off their makeup, their faces scrubbed clean. My heart nearly burst with relief.

"Interesting," I said simply.

"*Interesting?*" The *hertsoh* stood, practically spitting bile. "Leirauh is *gone!*"

I glanced over at Fritz and the *freinnen* again. "You do seem to be missing one."

My tone was light. My body was shaking in fear. I refused to give in to it.

Leirauh is free, Leirauh is free, I told myself again and again.

And I had chosen this.

They're not going to cook you, Cobie had told me once upon a time, another night, in another ballroom.

The *hertsoh* might actually cook me alive. I was drowning in dread; I was in the hands of Imperiya soldiers. Anything could happen in this court.

Maximilian was entirely unlike cold Alfödr. The *konge* had been controlling and self-righteous—and possessed of basic decency. The same could not be said of the *hertsoh*.

Duke Maximilian rose and stomped off the dais, spitting something in Yotne at his children. Instinctively, I turned to Perrault, who rushed to my side, clinging to the edges of a pink silk dressing gown and looking terrified at Lang's split lip bleeding onto his shirt, at Anya's hair, full of leaves from where she'd been pushed to the ground. "What's he saying?"

Perrault winced. "He's asking the *reichsfürst* and *freinnen* if they had anything to do with her leaving. With—Leirauh."

"*Ni, Batyushka*," said each of the children, one after another. *No, Papa. No, Papa.*

They lied convincingly. Like children who'd had months—years—of practice lying to a parent.

My momma had loved me with her whole soul. Daddy loved me more than his own life. My godmother saw the truth in me and let me talk about it in my own time. They would never hurt me or debase me the way this man did the children he was meant to care for. I was a terrible liar, because I trusted my family.

The practiced deception of Fritz and the *freinnen* hurt my heart.

It made me even more determined not to cower when the *hertsoh* loped over to me, shaking in his anger. I would betray no fear.

I looked him in the eyes.

"Do you know where Leirauh is?"

"No."

"Do you know how she got away?"

I swallowed. "Yes."

The *hertsoh* swore, spittle flying, handsome face creasing in anger. "I knew I should never have let you pass through my doors," he hissed. "My bride has disappeared, because of *you*!"

"Leirauh's safe from you," I said. "I won't be sorry for that, whatever you do to me, you despicable lizard of a man."

The throne room was silent. I took myself in hand, stood my ground the way Cobie and Homer had always done, lifted my chin and hid my feelings, as Yu had shown me to.

And when I opened my mouth, Perrault's words came out.

Pride had answered, in Asgard, to his display of respect. I had to hope, here, that the *hertsoh*'s tantrum would answer to authority. To threats.

It was a risk to invoke her name. But Maximilian behaved as if he was god of his whole universe, dwelling as he did on the fringes of the Imperiya.

Perhaps he needed to be reminded that there was still a tsarytsya at its center, and he was accountable to her for his actions.

"I was to marry into your family," I said, contemptuous. "I was brought here at the invitation of the tsarytsya herself, and what do I find? A court in ruins, a rotting castle, and her *hertsoh* attempting to marry a girl he raised as his daughter?" I spat at his feet. "Disgusting. A crime against nature. I can't imagine what your empress was thinking."

"What the tsarytsya was thinking? What do you know of her court and her ways, girl?" The *hertsoh* gave a wild laugh. It chilled my bones like freezing rain. Then the duke paused and studied me, his body going still but his eyes glittering. "Would you like to ask her?"

I knew, suddenly, that I had made a fatal mistake.

Maximilian had been prepared to deal with me on his own. The tsarytsya was a gray shadow in the corner, as omnipresent and as ignored as the mildew on the walls. Far-flung as we were here, she was a distant point on the map.

But I had spoken her name. Unprompted, I had conjured her presence.

The temperature in the room seemed to drop. My feet skidded a little on the mosaic floor, as if the tiles had unexpectedly iced over. Or perhaps my knees had just given out.

I'd avoided her gaze so carefully for so long. The tsarytsya had issued my invitation; but I could have let her forget me.

And like a fool, I had spoken her name, powerful as any incantation, foul and potent as any curse.

In all the tales, to speak a monster's name was to invite it in. I should have known.

I glanced over at Lang and found him watching me in abject horror. *No*, he mouthed. *No*. But the damage had been done.

The *hertsoh* nodded at one of the gray-uniformed guards. "Escort our guest to Grandmother Wolf's court. See if *nasha tsarytsya* takes greater issue with the seneschal-elect's rabble-rousing and fraternizing with the enemy, or with my choice of wife." He paused. "Her maid, too. A great lady like herself must not be without her companion." Then he made to return to bed.

The soldiers began to haul Cobie and me toward the door. "No!" I shouted, just as Margarethe shouted, "Wait!"

The *hertsoh* paused in the doorframe.

"You can't punish my friend," I said breathlessly. "This is not her fault."

"We both knew what this could cost us, and we chose it,"

Cobie said, voice low and tight. "Don't you dare forget that we chose this. Don't let them take that away, that we did this *for* someone."

The *hertsoh* waved a hand. "But I *can* punish her." He paused. "Also, I don't care." Above his head, chubby angels with mold-spotted faces clung to faded banners and looked on in sad confusion. "And you—what?" he asked Margarethe, irritated.

"I'd like to speak with the seneschal-elect. She deserves to know exactly what we think of her," said the oldest of the *freinnen*. Her tone was laced with venom. I cringed.

"Very well." The *hertsoh* rolled his eyes. He waved a hand, and the Imperiya soldier let me go. "Twist the knife, as I suppose you must. *Then* take her."

Slowly, slowly, I dragged myself to the head of the line of Hertsoh Maximilian's daughters, and faced his eldest.

Margarethe gripped my arms in her fists, thin fingers straining around the sleeves of my gown. The beads in my epaulettes rattled as she shook me.

Her face was strained, furious, but her voice was low.

"Thank you," she whispered. "Thank you. I will never be able to thank you enough for freeing my sister." She wet her lips. "We will do for you what we can."

Fritz came to his sister's side. His light brown eyes were blank, but I saw beneath the expression in the clear light of dawn.

"You manipulated me, I think," he said. "There in the beginning."

"I also got underfoot," I agreed. "And interfered with your work."

"And I'll never be able to repay you for any of it." Fritz glanced around and leaned near to me. "Don't forget our call sign. *Fur die Freiheit. Fur die Wildnis.* I will plead your case to Gretel and to whomever else I can." He paused. "I am sorry, Selah."

"No. I chose this. I choose this," I said. "For Leirauh."

"It was expertly done. Clever girl." Fritz smiled, just a little. "You will need all your cleverness now, I'm afraid."

He squeezed my hand once more. And then I turned to the *Beholder's* crew.

Basile. Vishnu. J.J. Jeanne. Will. Yasumaro.

Perrault. Homer. Skop. Anya. Andersen. Yu.

Lang.

My story. My home. My family. I wished them far from this place. I never wanted to leave them.

Homer wrapped me in a hug, iron muscles and iron beard sheltering me for the briefest of moments. When he drew back, he tapped one of the black pearls in my tiara, gray eyes serious. "You deserve this crown, and everything it means."

The others embraced me as well, kissed my cheeks goodbye. Will cried as he hugged Cobie, and guilt surged over me afresh. Yu told me he was sorry.

"Don't be," I said fiercely. "I'm not. I'm proud of what we've done."

"I'm proud, too." He scraped a hand over his short black hair. "Despite it all."

All except for Cobie. "You were going to stay out of this," I said to her. I couldn't keep the desperation out of my voice. "You and Will."

Cobie shook her head. "We stick together," she said simply.

For the first time since we'd been captured, I had to fight back tears.

Perrault approached, looking baffled, and I felt an unexpected pang of sadness. "What will you say to Alessandra?" I asked. "No fiancé to present to her, after all this."

But his expression didn't lighten. "Everyone you loved failed you," he said. "And I helped them."

"Haven't you been listening?" I gripped Perrault's elbows, forcing him to meet my eyes. "I would not have missed this journey." I paused to glance over at Lang.

No. I trusted Perrault. It had to be him.

I lowered my voice. "Perrault—find my radio. Contact Norge—tell Torden what happened. Tell England. It's on my bed, in the book in my cabin, and—"

"Enough," growled the guard standing just behind us, pushing Perrault away. The protocol officer stumbled back to join the crew, eyes wide.

Lang came to me last.

His dark hair was tousled. Dirt streaked his white shirt, and his left eye was a tender purple and swollen shut. He rolled his wrists as his guard released him, just for a moment.

"I'm so sorry," I breathed.

"It's not your fault," Lang said. "It's not."

But it was.

Back in Asgard and before, Lang had been the one to keep the truth from me; he was the reason we'd been cast out for traitors. This time, I was the one who had kept my cards too close. The reins had been in my hands when things went off course.

Perhaps we wouldn't have been discovered if I'd left Lang in charge. Perhaps we'd all be safe aboard now, sailing home, toward my father.

Or perhaps they'd been watching our ship since we'd arrived. Perhaps my choices would've made no difference.

But one thing would have been different, certainly: Leirauh's fate.

Lang's hands were stained with mud now as they'd been stained with ink and charcoal the first time I'd met him. His fingers curled slowly, carefully around mine.

"England. Norge. Now Shvartsval'd." I gave a sad little laugh. "Again, the dignified exit eludes me."

"You're exquisite," he blurted. "You're a wreck. You have absolutely wrecked me."

I couldn't catch my breath. "What?"

"You're every midnight I've seen these past months. Every sunrise." He swallowed hard. "Every day—I tried. I tried to find the right time to talk to you, but I could never quite—"

It hurt too much. "Lang, we don't have to—"

"I never got my chance," he cut me off quietly. "No one else ever had a chance, after you met *him*."

I knew who he meant.

Lang traced my engagement ring where it rested on my index finger. "This could never have been mine. But maybe—" I glanced up and found his dark eyes memorizing me. "But maybe this—this, just once—could be mine."

Lang bent his head, slowly, giving me a chance to pull away. I blinked at him but didn't move.

In one breath, two, his lips were on mine.

His mouth was as warm as a summer night, salty as the ocean with his sweat and tears. His hands—an artist's hands—cupped my neck, wound themselves into the soft hairs at my nape. I moved slow, careful, gentle, cautious of his bruises, but still, I felt him wince; his upturned nose nudged my cheek, lashes fluttering against my skin.

Slowly, I felt him tug the engagement ring from my finger, press it into my cupped hand. "Hide this, or they'll take it," he whispered against my jaw, and I dropped it quickly into my bodice.

When we broke away, I looked into Lang's face one last time. Two soft eyelashes had fallen into the hollow beneath his unmarred right eye.

I swiped the lashes from his skin and blew them off into the air.

Anya clung to Skop, her fingers tight around his shoulders. One of her braids was coming loose, and she was fighting back tears.

"You're shield-maidens," she said. "Torden would be so proud."

Torden. My stomach clenched.

Our odds had already been long. I doubted now, more than ever, that I'd ever see him again.

Would he ever hear what had happened to me? Would my father? Would I be able to tell them of my fate, or would the

Imperiya swallow us whole, leaving no trace behind?

I couldn't bear to watch Anya weep. I steeled myself to leave.

But when I turned to face my guards again, Anya stepped between Cobie and me, her face resolute.

"I conspired with them," she said to the guards. "Take me, too."

My jaw worked, horrified, but I couldn't speak, couldn't move. And then the shackles hit her skin.

"No!" I blurted. "No. No." I turned to the guards. "She's lying. She's done nothing wrong. She's— Don't—" I lunged toward Anya, scrabbling ineffectually to remove her cuffs. But the guards only shoved me away.

After all, who would falsely admit to treason? Who would give themselves up for a crime of which they were innocent, just to protect a friend?

"Anya." My voice shook, my panic rising. "Anya, don't do this. You have Skop. You can be free. You can be happy."

"I did, and I could." Her words came out steady. "But an ending with you carried off by enemy soldiers is not a happy ending, Selah. You are my sister, and I will see this through with you."

Tears gathered in my eyes. "But I chose this," I said. "I never wanted anyone else to get hurt."

"Yes. And now—" Anya swallowed and cast a glance at Skop, then back to Cobie and me. "And now, I'm choosing you."

All the money that e'er I had,
I spent it in good company;
And all the harm that e'er I done—
Alas! It is to none but me,
And all I've done for the want of wit
To memory now I can't recall
So fill to me the parting glass
Good night—and joy be with you all.

. . . All the comrades e'er I had
They're sorry for me going 'way
All the sweethearts e'er I had
They'd wish me one more day to stay;
But since it came unto me lot—
That I should rise and you should not
I gently rise and with a smile
Good night—and joy be with you all.
—"The Parting Glass," folk song of Alba

28

THE IMPERIYA YOTNE: THE GRAY ROAD

Cobie, Anya, and I walked a hundred nights behind the wagons carrying the soldiers and their gear.

It couldn't have been a hundred. Of course I knew that.

But then, it had to have been a hundred. A thousand. In no fewer than a thousand nights could the black gown in which I'd sat down to negotiate with Gretel have become the rag I wore, ripped along its hem, stinking with my sweat, muddy with the dirt of the road and the rain that beat down on us mercilessly. Our wrists chafed under the shackles binding us to the wagon, growing first sore, then raw, then bloody when the skin broke.

Anya's fair hair became matted and filthy; Cobie had to hack a slit in her dress so she could walk. My elegant party shoes grew dusty in the dirt, filthy in the mud, breaking against the cobblestones where the road was paved. Anya was worst off; she'd been barefooted when we'd been captured.

We took turns wearing the two pairs of shoes between us. Whoever went without padded her soles in fabric ripped from our gowns. It didn't matter; our feet were soon torn and bleeding. A trail of red leaked behind us on the Gray Road.

That was the English for what the soldiers called the path we walked. They spoke only Yotne, which neither Cobie nor I understood. Anya knew a little, and what she heard made her face grow pale. After a few days of asking her what she could gather from them—where we were going, how long we would be on our way—I stopped asking her to translate.

They'd said our destination was Stupka-Zamok, and I already knew what that meant. It was the tsarytsya's capital, the name of her house and of the city in its shadow, of the heart of her empire.

It meant that we were lost already.

Every step we took through the Imperiya's conquered lands felt like a step I would never be able to take back. We crossed out of Shvartsval'd and across the rest of old Deutschland, which the Imperiya had sectioned off into new *terytoriy*. From there, I didn't know where we went; I didn't recognize the names of the places.

Anya, Cobie, and I spent our nights in barns and farmyards and cellars, hungry and cold. But the soldiers wanted for nothing. In every village we passed, they walked into farms and pubs and shops, demanding they be served immediately, taking bottles of wine or loaves of bread or fresh clothes or shoes. They never paid.

In one hamlet, they found a stash of books hidden in its headwoman's home. They cut her throat.

Just beyond the edges of a village, they found a squad of deserted Imperiya soldiers living alone in the woods. They locked them inside their hut and set it ablaze.

Once, perhaps worst of all, they found a couple had been harboring three children in secret and had not informed the town's governor, another one of the tsarytsya's puppets. As the soldiers surrounded the house, I'd gotten to my feet, horrified, as if to chase them away like stray dogs.

I'd passed out from rising too quickly.

Anya and Cobie wouldn't tell me what happened to the children.

I had heard of the Imperiya's cruelty. But to witness it, unchecked and unbounded, was another thing entirely. I prayed for the souls of the dead every night before I fell asleep.

After they emptied a farm's larder or walked from a pub having eaten and drunk until their bellies were swollen and their lips stained, the soldiers marched on, caring nothing for what they left behind them, tipping their heads back at the sky and howling at the moon.

The road wound one night through a beautiful, antique city with buildings of ancient stone and lampposts out of a fairy tale. But the lampposts were clouded with ash, as useless by night as by day, and the stones were black and sour pink with mold and mildew. My heart ached at the sight of a lovely old building whose rainbow windows had been smashed and boarded up.

It put me in mind of Winchester Cathedral. Here, as there, I couldn't tell if it was a church or a library. But it didn't matter. The tsarytsya's soldiers had sacked it.

A gray sky hovered above, as if the clouds were worried enough to want to keep close but afraid to come too near. They, too, saw what the Imperiya had done.

We crossed a river to enter the city, traveling via the only bridge still standing. Anya broke into sobs when she heard the soldiers call the city Prakha.

One of them slapped her across the face and told her, in words even I understood, to stop making noise. Anya put her tears away then.

I tried to ask her what was wrong—Cobie had raised her eyebrows and glanced around us, as if to ask *what isn't wrong?*— but Anya couldn't bring herself to explain. Not then, and not as we lay in our cell while the soldiers went out. By the time they returned, smelling of wine and making filthy-sounding jokes, Anya had cried herself to sleep.

Only a night later, as we lay huddled together a few yards away from a campfire, did she explain.

"My mother always told me Prakha was a city of magic," she whispered, tears chasing trails down her filthy cheeks, clinging to her fair lashes. "When I was little, I asked if she would take Fredrik and me someday. She said that of course she would—that I could go to the city and wander its bridges and its streets and hear its musicians play. That even its stones would love me."

Something low and terrible clenched in the pit of my stomach.

The city would have loved Anya. It was impossible not to love Anya.

But its bridges were too ruined for happy wandering, and its stones were too shattered to care for her beauty and kindness.

"That was before, of course," she finished brokenly. "And now my mother is gone, and now Prakha is, too."

We didn't speak after that. We just scooted closer together, the three of us with our rag-wrapped feet and our torn dresses, like a litter of hungry pups waiting for their mother to come home.

Day after day we walked the road.

In another life, I might have thought the country beautiful. The leaves on the trees that lined our way were green where they hadn't been cut down; the villages we passed looked utterly idyllic, where they weren't reduced to ash.

Some days, we climbed mountains covered in stones that stabbed at our sore feet; others, we were forced to ford rivers of muddy water that stung the cuts in our skin. Nightly, I worried over our scrapes and blisters, afraid infection would set into the places where we were broken. Cobie brushed me off, trying to be strong for all of us; but I woke up in the middle of the night and found her missing, once. I came upon her near the place the soldiers had established as a latrine, leaning against a tree, staring away into nothing.

She wasn't crying. I took her by the arm and led her back to camp.

Cobie just lay down next to me, her back against the stony ground, eyes wide on the stars that shone down on us without mercy.

I tried to sleep. But I was ravenous, my stomach filled with nothing but the grasping pains that plagued me all day and the few bites of hard bread the soldiers fed us at night. We had learned better than to try and gather anything on the road; one day, the three of us had picked up acorns as we hurried behind the wagon, scarfing them as the soldiers paused for lunch.

The soldiers had not let us stop hours later when we could hardly walk for retching, for the cramps that racked our stomachs.

And though my legs burned—we were covering twenty or twenty-five miles a day, at least—the ache in my heart was more potent.

For Potomac, its warm summer nights and fireflies. For the *Beholder*, its gentle rocking like a lullaby. For food, and my books, and candles at night to see by.

I missed my rosary. The soldiers had taken it, and Margarethe's crown, when they had searched us on the road that first day. My ring was safe only because I'd braided it hurriedly into my hair the first time the guards had stopped to relieve themselves.

Most of all, I missed my family. My father. My godmother. Lang, and the rest of the crew, and Torden.

I carried his ring in my hair and Lang's kiss on my lips and wondered if either of them ever thought of me, if Perrault had gotten word to our friends or my godmother.

I wondered if I'd drop into the Imperiya's jaws and be forgotten entirely.

I chose this, I reminded myself, with every step throbbing in my swollen feet. *I chose this. I chose this.*

Leirauh's freedom gave me confidence that I'd done what was right. But only the comfort of Cobie's and Anya's presence was enough to keep me moving forward.

We walked on. My throat was dry from thirst. My feet throbbed and bled. My wrists chafed with even the slightest movement, as if glass were buried beneath my skin.

The same, day after day.

But one night, as the sun began to set, a new sight appeared on the horizon.

A city, jagged as a wolf's claws, its stones gray as ash. It rose over a gate made of black iron spears, a skull atop each one.

Anya wept as she had in Prakha. But I knew she had never hoped to wander these stones.

"They call her house Stupka-Zamok," she said quietly,

wiping her face with the backs of her dirty hands. "They call it the Mortar."

We had fallen off the edge of the world we had known. We had come to the source of the decay we had so long feared.

We had come to the land of shadows.

MIDNIGHT

When Baba Yaga locks the door,
Children pass thereby no more.
—"Baba Yaga and the Wounded Whelps," Yotne tale

29

YOTUNKHEYM, THE IMPERIYA YOTNE: STUPKA-ZAMOK

The sight of the skulls brought a scream to my lips, but I didn't let it break loose from my mouth and into the air.

I gripped Cobie's hand as we walked closer, Anya ahead of us.

I'd heard the word *bone* used as a color before. Hannelore had argued one night with Ingrid over whether a gown was *cream* or *eggshell* or *ecru* or *bone*. I hadn't realized there was any difference between the shades.

The skulls mounted atop the spears varied from sun-bleached white to faded gray to charred black.

Bone was, in fact, many shades. But every skull of every shade watched me with the same hollow eyes.

Cobie made a sound—a vague catching in her throat—and

I squeezed her hand. Anya drew inexorably toward the grue-some fence as if drifting on a nightmare, unable to look away from the bones lifted high before us.

One of the guards shoved Anya, barking something I didn't understand. And the gates opened.

The homes we'd passed on our journey were different, place to place. Some had been little white plaster things, red-tile roofs draped atop them like blankets. Some had been brown wood cabins; others had been cozy lodges of red brick, or of drystone, with little green lichens sprouting along the seams between the rocks.

I'd expected ruins here. I'd expected age, decay, water stains. All the Gothic mystery tied to childhood dreams of witches and dark queens, of the hungry headswoman who became the tsarytsya.

My childhood imagination was not disappointed.

We entered a city of a thousand little fortresses, each of gray and black stone, each of them armed to the teeth. A hedge of wooden and iron spikes surrounded the nearest house; algae grew over a miniature moat surrounding another. An under-fed dog with a mud-caked coat barked and snapped at us from behind the fence of a third. The houses grew larger, taller, and sharper as we walked on, many surrounded by uniformed guards.

Every last one was dressed in gray. Leaning against walls and crouched behind fences and jeering at us as we walked past in chains.

There had been little gray anywhere in Norge. It had been

a world of blue—blue-eyed boys, blue skies, blue Bilröst—
banked in fields of gold.

England had been gray. But England had also been green—
its sky full of mist and its earth the color of an emerald,
scattered with copses of trees and rose gardens and patches of
lavender. England's gray had been the gray of a sky just before a
gentle rain, the gray of a pearl or the wing of a dove.

This city was the gray of smoke and ash belching from
teetering chimneys. The gray of a wolf's pelt. The gray of unre-
lenting stone. And there was no green to be found inside its
skull-topped gates.

More uniforms pushed past us as we were hauled through
Stupka-Zamok's streets, narrow and twisting between the
houses that towered overhead like broken teeth. Soldiers in
clusters strode around us, calling out to one another in sharp,
clear voices; soldiers in formation marched past. Each time,
we and the crowds of shouting and shoving commoners had to
wait for their ranks to pass so we could carry on.

Once, we paused before a dozen soldiers being dragged on
leads through town by a pack of their gray-uniformed fellows.
Anya shut her eyes, listening hard as the bound men cried out,
as their captors scoffed and insulted them.

"Deserters," she finally whispered. "Baba Yaga does not look
kindly on those who forsake her service."

In the villages we had passed, we had met gauntness, hollow
eyes, starving ribs. I had anticipated more of the same here. But
if the gazes of the people of Stupka-Zamok were a little strained
as they whispered and looked away, pressing close together to

avoid us in the cramped, winding streets, they looked well-fed inside their gray clothes.

I saw no children anywhere.

And above the soldiers and the streets and the roofs of the hundred private fortresses, a great house rose stories high. Clouds hung heavy and gray overhead, and large birds of prey circled low.

I thought of every fairy tale I'd ever read, and I knew. A witch lived in that house.

It was a high tower of merciless gray at the choked, spiky heart of her world, skinny as a pike but for the top two floors, which bulged out into a wide, flat-topped disc. Windows dotted each floor, enough to see everything happening in the city below. Discordant statuary and fountains were scattered around the tower's base, as if plunked there as an afterthought.

Remembering the tale I'd found in the Roots as a child, the whispered warning circulated by the tsarytsya's opponents, I called up the picture of her storied hut: a cottage on chicken legs, groaning and shrieking high above the ground. That much was true; the disc at the top did almost seem to stand on a long, skinny leg over the city. And though the tower did not move as Baba Yaga's hut did, the city around us grated and screeched with harsh sounds, with the whine of rusty metal on hard stone.

But the little whelps in the story had had to ask Baba Yaga's *yzbushka* to turn away from the forest and to look upon them, and in this, reality differed from the fairy tale.

Baba Yaga's tower had eyes in every direction. And unlike the children in the tale, I had no hope we'd find the comforts of hearth and home inside.

We stood before great iron doors carved top and bottom. One of our guards stamped twice on the stone porch, and the doors swung, creaking, to admit us. I bit back a gasp of relief as my feet met the cold slate floor of the foyer, clear of shattered glass and debris. My shoes had broken beyond repair that afternoon, and I'd walked the last few miles barefoot.

I held Anya's and Cobie's hands, as if we were little girls playing a game, and stared upward. Fourteen stone floors were stacked like iron rings above us, bridged by a delicate-looking iron staircase and echoing with harsh Yotne words. Dozens of windows admitted a dull, smoky gray light.

And everywhere, everywhere, moving around and around, the gray uniforms of Imperiya servants and soldiers. The effect was dizzying; I swayed.

Cobie wrapped an arm around my waist, her strength barely enough to hold me upright. I could feel the places where, in four weeks' time, my gown had loosened and my frame grown thinner. Looking at my friends—my beautiful friends, with their dirty fingernails and greasy hair and their bodies grown gaunt—I couldn't believe I had ever envied their slimness. Hunger had made me wiser.

The door slammed shut behind us, and a bar swung down into place against it with a heavy *clang*.

I jumped and glanced back at the doors and realized only then that the carvings at their top and bottom were teeth.

Gripping Anya's hand, I turned back around. Her face was pale and somber, her blue eyes too big. I knew we were thinking the same thing.

When Baba Yaga locks the door,

Children pass thereby no more.

My fingers dragged my empty pockets, scrabbling for a rosary that wasn't there as we crossed the wide atrium of Baba Yaga's house to the narrow iron stairway, just wide enough for two to pass, at the center of the tower. Shafts of light cut through the windows as the guards forced us up the steps. Their glass was stained, like the windows in a church, but where the windows in Saint Christopher's in Potomac and the cathedral in Winchester had shimmered with color, the ones in Baba Yaga's house were gray like quartz. Artfully leaded wolves and teeth and towering plumes of smoke lurked at their edges.

Through the windows, I saw the citizens of Stupka-Zamok going about their lives and business. I wondered if they knew what happened outside the walls of their city or inside their tsarytsya's house. I wondered if they cared.

My shackles clinked on my wrists as we climbed, long cold chains clattering against the bannister and dragging between my legs. Hunger gnawed at my belly and bones.

I quit counting the steps after a hundred and fourteen, because that was when my feet began to leave bloody prints on the iron latticework. I stopped, dragging my soles over my shins, trying not to whimper, trying to wipe up the blood.

One of the guards cursed and butted me with his gun, and I couldn't stifle my cry.

My nose was running when we reached the second story from the top of the tower. Most of the floors we had passed were ringed with doors, but this one had just two, each a high thing

204

made of smooth wood the color of a shadow. Like her front door, this one was carved top and bottom with long, sharp teeth.

A sentry opened the door, and we found Baba Yaga holding court inside.

The walls of the tsarytsya's throne room were gray stone, punctuated with windows of the same smoky leaded glass. Mismatched oil paintings and marble busts and terra-cotta vases and ragged tapestries dotted the walls and filled pedestals across the room. Men and women in gray garments, their elegance betraying their rank above the citizens outside the tower, filled the spaces between the miscellaneous artwork.

I wanted to grip the doorframe and force our guards to pry me loose. But Anya slipped her hand into mine, and I put my hand on Cobie's shoulder, and we walked forward. The room went quiet.

"Ah," said Baba Yaga, surveying us. I kept very, very still.

The tsarytsya of the Imperiya Yotne was tall and thin, with pale, papery skin and long gray hair that hung loose down her back. She had a stately, high-bridged nose and remarkable eyes—not for their color, which I'd wondered about so many weeks before; they were an ordinary-enough shade of brown.

Grandmother Wolf's eyes were *hungry*.

The tsarytsya's throne was not built of finger bones, as the chair in the Baba Yaga story was; it was a high-backed chair of iron wrought into twisting patterns like smoke. She sat tall in its rigid seat, and a brilliant silver crown studded with emeralds and sapphires rested on her brow. She took in each of us in turn as a guard said something quietly in her ear.

"Your names," she called. Her voice was low, for a woman's; it bubbled and popped unexpectedly, like brew in a cauldron.

I stepped forward, chains rattling against my legs. "Selah—"

But Anya lifted her chin and followed me, before I could say any more. "Anya, Prinsessa of Varsinais-Suomi, lately of the house of Asgard." The crowd lining the room began to murmur, their eyes darting back and forth.

Anya pretended not to notice, but I saw the deep breath she drew in through her nose, the hard swallow at her throat as she kept her gaze on the woman on the throne.

"I'm Cobie Grimm." Cobie tossed the words out.

Anya was still holding my hand. She gave my fingers a squeeze, and our shackles clanked together. My free hand reached for Torden's ring in the matted hair at my nape, searching for comfort.

"Hmm. English. You are all a long way from home," said the tsarytsya. "You, less so, *Prinsessa* Anya, but what a surprise to see you, nonetheless." She emphasized Anya's title, but her gaze wandered to me, as if she couldn't quite place me.

Anya had interrupted me on purpose. She was protecting me again, distracting the tsarytsya and the court with her name and title.

When none of us said anything more, the tsarytsya shifted in her seat, tone growing businesslike. "Come you here of your own accord, or are you compelled?"

I stiffened. This, at least, was exactly what the Baba Yaga of the story had said.

I straightened my shoulders and told the tsarytsya what I

had told myself again and again on the Gray Road to her house. "I chose this."

She cocked her head amid the startled murmurs of the crowd, pointing a bony finger at Anya and then at Cobie. "And you?"

"Yes," Cobie said, without a moment's hesitation.

Anya nodded. "Yes."

Baba Yaga took us all in a moment longer, the silver crown listing over her pale brow. Then she jerked her head at a guard. "Make them useful."

"*Tak tochno, moya tsarytsya.*" He brought his heels together sharply and hustled us from the room.

I cast a glance over my shoulder as we passed from the throne room, back at the bloody footprints I'd left on the slate floor.

I determined then and there that it was the only blood I or my friends would shed in this house. We would survive and get back to the ones we loved.

My father was waiting for me. My new little sibling was waiting for me. Fritz had been right: I would have to be clever to live long enough to see them again.

If you're one step ahead of them, Penelope had taught me, *they still haven't caught you.*

The tsarytsya was still watching us as we left—still eyeing *me*, as if she were a haruspex and I her sacrifice, no more than organs and entrails laid out before her divining gaze.

And the look in her eyes chilled me to the bone.

30

The guard took us to the kitchens and left us. A dozen women at least were hurrying around the crowded set of rooms, but one—a tall, pretty woman around thirty, with dark hair and a smattering of freckles on her pale cheeks—looked us over, drawing back in horror at my bloody footprints on her floors. She tried a couple of different languages before landing on one we understood.

"You must wash," she said, a little impatient.

A sink full of plates and cups and pans caught my eye. "Wash the dishes?" I asked.

"*Ni!*" the woman burst out, flinging a string of exclamations at me I didn't understand. "Go wash yourselves." She motioned us toward a huge tub of water in the next room. A scullery maid passed us a cake of soap, and one at a time, we began to clean ourselves, wincing at the water's icy temperature, hissing in pain as the lye soap stung our broken skin.

When I climbed out and pulled on my new plain gray shift, I finger-combed my hair and quickly braided Torden's ring back into it, tying the end with a thread—the last relic of my ruined gown before another maid tossed it onto the fire. I tried to swallow the lump in my throat as the dress smoldered on the logs, tried not to think of how I'd felt in it when Lang kissed me goodbye, when I sat down to meet with Gretel.

The cook was sweating before the stove and the great oven at the center of the kitchen, ringed by worktables, surrounded above by hanging cast-iron pots and bunches of dried herbs. She dragged the back of her hand across her forehead and then did point to the pile of dishes. The cracked porcelain sink was full of pans filmed with fat, with dirty dishes coated in gravy and gristle. "You three—wash."

My bones ached, and I wanted nothing more than to lie down before the fire and sleep for a hundred years. But we were clean, we were together, and we had traded the company of male soldiers on the road for that of women in a kitchen. These were blessings.

Most important of all, Anya had protected me. With luck, it was possible that the tsarytsya might never learn who I truly was—that we could exist just beyond the bounds of her notice while we lived in her house.

I tried not to think about how long that might be. I tried not to dwell on what Anya's announcement of her presence might cost her. I tried to tell myself a house this large was bound to be full of gaps, and that we would stay alive until we could find one and slip through it.

I didn't ask the house to hide me, as Burg Rheinfels and the Shvartsval'd woods had pretended they would. I'd learned not to trust a place that felt safe.

Cobie and Anya and I—we were our only shelter. I asked only for a door. For an escape.

I would watch. I would wait patiently. And when the time came, we would run.

For now, we set to work, me washing, Anya rinsing, Cobie drying. The cooks were plating dinner by the time we finished. My stomach growled and I tried not to stare at the dumplings, the brilliant red-pink soup, and what appeared to be lard sliced onto bread. Two of them disappeared upstairs carrying trays, one hauling an enormous thing like a silver vase full of hot coals and scalding water.

The pots and pans went immediately into the sink, and I was prepared to be ordered back to washing. I was grateful when the head cook beckoned to us instead and ladled each of us a bowl of something hot, like grits with cheese and mushrooms in it.

It was gone too soon, but the cook was probably wise to give us no more than a half cup each. I didn't fancy waking up in the middle of the night to vomit beside the fire.

I turned to Anya. "How do you say *thank you?*"

She cut me a wry glance. "*Spasibo.*"

"*Spasibo,*" I repeated to the cook.

She nodded, not ungraciously, pushing back flyaway strands of her dark hair. Then the cook pointed again to the mountain of dishes in the sink. "Wash."

* * *

My arms were trembling when we finished our chores hours later. The cooks and serving maids had long since left, and the kitchen had cooled considerably; someone had banked the fire in the great oven. Cobie, Anya, and I lay down close together on its hearth.

Anya's hair was pale gold by its faint light; Cobie's brow, in sleep, was finally smooth. I wished they were far away, safe, but I was thankful they were beside me.

I longed for a story. But absent my godmother's book, I told myself the ones I already knew—the tales I'd read, and the ones I'd lived. As the embers burned low in the fire, I thought of the way Torden's hair looked in the sunshine. Of his confident hands on his weapons and on my waist, and the way he'd joked with his brothers.

Thinking of Torden made me think of Lang—Lang and his jealousy, his competition, his kiss that had smelled of salt and summer. I'd forgotten my guilt on the Gray Road, but sifting through my memories brought it back.

Would Torden come for me, or was he too devoted to his father to leave home?

Would Lang come? Or was he bound up in some fresh endeavor now—in something new that had caught his attention, or some other prior commitment he'd hidden from me?

Had his kiss been a goodbye, or a promise?

I hoped the crew, at least, would push for our rescue. I had been so angry at them—but they were my friends.

I had read the old tales. I knew friends made along the way

mattered at the story's end, and that to be generous to friends and strangers alike was to pave one's own way to a happy ending. Gods and queens and powerful fae rewarded those who proved themselves less cruel and selfish than the world said was only practical, only fair.

I had seen cruelty in abundance, and we had much to fear. But threatened though we were on all sides, we were still whole, still not broken or alone. My friends and I had passed through the gate of bones, and still, against terrible odds, we lived.

Sleep dragged at me. But I couldn't rest yet.

I tore a very thin strip from the hem of my shift, though it was already threadbare and short. In the ragged cloth I tied careful knots in sets of ten, then joined the ends; a few more knots and two crossed splinters finished my makeshift rosary. In the silent kitchen, I began to pray.

I poured out my thanks for the fire, for the bath and the food and the door between us and the wolves beyond. Most of all, I offered my gratitude for the friends safe at my side and the ones I believed with all my heart would come for me.

I would hope. I would wait.

We were in a wicked, brutal house, a cold cast-iron cage, and we would survive it. But I would not let it make me brutal. I would not let it make me cold.

31

We woke to the clanging of pots and pans, ashes on our cheeks and arms and feet.

I was leaden with sleep. I'd been dreaming of the *Beholder*, of working in the galley with Will and of the candle I'd stolen that Lang had blown out.

"*Zolushka*," muttered one of the maids. The head cook drew back at this, surprised, and dealt her a sharp answer.

I didn't understand their Yotne words. But the maid's was clearly an insult, and the cook's was clearly a reproof.

"*Spasibo*," I said to the cook quietly.

She gave me a bracing nod, then pointed at a pile of potatoes beside the sink. "Wash."

It was her most frequent order, and the nickname I silently began calling her.

We scrubbed potatoes until Wash and the rest of the cooks looked like potatoes. As soon as we finished scrubbing one pile,

213

another was placed before us. Potatoes were peeled, grated, boiled, mashed, fried into pancakes, stuffed into the dumplings they called pelmeni. When there were no more potatoes to wash, there were dishes.

I was used to the easy timbre of work in the galley. But there had been two of us in the *Beholder*'s kitchen, and a mere fifteen souls aboard; two dozen women worked in the tsarytsya's kitchen and laundry, speaking as many languages, running a tower that housed hundreds—courtiers, soldiers, advisers, and Baba Yaga herself. There were no breaks in our labor; the work was constant. Wash cooked with all the ceaseless efficiency of an army general, with all the eye to taste of a parent feeding their family, clucking like a mother hen to move us from task to task.

I wondered if Wash liked kitchen work, and where she'd learned it. Had she grown up the daughter of a great house, and learned from her own cook? Had her father or mother taught her? Or had she learned as she worked, perhaps in this very cellar?

My mind turned the questions over like a spinning wheel as the three of us scrubbed dishes for hours. And then Wash issued a new order.

"You," she said to Cobie, Anya, and me, then issued a long command in Yotne.

"*Ya—idu?*" Anya asked haltingly, pointing at herself. She spoke the Yotne words with the cadence of someone who'd learned a few bits of a language here and there—just enough to ask for something to drink or count to ten.

Wash nodded. "*Tak.* You three. Beds and towels—change them."

I followed Anya out of the basement and up the stairs, over-size basket gripped tightly in my hands, dreading the inevitable sight of soldiers again. When we reached the first floor, Cobie glanced around the open foyer, then nodded at the house's great front door.

Anya nodded. "Now. Let's go."

I felt like I'd been doused in cold water. "Now? We're—just—now?" I'd told myself we would escape; but I'd banked on preparation, on allies. On a moment to get my feet beneath me.

"We've got to get *out* of here," Cobie said tightly. "The cook may never let us go again."

"Okay," I breathed. My heart was hammering in my chest, but she was right. We had to try.

I had seen the way Baba Yaga and her court had looked at Anya. And it was only a matter of time before she recognized me.

I had run out of time and tick marks long ago. There was no knowing how much longer Daddy had left.

The three of us walked toward the door, heads down, baskets bumping against our hips. I prayed for gaps to open up and hide us.

I didn't know where we'd go, if we got out. But anywhere was safer than Baba Yaga's Mortar.

One step at a time. One blistered foot forward, stone past stone.

"Aghov! Stop!"

I glanced up; a guard stood before the door, his hand out-stretched, barking at us in rapid Yotne.

Of course. Of course the front door would be guarded. It

had been when we arrived. My heart sank a little.

"*Mitä?*" Anya let her eyes go wide, her voice almost childishly high as she babbled a string of language that didn't sound like Yotne.

The guard's brow furrowed. "*Fins'kyy?*"

The Yotne called Anya's childhood home *Finlyandi*; she must have addressed him in her mother tongue. She nodded, and his scowl softened a little bit.

He was young—just a boy our age, no older than Torden or Aleksei. His brown hair was shaved nearly to his skull so it looked soft as a peach. But when he put his hands on his hips, the wolf tattoo on his forearm flexed, and I remembered where we were.

Anya asked a few more halting questions, and the guard ushered us back toward the stairs. *One more floor*, he seemed to be saying with a smile.

Cobie and I made for the staircase, but Anya paused, blond lashes batting over blue eyes sweet as a baby's. She asked him a question, and he grinned crookedly, crossing his arms around his rifle.

"Anya," she said, curtsying.

"Ivan." He pressed a hand to his chest and gave a little bow. The wolf on his forearm shifted with his muscles.

Anya nodded, seeming to blush before hauling us up the stairs, giggling.

"What was that all about?" Cobie glowered at her as we climbed the stairs.

We reached the landing of the first floor, and Anya went stone-faced.

"Reconnaissance." Then she turned into the nearest bedroom and began to strip sheets off the mattress.

Ivan, Anya informed us quietly as we worked, was at his regular post this morning. We had caught him during the brief half hour he was alone, when his fellow soldiers took their noon meal. "He said he's there from sunrise to three in the afternoon, and that he had to stay on duty during lunch, because he's the freshest recruit. He thought I was flirting."

"I did, too," Cobie admitted.

Anya balled up a sheet and threw it at her, accusatory. "That boy is our enemy, Cobie Grimm." She glided to the washbasin and gathered up the wet towels, piling them into her basket. "Besides, Skop's waiting for me. Somewhere out there."

She swallowed hard and stared out the window, at a river the color of pewter winding beyond the city wall. My gaze followed hers, and I knew I was searching for the *Beholder*, as I searched for her everywhere I went. But she had no way of finding me, so high in this tower, caught in Stupka-Zamok's sharp teeth.

We pulled sheets from beds, cases from pillows, towels from washbasins, replaced them all. Room after room, floor after floor. Some belonged to courtiers, some to staff, others to soldiers.

I was grateful not to meet any of Ivan's fellows in their quarters.

The stairs rattled beneath our weight as we hauled ourselves up and down their length. "Who built a staircase this narrow for a house so large? What a nuisance." Anya clicked her tongue as we huddled against the railing yet again for half a dozen soldiers to troop past, whistling appreciatively at us; I had to pinch Cobie on the arm to stop her snarling at them.

"Be smart," I whispered. "Save all that up for later."

Cobie's lip curled, but she nodded, and we carried on.

The second floor from the topmost, we knew from our first day, held the tsarytsya's throne room and her grand dining room; we bypassed it and carried on to the top floor. But a uniformed guard at the door shook his head. "*Ni. Nasha tsarytsya* sleeps."

But the door opened behind him. We met the eyes of the tsarytsya, their red rims the only color in her pale, bony face.

I expected her to turn us away. To order us downstairs, never to return to her chambers again. After all, she knew Anya's name. She knew her allegiance. She knew how dangerous a shield-maiden could be.

But Baba Yaga only eyed us dismissively, as if she were staring down a huddle of sheep alone with no shepherd. "Come back tomorrow," she said, and shut the door.

Back down in the kitchens, the cook eyed our piles of dirty linens with grim approval. Freckled arms elbow-deep in a batch of dough, she nodded to the laundry door.

"I know, I know," I mumbled.

"Wash," we said simultaneously.

The laundry was empty. Sheets and towels formed mountain ranges at one side of the room; the other was a forest of lines and clothespins. I took a cake of harsh soap and dunked a pillowcase in one of the great tubs.

The soap stung, humidity clung to the stone walls, and the room soon grew so hot from the fires under the tubs I wished I could work in my underwear. But here, at least, we were free to talk.

"So there are fourteen floors," Cobie whispered. "Top floor is Baba Yaga's room. Second from the top—the thirteenth—is her throne room and her dining room."

"Two through twelve are the bedrooms and offices of personnel and guards," I added, scrubbing the soap cake over a sheet. "We didn't go into any of the offices—should we have?"

"Maybe," Anya said. "We'll have to wait and see if the cook sends us up to empty rubbish, to take up meals."

My arms fell still, tangled beneath a heavy, wet sheet. "How are we going to get out?" I asked softly. "I wish the two of you hadn't come. I wish you weren't trapped here with me. I—" My words caught in my throat. "I think we might survive this. But escape? There's only one exit, and it's under guard. And besides, where would we go?"

Weeks of starving and the day's hard work had left me weary, and weariness made me doubtful. Would I ever see my home again? My father, my godmother? Would I ever meet my little brother or sister?

"I'd want to follow the river north to the sea, but we'd be caught," Anya said. "Rivers mean towns, and towns mean guards. If we can get our hands on a map and try to find neutral territory, we can attempt to contact the *Beholder* somehow."

"We'd do best to stay in the woods and the wild and get back to Norge that way—I know, I know." Cobie grimaced as Anya made a face. "But the Shield's house is secure. From there we could hail the *Beholder* and wait."

To hide in Asgard, huddled behind the Shield of the North with Torden at my side and Anya's brothers around us? It sounded like a dream—a coward's dream, but bliss nonetheless. I fought down my aching. "Perrault said he would contact Alfödr. They may already know where we are."

"Here's what I really want to know," Cobie continued. "What's the tsarytsya's plan if someone attacks this place? That staircase is barely wide enough for two of us to walk up side by side. If there were an emergency, people would die."

"Maybe she doesn't care about the people who serve her," I said quietly.

"Does she care about herself?" Anya muttered. "Because her room is on the top floor."

"Maybe there's an exit from the roof," Cobie said.

I swallowed, feeling my shoulders sag. "Or perhaps she believes the tower is impregnable. Her city is well guarded, and her house is a pillar of stone."

Cobie set her jaw and dropped her clothes in the tub. "Maybe she thinks it is," she said, taking each of our hands, her own slick with soap and water. "Maybe she feels untouchable here, behind all her spears and skulls. But never forget that as secure as this place is, and as unafraid of us as she may feel, we are already inside. And now, we know where she sleeps."

32

Wash set us to work again the next day. I renewed my vows to watch and wait and observe with every step up and down the rattling stairs.

Stupka-Zamok bore no resemblance to Winchester Castle or to the Neukatzenelnbogen. Those were peacetime palaces for royal courts, beautiful monuments to the glory of their noble lords—though Katz Castle had been left to rot.

Now, *there* was a place with gaps aplenty, where any number of things might slip out.

If anything, Stupka-Zamok reminded me of Asgard. Konge Alfödr's house was surely airier, broader built, more cheerful altogether; but it had the look of a place continually refortified. Asgard was not a palace, or even a castle. It was a fortress, safeguarded by its mountaintop height and its stone walls and Alfödr's *thegns* and *drengs*.

Stupka-Zamok lacked Asgard's natural protections. But

it was a fortress all the same, surrounded by a jagged city of teeth and spears and bones. Its only concession to the beautiful palaces I'd visited along my way was the treasure heaped everywhere; but that had been done artlessly, tastelessly, the work of thieves and not curators.

At least I had an answer, now, to where the portraiture and gilt and statuary torn from the walls of Katz Castle—and, likely, a hundred other great houses—had gone.

We reached the top floor far too soon, and found the tsarytsya's door already open.

The room was half a great ring, like the tsarytsya's throne room below. It, too, was dotted with mismatched busts and statues of every shape and size; the walls were covered with framed paintings and woven tapestries ill-suited to the castle's design and to one another.

At the heart of the space was a gray wooden table, flanked by chairs. Baba Yaga sat at its center, her eyes fixed on a board. Two women sat across from her, both in gray Imperiya uniforms.

One of the soldiers wore a wide black band above her elbow and another around her shiny, dark hair. She was pale-skinned, slim, and looked to be in her late thirties; a few gray strands shone in her braid, but her dark eyes were keen as flint.

The other looked younger—not quite thirty. She had a lean face, with a chiseled jaw and freckles on her nose and cheeks, and she wore a red band around her arm and around the short peach fuzz that covered her scalp. Her limbs were muscled, her skin tanned, and she had the look of a lioness: patient, thorough, relentless.

222

The room was silent but for a maid who sat before the fire-place, scooping out ashes, her little spade clanking and scraping against the stones and her bucket. The woman in the black band shifted in her seat, her jaw twitching.

Cobie, Anya, and I stood stock-still until the tsarytsya raised her eyes to us, irritated.

"Through there," she said, lifting her chin at a door.

"No, wait." The dark-haired woman pointed idly at me. "I need her." Then she beckoned to the girl at the fireplace.

Cobie and Anya passed through the door, glancing back at me with eyes wide. I shook my head, confused, and waited as the scullery maid at the fireplace drew near to the dark-haired soldier. The girl's shovel dangled limply from her fingers; strands of mousy hair had come loose from the knot at her neck and hung around her face.

The dark-haired woman said something in Yotne, to which the maid only shook her head. She tried another language, and then another, and then said in English, "Do you want me to lose this game?" To this, finally, the girl shook her head vigorously.

"No, no, my lady Polunoshchna." Her voice shook, but my heart throbbed a little—I hadn't known any of the other maids were English speakers. How had she come to be here? Was the tsarytsya's reach truly so limitless?

The soldier held out her hand, and the girl passed her the little shovel she'd been using to clean the fireplace. "I am not *Lady Polunoshchna*," she said, dealing the girl a stunning blow across the elbow with the back of the spade. "I am your General Midnight."

"Yes, yes, General," the girl gasped, clutching her arm.

"And I ask you again, do you want me to lose?" Polunoshchna gestured at the game board, dark braid swinging behind her. The girl bit her lip, and Polunoshchna raised the shovel again, aiming this time for the girl's neck.

"Stop it!" I shouted. "Control yourself!"

All four pairs of eyes turned to meet mine.

"Who are you?" Polunoshchna demanded.

I wet my lips. "I'm no one," I said. "Send her away. You need someone to clean the fireplace, I'll clean it."

She studied me for a long moment, nostrils flared, and I wondered if Polunoshchna and the tsarytsya would let my nonanswer stand. Polunoshchna had just demonstrated such breathtaking selfishness, I banked on her not much caring.

The tsarytsya was harder to read, especially as I was studiously avoiding her eyes.

"Fine. Go," Polunoshchna snapped at the scullery maid, who ran from the room, still cradling her elbow. The general tossed me the spade, and I bent to collect it from where it clattered to the stone floor. "Do it silently. And close that door," she added, nodding at the room where Cobie and Anya were quietly cleaning.

I shut it silently, then sat before the fireplace, ash bucket by my side. Baba Yaga and the two women continued to play.

"It is your turn, Vechirnya," said the tsarytsya. I glanced carefully over my shoulder and watched Vechirnya, the woman with the shaved head, reach for the dice and declare something in Yotne to Polunoshchna. The two women rolled a die twice each, and then Vechirnya reached forward, sweeping General Midnight's

224

pieces from the board and replacing them with her own.

Quietly as I could, I cleaned the fireplace, climbing onto the hearth to reach the ashes in its depths and sweep the soot from its walls, listening as they played on. Vechirnya and Polunoshchna spoke in Yotne at first, but Baba Yaga drew them back to English.

It made no sense. Perrault had been very clear that the tsarytsya insisted on Yotne. If she preferred English at the moment, I feared it was for some very particular reason.

When I was finished, I stood a respectful few feet from the board, waiting for Cobie and Anya and watching.

The game was played over a map of the world—of sorts. But the continents were misshapen and covered with pebbles, and their die seemed to have more than six sides.

"I challenge you for the Bear Whelp's paw," General Midnight sneered at Vechirnya. She moved a few pebbles into the other soldier's space.

As I studied their maneuvers, my hand crept unbidden to the back of my head where Torden's ring was nestled in my braid.

"Do you have lice?" Polunoshchna snapped at me. "Stop fidgeting, before I shave your head like Vechirnya's!"

I flushed and yanked my hand from my hair and wished again I were a thousand miles from this tower.

"Tooth and Claw, girl," said Vechirnya to me, lifting an eyebrow at my poorly disguised interest. Her voice was low and frank and refreshingly not laced with venom. "Have you ever played?"

I shook my head. She held something out to me, one of the pebbles, and I took it.

It was not a pebble, I found as I held it in my hand. It was a claw, from a dog or a cat perhaps, dyed red as blood. All the game pieces were claws and teeth, as the name implied.

I studied Vechirnya's gray uniform, the red band around her arm and her head. "No, General . . ."

"Sunset," she supplied.

"No, my General Sunset. I have never played."

She passed me the die next, pointing out its sides, counting out their meanings. "*Nul'—odyn—dva—tri—*" On and on she counted, from zero to nine, apparently enjoying the sight of my head swimming.

She was brilliant, and cool. I strove to mimic her.

Midnight glanced over at us. "You're distracting me," she snarled. I withdrew a few paces as they each rolled again. When they were done, Sunset nodded briskly, pleased, and swept Midnight's claws and teeth again from the map. Midnight sat back, arms crossed.

Her pieces, I deduced, were the black ones scattered far and wide across the board. I frowned, considering.

"What is it, girl?" asked the tsarytsya.

I started and shook my head. But she arched her brow, demanding my answer. Her gray hair shone in the smoky light of the window.

I couldn't speak to the tsarytsya; I could hardly meet her eyes for more than a moment. I turned to Polunoshchna, my hands shaking. "My General Midnight, would it not be wiser to concentrate your armies?" I asked. "You seem to have fewer. Shouldn't you cluster them together and shrink your border, to better defend your territory?"

"That is not the way of Wolves," spat Midnight. "I take what I will, lack of numbers be damned. Now close your mouth, *Zolushka*, or I will beat you as I beat that other bit of kitchen trash."

I thought of the scullery maid's gasp of pain when Midnight struck her, of the girl cradling her injured elbow, and felt my anger rise. "You take what you will, and you lose it just as easily," I said tightly. "And if you can't win the game with a little noise in the background, the fault is with your focus, not with the world around you."

General Midnight rose and slapped me across the face.

"Polunoshchna!" the tsarytsya barked. "Enough. Go."

"*Noh, moya tsarytsya*—"

"*Zabyraysya*," droned Baba Yaga. "Begone. I am bored. You too, Vechirnya."

I worked my jaw. Blood leaked in my mouth where Polunoshchna had struck me.

"*Tak tochno, moya tsarytsya*," said Sunset and Midnight, the former resigned, the latter enraged. Both generals rose, bowed, and left.

The tsarytsya turned her eyes on me. "You," she said. "Sit."

33

I pulled out a chair and sat down across from Baba Yaga.

"Tell me again your name," she said.

My limbs shook. "Selah."

"Selah from where?"

I swallowed hard. I was afraid to lie, but if she wanted truth, she would have to pry it out of me piece by piece. "From Potomac."

"And where is Potomac, Zolushka?" The tsarytsya pushed the board a little closer to me.

I'd been right; they'd been playing on a map of the world, but the continents were formed of animals. Africa was a great ox, its horns curling at the lower tip of the continent. Europe was a fat sheep, Zhōng Guó a plump rabbit, South Asia and the Pacific Islands a scattered herd of deer, Australia a clump of fish. Ranneniy Shenok, far in the north, was a bear's whelp. The Imperiya Yotne, at the map's center, was a wolf. And the

New World, far to the west, was a phoenix. Its wings were stretched wide, its tail feathers plumed, its head turned to the left.

There lay the world before the tsarytsya, hers for the taking.

And there lay my home. Far away and safe and *mine*, and I did not want to show her how to find it.

"My name is Selah," I said again, stalling.

"I can call you what I wish." Baba Yaga furrowed her brow, then smiled, disdainful. "As you are not a child of my Imperiya, I assume you've been nursed with the old tales, pacified with them from your infancy. To speak a name is to invoke meaning."

"There are no names in the old tales," I said, crossing my arms. "Only figures. They can be about anyone, about anywhere."

I was stalling. There *were* names in the old stories—beautiful Belle, intrepid Jack, a litany of gods and goddesses. But more common were the figures who appeared again and again: the wicked queen, the wise old crone, the third daughter sent to seek her fortune.

Mostly, I was being contrary because she'd been condescending, and it made me angry. The old tales—the stories Momma had taught me—were not milk sops for crying children. They were meat and power and truth, and she had no *idea* what they meant.

"Zolushka is not a name. It is what you are. It means 'ash-girl.'" Baba Yaga stared me down. "Now tell me who you are and where you are from and what you are doing in my house."

I was nearly nauseated with fear. The sickening terror made me less guarded, somehow. "The stories would say never give your true name to a stranger," I blurted. "Why should I tell you?"

"I shall not be a stranger for long." Grandmother Wolf never took her eyes off me. "And you should tell me, because I already know."

She did. I wasn't sure how, but her face told me she knew who I was.

My heart collapsed, and I pointed a shaking finger at the tip of the phoenix's eastern wing.

"Ah, yes." Baba Yaga's eyes lit with recognition, and she sat back, satisfied. "The stepdaughter."

My tongue tripped over itself. "I—I don't know—"

"You were to be bride to that boy in Shvartsval'd." She smiled, revealing long, straight teeth.

Bear. Torden. Fritz.

"He was one of my many suitors." Sweat filmed my palms.

"It had slipped my memory," she said. "You were so guarded, I was curious. I searched my correspondence, and your stepmother's letters reminded me." She smiled slightly. "She must hate you mightily, to propose a marriage alliance so far from your country."

The words were like a blow to my stomach. I knew Alessandra had written to the tsarytsya—how else could the suit have been arranged? But I ached to be confronted yet again with how truly, how powerfully, my stepmother hated me.

I swallowed hard, forcing myself to think of Torden. Of the

good that had come from the harm Alessandra had done me. Of red hair and red-gold lashes and freckles and strong, kind hands.

"Or she must have greatly desired to ally with my Imperiya," the tsarytsya added lightly, when I did not reply. "Indeed, I hope soon to reach your side of the ocean. An alliance between us would have made for very light terms for your *terytoriya*." She paused, considering me. "That could still happen. I could find you a husband in my court. You could have your freedom again."

"No."

I made it a full sentence. Baba Yaga waited for more—for pleas, or an explanation. But I said nothing else.

Her face grew cold, businesslike. "The girl you defended. Why? What is she to you?"

"Because General Midnight beat her with a shovel when she started losing a board game," I answered as steadily as I could. Where were Cobie and Anya?

She smiled at this. "We take Tooth and Claw very seriously. It helps us sharpen our own." She held up her hands; her nails were filed to points. Then her face grew thoughtful. "Do you think you could have won, with as few armies as Polunoshchna possessed?"

"I don't know," I hesitated. "But her lack of strategy couldn't have helped."

"There are a hundred girls in the world like that serving girl," the tsarytsya said thoughtfully. "Vasylysa came from a town on the border between the land of the Whelp and the

Wolves. Her father was a headman, and she wanted to be just like him."

I sat forward, curious against my own will. It had been ages since I'd had a story.

"But?" I asked.

"But she lost her mother," Baba Yaga answered. "And her stepmother grew tired of her, just like yours did." I drew back as if stung.

The tsarytsya smiled cruelly.

"Go," she said. "Rejoin the girl in the kitchens, where you belong."

Anya and Cobie were in the laundry when I returned. Vasylysa was peeling potatoes; a bruise was forming near her elbow where Polunoshchna had struck her. She gave me a weak smile, and I returned it.

"Where have you been?" Cobie hissed, dropping the towel she was scrubbing and pulling me into the laundry. "We left through the wrong door and couldn't go back to find you."

"Playing dice with my life," I said, showing her my shaking hands. Anya took them in her own and drew me close to the tub as I related my conversation with Baba Yaga and her generals. "What about you? What was her room like?" I asked, taking up the washing alongside them.

They had searched it as rapidly as they could after Polunoshchna ordered them to shut the door, rummaging first through her closets and then her desk. "A few of the papers seemed to be important," Cobie said.

"One on top of a stack looked like a report," Anya added. "There were notes all over it, and a lot of it was crossed out and rewritten. Some of the words matched the ones on the map over her desk."

"A map?" I asked. "Can you read it? Could we use it, if we got away?" My heart rose like a shot, painful and sharp, at the thought of Torden and the *Beholder* and home.

Anya shook her head, grimacing as the lye soap stung a cut on her hand. "I can't read the map, or the papers," she confessed. She cut a glance at Cobie. "But we found something else."

"What? What is it?" I shook my head, waiting for them to spit it out.

"Books," Cobie said in a rush. "She's hoarding them. She's got dozens."

The books that had gotten the headwoman on the Gray Road brutally murdered. The books stolen from the shelves of Katz Castle. The storybook I'd had to leave behind on the *Beholder*. Their weight seemed to collapse all upon me at once.

I couldn't form a response. But I shouldn't have been surprised.

There was no end to what Grandmother Wolf would catch between her jaws and carry away.

34

Wash was in high dudgeon the next morning. Two of the maids hadn't shown up to work, and one of the cooks had sliced open her hand peeling potatoes, so Wash cooked at double time; but even she made mistakes in her hurry. Once, she threw up her hands and tossed a whole batch of pelmeni dough into the bin, muttering about *chebureki* and her mind being elsewhere. Wash dragged the back of her wrist across her forehead, looking exhausted.

I didn't know what chebureki was; we'd never made it in Baba Yaga's kitchens. Perhaps it was food from Wash's home.

I wondered if she'd been so tired that she'd forgotten herself. Forgotten where she was and who she was supposed to be feeding.

This was the problem with our repetitive chores: they kept the hands busy and left the mind far too free to wander.

But Wash didn't say anything else. She made up more

dough and rolled it out and was soon frying pelmeni in such a frenzy that I asked if I could help. She shook her head, tossing something off in Yotne.

"She doesn't want us burning the castle down," Anya translated.

I laughed at this—before my too-limber memory reminded me someone else had warned me once of just the same thing. *You wouldn't mean to do anything,* Lang had said. *But a single stray spark could burn us alive.*

I'd stolen eyelashes from his cheek, and he had pressed his temple to mine. He'd kissed me, hands in my hair.

We had too much time to think.

Were the crew coming for us? Had they carried on down the Canal Route, into the Mediterranean Sea, and made for home? Or, perhaps, east for Zhōng Guó?

Did I even want them to put themselves at risk rushing in to save us? It could provoke retribution from Stupka-Zamok. It assumed Cobie, Anya, and I could not free ourselves.

I didn't know if I wanted someone to charge in and save us. I only wished I knew the ones I loved were as lonely for me as I was for them, left as I was only with their memories and my battered knees and knuckles.

My faraway thoughts haunted me all that day as we worked. As we plated supper I eyed the stovetop, spattered with grease from feeding the endless appetites of Baba Yaga and her people.

A single stray spark.

I wondered how many sparks I would have to light to burn this place to the ground.

And whether, if Baba Yaga's house burned, it would take me with it.

Baba Yaga, who outlawed belief in anyone but her. Baba Yaga, who forbade her people to sing or make music. Baba Yaga, who took children from their families to raise them as she saw fit.

Who had books upon books in her own room for her own use.

Not that I imagined she took any particular pleasure in them. But study was necessary to any ruler's success; Momma and Daddy had insisted on that, and the nuns had worked hard to teach me.

I thought of Bear's library. Of the tapestries clinging to Valaskjálf's walls, so the deeds of the brave could never be forgotten. But the need to learn ran deeper. Study wasn't crucial only for the powerful, just as good, hard work wasn't good only for the poor.

But the tsarytsya knew best.

Did her people really believe that? I doubted it rang true far out in the empire, but what of her people in this city? They had looked healthy and well-fed, protected in their little private fortresses—but were they content?

Twice, now, we'd seen packs of her own wolves deserting her.

I wondered if there were more here in Yotunkheym who resented her rule. Any who, like the Waldleute in Shvartsval'd, rebelled against her in secret, who we might call on to help us.

Fearful though I was, I longed to go to the tsarytsya's room.

To search its hiding places and to dig out the books she hoarded like a dragon.

I longed to let her feel my fire.

Cobie and Anya had tidied her room again that day. As we plated dinner, they told me they had something.

"You," Wash called across the kitchen, tucking stray wisps of black hair behind her ears. She pointed at the three of us as we finished pouring the last of the bloody-red soup into bowls.

"Wash?" I asked. I was eager for the kitchen to be empty. I wanted to see what they'd retrieved from Baba Yaga's lair.

Wash frowned. "No. Go. Serve." She gestured from the bowls to the stairs.

"Us? Serve dinner?" Anya asked.

"*Tak. Spasibo*," Wash added.

"Um, okay," I stammered. We'd never served before.

I raced for the trays I'd seen the maids use. "Okay, okay, okay." We set eighteen bowls of borscht onto them and started up the stairs. They were heavy; I tried not to look down as we climbed and climbed. Baba Yaga, I suspected, would not look indulgently on a dinner spilled down her stairs instead of served at her table.

Suddenly, Cobie paused on a landing at the head of our line. She glanced around.

"What are you doing?" I demanded. "We have to go!"

"Wash said dinner is already late," Anya said. For lack of a name for the head cook, I had shared my nickname with her and Cobie.

Cobie shook her head. "I wish we could poison the food. We

could do it all right now, all the bowls, then run."

"Are you crazy?" Anya demanded. "Poison the food? And lose our heads to the tsarytsya's guards here and now?"

"We wouldn't be punished if they all died," Cobie argued. "The castle would be in chaos. We could get away in the melee."

"Are we going to feed her guards, too?" I demanded in a whisper. "She'll have sentries posted at the dining room door. And what if the poison didn't work on everyone? And since when are we *killing* people?"

"Selah." Anya rounded on me. "She's killed thousands. Thousands upon thousands."

I froze, suddenly cold despite the sweat on my skin from cooking and carrying. "But we aren't the arbiters of justice. We aren't government, we aren't God."

"We are government, actually," Anya said, blue eyes large and serious. "You will be, someday. I will be, too."

"Either way, we're prisoners, and this is war. How are we getting out of here, if not by attacking her?" Cobie asked.

I had no answer for that.

I could only think that Daddy would understand me giving arms to resistance fighters, but poison—he was being poisoned himself. How could he ever understand or forgive me that?

I couldn't countenance it. "Let's just go serve dinner."

We climbed and climbed to the thirteenth floor and didn't speak again. A guard opened the door opposite the throne room, and we passed inside.

A long ash-gray table, identical to the one in the tsarytsya's salon, was surrounded by guests; empty chargers sat before them. "Finally," the tsarytsya intoned.

I put my tray down on a sideboard and nodded Anya toward the table. She walked slowly from guest to guest as I set bowls from her tray before them.

"My General Midnight," I murmured as I served her, seated on Baba Yaga's right. "My General Sunset."

Vechirnya gave me the barest nod. She wore a gray coverall that left her lean arms bare, but for the red band around her bicep. Her arms were tanned, their hair blond from days in the sun.

"Zolushka," Polunoshchna sneered. Her dark hair was shiny and perfect and clean. I felt filthy before her.

The seat on the tsarytsya's left was empty; she gestured for me to put the soup bowl down anyway. "He'll be along," she said, waving a papery-skinned hand.

Past a host of gray-clad guests, three children sat at the table's far end, dressed in repulsive child-size replicas of Imperiya military uniforms. My stomach dipped convulsively at the two little boys and girl like military-style dolls.

I glanced from the children hungrily spooning up soup— the girl trying to hide the drop she'd spilled on her trousers, one of the boys' stomach growling even as he ate—to Cobie and Anya, and I knew we were all thinking the same thing: we were glad, after all, that we hadn't had anything like poison to hand.

I could barely look at the children. They were the starving-eyed little boy and girl from the fairy tale made flesh.

So eager to lap up their food. So eager to accept warmth wherever they found it. So unaware Grandmother Wolf would open her jaws soon and swallow them whole.

Down in the kitchens, I gasped for breath, overwhelmed by nerves, by the guests ignoring me even as they sneered at me. By General Midnight's open disdain.

Zolushka.

"Did you understand anything they said?" Cobie asked.

Anya pursed her lips. "*Soon*, the tsarytsya kept saying."

We piled plates of dumplings on our trays and made to return upstairs.

We served more smoothly this time. I set down pelmeni and Cobie collected empty bowls of borscht. I couldn't help noticing how red were the mouths of everyone around the table.

We came again, at last, to the empty seat.

I glanced at Cobie. She shrugged and picked up the full bowl, and I set the plate of dumplings down on the charger.

The door swung open behind us. "*O net!*" exclaimed a familiar voice. "*Ya ostalsya bezh borscht.*"

Cobie looked up first, and the bowl of soup fell from her hands, crashing to the floor in an explosion of gray ceramic and bloodred soup. Anya and I turned.

Aleksei was framed in the doorway, pale and dark-haired and fine-boned as ever. His expression shifted from insouciance to shock when he saw us.

"Aleksei," Anya whispered. "What are you doing here?"

Aleksei's eyes darted to the tsarytsya's, their sharpness at odds with the lazy tone of his question to her in Yotne.

"*Angliyskiy*, please," Baba Yaga said, lifting her fork and knife. "It's only polite in front of our guests."

We weren't guests, but I barely registered the words. I could hardly think.

This was wrong. All wrong.

"Aleksei?" Anya asked again. She looked stricken.

"I invited him," the tsarytsya said, but she was watching me. "I saw how poorly he fared at Alfödr's court, and how much worse things would become for him."

"And you accepted her invitation?" Cobie demanded.

My brain reeled.

Baba Yaga ignored her. "Come you of your own accord, or are you compelled?" she asked Aleksei, examining the knife in her hand.

"Of my own compulsion, *moya tsarytsya*." Aleksei bowed low and gave her a grin, his pale face contorting with the expression.

She smiled. "Then I welcome you with open arms, Aleksei Stupka. I am pleased you finally see this is where you belong."

Aleksei. Aleksei Asgard was here, answering now to *Stupka*—a son of Stupka-Zamok. A son of the Mortar.

"*Her.*" Anya's voice grated, harsh. "Here, with her. After everything our father did to keep us safe."

"*Our father*," Aleksei mused. "What did he do for us?"

"He took us in," Anya growled. "He kept us safe."

"He kept *himself* safe," Aleksei snapped. "And he was ready to offer you up like a brood mare at the first chance."

"And what of our brothers?" Anya shouted.

Torden. Fredrik. Bragi. Hermódr. Their names were seared on my heart.

"They chose him!" Aleksei fired back. "And now, I'm on my own side."

Anya's nostrils flared, furious, the blue vein pulsing in her forehead. The tsarytsya's fine eyebrows were arched, her gaze on Aleksei and on us.

Anya charged at Aleksei and shoved him to the stone floor. The dinner guests gasped; even the guards were frozen in astonishment.

This was not Valaskjálf, prone to laughter and cheers in the event of a scuffle. And this was no tussle between brothers.

One of the little boys at the end of the table scrambled out of his chair and hid behind it. I wanted to scoop him into my arms. I wanted none of this to be real.

Anya straddled Aleksei, pinning down his knees and his left shoulder, and punched him in the mouth. She hit him until her knuckles and Aleksei's teeth matched the bloodred mouths of Baba Yaga's dinner guests. At a word from Baba Yaga, the guards recovered themselves and dragged her off him.

Aleksei stood and brushed himself off, spitting a broken bit of tooth onto the floor. I clutched Cobie's hand. My breath came in gasps.

"Traitor!" Anya screamed as the guards hauled her out the door. "Patricidal son, treacherous brother, backstabbing friend—"

The door slammed shut behind her, but I could hear Anya—beautiful, golden-haired Anya, my friend, the princess—screaming herself hoarse all the way down the stairs.

Aleksei drew out his chair over the shattered porcelain and

the spilled borscht at his feet, seated himself, and began to eat his pelmeni.

The neck of his uniform was torn, and the nose of the wolf tattoo nudged up his neck and above his collar.

"It's so frightfully dull playing soldier in Norge, *moya tsary-tsya*. Standing up alongside the fairy-tale princes on their white horses." Aleksei rubbed his hands together. "I find I'm ready to run with the Wolves."

35

We returned to the kitchen to find the soldiers shackling Anya's wrists, ignoring Wash as she railed at them. Her words were in Yotne, but I couldn't mistake her gestures, her angry dark eyes, the sweep of her chapped hand toward Anya.

How am I to serve the tsarytsya with her servants bound? she seemed to demand.

The guards ignored her. Hot tears pooled in Anya's eyes, and her nostrils flared, furious. Vasylysa gaped as she stirred a pot of something over the stove, her hands slowing until the smell of burning grain filled the air.

When the guards were gone, Wash examined the skin beneath Anya's shackles and shook her head, ferocious. The injuries from the cuffs we'd worn on our journey from Shvartsval'd had only just begun to heal.

Anya's chains clanked with her every movement.

Wash drew in a sharp breath through her nose and gestured

from Cobie and me to the main course, rows of plates of buttery chicken. "*Kurka*. Take it upstairs." Then she nodded at Anya, pointing at the samovar. "*Chay*." I knew that word: *tea*.

We left Anya to follow her orders. But I wished we could stay to talk to her about what had just happened.

Anya's brother was here. In Baba Yaga's house, ready to betray her family.

"I can't believe it," Cobie whispered over my shoulder as I climbed the stairs ahead of her. "I can't believe he's here."

I swallowed, thinking of Aleksei in Norge. Dressed in a gray Imperiya uniform as Konge Alfödr shouted at him. Provoking his brothers to fury. Disappointing his king again and again despite all his efforts, until he didn't care to try anymore.

"The worst of it is," I said, "I can."

In the dining room, we served in silence, taking up dirty plates and setting the chicken down before the guests.

When I came to Aleksei's place, I wanted to spit in his food. I wanted to smash the plate over his head. How dare he come here, with other choices left to him?

"I believe I have a place for you among my ranks, Aleksei," said Baba Yaga. I nearly tripped at her words; Cobie steadied me.

"Indeed, *moya tsarytsya?*" Aleksei asked.

"I have my Vechirnya, my General Sunset, and my Polunoshchna, my General Midnight," said the tsarytsya, taking a bite. "But I lack a Rankovyy."

Midnight dropped her fork with a *clank* and turned a vicious gaze on Aleksei. Baba Yaga did not acknowledge this.

"Your General Dawn?" Aleksei asked. I could almost see him translate the word, as if he'd spoken English and Norsk for so long that Yotne was foreign to him. "But what does—what would that mean?"

"You shall be my Bright Dawn, the harbinger of Yotunkheym's glorious future," the tsarytsya said. "You will wear white and rear my wolf cubs."

Aleksei's mouth curled into a broad, ghastly grin.

The tsarytsya's guests murmured among themselves. "Why me?" Aleksei finally asked, cocking his head, sprightly and dangerous. "Why make me Rankovyy beside Vechirnya and Polunoshchna? They've served you since my father's time." He nodded at Midnight and Sunset, deferential.

"Them?" Baba Yaga smirked. "I suppose they have."

Midnight's jaw tightened, and Sunset looked sharply from the tsarytsya's face to Aleksei's.

The tsarytsya sighed and rolled her eyes. "Because my former General Dawn is dead, and because I have promised Vechirnya and Polunoshchna a replacement quickly so that they may grow the ranks of our armies, and because I like your instinct," she finally said. "You did not like your place in the Shield's house, and so you took to another house with no compunction. You take what you will, as a Wolf should. And you will teach my cubs to do the same." She nodded down the table at the children still eating quietly, and I had to curl my fingers tightly around the tray in my hands to keep from dropping it.

"Very well, *moya tsarytsya*," Aleksei answered, nodding at Baba Yaga and at her generals. "I will guard your litter." Sunset pursed her lips, scratching at the short fuzz of her hair with tanned fingers. Midnight was entirely still.

"You are not just to guard them," Baba Yaga said, suddenly aggressive. "You are to grow their numbers. You are to whet my wolf cubs' appetites and sharpen their claws." She sat back, plate empty but for the bones. "Do not forget that fact, Aleksei, or I may have to dispose of you. You will show me what you've done the night of the full moon."

Confusion flashed across Aleksei's face, but he schooled himself and nodded. "I will not forget it, *moya tsarytsya*. On the night of the full moon, you will see how well I remember."

Baba Yaga's smile curled. "Very good, my General Dawn."

We took one more trip between the dining room and the kitchen. I avoided Aleksei's gaze as Cobie and I collected the last of the bowls and plates.

He was too familiar. He knew us, spoke the secret language of our friendship.

We would have to be careful around him. His presence changed our chances of escape—and everything else.

Because Aleksei shouldn't be here. He shouldn't be at this table, opposite General Sunset and General Midnight and their witch queen. He shouldn't be in this house at all—at the side of the woman who he'd told me himself stole children from their families, the mortal enemy of the man who'd raised him up from childhood.

He should be in Asgard, where I would give anything to be. He should be beside his brother, the boy I loved. He should be with his father, since he'd been lucky enough not to be expelled from the only home he knew.

Never mind that Konge Alfödr wasn't an affectionate father. Never mind that he was harsh, stern, unforgiving, single-minded, pragmatic to the point of coldness. To his mind, he was cold because he had to make difficult choices. He was stern because his people were counting on him. He was pragmatic because, as Shield of the North, he could not be otherwise.

Fleetingly, I wondered if the tsarytsya had told herself the same thing as she first took revenge on Ranneniy Shenok and then took the rest of Europe: that it did not matter that she had been vicious. That her people's larder had been empty, and she had filled it, and what else mattered?

Potomac had wanted, as well. My father's answer had been to plant trees alongside the Anacostia River, to see that the public fields flourished.

He had looked after his own. But he had done it with the sweat of his brow, not by taking from others what was not his.

How I ached for him.

I didn't look at any of the guests as I served them from the samovar of tea, as I served them *kisel* and lemon and small cakes.

Let them feast while the rest of their people starved and feared and grieved. Let them feast—for now.

36

I should've known we couldn't avoid him. None of Anya's brothers could stay away from a fight for long.

After the tsarytsya's dinner guests had retired, after Wash had reluctantly chained Anya to the hearth with the key the guards had given her, after we finished our own small suppers and curled up before the oven to sleep, he sauntered down the stairs and into the kitchen, as curious and comfortable here in Baba Yaga's basement as he had been in Konge Alföðr's great hall.

Anya lurched to stand, her chains yanking her backward. "What are you doing here?" she snarled.

"What am I doing here?" Aleksei demanded. "What are you doing here?"

"Didn't the tsarytsya tell you?" I asked dully. "We were captured as rebels in the Shvartsval'd. She brought us here. I suppose we're lucky we're in her kitchens and not in prison."

Aleksei gave a wry laugh. "The tsarytsya doesn't have prisons. A waste of materials and manpower. Her captives are useful or they are dead." His gaze sharpened. "Please don't find yourselves the latter."

"What do you care?" Cobie snapped. "You're here betraying your father and the country that took you in. Why should we matter more to you than they do?"

"Are you an idiot?" Aleksei snapped. "I was never going to be perfect Torden. Or Tyr, never asking Alfödr any questions. Or you, Anya, with all your charms."

"Aleksei, you had your place in our family, just as I did!" Anya burst out.

"I thought I did." Aleksei's voice was dark. "But I'm not Alfödr's son. He made it clear that I would never be enough. That he only ever set a place for me at his table to keep me from hers." He pointed toward the ceiling, gesturing not at the stones above our heads but at the dining room table far above. Then he smiled. "I wanted to be somewhere I mattered. And I was right. Here I am, received with a hero's welcome."

"And your brothers?" I asked. "Do they deserve your betrayal?" *Torden, Bragi, Hermódr, Fredrik.* Their names reverberated through me like a heartbeat. I pointed at Anya, at the shackles that bound her to the hearth. "Did you think about what the Imperiya is *really* like, what *really* happens as its power grows, when you threw your fit and stomped out of your father's house to prove a point?"

"Don't talk to me about proving points and throwing fits," Aleksei spat. "I heard all about your display the night of the

Midsummer bonfires. You stood up to my father to prove a point, yourself."

"Yes!" I bellowed, stomping toward him. "I did! To prove the point that I would do anything to protect my people. That individual hearts were not meant to be sacrificed on the altar of the greater good. You came here to rub your hurt and your neglect in your father's face, and believe me, I understand." I laughed, utterly humorless. "Or rather, I would have understood. If you'd sunken a boat, or stolen a horse, or gotten caught in some embarrassing public affair. But this?" My chest rose and fell, anger chasing my heartbeat into a gallop. "This isn't making a point. This is treason, and there will be consequences."

"I am beyond my father's power," Aleksei bit out. "He can't humiliate me here."

"I meant for other people!" I shot back. "Consequences for *other people*, Aleksei. For Asgard. For your brothers and sister. You're looking at the first of them right now." I pointed at Anya's chains, and Aleksei blinked at me, something coming unmoored and uncertain in his expression.

For a long moment, none of us spoke. The only sound in the kitchen was of our breathing, echoing off the stones.

Anya spoke into the silence. "Will you really be her General Bright Dawn, Aleksei?"

"And what does all that mean?" Cobie's voice was troubled. "Sunset, Midnight, Dawn?"

"Huginn and Muninn say that if Stupka-Zamok is the mortar, her armies—the *pestykk*—are the pestle," Anya said.

"She uses them to grind down her enemies. General Sunset, Vechirnya, leads them, and night falls with their coming."

But it wasn't Sunset I feared most. "And Polunoshchna?" I asked.

"General Midnight is the head of the secret police," Aleksei said. "Her informer, much as Huginn and Muninn serve our father."

I stiffened.

You look like Midnight herself, Margarethe had complimented me.

Hope that you never meet her.

"It's not the same, and you know it," Anya spat.

"And you?" Cobie asked.

"As Rankovyy, General Dawn, I will raise the little *pestykk, nasha tsarytsya's* soldiers in training. They will fill her army's ranks someday." Aleksei drew himself up, reciting the words to us as if the tsarytsya had just taught them to him. "The Yotunkheym litter live in a house not far from here, piled up all together, raising one another like Wolves. Not unlike the way we raised ourselves," Aleksei added pointedly at Anya.

Anya only shook her head.

Aleksei sighed, conciliatory. "Look, if you must know, I privately think the tsarytsya ought to leave children with their families. It seems wisest not to address that point with her now, while I remain at loose ends in her house." He swallowed. "As I said, Baba Yaga does not favor the useless."

"And what about us, Aleksei?" I asked. "If Grandmother Wolf asks for details about the girls living in her kitchens, will you make yourself of use to her?"

"Of course not." Aleksei scowled, as if this was a ridiculous question.

But I didn't trust him.

Aleksei wasn't the wolf tattooed at his neck. He was the snake inked around his arm. He was a low, cold-blooded, creeping thing, who would slip away from trouble and danger and shed his skins as often as he needed.

"And what happens on the full moon?" I asked.

His jaw tightened. "A celebration. Each month, on the full moon, the Wolves come out to sharpen their claws."

"So, you don't know," Cobie deadpanned. He ignored her.

"Do you really think it will be the same here, Aleksei?" Anya asked.

He swallowed. But I was tired of his carefully pinned-together answers.

"No." I made my voice unforgiving as Baba Yaga's stone walls and pointed at the kitchen door. "No. Get out."

Aleksei left us, and I turned to Anya and Cobie. "Now, show me what you found in Baba Yaga's den today."

37

Cobie disappeared into the laundry room and returned bearing a paper scribbled with writing, which she passed over to me.

"It's a list," she explained, "but we don't know what it means."

I pressed my lips together and squinted, drawing close to the oven so I could see.

Two columns opposed one another, the left-hand one clean, the items on the right crossed out again and again.

Realization struck me. "These are numbers," I said, pointing to the scratched-out items on the right. Numbers that had been changed—altered, or updated, perhaps, again and again.

"Yes, I thought—but how did you know that?" Anya looked surprised.

A wry grin stretched across my face. "Vechirnya taught me." I mimed rolling dice. Cobie smiled, sharp as any wolf. "Anya, can't you count in Yotne?"

"Out loud, yes," she said, "but I can't read anything."

Vechirnya had only shown me the once. But I had kept watching as they played.

I'd always been an excellent student.

I took up the pencil they'd stolen and set to work, counting to myself as General Sunset had on the dice while they played Tooth and Claw.

The numbers I translated ranged from the thousands to the hundreds; the figures grew smaller with every scratched-out correction. My first guess, from years spent looking over Daddy's shoulder, was that it was a list of accounts. I frowned. "Is it money?"

Anya shook her head. "I don't know what these words on the left mean, but if this were money, they'd have this symbol beside them." She drew three quick lines, little hash marks, one after another. "They deal in *nulya* here. It means 'scratch.'"

I sat back, the figures swimming before my eyes.

So often since I'd left home, words had been lost to me, but meanings had been clear. The taunts of Imperiya soldiers, the chatter of the *freinnen*, the boasts of Konge Alfödr's *heerthmen* in his great hall. Even where their speech meant nothing, their faces and their voices guided me toward their intent.

I stared at the numbers I'd translated.

For once, I possessed the facts. But their significance was beyond my grasp.

I sat the next morning on the hearth of the great oven, my back warming against its bricks. Cobie and Anya were still asleep. I'd woken from a nightmare.

One by one, the knots of my makeshift rosary slipped over the pads of my fingers.

In my dream, Torden had found me kissing Lang, my cheeks and waist smeared with charcoal from his fingers. I'd chased Torden over the Gray Road, but he hadn't looked back, no matter how fast I ran.

My feelings were a maelstrom. I was sick with guilt from the dream, drowning in Aleksei's betrayal. Strangest of all, I was unable to read for the first time in my life.

The written word had never been closed off to me. Speech, either, before this trip. I'd never felt such empathy for travelers. For immigrants. For strangers in strange lands.

My godmother's book had been a map, out on the ocean. The paper we'd found might be one for us, as well. But I lacked the understanding to use it.

Doubt clung to my bones. I prayed for the faith to believe that light would come.

I didn't hear anyone enter the kitchen. But when I opened my eyes for a moment, to move to the next decade of knots, Wash stood tall above me.

My rosary fell into my lap. I felt all the blood drain from my face.

My mouth dropped open, searching for an excuse, and my hands shook.

Wash had been gentle with Anya. But she might be less forgiving of this. I hoped whatever punishment this earned me wouldn't affect the others.

Wash's dark eyes gave away nothing. Finally, I just said, "Please."

She picked me up by my elbow, not gripping me but guiding me. "Come."

My thoughts raced. My heart turned to water. What a coward I was.

Wash led me on through the kitchen, through the laundry, and into a closet I'd never noticed. I shuffled over the threshold, ready for the locks to fall shut behind me, as they had so many times in Shvartsval'd. To my surprise, she followed me inside.

"What—?" I began.

"Pray in here only," Wash said quietly.

I said nothing. My jaw worked but produced no sound.

Wash stared at me, as if trying to make a decision. She gestured to a basin of water, a scarf, and a rug rolled up in the darkest corner of the closet—a worn old thing she'd probably rescued from a courtier's room or a soldier's office. I crouched beside it, peering closer. A prayer rug.

My breath left my chest in a whoosh.

I'd thought I was the only one with a secret. The only one resisting in this way. How foolish I had been.

"This is a safe place to pray." Wash glanced again at the closed door. "Not out there. I am finished this morning. So now—you pray here. I will keep watch outside."

I stared at her broad cheekbones constellated with freckles, her skin only a little lined, as my mother's had been before I'd lost her.

Wash frowned, as if she wasn't sure I understood. Her chapped hand cupped my shoulder. "You must be more careful."

I blinked furiously. "Thank you. *Spasibo*."

"Do not cry," Wash said, not ungently. "Hurry."

Wash returned to her prayer closet later—five times in one day, in keeping with Muslim tradition. Once, as I watched her slip away, two of the other cooks met my gaze, their own eyes defiant—as if daring me to question her absence. Another time, Vasylysa closed the door behind Wash when it hadn't shut properly.

I wasn't sure how safe or dangerous it was to be Muslim in the world beyond the Imperiya. Probably, it depended on where you lived. I'd never met anyone of Wash's faith in Potomac, and the world was wide—and how little I knew about it, about what lay beyond my home's borders and shores, was becoming clearer every day. What I did know was that here, inside the witch's castle, her worship was a stunning act of resistance.

As she returned to the sheets she'd been scrubbing, Vasylysa and I exchanged a single, brief nod of understanding. The women in this cellar protected one another. *This is a safe place*, they all seemed to say with their silence.

It made me wonder how many other secrets might be safe here.

38

My muscles were burning before the sun had climbed halfway to noon the next day.

Up and down the stairs we climbed, avoiding the eyes of the soldiers by the front door who nudged Ivan every time we passed. He greeted Anya, his voice cracking.

I ignored them. We were busy. Baba Yaga needed clean sheets and towels again, needed her chamber pot emptied, needed her empty tea glasses tidied away. Anya winced with every movement, her chains clanking as she worked, her shackles chafing her wrists.

The sentry didn't even look at our faces as we approached the tsarytsya's bedroom. He saw our baskets and rags and stepped aside at once.

Inside were a great bed, desk, and wardrobe. All were of the finest, all in the utmost order, surrounded by pilfered statuary and artwork.

I knew I had no time to waste, but I stepped near to one painting, drawn by recognition. Angels and shepherdesses floated beatifically against a powder-blue background, framed in gold.

"Selah?" Cobie asked.

"This was stolen from Katz Castle," I said, not turning. "I'm sure of it."

Along the wall immediately to my left, a row of skulls wore a series of crowns, each more elaborate than the last. One was bareheaded. Perhaps it was home to the crown she wore today.

I hoped the skulls hadn't belonged to the crowns' original wearers—though, what did it matter? They were *someone's* skulls.

"Selah," Cobie said again, insistent. This time, I turned.

She leaned across the tsarytsya's huge bed as if to strip its sheets, reaching for the headboard. It gave, and I gave a gasp, racing to Cobie's side.

"You broke her bed," I whispered in horror. "She's going to kill us."

But she hadn't broken it. Cabinet doors opened along a seam in the headboard's dark wood surface. The inside was lined with books—books upon books, covered with leather and canvas and gold foil. Some of them were in English. Most were in Yotne. Some were in old Deutsch or Arabiyya or Nihongo.

Cobie and Anya had warned me, but I wasn't prepared. The sight of them, gleaming and cozy on their shelves, filled me with joy. And with fury.

I wanted to clutch the books to my chest. I wanted to steal them. I wanted to sit down on the tsarytsya's bed and read them one by one.

I wanted to open a window and toss them to the ground outside, pages flying, to let her people know what a hypocrite their empress was.

I did none of these things.

Carefully, carefully, setting her unwashed sheet back over the mattress, I braced my dirty feet and balanced as I pored over the spines, hoping I'd find what I needed. What I suspected she might have.

"Here's something else." Anya stood beside Baba Yaga's desk, blue eyes wide, a drop cloth in her hand.

A radio sat along its edge.

A radio. My brain was reeling.

Could I hail the *Beholder*, or the Waldleute? Or Torden? Or my godmother?—but I heard the tsarytsya's voice on the other side of the door, in her sitting room.

I climbed down, shut the cabinet doors, wrapped a book in the used sheet, and remade the bed with clean linens as quickly as I could. Cobie stared at me, horrified.

"Do you know how much trouble we could get in? For a *book?*" she demanded.

I ignored her, stuffing the sheet and its contents into the bottom of a basket. "Cobie, can you read old Deutsch as well as you speak it?"

She drew back. "What?"

Before I could explain, the door swung open.

"Little Zolushka. I knew I smelled you," General Midnight said with a smile. "*Nasha tsarytsya* would like a fourth for our game."

39

"Stand there," Baba Yaga said to Cobie and Anya, gesturing along the wall. She wore gray as always, but today a silver-and-diamond coronet ringed her head.

Cobie and Anya retreated between two statues that both looked like Roman emperors.

General Midnight sat beside Sunset; across from her sat Aleksei, the new General Dawn. I glanced at the tsarytsya, confused. "But you already have four players."

She gave an icy smile and gestured to the seat opposite General Midnight. "You take my place today, little ash-girl."

That smile left me cold to the bone. I sat.

"First," said General Sunset, "we roll." She held up the die in her lean, efficient fingers for me to see, then put it into Aleksei's hand.

Dawn, Sunset, Midnight. Aleksei rolled a seven, Sunset a six. Midnight crowed when she rolled a nine, the highest value on the die, and again when I rolled a three.

"I will go first," said Polunoshchna, leaning across the table to narrow her eyes at me, "and you will go last."

They quickly gathered their claws and teeth before them. White for Dawn. Red for Sunset. Black for Midnight. The little pile heaped before me was gray.

Midnight lifted her chin, pugnacious and challenging, as she plunked a claw in the heart of the wolf. Sunset rolled her eyes and set a red tooth in Australia.

Baba Yaga laid a papery hand on Aleksei's shoulder at my side. "It is your turn, my Rankovyy." He swallowed and shook himself and placed a claw somewhere near the southern end of Africa.

Sunset, Midnight, and Dawn turned to look at me.

I didn't know what to do, or what I was doing here at all. Hands shaking, I set a piece at the heart of the phoenix. Midnight sneered and took her turn.

The game tore ahead after that, each of us sinking our claws and teeth into territories across the map. I could feel Baba Yaga's breath down the back of my neck, searching my face and my moves for *something*, but I didn't know what.

Then came the attacks.

To take a *terytoriya*, players moved claws into territories adjacent their own, and a few rolls of the die decided whose claim won.

Tooth and Claw was simple enough. But I loathed it.

I didn't even want to pretend to take places that didn't belong to me. Even staking claims across the New World—places that belonged to other tribes, to other kingdoms—twisted my gut. More than anything, I wished Anya wasn't standing along the wall, forced to watch a game about the horror that had been her childhood. I wondered if the tsarytsya could feel the disgust radiating off me.

Did she hope to learn what kingdoms I cared for? Was she rattling me for her own enjoyment? Watching to see whether Polunoshchna or I would strike first, or if Anya would lunge at Aleksei again? I could divine nothing from her pacing about the room, except that while I played, she was playing a game of her own, and it terrified me.

It was fortunate that the others had little interest in the New World, because I played ineptly. Sunset was occupied with a strategy I didn't understand, but Midnight was relentless and obvious, obsessed with the territories on the map that represented her immediate environs. She took first Yotunkheym, and then Ranneniy Shenok, and then grappled with Aleksei for the fat sheep representing Europe. But after Midnight laid claim to Den Norden, she turned her eyes on the New World.

I moved all my armies to the phoenix's shoulders, her only means of entrance to my continent. Again and again, I fought her off. The die was a cold bit of bone in my hands, the claws rattling dryly across the board. Vasylysa had built up the fire again—silent as a mouse this time, her watery blue eyes darting around—and I felt sweaty in my shift, felt frantic with Midnight glaring at me.

Most of all, I felt the throbbing call of the book at the bottom of Cobie's basket.

Suddenly, the door burst open. A cadre of guards entered, two men gripped between them. Both were injured, one with a gash in his thigh that stained his pant leg an ominous brown-red. Baba Yaga and the generals rose.

"We are occupied," said the tsarytsya. Her voice was cold.

The soldier answered her in Yotne, looking confused. Baba Yaga arched her eyebrows and nodded her head at me, as she had once before. "*Angliyskiy*, please, for our guest."

Angliyskiy. English. Aleksei stole a glance in my direction, brow furrowed.

"We think they ran from Zatemnennya," the guard said.

I frowned at Aleksei. He paused, translating in his mind. *The eclipse*, he mouthed a beat later.

This made no sense to me, but the tsarytsya turned to the men. "Come you here of your own accord," she asked, "or are you compelled?"

One of the men did not answer. The other cried out in Yotne, clutching his bleeding thigh; he strained toward the door, pleading to be released.

Baba Yaga sighed, pulling a long dagger from her belt. "Compelled, then."

In two swift moves, she clawed their heads from their bodies. Blood painted the walls.

Cobie cried out. My stomach heaved. I pressed my lips together, tried to look away. But the empty eyes of the man who had not spoken stared up at me, precious scarlet lifeblood leaking out onto the stones.

We had been playing a game a moment before, and now two men lay dead on the floor. It seemed impossible.

I wished for a priest or an imam or a rabbi or a mere moment of silence. I wished for my father. I wanted to flee to the kitchens. I wanted to go home.

Without thinking, I gripped Aleksei's hand at my side. He squeezed it, meeting my eyes, his pale face set like stone.

Then he glanced at Sunset and Midnight behind us and released me.

Baba Yaga turned to the four of us, shaking her head again, gesturing for us to sit. "I have no use for the compelled."

I settled into my chair, afraid I'd be sick.

What difference does it make? I wanted to demand. In a world where the tsarytsya took what she would, where her word was law and she the only god there was, who could say whether anyone chose or had their choices made for them?

But watching the men's blood leak across the slate, I realized what she had been asking. *Are you bounty,* she meant, *or are you a hunter? Are you a wolf, or are you prey?*

I had not realized there was a correct answer to give her, when we arrived. I had not known what the consequences would be if we answered wrongly. That those men could have been Cobie, or me, or Anya, if we'd mumbled a reply that displeased the tsarytsya.

Had she put this question to everyone in the castle? To

the women in the kitchens? To Wash? How had they known what to say? How had any of us found ourselves in this tower of nightmares?

I was playing her game and knew none of the rules and suddenly fear felt so thick in the air I could scarcely breathe.

We had to get out of here. We had to get clear of this place before it was one of us dead on the floor.

The tsarytsya was watching me closely, but her face gave nothing away.

"It is your turn, Rankovyy," said Sunset.

But Baba Yaga sighed, sounding almost dissatisfied. "Enough. I'm tired."

Relief filled my lungs. I could leave. I pushed my chair back, trying to curtsy even as I rose.

"Wait," Midnight barked at me, holding up a hand, already counting rapidly—her claws, Sunset's, Aleksei's, and mine. She clenched her fist around a palmful of pieces, dark hair swinging over her shoulders, her eyes angry.

"Who—" Sunset asked.

"You won, Vechirnya," the tsarytsya said. "Zolushka was second."

"Did you think you'd won?" Midnight sneered at me, though I'd said nothing. "Sunset always wins."

I drew back. "I didn't think I'd—"

"I have my tactics," Sunset explained to me quietly. Her full brow drew together seriously as she spoke. "You chose a different one, of course—but the New World was a wise place to begin." She raised a hand in something like congratulation.

"And of course, Sunset always wins," said the tsarytsya. "She is the head of my *pestykk*, and as Zolushka said, Midnight, you lack control." General Midnight scowled at me; I tried not to shrink in my seat. Baba Yaga's voice grew cold. "And if she had won, you three would be lying dead alongside those traitors' bodies, because she is a child from nowhere."

"Even so." Midnight swallowed, leaning across the table at me. "You lost. So you lose."

"Lose what?" I pulled farther away from her, shoulder blades pressing into the back of my chair. Alarm shrilled up my spine. "I have nothing. I didn't know we were playing for stakes."

"At this table, there are always stakes," Sunset said, organizing her pieces and leveling me with a glance. "And you accepted that seat."

Had I? I'd had little choice—but Baba Yaga had no use for the compelled, and I would do myself no favors arguing to the contrary.

"What if I didn't lose, on my own terms?" I squared my shoulders, trying to mask my own desperation. "I did what I set out to do. I defended an entire continent. Number of territories be damned, I say I won."

Baba Yaga slowly began to clap. Her cold laughter howled through the room. "Very good, Zolushka," she said. "Spirited, indeed. A worthy addition to my table. *Focused*." She emphasized the word, staring pointedly at Polunoshchna.

I did not care for the tsarytsya's flattery. And I did not

thank her for giving her general greater cause to hate me.

"I will grant you this," said the tsarytsya. "You have still lost, but you may choose what you forfeit."

I shook my head, jaw tightening. "What does that mean?"

Cobie and Anya had been standing quietly against the wall for the better part of an hour. Baba Yaga nodded at them now. "Choose. We need fresh blood for the full moon tonight."

40

Fear and nausea shot through me. I fought to control my reaction. "What does that mean?" I asked again slowly.

"Tonight, we will sharpen our claws." Polunoshchna's smile was dark. "Every full moon, we meet in the courtyard to winnow the pack. The best rise. The worst fall."

"We fight," Vechirnya said evenly, rolling her eyes at Polunoshchna. "We open the ring, and members of every class participate."

I met the eyes of my two best friends in utter horror. Blood still painted the walls and the floor; its copper scent had sent my stomach reeling. "No," I said to Baba Yaga, horrified. "No, I can't."

What kind of fighting would it be? How long would it last—till first blood, to the death? My brain raced with questions, and I fought not to let them show. I didn't dare look at

Aleksei beside me, for fear of giving myself away.

Both Anya and Cobie watched me, their expressions guarded. Were they each asking me to choose them, or wishing it wouldn't be them, or both? My panic rose.

Could I ask to fight, myself? Or if I refused, would Baba Yaga simply pick one of them for me?

"I will choose." Across from me, Midnight stood up, eager.

Sunset rolled her eyes. "You lost worse than she did."

I glanced between Midnight and Sunset, loathing the way Baba Yaga pitted them against one another—for what? Her own entertainment? To keep them malleable and dependent on her? To keep them from uniting against her?

Did she mean to make me treat my friends—my sisters— the same way?

I assessed the facts as calmly as I could, and chose.

"Cobie." The word broke from my mouth. "Cobie will fight tonight."

I felt Aleksei relax at my side. Anya clenched her teeth and shook her head.

"Very good," Baba Yaga said, almost smiling at me. "Well and quickly chosen."

I said nothing.

"Now," she said, waving a hand at the blood spattered on the floor and the wall. "Clean this up."

The empress and her generals swept from the room without a backward glance.

* * *

We scrubbed the stones on our hands and knees. The blood of the dead men was everywhere. Neither Anya nor Cobie spoke to me.

I hoped the murdered men would find peace. I prayed theirs were the last deaths I would be forced to watch for a long, long time.

With the full moon so close at hand, I doubted that prayer would be answered as I hoped.

"I can't believe you didn't pick me," Anya muttered in the direction of the floor. "I can fight. You know I can fight."

"Of course I know you can fight," I said. "I've seen you take down every single one of your brothers and my first mate. You're a shield-maiden."

Anya, fighting with her brothers. Torden, teaching me to shoot, his broad hands on my shoulders. The memories and the moments of racking loss came again and again, and they never hurt any less.

"And yet you still picked Cobie, because she—what? She used to wear a knife everywhere?"

"I'm right here," Cobie protested, sitting back on her knees. Both of us shushed her.

Anya's wrists were scraped and abraded from the shackles she still wore, but she was an excellent fighter. I'd never seen Cobie fight, but I'd seen the friendly grip she kept on her knife, and I knew she was strong.

But I had also seen the eyes of the court on Anya when we arrived, and that was what had decided for me.

I worked at a congealed patch of blood on the floor, fighting back nausea. "This wasn't about who was the better fighter," I finally replied.

Anya said nothing, only scrubbed harder, her chains clanking against the floor.

"You're the *prinsessa* from the North, and the Wolves hate the Shield," I pressed. "What if the tsarytsya or the generals had used that to start something with the crowd? Or to pit you against someone unbeatable? It would have been a hundred times worse for you out there. They would be delighted to watch you fall."

"She's right," Cobie said. "No one knows who I am. They'll fight me, but they won't hate me."

Anya winced as the lye soap burned her ruined wrists. "Of course Selah is right," she said flatly. "I am still angry."

The three of us watched each other for a long moment. "I was never angry, before," I finally said, swallowing. "Now it feels like I'm angry all the time."

Cobie, Anya, and I cleaned the blood from the floor and the walls, but it clung to our hands and knees when we were done.

I wanted nothing more than to bathe myself and burn the rags we'd used. But we found our way down the stairs blocked again.

I was beginning to believe Baba Yaga was everywhere.

We drew against the railing, hoping she would continue climbing and we could carry on. But she stepped close to me—too close. The diamonds in her stolen crown winked at me.

"Do you think you're special, Selah, seneschal-elect?"

I stiffened. "No, *moya tsarytsya*." The honorific was bitter in my mouth.

"You are." She climbed up one, two steps, until she could lean over me. "You are the girl in a story."

My limbs shook as I lifted my eyes to hers. "There are many girls in many stories."

Baba Yaga laughed. "True. But only heroines are tested."

I shook my head. "Am I being tested?" I didn't know what she meant. I didn't know what she wanted. Cobie and Anya hesitated behind me. The book I'd stolen hours ago screamed out in the silence from its place in Cobie's basket.

"Vasylysa was tested, too," Baba Yaga said, narrowing her eyes. "Once upon a time. Her stepmother sent her to a town over the border called Medved, bearing nothing more than a sack of potatoes with which to make trade, and told her to come back with all they and their neighbors needed. It was training, she said, for her future as the leader of her village."

I didn't know what to say. I didn't know what she was talking about, or why she continued to harp on the story of a girl in the kitchens I'd hardly spoken to.

Was the girl a particularly hated prisoner? Was she kin to Baba Yaga, some kind of spy? What was the tsarytsya trying to tell me?

"And did she?" I asked.

Baba Yaga scoffed. "Of course she didn't." She pushed past me up the stairs, making for her chambers. "She was captured, just as you were."

41

Aleksei descended to the kitchens that afternoon. "Do you have your knife?" he asked Cobie, with no preamble.

She didn't look at him. "What do you care?"

"I want you to have a fair chance." Aleksei crossed his arms, shifting uncomfortably.

"Why the full moon?" I demanded. "And what's happening on the eclipse?"

"Zatemnennya?" Aleksei shrugged, abstract. "It's a lunar eclipse, one month from now. It's . . . significant. Busy, and bordering on religious, I think."

Anya dropped the dish she'd been washing. It clattered in the sink. A few of the maids and cooks glanced over, concerned, then dropped their gazes quickly at the sight of Rankovyy in their midst.

"And what will you be doing tonight, Aleksei?" Anya asked, expression hard.

"Seeing to the little *pestykk*." His eyes darted away, guilty.

"To the *children*?" Anya fired back at him. "To the children she calls her little pestles, who will grind those who resist into dust? The *children* she's indoctrinated?"

"Every member of the *pestykk* comes of their own volition," Aleksei said, righteously indignant.

"We've all seen that there's only one answer when the tsarytsa asks a question," I said, pitching my voice low. "Besides, there are some choices children can't make."

"They choose what you were spared!" Anya raged. I put out a hand to quiet her, but she was not to be soothed. "You were allowed to grow up happy and free with a *family*. We were taught discipline, humility, hard work—in safety."

At this, Aleksei finally seemed to grow frustrated. "And I will teach these children the same!"

"Can you teach them justice?" Anya demanded. "When the tsarytsya tells her people that they will never grow hungry, because the whole world is theirs to eat? That whatever they can take belongs to them by right, because that is the way of Wolves? Can you teach them kindness, when the tsarytsya tells them that the world is brutal and their teeth and claws must be kept sharp?"

"How do you know—?" Aleksei began.

"Because I ran from it!" Anya shouted. "Because she came for Varsinais-Suomi and killed my parents and changed our country's name! Because I looked over my shoulder while I ran, and I saw—I *saw*—what she did." Anya was breathing hard, a vein in her forehead pulsing.

"Anya." Aleksei swallowed, face looking drawn in the dim kitchens. "I have a place, and I'm proud of it. I have power now. I can use it to help you."

A few nights before, I'd fallen asleep by the fire, thinking about how the kings and the fae and the gods of the old stories rewarded the good, the brave, the kind.

I hadn't let myself think that night of who else they sometimes seemed to reward.

It was not only the virtuous, the generous, the hospitable, the humble.

Sometimes fools and liars won the day. Sometimes con men's tricks succeeded.

Sometimes the wolves were sated, and the innocent were lost.

"If you are proud of this, then you are not the brother I knew, and I don't want your help," Anya bit out. "I never wanted to draw lines between us. But if you can't see how horrible this is—the things she wants to teach them, the things *you are going to help teach them*—then I don't know who you are anymore."

Aleksei's face hardened, and he paused for a long moment before tugging a knife from his waistband and passing it hilt-first to Cobie. "Take this, anyway."

Vasylysa and another pair of maids saw her take it from his hands. But I saw from their looks that they would say nothing. As they said nothing of Wash's prayers, or of mine. As they must have taken in Vasylysa herself after she failed her stepmother's "testing."

I'd never seen Anya cry before. But after Aleksei left, tears began to roll down her cheeks.

And dread took shape inside me, pale and sharp as the light of the full moon on a blade.

42

We heard the masses beneath the full moon before we saw it in the skies above.

It was nearly ten at night when Anya and I trailed Cobie and her guards up the stairs and out the front door. A crowd filled the white-lit courtyard before Baba Yaga's house, soldiers and commoners and—my stomach dropped—hundreds of children in military uniforms. They stood in ranks to the side of an open circle in the courtyard, arms rigid at their sides, chins high.

The guards hauled Cobie to one side of the circle, and the crowd swallowed Anya and me. My panic swelled as we were pushed away; the need to go back and protect Cobie was a hook in my gut.

Fear pounded in my veins. What if I'd picked wrong? What if this ring—empty now but for the cold light of the moon—broke Cobie in some way I couldn't fix or take back?

I couldn't handle any more guilt.

"We need to get back to her," Anya panted. "I want to talk strategy. I want to watch some fights and help her decide what tack she'll take."

"Yes," I agreed at once. This would help. We could still help Cobie.

We shouldered and shoved our way back toward her, pushing through the hordes of men, ignoring wolf whistles and sly comments and slapping away wandering hands. Someone spilled a glass of beer down Anya's shift, and she turned to snarl at its bearer—then quickly falsified a broad, flirtatious smile.

"Ivan?" she chirped.

"*Ivan?*" his friends mimicked, jostling him and laughing. A flush crept from Ivan's neck to his peach-fuzz hairline. They all smelled sour, like too much alcohol and unwashed uniforms.

They scared me. I wanted to hide.

But gears were turning behind Anya's doe eyes. She pointed to Cobie, leaning close to Ivan. He nodded, then draped an arm over Anya's shoulder. I was impressed that she didn't shrug him off at once.

"What did he say?" I muttered, leaning close to her.

"He'll take us to her in a minute—the first fight's about to start," she whispered.

I looked around for soldiers getting ready for a match, but the tsarytsya moved instead to the ranks of the little *pestykk*. Aleksei moved with her.

He wore a gray uniform with a white band around his upper arm and another around his hair. He was a triplet to General

Midnight and General Sunset.

The children in their rows were healthy, their cheeks full, their eyes bright. Baba Yaga inspected them, seeming to correct one here, to compliment one there. One and all, they swelled with satisfaction beneath her gaze.

It was worse than the uniforms. It made me sick to watch her convince the safe, well-fed children of her city that the world was out to destroy them, and that they would have to be brutal and take what they could in order to survive it.

Finally, the tsarytsya turned to Aleksei and asked him a question. I didn't understand what she said. But Anya's face paled.

Aleksei's throat bobbed. He put a hand on the shoulder of one boy and one girl, both probably about eleven, about the same size. Baba Yaga nodded, efficient, and the children emerged into the circle.

I couldn't stifle a cry when I realized what he'd done.

Aleksei had chosen the children who would fight.

Anya reached for my hand. I seized it, my fingers shaking. Consumed with horror.

I hadn't believed Aleksei was one of them—not really. But he was. He wasn't just taking the tsarytsya's orders; he was issuing his own, adding to the hell that was life for these children, for this miserable gray city.

Grandmother Wolf tipped her head back and howled.

The crowd followed her.

The sound had frightened me when it had been merely the cries of a few guards on the Gray Road. This—the animal screams of a crowd beneath the white moon—turned my heart to water.

And then the children began to fight.

The match was ugly. The boy and the girl fought with a certainty that turned my stomach. But their movements were clumsy, ham-fisted—unchoreographed, nothing like the practice matches above the fjord in Norge.

The Asgard boys had bantered as they sparred, trying to sharpen one another. These children fought to win.

The girl's fists were so small and the boy's arms were thin and birdlike and their fight seemed to go on forever, forever, forever.

Finally, the boy caught the girl around the waist and wrestled her to the ground. He pinned one shoulder and punched her in the nose again and again, until blood stained his wrist and she rolled her head to the side so as not to drown in its flow.

The boy kept punching her, striking her in the ear.

I had clung to hope since I had left Potomac. Tried to be brave. But watching a crowd of men cheer as children beat one another, I wanted to go back to the kitchens. To curl up in the ashes and surrender.

Mostly, I wished for Torden. I wanted to bury my face in his chest and not look at a world that proved itself more brutal at every turn.

When Cobie and Anya had suggested it, I had balked at poisoning Baba Yaga. But watching the brutal spectacle before me, it seemed like justice. I didn't think I'd stay my hand now, if I had the chance to deal it out.

I wanted to raze her tower, turn the gray uniforms to ash, return every child she'd conscripted to the ones who loved them.

> When Baba Yaga locks the door,
> Children pass thereby no more.

This city was as foul and dark and decaying as the witch's house in the nursery rhyme. For the first time, it did not feel enough to put this ruthless empire at my back.

The girl's head snapped back a final time, and the boy stood. Blood spattered his face and his knuckles.

Baba Yaga loped forward and lifted his hand high, calling something out in her low, rasping voice, and the crowd howled again. Fury and repulsion roiled through me. I was afraid my bowels would loose themselves of their own accord.

"Selah, the girl's still breathing," Anya whispered. "She's getting up."

"Thank God." I swallowed hard. "Anya, we have to get to Cobie. We need to talk to her before—"

Anya nodded sharply. She put a hand on Ivan's arm, let her voice grow high and frightened as she pointed to Cobie. I grimaced and looked away, searching the mob for anyone—any single face—who didn't approve of this butchery.

My gaze lit on a cluster of women near the back of the crowd. At least twenty of them stood together, some in finery, some ragged, their skin of every color from pale white to deep brown. They were mostly in their twenties and thirties.

I wasn't a mother, but I'd had one, for a brief, blessed time. And I remembered the way she'd looked at me.

The women were watching the little *pestykk* with hunger in their eyes—a mother's hunger. A mother's fear for the children, still in their parade lines, being groomed into monsters. And a mother's rage toward those guilty. Toward the tsarytsya, and Aleksei.

He looked like a ghost beside Baba Yaga. She was fierce and alive and bloodthirsty, and Aleksei looked a mere shade away from disappearing altogether.

One of the women met my eyes, her starving gaze so intense that I stepped back, tripped, and fell. The stones of the courtyard sliced at my hands. Someone trod on my leg.

"Selah!" Anya crouched beside me, calling up to Ivan.

I didn't want him to touch me. But as Ivan helped me rise, blood seeping from my palms, I let the tears I wanted to cry fill my eyes.

I held out my bleeding hands to Ivan and his soldier friends and wailed like a child.

Anya clung to Ivan's bicep, pleading with him and pointing to Cobie. Ivan scrubbed a hand over his peach fuzz and sighed, finally conceding.

While his friends rolled their eyes, annoyed at my whimpering, Anya and I exchanged a sharp, victorious glance. "Got him," I murmured, still sniffling, as Ivan shouldered his way through the crowd ahead of us.

When we reached Cobie's side, Anya seized her arm with no warning. "I can still take your place."

Cobie shook her head. "No. I'm—I'm ready." She glanced down at my hands. "Selah, what happened?"

"Oh, nothing," I said, dismissing my bleeding palms.

Anya and Cobie swapped a significant look. "You should go inside and clean up," Anya said.

"What—no!" I blurted to Cobie. "I have to stay, you could be called any minute—"

"And I don't want you to watch," Cobie broke in. Her dark hair shone in the moonlight.

I drew back a little, wounded. "You don't want me here?"

Cobie glanced between Anya and me. "I don't want either of you here. But especially not you."

I scoffed, fighting to hide my hurt. "But Anya's all right?" It felt petty, at a time like this. But I was stung nonetheless.

"Anya's better with this than you are," Cobie said quietly, putting her small tanned hand on my shoulder. She swallowed. "I don't want you to look at me differently after this."

"I wouldn't!"

"You might," Cobie said. "I'm going to do what I have to do not to die, and—you might change your mind about me."

"I would never," I said, vehement. "You know I would never, Cobie."

Anya drew Cobie and me close, pretending to hug us. "The castle is empty, Selah," she whispered. "And Baba Yaga and most of her guards are outside. Don't waste this chance." She darted her eyes at the top of the tower, to the room where Baba Yaga slept. I straightened, my eyes widening.

The radio.

"Are you certain?" I took Cobie by the arms. "I don't want to leave you."

"Go, Selah. This is Wolf territory. I don't want you to watch me fight them off." Cobie's throat tightened. "Because when I fight, I don't lose. And winning is an ugly business."

43

Fear hammered at my heart as I left Cobie behind.

It felt like yet another betrayal that would sit on my conscience—to abandon her to the howling Wolves outside. But this chance might never come again.

The tower was quiet as a tomb after the rage of the crowd in the courtyard. I raced into the kitchen to clean and bandage my cuts, to wipe away all the blood on my hands.

It would not do to leave any trace of my presence behind.

Then I gathered up a basket of rags and soap and made for the stairs.

For once, the way was clear. The steps creaked beneath me as I climbed, trying to look bored, like I was going about my business. One story after another passed me by, until I came to her door.

I'd seen a few guards here and there, most looking as if they were on their way to the toilet or to bed after overindulging, and I'd expected to meet at least one outside Baba Yaga's bedroom door. But there was no one. The hall was empty. And there was no one to stop me from pushing into her room and striding toward the radio.

I'd hardly allowed myself to contemplate what I'd do when I reached the top of the stairs. My hands shook, hovering over the dial.

I needed to hail the *Beholder*. I needed to reach out to my friends at Asgard and to Winchester. I needed to make contact with the resistance and plead for their aid.

My heart urged me to search first for Torden, and that decided it. But I didn't know what frequency Asgard would use to communicate, if they were using radios at all.

I had to try. I switched the radio on and began slowly, slowly, to scroll.

Voices rolled past me like waves on the ocean. I closed my eyes and strained my ears, searching for the sounds of the Norsk words I wish I knew better.

I searched from one end of the spectrum to the other, and heard no trace of them.

I steeled myself and tried another tack. Fritz and Gretel had communicated via a channel not far from my godmother's; I would search for them there. I turned the dial gradually, holding my breath.

But there was nothing.

I was entirely alone.

Hopelessness pooled in the pit of my stomach. Without knowing what channel England or Norge or the resistance used, I couldn't reach them. The radio was useless to me as a tool to escape.

Slowly, I unbound my tangled hair, unbraided Torden's ring from where it was hidden. I slid it on and off my finger for a few long moments, trying not to cry.

I dared remain only a few more minutes. Escape denied me, I chose comfort. I turned the dial one more time.

"Godmother Althea?" I asked the air. "Godmother, are you there?"

There was a sound like a snap and a creak, and I jumped. But Baba Yaga's room was still quiet.

"Selah?"

I turned back to the radio, my blood surging. "Perrault?" I demanded, falling to my knees. I should have realized my own radio would still be tuned to the channel my godmother had chosen. "Perrault, is that you?"

"Oh, heaven," Perrault blurted raggedly. "You're alive."

"Just barely." My voice was grim. "Perrault, I don't have long. Where are you?"

"We're in Asgard." His voice broke. "Selah, I feared you were dead."

I couldn't tell him I'd had to buy this time with blood.

"You made it?" I breathed.

"We repaired here after leaving Shvartsval'd. It seemed the safest place to be while we sorted out how to free you," Perrault said. "We're not in the fortress itself; Alfödr wouldn't let us remain there. We're at the outpost he's building, a place called Flørli. He's built a forge here, and a radio tower."

The tower. Of course.

"Perrault, did you have any luck?" I asked. "Were you able to speak to Konge Alfödr and King Constantine about what happened?"

It felt shameful to beg. But Cobie was not fighting out beneath the full moon so I could cling to my pride.

I had sworn to myself that we would lose no more blood in this house. And tonight, I had failed at keeping that promise. I would not let it go unkept again.

Perrault cleared his throat. "I tried, Seneschal-elect. The English court has moved to London for the autumn; King Constantine did not look kindly on attempts to pull them into a war he wants no part of."

The English king's unwillingness to engage did not surprise me. So many months ago, Constantine and Bertilak and I had talked of Saint George and his dragon and the chasm between the old tale and the way they told it now. The Saint George of old had ridden abroad, searching for dragons to slay.

He had been a meddler. He had learned better.

The Saint George of Constantine's England remained at home. He defended his own and did not trouble that which was not his. Of course he would not ride across a continent and invite trouble when none stood at his door.

"And Alfödr?" I asked.

"He's not a trusting man." Perrault's voice wavered. "I'm trying, Selah."

These were grand requests to tenuous contacts, in far-flung places—and most of them bore me little love.

My hope was a shallow little well.

"I know. I know. Thank you," I said quickly. "How is Torden? Have you spoken to my godmother?"

Perrault took a long breath. "I've spoken to Sister Althea. She'll be relieved to hear you're not—that you're well," he corrected hastily. "She said nothing of your father, but I will ask for an account of his condition."

"Yes, please. And my stepmother, and the baby. And— Torden?" I closed my eyes.

"He isn't here," Perrault said. I could picture my sometime protocol officer, his head cocked to one side, his dark eyes probing. "Alfödr won't disclose where he's gone, but I suspect he's made his way to Iceland. I heard the king speak of it one night just after we arrived." Hodr, Torden's youngest brother, was being kept in Iceland. Torden was a devoted brother; it made sense he would go.

"Thank you for being there, Perrault," I said into the quiet. "Thank you for being there when I needed to speak to someone."

"I keep the radio with me all the time. Just in case." There was no charm or pride in his voice. "I helped her force you from home. So it's my job to bring you back."

"Your job?" I laughed. So many people were more to blame than Perrault for my present circumstances.

"He's reeling, Selah," Perrault said quietly, and I knew he meant Lang. "I didn't know what his plans were before, but he didn't expect them to go so badly wrong."

I touched my mouth, thinking of Lang's kiss goodbye,

remembering how long it had been since I'd felt his eyes on me. Then something snapped in me.

Lang was reeling? I was the one who'd been carried off by the tsarytsya's Wolves. I was the one hiding out while Cobie paid for my loss with her own blood.

I shook myself. I had no time for pettiness.

"One more thing, Perrault," I said. "Speak to Fritz. He'll be using a frequency not far from this one. See if he's spoken to Gretel on our behalf—or perhaps you'll reach Gretel herself. Tell them—" I swallowed, thinking hard.

Of the stolen children in their ranks down below. Of the murdered men and women we'd seen on the Gray Road and here in Baba Yaga's house.

Escape would mean safety for my friends and me, but for no one else I'd seen suffering.

It felt too small a hope. I wanted more.

"Tell them that the city will be in chaos on the night of the eclipse. It's some major event in four weeks. If you work with them, and any resources Alfödr will give you, we might have a chance."

A chance of *what*, I didn't say. My wants were too large, too high, too great.

"I will search for them," Perrault vowed.

He would try. And I would try. I would plead with every friend I had, grasp at every chance I saw.

Baba Yaga had achieved her position by taking. And Alessandra had done the same: she had taken our mortal enemy and made of her a tool.

And I had been watching them. I had learned from the best, the most cunning, the most vicious: I would mimic them, and befriend everyone they had wronged, and make of us a force to be reckoned with.

I bid Perrault farewell and returned the radio to its original frequency and switched it off. When I'd bound up my hair and the ring again, I left the tower, the din inside its walls rising once more.

The soldiers on the stairs stared at me in curiosity or blood-drunk lechery as I left the tsarytsya's rooms. I dipped my head, looking meek as a lamb, giving no hint of what I'd been up to.

But I was living among Wolves. And I was learning how to behave like a Wolf myself.

44

I could have worn a path in the kitchen floor with my pacing. When Cobie and Anya returned, I nearly lunged at them.

"Are you all right?" I blurted. I hovered over Cobie, taking in the blood and dirt on her shift, her scraped knees, the cut on her cheek.

"She's all right." Anya guided Cobie to the hearth. "Just took a few knocks to the head."

Cobie had told me she didn't want me to see her fight, and I wondered if I should bite back my questions and spare Cobie their answers. But I couldn't bear not to know. Not when tonight was my fault.

"Did you—did you have to kill anyone?" I asked gravely.

Cobie laughed, sounding dazed. "No. He wasn't a very interesting fighter, and he didn't expect me to be, either."

I swallowed. "Did you win?"

The corner of Cobie's mouth curved. "Yes."

"Did he have a knife, too?" I asked.

"He had three," Anya said.

I stared between them. We were lucky Aleksei had visited that afternoon.

"Did you get through to anyone?" Anya suddenly asked.

"Yes." I nodded eagerly. "I spoke to Perrault."

Anya's brow creased. "Perrault? Not—"

"No." I cut her off, my cheeks flaming. I tried to imagine Lang contacting Bear for help, or Torden's brothers, and found I couldn't.

Quickly, I related what Perrault and I had discussed—King Constantine's reticence, Perrault's pleading our case to Konge Alfödr and Fritz. "They're with your father," I finished, nodding to Anya. "I made the best use of the quiet that I could." I paused. "And speaking of making use of the quiet—"

I slipped into the laundry and pried the loose stone from the floor. When I returned, I spread over the hearth the paper we'd copied and cradled the book in my hands, feeling the cloth of the spine, the foil smooth beneath my fingers. My throat tightened; it had been so long.

The book felt like strength in my palms.

"All right," I said. "Anya, you couldn't read the numbers— but can you write the alphabet?"

Anya frowned. "I think so." She took the pencil we'd stolen and copied the letters out, slow and careful.

When she was done, I set to work.

The first line on the paper read Верхній Північний. I didn't even know what sounds the word would make, and some of the letters looked nearly alike. But I found first one letter in Anya's alphabet, and then another, and then I began to flip through the book in my hands, sifting through the symbols one at a time.

I ran my finger over the translation. "This word"—I pointed to Верхній—"in Yotne translates to *ober* in Deutsch."

Cobie stared at me. "You found a dictionary."

I nodded. "A translation dictionary. There wasn't one that translated Yotne to English, but there was one for Yotne and Deutsch. If you know these Deutsch words, we can use it to translate this column."

"Upper," Cobie said, nodding, surprised and eager. "*Ober* means 'upper,' or 'high.'"

Elation buzzed in my veins. "Okay." I flipped tentatively through the pages again, my eyes cutting back and forth between the alphabet and the column of words and the dictionary. Північний translated to *nördlichen* in Deutsch—"northern."

"Upper Northern!" Anya proclaimed, triumphant.

One line in the column. One line after another.

Even racing against time in Baba Yaga's room, Anya had copied the report carefully. But though we were able to translate most of the words, we still didn't know what the document *meant*. My euphoria began to evaporate, leaving disappointment in its wake.

Upper Northern	~~18,693~~
	~~13,483~~
	11,161

Northwestern	~~6,294~~
	~~3,449~~
	2,978
Far Western	~~5,922~~
	1,121
Near Western	~~3,292~~
	2,254
Southwestern	~~1,985~~
	~~1,144~~
	898
Mediterranean	~~2,439~~
	1,080
Eastern	~~1,548~~
	~~828~~
	653
Far Eastern	~~1,025~~
	825
Central	~~1,850~~
	~~1,203~~
	858

"Well, we've established it's probably not money. Could they be . . . distances? Between . . ." I racked my brain. "Between military outposts?"

Cobie chewed her lip. "The Imperiya Yotne stretches west of old Deutschland and well into the Ranneniy Shenok—almost to Alyaska. It could be."

"And the words were scattered more or less evenly across the map," I added. "The way you'd space garrisons."

But Anya shook her head. "Still, it's too few. Nine fortresses in the whole Imperiya?"

I sat back, dispirited.

Were we just pretending to be spies? Pretending that anything we could learn here would matter?

Something dark and doubtful whispered it was far likelier we would live in the tsarytsya's kitchens until someone Perrault contacted deigned to rescue us. Or until we were forced to fight in her ring again, and our luck ran out.

We got ready for bed a little diminished, washing Cobie's cuts and scrapes with lye and water and binding them up. Then we climbed onto the hearth, utterly exhausted, poured out like water as we were every other day.

Someone entered the kitchen as we lay down.

I shot up, and Anya behind me.

Aleksei lifted his pale face. It was streaked with tears. "You were right," he said, crossing the threshold. "You were all right."

45

I stiffened, fearing Anya would do as she had done the first time she saw him at the tsarytsya's table. Run at him, claws out, snarling.

But she took one look at Aleksei's face, streaked with tears, pale with horror, and rushed to his side. "What's wrong?" Her hand was tense on his arm.

"Don't," he groaned, pulling away. "I don't deserve it."

"Aleksei?" Cobie sat up, voice cautious. "What happened?"

Anya's brother wiped his eyes on his sleeve. I could hear his teeth grinding in his mouth. "The little *pestykk*—the children," he said. "What happened tonight—"

"You mean forcing children to beat one another senseless?" Cobie said sharply. "That's your job, Rankovyy. You were so proud of it before."

"I wasn't," Aleksei said, shaking his head. His eyes were bloodshot and red-rimmed, as if he'd been drinking or crying, or perhaps both. Aleksei convulsed, then dashed for the scraps bucket in the corner, evacuating his stomach in low, choking gasps.

He was a horrible sight.

Anya bit her lip as he sat beside her on the hearth. "Why, Aleksei? Why did you take the position?"

"To prove I belonged here," he said. "Because if I don't belong here, I don't belong anywhere."

Aleksei had set out, as I had, unwanted at home, as I had been. He had thought he knew what to expect at Stupka-Zamok, as I had.

We'd both had our expectations set afire before our eyes.

"It wasn't your idea to make the children fight, was it?" Anya began, uncertain. "If you didn't propose it, then it's not your—"

"No." Aleksei cut her off swiftly. "I didn't. But don't make excuses for me, Anya. I'm guilty. I'm sick to death at myself." He passed a hand over his dark hair, tugging the white band off his brow and looking as if he wished to toss it into the flames.

"You chose which children would fight," I said. I tried to keep the accusation from my voice, but we had witnessed a horror.

Aleksei nodded, eyes on the bricks. "She had told me I had to. I tried—" He broke off, and I feared he'd retch again. "I hoped it'd be like sparring at home. I chose two friends. I hoped they'd be gentler with each other. Fairer. But this place ruins everything."

"You tried," Anya whispered.

301

It was strange to see Anya so changed in the space of a few hours. But if the Asgard siblings fought hard, they forgave quickly—especially if one of them was in pain.

But Aleksei refused to be comforted. "No. I knew. I knew it wouldn't be like home," he said, wincing at some invisible pain. "You tried to tell me what this place would be like. What kind of childhood Pappa spared me. What I'd be joining, if I joined them. And I could've stood up to her. I could have said no."

Home. Pappa.

His heart was in Asgard again, as mine had been all along.

"So leave," I said in a low voice. "Leave this place. You aren't a prisoner. You can go home if you want."

Aleksei smiled pityingly. "Ever the hopeful one, Selah."

"Now is not the time to feel sorry for yourself," Cobie snapped. Then she closed her eyes, softening ever so slightly. "I'm sorry. But you have freedom here. You can walk around unquestioned. You can get word to your father. You can get us out of here."

"Pappa will take you back," Anya urged him. "He'll just be glad to have you home."

"At the very least, he'll take your information," Cobie added. "You speak Yotne. I'm sure you've learned things here worth bargaining with."

Aleksei raised his eyebrows, wry. "And, Cobie, ever the whimsical optimist."

Yotne. My mind worked slowly, then stilled. "You speak Yotne!"

I dashed away to the laundry, hearing Aleksei's question and Anya's murmured explanation as I scrabbled for our dictionary and paper. But once I laid hands on them, I paused.

Could we really trust Aleksei?

He mourned the events of the night; that, I believed. But would he get over his tears tomorrow? Would he change his mind as abruptly as he had so many times before?

Would we come to regret putting our faith in Torden's most unpredictable brother?

I forced the thoughts away. We had few enough allies here. We couldn't afford to question each other.

When I returned with the paper, Aleksei was waiting.

"Tell me what you make of this," I said.

Aleksei studied our translation, squinting once or twice at Anya's rendering, pale fingers a little shaky around the paper. "Where did you get this?" he asked, tone bare with shock.

"Some papers in her room. What are the numbers?" I blurted. "Did we translate the words right?"

"More or less. I think—" Aleksei frowned, pushing a hand through his black hair. "But it doesn't make any sense." Quickly, we explained the route we'd taken from Yotne to Deutsch via the dictionary, then from Deutsch to English with Cobie's help.

"And where did you get the—" He froze, seeing the volume in my hand. "Did you get the dictionary from her room, as well?"

I nodded, and he let out a slow breath.

"I need to think. Do some investigation of my own. But the tsarytsya will certainly know the book is missing," he said.

"You can't be found with it, and you can't risk returning it. You have to destroy it."

Everything in me revolted at the idea. "What? No!"

Cobie and Anya exchanged a glance. "Selah, maybe we should," Anya said tentatively.

"You *cannot* be found with this in your possession," Aleksei said forcefully. "It is illegal property, and it is proof that the tsarytsya ignores her own law. She would put you to death without a second thought, regardless of whatever game she's playing with you."

My hands shook as they ran over its cover, an unfortunate mustard yellow, water-stained and spotted with age. But it was the only book I'd held in months. Just having it near had given me strength and comfort.

"I can't even read it." Tears sprang into my eyes. "But it felt like an advantage. Like a little bit of power to wield against all of hers."

"That's why she's banned them." Aleksei's voice was dark. "If you have knowledge, you feel powerful, and you *are* powerful."

"It made me think of another world," I said, dragging my wrist across my eyes. "A place apart from her. That's what's anathema to her."

No God but her. No story but the one she chose to tell. No world but the one she had built. And the poor little volume in my hand undermined it all.

Aleksei squeezed my elbow but didn't speak. His mouth was a thin line in his bone-white, bone-thin face.

I thrust the book at him. "Here. I—can't," I said. "I know I should, but I can't."

Aleksei gave me a grim look, took the dictionary, and tossed it into the oven's flames.

I wept silently as I watched it burn.

Anya hugged my head to her shoulder. "Don't look, *kultaseni*. Don't look at it."

Kultaseni. She'd used the word before. She'd told us it meant "sweetheart" or "dear" in Suomi. Not quite *elskede*—"my love," in Norsk.

Torden had called me that. *Elskede*.

The word had warmed me then. But it was a fire inside me now. I drew near it to keep from freezing.

O! Mo laoch mo ghile mear;
O! Mo ghaodhal, mo ghile mear;
Aon t-suan chum séin ní bh-fuaras féin;
Ó chuaidh a g-céin mo ghile mear!

My hero brave, *mo ghile, mear,*
My kindred love, *mo ghile, mear;*
What wringing woes my bosom knows,
Since cross'd the seas *mo ghile, mear!*
—John O'Tuomy

46

We trudged out of the basement heavy as the gray skies and the gray walls around us. A week had come and gone since I'd spoken with Perrault; most of Cobie's scrapes and bruises had healed.

I'd slept poorly, dreaming of Potomac aflame and swallowed by Grandmother Wolf.

I followed the girls up the stairs, preparing myself to ignore the soldiers. The day before, Ivan had whistled and fanned himself as Anya walked past. The other soldiers had snickered and called out to her, and Anya's smile had been furious, for anyone who looked and actually cared to see.

Today, I wouldn't spare them even a glance. But when Anya dropped her breakfast tray, eyes on Ivan's post, I was startled out of my resolve.

I blinked once. Twice. My heart began to beat like thunder, even as my breath hung in suspense.

Most of the guards at the door were the regulars—Ivan among them.

Torden Asgard was new to their number.

His beard was shaved. His hair was cut close to his skull and dyed a few shades lighter, and his tattoos were hidden beneath the hideous gray uniform he must have stolen off an Imperiya soldier's back. But he was Torden.

My Torden. *Elskede.* My beloved, standing not ten feet away, here in Baba Yaga's house.

Ivan stepped forward, helping Anya pick up the broken plates and scattered loaves of bread. He smiled and spoke to her in Yotne, and Anya didn't avoid brushing against him as she gathered herself and rose.

I couldn't stop staring at Torden. Whatever else about him was different, his brown eyes were unchanged.

He was here. He had come for me.

Everything in me strained toward him. But Cobie pinched me, and I dropped my eyes to the samovar in my shaking hands.

Tray in hand again, Anya cocked her head to one side, looking flirtatious and pretty and foolish as the day was long. But I saw the gears working behind her eyes.

She leaned close to Ivan and bit her lip. I caught only one word—*vécherom.*

It sounded like *vechirnya.* It meant "tonight."

Ivan's face lit up like a candle. He answered eagerly, nodding at his fellow soldiers and gesturing beyond the door, looking hopeful enough to float off the ground.

I risked another glance at Torden, and one of the soldiers

nudged him and nodded at me. And when Torden crossed his arms and eyed me top to toe and grinned a long, slow grin, there was nothing pretended about my foolish smile or the heat that swept me from neck to hairline.

"*Vécherom*," Anya said to them again. I nodded and followed my friends back to the kitchens, my heart pounding.

We would see them—we would see Torden—that night.

"He's here. I can't believe it. I can't believe he's here," I babbled as we wiped off the bread loaves and replaced the broken plates.

Vasylysa headed toward the stairs with a broom to sweep up the smashed dishes. "Good news?" she asked shyly.

I grinned broadly. "Good news," I agreed.

Wash just barely swallowed her smile when she saw we'd merely brushed off the dropped loaves. "Go," she ordered us.

We did as we were told, and I hardly felt the weight of the samovar. Anya winked at Ivan again and they traded comments as we rounded past the front door.

My heart hammered and I looked like a fool, staring at Torden, but I didn't care.

Torden. Torden was here.

As we reached the dining room, I squeezed the handles of the samovar, forcing myself to focus. "There you are," barked Polunoshchna. She sat at the center of the table, next to Vechirnya, Baba Yaga, and Aleksei, with the court all around.

They were playing Tooth and Claw again. This time, with an audience.

We said nothing. Anya, Cobie, and I served breakfast and

poured tea in silence, slowly rounding the table, not interfering with the game.

We came to Aleksei last. He glanced up at me as we served him, scratching the wolf tattoo at the back of his neck as though it itched. I tried not to look at him.

The story I'd read as a child said that a Wolf always knew other Wolves. That Baba Yaga could smell her enemies.

I wondered if the tsarytsya could sense a change in Aleksei. If she could tell, merely from the way he looked at the three of us, the shift in his loyalties from the week before.

Cobie set down a bowl of apples, and Sunset mimed peeling one, asking her a question in Yotne. When Cobie shook her head, Sunset switched to English. "Knife?"

But Cobie only shook her head again.

There had certainly been a knife on her tray. I kept my face blank and poured more tea. The tsarytsya took a bright red apple and set it on her little plate, rolling it around contemplatively as she studied the game board.

Anya, Cobie, and I made for the door, preparing to wait in the kitchen until it was time to clear away. "Stop," said General Midnight. I turned.

She nodded at me. "You. I want you to watch. The others can go."

Anya and Cobie hesitated.

"Go," Aleksei ordered them. His tone was ugly; it made my stomach clench. Had he already forgotten his remorse?

No, I told myself sternly. He had to behave this way in front of the tsarytsya. My friends left the dining room.

I took the place General Midnight indicated behind her chair. And then I studied the board.

Polunoshchna's black claws were scattered, once again. She had laid claim to the places General Sunset had staked out during our previous match, as if trying to mimic her strategy.

She had also laid claim to much of the New World, as if copying mine.

Sunset had begun this time in Australia and was slowly and patiently deposing Polunoshchna wherever she met her armies. Aleksei seemed to have no particular plan.

Baba Yaga had laid claim to the Imperiya and Ranneniy Shenok. But she was moving now toward Alyaska, on Ranneniy Shenok's border.

I did not like the sight of her gray claws and teeth approaching the New World. It was too close to my dreams of her in Potomac.

"You'll forgive us for not inviting you to play today, Zolushka," Polunoshchna sneered at me over her shoulder.

"I didn't ask to join you the first time," I said evenly.

I felt Baba Yaga watching me, felt Polunoshchna waiting for me to show some emotion. But I would not be baited.

Polunoshchna's expression soured as Vechirnya swept away a few of her black armies and replaced them with her red ones.

The board was extremely red. I hoped General Sunset was less talented as a real-life commander than she was at Tooth and Claw.

"Any suggestions?" Midnight scowled at me.

"No, my General Midnight."

313

I kept my tone quiet and servile. I didn't want to anger her. I didn't care about her at all.

She arched her eyebrows at me.

Then she turned back to the game board, picked it up by the edge, and flicked her wrists. Claws of all colors scattered across the table and into the air.

Aleksei and Sunset exclaimed in Yotne, both scooting back a little from the table and from the flying claws and teeth.

Baba Yaga said nothing. She toyed with the apple on her little plate, spinning and studying it as if she could see the entire world in its sphere.

Midnight turned in her chair to face me. "Since you couldn't offer *me* any advice, allow me to offer you some." Her eyes were narrow and dark as pits. "It doesn't matter what you do. It doesn't matter if you think you know how to win. It doesn't matter how smart you are, how young you are, how bright are the stars in your eyes." She stood up and stepped closer to me.

"I am General Midnight. I am Polunoshchna, a queen among Wolves, head of the tsarytsya's secret police, and you are alone. I can always, always take whatever you think you've built, and upend it with the slightest brush of my fingers." She was breathing heavily, her eyes almost black with anger. "You understand, don't you?"

I understood nothing. She would beat nothing out of me. I would cease to believe nothing.

Torden, my Torden, was downstairs, because he had come for me. And the *Beholder* was on its way. They would be here the night of the eclipse, ready to rescue us all—perhaps more.

I was not alone. Midnight was wrong.

I bent to begin picking up the mess she had made.

"Polunoshchna," Baba Yaga said mildly. "You've upended our game."

"Yes, *moya tsarytsya*," she said.

I remained crouched, gathering teeth and claws into my apron.

"I think Selah will take your place next time," Baba Yaga said evenly.

I stood and nearly dropped all that I'd tidied up. "What?"

"What?" Midnight demanded.

The tsarytsya rose, and with her, her breakfast guests. "In three days, Selah." Baba Yaga crossed behind Polunoshchna and laid a bony hand on her shoulder, her tone cold as ice. "I have no children of my own. That choice was deliberate. I have no desire to play with them."

She swept from the dining room and took her courtiers with her. Sunset stepped over a little heap of black claws that had fallen on the floor and followed.

"Clean that up," the tsarytsya called over her shoulder.

I bent and carried on tidying up claws. My hands were shaking.

Only Aleksei and Midnight remained.

Aleksei poured himself another glass of tea from the samovar, warming his palms around it, gazing idly out of the smoky-quartz tower windows. His gray uniform fitted him perfectly.

"Why so tense, Polunoshchna?" Aleksei asked without turning.

"I'm not tense," Midnight bit out, three sharp syllables as dark as her hair. "I do not know what's come over *nasha tsary-tsya*."

I didn't know if she was looking at me. I kept tidying up.

"Doubtless she's out of sorts because of—well. You know," Aleksei said meaningfully.

"I don't know what you mean." Midnight was sullen.

"But of course you do." Aleksei's tone was agreeable. "Polunoshchna, why is Vechirnya home at all?"

"Rankovyy! We can't—" She cut a glance at me, nostrils flaring in anger, and bit out a long reproach in Yotne.

But Aleksei merely scoffed, and carried on in English. "She's a child, and a fool. She fell head over heels for my stupidest brother, then lost him helping my sister run away for love."

"*Former* brother," Midnight corrected him coolly.

"Of course," Aleksei agreed.

I stole a glance up at him, and my heart kicked in my chest.

Aleksei's natural state was eager, alert, witty, morbidly curious. But at the moment, every line of his lanky form was relaxed, draped casually against the window ledge.

This was Aleksei's scheming face.

I bit back a grin and kept cleaning furiously.

"Old habits die hard," he said indolently. "Trusting people, for example, even when it's become clear they're failing. Clinging to old allegiances when it's obviously time for new ones."

Midnight spat. Aleksei's smile curled.

"So I was right," he said. She made a face, and Aleksei's grin widened. "Oh, my dear Polunoshchna, you may live and work and do the unspeakable by dark, but the dawn is *my* time. Seeing clearly into the future is my job."

"I have my suspicions." Midnight poured herself another glass of tea and spooned *kisel* into it, eyes narrowing. "Why should I share them with you, Rankovyy?"

"Because it's dull to keep secrets." Aleksei's smile grew lazy. "And because *nasha tsarytsya* and Vechirnya aren't confiding in you. Why should *you* not cultivate a confidant?" He laughed, easy as could be. "Besides, it's not treason to tell me if you've had to work out the truth yourself."

At this, Midnight laughed, too. She didn't look young in the gray dawn, as Aleksei did. But the wrinkles on her forehead and the gray in her hair only made her more formidable.

They spoke of wisdom. Of experience. Those things made her dangerous.

"Our numbers are shrinking," Midnight finally said to Aleksei, taking a long slug of her tea and looking as if she wished it were something stronger. "Our little *pestykk* are growing and refilling our ranks more slowly than ever, and desertion is on the rise. And somehow, Vechirnya's position still remains safe." Her mouth curled in a snarl. "She is home to discuss *nasha tsarytsya*'s new plan."

My head swam at her words. Somehow, Aleksei didn't react.

"And yet they punish you," he said, his tone all wonder. "She sends all her *zuby*, all her men, to the Upper North, preserves none for the rest of her Imperiya, wonders why things are falling apart, and still—Sunset is the one who can do no wrong."

"I'm on the outside today, but I'll be back." Midnight came to stand over me and flashed a surly smile. I stared up the length of her gray uniform, hands trembling, clutching the game pieces I'd collected. "Just remember this, Zolushka: Her favor is fickle. You may have it now, but it will not last."

Polunoshchna crouched at my side and slapped a few claws out of my grasp before grinding them beneath her boot.

"You are her toy today," she said in a cruel whisper. "And you will be broken and forgotten tomorrow."

47

Desertion. The tsarytsya's armies were deserting her.

I passed Torden standing guard twice more, wishing every moment that I could rush to him and kiss him and tell him everything I'd heard. I hated waiting. I hated feeling the eyes of the soldiers on me.

With beautiful Anya always at my side, the guards had hardly noticed me before. But by the end of the morning, Torden and I were their favorite joke.

I'd instructed myself sternly not to stare or smile like a fool. But I tripped over my own feet twice and ran bodily into Anya once while gawking at him, and midmorning, his fellow guards had to try four times to get his attention before Torden noticed, because he was watching me descend the stairs.

That had been the second time I tripped over my own feet.

"You're going to give us away," Cobie hissed at me, not ungently.

The guards were merciless. Torden flushed bright red, tongue-tied as he tried to defend himself. It only made me want to close the distance between us more.

My disappointment was bitter when the door guard changed at three that afternoon; I couldn't chase the hours away quickly enough, scrubbing linens and serving meals into the early evening.

Finally, an hour after sundown, Ivan met us at the castle's front doors. My insides quivered as we passed over the threshold and into the night.

We hadn't stepped beyond the castle doors in nearly a month. But Ivan was our ticket through the town, over slate-paved streets and through rubbish-lined alleys, past a hundred private fortresses to a tavern halfway between the tsarytsya's house and the town's skull-topped walls. A red setting sun was painted over the tavern's front door.

As we passed inside, I wondered if Ivan would be our ticket out of the city, as well.

The public house was noisy and smelled like fat and beer—like Valaskjálf with none of its cheer or warmth. Straw and dirt were strewn across the floor, and the soldiers' shaved heads barely cleared the low-beamed ceiling.

But the tavern possessed one crucial similarity to Alfödr's great hall: a boy with rose-gold lashes and freckled hands whose gaze found me the second I entered the room.

Standing in a circle of guards, he took a long drink from his glass, eyes warm on mine, and for a moment I was back in Asgard. I was wearing a gown instead of rags, and Torden's

320

uniform jacket was royal blue instead of gray, and there was a ring in his hand and a question he wanted to ask me.

I lived in that memory for a long moment before Ivan hailed him and Torden strode over.

Torden bought Ivan and his friends round after round of drinks that evening. They leaned against the bar, swapping stories, their voices and gestures progressively louder and more exaggerated as they drank. Cobie was barely a step above sulky as the soldiers flirted and toyed with her shiny, dark hair, but Anya never dropped her adoring smile or ceased clinging to Ivan's arm, though she firmly removed his hands when they began to wander. Truly, it was an inspiring performance.

Torden and I had begun the night on opposite sides of our circle. I bit my lip, trying not to smile too broadly as he told an obviously embroidered story; I felt him watching as I deflected occasional slurred comments from the other soldiers.

But with every drink downed and story told, the order of the group shuffled, and finally, Torden was at my side.

I wanted to kiss him so badly. I didn't think I'd even mind the hideous gray uniform.

As Ivan began to sing to Anya, overcome with alcohol and her inexorable charm, Torden propped an elbow on the bar and smiled down at me.

"Can I buy you a drink?" he asked in English, pitching his words playfully, flirtatiously, as though we were strangers meeting in a pub for the first time. "What is your name?"

"They call me Zolushka at the tsarytsya's house." I tried to keep my voice light, but I could barely breathe.

"I won't call you that," Torden said softly, bending toward my ear, brushing a bit of ash off my cheekbone. "My name is Ivan," he added.

"How convenient." I nodded at Ivan, whose arm was draped around Anya. He was trying very hard to articulate something to his neighbor. "*His* name is Ivan."

"Yes," Torden agreed, leaning a little closer, smiling mischievously. "Lots of us are named Ivan. It's a very common name."

He took my hand and laced his fingers through mine, his eyes going still and soft.

This place and the people in it were all wrong, but nothing had changed between us—not the earnest way he looked at me and not the inescapable pull between us. I ached to bury my face in his chest and hide in his arms for a while.

He was a storybook prince in disguise. He had come here for me.

"Selah," Cobie suddenly hissed. "Selah. Behind you."

I jumped, dropping Torden's hand, and glanced around. Sitting at a table, their attention snagged on the real Ivan's steadily rising pitch, were Polunoshchna and Aleksei.

When I faced the bar again, Torden was gone.

"Are all the hearths swept, then, little Zolushka?" Polunoshchna's voice was close, grating on my ears, making me tremble.

But I turned, and I faced her.

I was beyond Baba Yaga's walls. Freedom loosed my tongue and made it reckless.

"Are there no more games to be lost back in Stupka-Zamok,

my General Midnight?" I asked pleasantly. A few of the soldiers hooted with laughter.

Polunoshchna's lip curled. And as she had the first day I met her, she lifted her hand to slap me.

"*Vot te na! Otakoyi!*" The soldiers exclaimed in protest, grabbing Polunoshchna's arm before she could hit me. One of them crossed his arms, sizing her up before he jerked his chin at me, his message clear: *She's with us. Back off.* Cobie and Anya stepped close to me.

"*Ya Polunoshchna,*" she snarled, wrenching away from the soldier.

I am your General Midnight.

I didn't like these soldiers, and I didn't trust their favor. But smug vindication settled comfortably in my stomach as the soldier waved a hand at their numbers around the room, yanking at the sleeve of his uniform. His reply to Midnight was defiant, containing a single word that I knew: *Vechirnya.*

A red sinking sun had been painted over the tavern door. And a closer look at the soldier's sleeve revealed the clumsy outline of a wolf, hand-sewn in red thread.

We answer to Sunset, he clearly meant. *Not to you.*

General Midnight's eyes were cold as she turned them on me. "You charm *nasha tsarytsya*, you charm our *zuby*. Why are they all so drawn to you, little Zolushka?" she spat. My hands shook.

Anya pressed against my side. I fumbled for her hand, clinging to it where no one could see. "Perhaps because I don't slap people unprovoked," I said, voice shaking. "Or upend games because I don't get my way."

General Midnight searched me with her gaze, turning out my pockets, looking for secrets. "Hide behind your soldier boys for now, kitchen trash," she said. "Soon enough, your spell over them will break."

Just then, Aleksei appeared at her side. "You three," he barked. "You shouldn't be out here."

"*Ya idu?*" Ivan pointed to himself hopefully. I didn't think he could walk a straight line to the door, let alone escort us anywhere.

The prospect made me hopeful. We could get clear of Ivan with no trouble.

"*Niet,*" Aleksei pronounced. "I will take the little ash-girls home."

I felt a flash of fear as he hauled us from the tavern.

Aleksei didn't speak to us as we raced through the darkened streets back to Baba Yaga's tower. I didn't know where Torden had gone, and I suddenly feared I wouldn't see him again. What if he had gone away? What if he'd been caught by Baba Yaga's real soldiers?

"Aren't you going to get us out?" I whispered to Aleksei.

"No," he said sharply, and my doubt of him spiked again. "I don't even know what you think you were doing in there with all those *zuby*—all those soldiers."

"Why not?" I demanded. I stopped outside the tsarytsya's courtyard.

"Do you have a plan?" he asked in a low voice. "Do you have supplies? Food? A *coat*? Winter is close and you are in the heart of the Imperiya. I would sooner you live at *nasha tsary-tsya*'s hearth than freeze or starve, free in the wilderness." He ushered us inside the front door, and I followed him to the basement, my shoulders slumped.

"That isn't your decision to make, you know," Cobie said through gritted teeth.

"Maybe not, but I'm not going to help you until I can be sure you won't die out there," Aleksei said pleasantly.

I stomped into the basement, feeling let down and weary.

And then came the voice I had been longing to hear.

48

"Selah," he said.

I turned. And there was Torden, framed in the kitchen doorway.

The sight of him cracked me open.

I ran to him, threw myself into his arms. Torden caught me, and I buried my face in his chest, beginning to sob.

"You're here," I cried. "You came."

Holding myself back from him in the tavern, then fearing harm had come to him—I'd thought I would burst. I didn't hold back now. I dug my fingers into the fabric of his uniform, balanced on my toes until he hitched me up around his waist.

"Of course I came," Torden said, his own voice broken. "Didn't you know I would come for you?"

"But I left." I wept and held him tighter, as if to pin him to this place in the universe. "You couldn't go with me."

"It doesn't matter." Torden's voice was low. "I heard you were here, and I had to come. My father didn't approve. But I didn't care."

I had wondered if I wanted Torden or Lang or anyone to rush in and rescue me.

I knew now it didn't matter if Torden had a strategy to get us safely away, or if he planned to fight our way out of this place.

It wasn't that he might get me out. It was that he had come for me.

Soot smeared across my face as I wiped my eyes with ash-covered hands and looked up at him in wonder. "You're here," I said again.

Torden didn't answer this time. He bent his head and kissed me.

I had spent weeks in the cold, crowding close to my friends and the hearth, aching for love, for warmth.

I could never be lost with my friends at my side and my prayers in my heart. But in Torden's arms, his mouth on mine, his hands cupping my waist fiercely, I'd never felt so found.

When we broke apart, I bent my head to his chest. "I wanted you," I said, my voice breaking. "I missed you so, so much."

"And I you." As he had in the tavern, Torden took my hand—first the right and then the left—and found them both bare. At once, I tugged the snarled lock from the nape of my neck where my ring was still braided and secure. I caught a glimmer of blue stones from the corner of my eye.

"I would never have lost it," I said quietly. "Or given it up."

"I wouldn't have cared. You are the one I feared was lost. The ring is—"

"Is my reminder of you in this place," I whispered. "I was glad to be able to save it."

At the sound of someone clearing his throat, I broke away and turned. Aleksei stood but a few feet away. Torden went stiff and still in my arms.

"I should have known," Aleksei said quietly.

"Hush, Aleksei," Anya said. She hugged Torden, and he hugged her back tightly, turning next to embrace Cobie, who squeezed him tight around the waist with an affection that surprised me.

But when he turned back to his brother, Torden's eyes went cold. "You left Pappa. You left Rihttá terrified."

"Let me explain," Aleksei said.

"After everything that's happened—"

"He didn't *want* me," Aleksei said, bony hands outstretched, taut with all the strain that racked his voice. "Fredrik and Anya were happy to bend to his will—"

"For a time," Anya said sharply.

"—but I couldn't be good enough for him. I could not be clay on his wheel," Aleksei finished, sounding desperate. "And—I will admit. I wanted to make a point."

"And you've made it," Torden said darkly.

"I have," Aleksei said. "And I regret it."

At my side, hand still in mine, Torden pressed his lips together. "I disagree with Pappa's choices. With many of them," he said. "I stood against him, coming here. And I see now that he was wrong to control Anya's life as he did, and wrong to attack Skop—to strike a guest in his own hall," he added, shaking his head. "But he wept the night Anya left. And your leaving broke him, Aleksei."

Aleksei looked up, surprised. "What?"

Torden chewed on his lip. "I heard him talking to Rihttá—four children lost in under a year, he said. He wondered what he could have done to so offend heaven." He swallowed. "Rihttá didn't answer. Pappa already knew what he'd done."

Baldr. Hodr. Anya. Aleksei.

Torden looked so tired. I put my palm to his cheek.

"Aleksei's making amends, Torden," Anya said quietly.

Torden frowned. "What do you mean?"

"Baba Yaga gave me charge of the little *pestykk*," Aleksei said, swallowing hard. "I am her General Rankovyy, her Bright Dawn." He looked away. "I accept responsibility for what I have done, but I haven't lived here since I was a very small boy. Even I could not have foreseen what this task would mean. What she would—ask me to be."

Torden said nothing.

Aleksei stepped forward, his face pale and fearful. "I was wrong, brother. I don't deserve to be forgiven, but I want to come home. I want to be sure I have a home to go back to."

"This is not your home?" Torden's brown eyes were grave.

"No," Aleksei said. He put more force behind the word than I could have expected. "No. I was wrong. Home is where my family is. My real family." He stepped toward

Torden again with that word—*real*.

He held out a hand, and the rest of us held our breath.

Torden took his hand, and pulled his brother toward him in a hug. I was still in his arms, and I certainly wasn't going to let go, so the embrace was the three of us instead of the two of them.

"Selah, are you crying?" Aleksei suddenly asked.

"No," I insisted, my voice damp with tears. Aleksei sputtered a laugh, and I smacked him. "This is an emotional reunion for all of us." But he only laughed harder, so I pushed him away. "I'm done sharing your brother, regardless," I grumbled.

Torden's laughter rolled through his frame, and I held on to him tighter.

I was never letting go.

Aleksei rolled his eyes and seized both of us by the arm, making for where Cobie sat by the hearth. "Come on. We need to discuss what you found." Torden's brow furrowed, confused.

"We discovered something in the tsarytsya's chambers," Anya explained.

"And Aleksei interrogated Midnight about it this morning," I said.

"You what?" Cobie demanded.

Aleksei twitched a shrug. "Subtly."

"So what is it?" Torden asked him. "What did you find?"

Anya retrieved the paper from the laundry and spread it out on the hearth, and the five of us crouched over it.

"Is it a supplies list?" Anya asked. "Munitions?"

330

"We thought it might be the distance of the outposts from . . . something," Cobie said vaguely.

Aleksei eyed me. "Do you think Midnight was lying today?"

I thought carefully. "Midnight is rattled. I doubt she could have lied so well just then." I pressed my lips together. "As I said, she lacks focus."

"I agree." Aleksei took a steadying breath and nodded at the papers on the hearth. "This is a census of the tsarytsya's armies."

Silence filled the kitchen for a long moment as we studied the numbers, crossed out again and again, continually shrinking.

"What?" Torden shook his head. "That's—this isn't possible. She can't be maintaining control with numbers this low."

"Let me explain," Aleksei said. He turned to me. "First of all, it's strange that Vechirnya is home at all. From what little I know, General Sunset lives in the field. Period."

"So why is she here?" Cobie asked.

"Because she's in crisis," Aleksei said. "Desertion is high, and Imperiya birth rates have been declining for some time. Baba Yaga's chickens have come home to roost."

"Why do birth rates matter?" Anya frowned.

"Fewer children entering the little *pestykk* means fewer soldiers down the line," Aleksei said.

Cobie shrugged. "And it makes sense that fewer people are having children. Who would have babies just to have them taken away from you? Who would want to have children at all in a place like this?"

"But reports were normal," Torden argued. "Huginn and Muninn haven't informed us of any change in Stupka-Zamok, any rise in defection."

"Morale will always be highest here because the tsarytsya prioritizes the well-being of her home," Aleksei said. "Unrest will arise here last."

I thought of the thousand little fortresses I'd observed out in the city, of the mothers I'd seen on the night of the full moon, watching their children and looking as though their hearts were broken and starved.

I wondered if *last* might be now.

"As for the defectors—those who succeed are very careful, and those who do not are killed. Word may never reach Pappa's informers," Aleksei added. He pushed a hand through his hair, scowling when he ran into the white band at his brow. "The tsarytsya has made her people fierce, but she hasn't made them loyal. Nothing holds her world together but her will."

"What do you mean?" Cobie frowned.

"Baba Yaga called Midnight a child this morning, demeaned her in front of everyone," I said slowly. "She's wedged me between her and Sunset, I think just to throw the generals off-balance. They aren't a family; they're on opposite sides of the board in real life, as well."

"The city is the same," Anya added, running her fingers over a seam between oven bricks. "Every house its own little fortress, the soldiers and the children divided among the three generals."

"This isn't a normal society," I said. "All the things that tie you to other people and make you better—family bonds, kinship with neighbors, religion and art and good stories—"

"None of it exists here," Aleksei finished.

The tsarytsya had scrubbed from her empire everything that encouraged people to be better than the worst of themselves. She had built herself a world, and she had peopled it with wolves.

"They believe, here, that if you can take something, it belongs to you," I said quietly, reaching for Torden's hand. "So she calls herself Grandmother Wolf, who took the Imperiya for them to grind down and devour. She hides how weak her position is. Because she's raised a city of wolves, and if they can take her Imperiya from *her*, they will."

Grim hope grew in me as I spoke the words.

Aleksei swallowed hard, then nodded again at the paper. "These numbers are a disaster for her." He pointed at the first label—*Upper Northern*. "This is the division of the *pestykk* stationed beyond the Norsk border. They are, by far, Baba Yaga's largest army."

"Well, that's to be expected," Cobie said. "Al-Maghreb and Masr guard against her far to the south, and Zhōng Guó is on the far side of Ranneniy Shenok, but the Shield of the North is the tsarytsya's strongest remaining opponent on the continent."

Torden shook his head, still wondering over the numbers. "But even in the Upper North, her largest division, the tsarytsya has a third fewer *pestykk* than Huginn and Muninn believed."

Aleksei nodded. "Her armies were vast early in her reign.

She inherited her role as headwoman from her father during a turbulent time. Her people's admiration united them—admiration for her viciousness during the war."

"And now that war is over, and times have changed," Cobie said, following Aleksei's thought. "But she's relied on rumor and inertia to maintain control, and people buy the lie."

Aleksei nodded. "Yes. And Sunset's armies press ever onward. No one will believe the tsarytsya is faltering as long as she keeps moving. She hopes to recoup her losses from desertion by conquering farther and faster." He swallowed hard. "I suspect you were meant to aid her in that plan, Selah."

I squeezed Torden's hand and he kissed my knuckles. "Alessandra expected the tsarytsya to take me off her hands. The tsarytsya hoped I would give her Potomac."

Never. I would *never*.

"Here's what concerns me." Anya leaned against the oven, legs drawn up. "The sizes of those armies—they're entirely unbalanced."

"Well, we explained that," I said, confused. "The Shield is in Den Norden; she keeps her largest army there."

"This doesn't feel like an attempt to balance his power," Anya disagreed. "Her armies are desperately small elsewhere. This feels like she's mounting an attack." She raised her brows at Aleksei. "Did Midnight give you any inkling about that?"

"Even jealous, Polunoshchna isn't quite that reckless," Aleksei said. "But with the element of surprise, the tsarytsya could take Asgard."

We all stared at one another for a long moment.

"If her plan is to rebuild her armies with captives, she'll fail,"
I blurted. "Alfödr's *drengs* and *thegns* would never join her. She
has to know that."

"Does she?" Cobie asked.

Torden scrubbed a hand through his hair, standing abruptly.
"Someone has to tell Pappa. He has the numbers—if only he
has the time to summon them from across Norge, rally them
to Asgard."

"Someone needs to tell everyone!" Anya exclaimed. "If people knew the truth—"

"The three of you aren't telling anyone anything. You're
about as subtle as a parade in the streets." Aleksei pointed at
Cobie. "And I wanted a word with you. You kept that knife."

Cobie put a hand to her thigh above the hemline of her
shift, where I suspected she'd bound it up. "I won't be defense-
less, Aleksei."

"If Sunset had searched you, you'd have been killed," he said
tightly. "The tsarytsya would not have hesitated to spill blood
over breakfast. They already call you *kikimora* upstairs."

"What does that mean?" I asked.

Aleksei gave a dry laugh. "*Kikimora* is a household spirit, a
vicious one. She does 'women's work'"—here he drew quotes
around his own words—"but in a terrible temper, and always
poorly." Then he rounded on Anya. "You, the soldiers call
vila. Nymph. Fae creature." He cleared his throat. "Be careful,
please. All of you."

I didn't have to ask what I was called upstairs.

Zolushka. Ash-girl.

I didn't care. At least the ashes were warm, in this tower of cold stone and colder people.

"I can radio Perrault again," I said. "I can warn them about the tsarytsya's impending attack, and see where our reinforcements are."

"Reinforcements?" Aleksei asked. I explained quickly that Perrault was pleading with Alfödr, seeking contact with the resistance through Gretel. "I told him about Zatemnennya. I said the city would be in chaos. Whatever we do, we'll do it that night." Escape—or something more.

"And I expected to be the hero, leading the charge to rescue you," Torden said, half teasing.

"You're a formidable army on your own, but I'd rather improve our odds." I bit my lip and looked up at him. "Do you need to go home, if the tsarytsya is coming?"

"No," Torden said quietly. "This will not take me away. I will never leave you again."

I didn't think. I stretched up to kiss him again, wrapping my arms tightly around his waist.

"Good grief," Aleksei groaned, passing a hand over his forehead. "You two are back to being absolutely useless now that you're together."

I stuck my tongue out at him, and Torden squeezed me tighter.

49

Torden stayed with me long after he should have left. We sat in the quiet of the laundry, burrowed in a pile of sheets, hip to hip, knee to knee, his arm around my shoulders.

I never wanted to stop touching him. I ran a finger down his forehead, over his nose, across his cupid's bow, over his lips.

"I feel like I'm dreaming," I whispered. "I've been dreaming so much since I've been here, I can't believe any of this is real."

"Are any of your dreams this good?" Torden laughed softly.

"No. Most of them are—" I swallowed, cutting myself off before I said *nightmares*.

Most nights I dreamed of my father, of his body shriveling up until it was nothing but bones. Some nights I dreamed of Potomac's fields aflame, of Arbor Hall's trees turned to pillars of ash.

Only once or twice had I dreamed of Torden, our bodies weightless in the lake above the Lysefjord, his hands hot on my waist despite the cool of the water.

"How did you even get here so quickly?" I asked quietly.

Torden studied our joined hands. "Huginn and Muninn got wind of your arrest within about two weeks of your being taken." His throat bobbed. "And I was on my way within hours."

"You just left?" I breathed.

"I should never have let you go in the first place." Torden's voice was low, frustrated. "I should have stood up to my father. Treason," he scoffed.

"Well." I cleared my throat. "It turns out Lang and the crew were ferrying arms from the *zǒngtǒng* to the resistance here in the Imperiya. They hadn't told me about it, but . . . I don't think they were wrong to do it."

Torden went very still. "Your ship was bearing weapons, and you didn't know about it?"

I shook my head, grimacing.

"Your captain—Lang—he brought contraband aboard, at the commission of a foreign power, and put you at risk without informing you or your family?" He started to rise, but I pulled him down, only just stifling a weary laugh.

"Torden, he's hundreds of miles away. What are you going to do? And—besides, I've already dealt with this. And I'd do it all again." Despite my protests, his eyes still burned with anger.

I expected him to pull away—to shift sideways, to need space to cool off. But Torden couldn't seem to get close enough to me. He gathered my legs across his lap and wrapped his arms around me, touching his forehead to mine. "If anything had happened to you because of him—" His jaw clenched. "Selah, I couldn't bear it. I would've never forgiven him."

"Shh." I took his hands in mine. "I'm fine. I'm all right."

"You are serving Baba Yaga at her very table," Torden said. Remorse was in every line of his face. "You are not all right. Aren't you afraid?"

I ran my fingers over his arms, breathing him in, thinking.

I'd told Torden once I was afraid of being made foolish. I'd run from England, from Bear and his family, who'd humiliated me. I'd run from Norge, too, from Konge Alfödr and his wrath.

Neither king worried me anymore. I had seen and suffered too much. And love had grown stronger than my fear of either.

"I was afraid I might never see you again," I whispered. "And here you are. My prayers answered. The hint of a happy ending already." I ran my palm over his cropped hair, smiling wanly. "What did you do while I was gone? What—what happened after I left?"

Torden sighed and settled me in closer to him. "I was running faster than ever. Beating Bragi and Hermódr in hand-to-hand, outshooting Fredrik. I worked with my hammer, Mjolnir, nearly every day—fought with him on the practice field and worked with him in the forge, in the Flørli outpost. That was the other change," Torden added. "Per the *valkjrya's* recommendations to fortify a place downriver from Asgard, we sent men there to work, to watch, and to monitor messages from the radio tower. I worked there with the *dvergar*, learning to forge weapons."

I gnawed on my lip. "It sounds like you did pretty well on

your own." My voice was thin.

It was ridiculous. I hadn't wanted him to suffer. I shook off my pettiness.

His Adam's apple bobbed. "Pappa drove Anya out because she loved someone else, and Aleksei had gone to the devil to spite my father, and you were destined to be bride to some other man. My family had crumbled before my eyes. And I could do nothing about it." His eyes shifted to mine. "So I tried to work, and tried to forget."

I wet my lips. "And did you?"

I was almost afraid of his answer. Because—what if he had? What if he was here only out of duty, out of guilt over what his father had done?

Torden's hands stole, possessive, around my waist. He shook his head, dark eyes sparking. "I felt you gone like a hunger," he said. "You were the first thought I had when I woke. The last when I went to sleep. I was trying to sweat you out."

My breath grew jagged. His eyelashes were rose gold in the light of the fire, bare inches away. Unbidden, my hand reached for his cheekbone, skating over the freckles on his pale skin and the copper stubble of his beard.

Torden bent, his nose brushing my jawline, and pressed a kiss soft as a breath against my neck. "I will never want anyone the way I want you." He kissed me once more, lingering over my fevered pulse as his fingers slipped into the hair at the nape of my neck. He worked at the snarled knots until he slid my ring free. "Ask me again. Ask me if I forgot you."

His kiss was like a burn. I wanted to let it scorch me alive.

But the feel of his lips on my skin made me think of the last person who had kissed me.

Sour guilt replaced the heat burning beneath my skin.

I swallowed. "I have to tell you something. I— For the sake of honesty."

Torden frowned. "You sound worried."

He was still concerned for me. Did I even deserve it? Had I betrayed him?

I gathered my courage. "After I left Norge, in the Shvartsval'd, something happened with Lang. It's—hard to define exactly what was going on, but I think there was always something there. Between us." I trained my gaze on my hands, afraid to look at Torden. "He kissed me before I left to come here."

I resisted the urge to justify, or explain, or apologize.

"Are you angry?" I lifted my eyes to his, preparing myself. "Does this change things?"

"His interest in you was always clear," said Torden. He toyed with my ring, his chest rising and falling, his mouth growing sulky. "Or it was to me, anyway."

"I haven't spoken to him since I left." Then an odd idea struck me. "Are you jealous?" I asked in a whisper. "I thought you'd be angry at me."

"I'm angry at him. I'd like to fight him with my bare hands and see if he tries to put his on you again," Torden said immediately. He paused. "So, yes, I think this is jealous."

Torden. Jealous. It gave me a wicked thrill.

His throat bobbed, and he began to braid the ring back into

341

my hair, his fingers tender against my neck, sending bolts of heat and chills over my skin.

When he was finished, I gripped his hand. Our threaded fingers dug into the sheets piled around us as I leaned close and pressed a slow kiss to the corner of his mouth.

We were in danger every moment we stayed together. But I was a maiden in a tower and the dragon was watching every moment and he, my prince, had come to put a sword in my hand.

And I could not help but feel powerful at the way he wanted me.

50

We served the tsarytsya and her generals in the formal dining room the next morning, eyes down, arms full. General Midnight made acid comments, and Aleksei was snide, and as we went up and down the stairs Ivan eyed Anya with a desperation that embarrassed me on his behalf.

I didn't care. Once we had assured ourselves the generals weren't going anywhere, Cobie, Anya, and I made for the tsarytsya's room. We had decided to give ourselves eight minutes. Any more than that, and the guard outside would begin to suspect.

Anya tore the sheets off the bed, working triple-time by herself as Cobie counted and watched the door. I went straight for the radio.

I noted the frequency it sat on first, then, painstakingly, I turned the radio dial, stumbling across chatter here and there on my way to 3.44.

My heart was in my throat. I needed to know if Perrault had pleaded our case to Asgard, and I had to warn Asgard that an attack was coming.

But when I reached my frequency, I found it empty.

The sound was the skate of runners over cobblestones, the merciless roar of a river. My stomach sank. Perrault wasn't there.

It cost us so much to come in here, every time. And today, it was for nothing.

"Nothing." I turned to Anya. "He's not manning the radio."

"Or they've left Asgard," Cobie said. "They could be beyond range of the tower."

"No," I breathed, horrified. "I don't know what frequency to use to contact Flørli. I didn't think to ask Torden. How will I warn them the tsarytsya is planning an attack?"

The hole in my logic gaped at me: I'd hoped the *Beholder* was on its way to me. What assurance had I had that there was a tower close to them?

I hadn't thought of it. Guilt left me weak. What if we had missed our only chance to warn Asgard?

"We'll come back. We'll do it another day." Cobie took a long breath. "You have six minutes. Do something with them." She pointed to Anya, who'd paused changing the sheets. "Don't stop. We only have six minutes."

I stared, horrified, at the radio.

With six minutes, I could reach out to Godmother Althea—but, no. Her frequency was 3.44, as well, and she wasn't there. I counted on my fingers; it was probably around two in the morning in Potomac. She and the sisters were asleep or at Matins, the prayer service that broke the night before Lauds at dawn.

I clenched my jaw and began, slowly, to turn the dial—straining after the chatter I caught, hoping I'd hear familiar voices.

And finally, I did.

"She is well," someone was saying.

"But you won't tell us where?" answered a boy's voice. "My sisters are—"

"You know I can't," said the first voice, a girl's—my chest seized.

The voice was Gretel's.

I cleared my throat. "You really ought to leave well enough alone, Hansel. Leirauh is safer where she is. That is, if Gretel kept her promise."

There was dead silence.

"Hansel?" I asked the quiet. "Gretel?"

"Selah?" Fritz blurted. "Is that you?"

"It is," I affirmed. "I'm here. With Cobie and Anya."

"You're where?"

I swallowed hard. "Baba Yaga's house."

Gretel swore. Fritz was silent.

Five minutes, Cobie mouthed to me, imperious.

"It's all right," I said hurriedly. "I—Gretel, did Perrault speak to you?"

"He did not."

"Fr—Hansel?" I asked.

"Not I," he said.

I chewed my lip. If Perrault hadn't been able to contact the *fürst* or the Waldleute, what else might have gone wrong? *Had they left Asgard, after all?*

There was no time to fret.

Perrault hadn't spoken with them. Torden was here—I would be fine. But we still had the chance to help the resistance free the city.

"Regardless," I said, "I have information for you."

"Well, don't keep me in suspense, princess." I couldn't see the leader of the Waldleute, but I could imagine her: eyes narrowed, chin lifted, one brow quirked.

Quickly I related to them what we had discovered—the depletion of the tsarytsya's armies in the east, west, and south, and at Stupka-Zamok. "So if you can coordinate an attack with the other arms of the resistance—"

"We could feasibly end her," Gretel said slowly.

"Yes, and there's more," I said. "One night soon, security in Stupka-Zamok is going to be very lax. If I could speak to local divisions of the resistance, we could take advantage of that. We—" I paused, uncertain. "We could take the city."

"You can't approach them, but I can," Gretel said immediately. "I will reach out to the Rusalki and the Leshii and the Vodyanoi. Speak to them on your behalf. They will find you and coordinate an assault."

"Who are they?" I asked.

"The Leshii are the woodfolk, the Vodyanoi the river dwellers," Gretel said. "And the Rusalki are the mothers."

I stopped short at this. "The mothers?"

"Yes." Gretel's voice turned bitter. "The mothers of stolen children."

"I've already seen them," I said slowly. "The night of the full moon, some of the children were forced to fight. The mothers came to watch."

"Good," Gretel said. "So you know who to watch for. Now, when is this happening?"

"The night of the lunar eclipse, in about three weeks," I said. "The phases of the moon are important here. I think it's a religious ceremony. They call it Zatemnennya."

A hand flailed in my periphery. *Three minutes*, Cobie said, holding up three fingers.

I was so distracted by Cobie that I didn't hear them at first. But Gretel and Fritz were hissing, protesting, horrified. "Zatemnennya?" Gretel demanded. "Is that what you said?"

"Yes," I answered, uncertain.

"Are you trying to get my people killed?"

"No!" I exclaimed. "What are you talking about? I'm trying to help!"

"I am not sending my people into the Mortar on Zatemnennya," Gretel said, forceful. "And if you're smart, you will spend the night behind a barred door."

"What is Zatemnennya?" I asked, confused, my panic rising. "I don't understand!"

"It is a revel, of sorts." Gretel's voice was grim. "I like you, Selah. Take my advice and don't make any plans for the eclipse. Stay inside."

Cobie dragged a finger across her throat. *Time to go.*

I desperately wanted to press Gretel for more information. But I was out of time.

"I have to go," I said. *"Fur die Freiheit."*

"Fur die Wildnis," said Gretel.

Fritz's voice was rusty when he finally spoke. "Stay safe, Selah."

51

I'd hoped Baba Yaga would forget. But when I took up her breakfast two days later—this time, to her private sitting room—she, Aleksei, and Sunset were ready. The board was set. And Midnight was not present.

I'd hardly slept for two nights. I'd lain awake, wondering how to find the Rusalki, since Gretel wouldn't help me. Wondering where Perrault and Lang and the *Beholder* and her crew were. Wondering what I'd summoned them into. If Lang came to rescue me, and they met harm because my ignorance led them into danger, I would never forgive myself.

The tsarytsya gestured to the last empty seat among them, at Aleksei's side, and pushed me Polunoshchna's pile of black claws. A few rolls of the die determined our order of play. Baba Yaga would go first; I, Sunset, and Aleksei would follow.

My head and heart were flitting from place to place. But

I was at table with Wolves. I had to focus. I had to control myself.

Baba Yaga set her first claw at the heart of the wolf. I put mine at the eastern wingtip of the New World.

She already knew where Potomac lay. I might as well let her know it was mine.

Sunset played as she always did—careful, cards close to her chest. Aleksei, too, kept to his modus operandi, which appeared to be to salt the board as randomly as possible with his white claws.

Sunset was playing to win, and Aleksei was playing to survive in Baba Yaga's court.

I was playing for my homeland.

As I had in our first game, I laid claim to the whole of the New World. But this time, I faced no competition for it from the others. With Polunoshchna gone, there was no one to be petty over territory they didn't think would help them win.

When the New World was entirely claimed, I put my black claws down in Den Norden, starting with Norge and Varsinais-Suomi.

For once, I was mimicking Midnight. I was letting everyone at the table know that these were my lands and they were my people, and they were not to be touched.

The tsarytsya lifted an eyebrow at me. I tried not to react. Before long, the board was full, and the attacks began.

The last time I had played, I had avoided attacking for as long as possible, using my turns to shift troops around within my borders. I abhorred empire, and I loved Potomac. I wanted only for us to be left to live, and to let others do the same.

But this wasn't real life. This was a dangerous game. So I played the tsarytsya's way. I attacked her first, striking the nose of the Bear Whelp, Ranneniy Shenok.

We rolled the die. I won.

I gave the tsarytsya a disinterested smile, as if pleased but not unduly so. Her returning smile was strained.

Vechirnya tensed at Baba Yaga's side, her lioness's eyes going still and seeking me out, as if seeing me for the first time.

Sunset set truly to work. She attacked me in Varsinais-Suomi. She won.

It was immediately clear that Sunset had not considered me a proper opponent before. She had held back. But Sunset ceased now to play gently, and I began to lose.

I played the best I could, but so much of winning was a roll of the die, not a matter of strategy. And for the part that was: I was inexperienced, and my opponents were the empress of a massive empire and her best general.

And Aleksei. "Cheer up, little Zolushka." He wrinkled his nose, tone snide. "At least this time you won't have to clean the game up off the floor when it's over."

"Rankovyy." The tsarytsya arched an eyebrow. "Smugness does not suit you any better than it did Polunoshchna."

I gave her a smile that seemed to peel my teeth away from my lips.

I had to win. I thought as hard as I could, tearing through my thoughts and experiences and every story I'd ever read for a strategy that would hand me the game.

When I'd last sat down with them, I'd mimicked Konge Alfödr and King Constantine without intending to. I had staked my claim for the land that I loved, and let the rest of the world do what it would. But my lessons learned from Saint George and the Shield of the North would only take me so far here.

The board began to glow with red claws and teeth. Sunset was better than me, and she was winning.

I realized, suddenly, certainly, that I could not win the game playing it properly. A very, very simple solution presented itself to me.

I would not play it properly.

I would strategize off the board. I would take a leaf out of Alessandra's book. Out of the *freinnen*'s.

"Is this game common in Yotunkheym?" I asked, poking around the map. Here and there I shifted the different-colored claws, squinting at the *terytoriy* beneath them as if trying to decide what to do next.

"Yes," Baba Yaga said. She nodded at Aleksei. "Even our little *pestykk* play it. It sharpens their claws."

"Like the full moon," I said. The bedroom door clanked open; Cobie and Anya emerged, piles of dirty linens in hand, murmuring betwixt themselves.

"What?" the tsarytsya asked, turning back to me.

"Like the full moon," I repeated. I was still twiddling claws around, debating my next move.

"Yes, exactly." Baba Yaga eyed me. "It is your turn, Zolushka."

I shook myself. "Oh. Yes, of course."

I moved black claws across the Baltic Sea to attack one of Sunset's red *terytoriy*, a corner of the Imperiya, then handed her the die. "Would you like to roll first?"

She squinted, assessing how many claws she had in the ear of the wolf, which would determine how many rolls she could make. Sunset frowned, casting her gaze around the board for a moment, then rolled.

I rolled next. I beat her. I claimed Latvya and Lytva.

Grimacing, Sunset relinquished her lands, then used her turn to adjust the distribution of her armies. For his, Aleksei fought a determined battle with Baba Yaga in the south of Africa; then Baba Yaga expanded her claim in Australia.

"So the eclipse," I asked, still casting about the board as I moved farther into the Imperiya, where more of Sunset's claws reigned. "It sounds like quite a hectic affair. What's it all about?" My stomach quivered with nerves as I tried to sound light and disinterested.

Neither Vechirnya nor the tsarytsya answered; Vechirnya assessed her armies in the territory I attacked, more frown lines creasing her tanned forehead.

She rolled.

I rolled.

I beat her.

I took Bilorus and turned it black. Sunset added the red claws of her defeated armies to the small pile of their fallen comrades beside the board.

"The eclipse," I asked again. "Is it a party? With . . . street vendors and a parade?"

Baba Yaga and Sunset laughed uproariously. I settled my palms over the board, my own forehead furrowing.

"What's so funny?" I demanded.

"Selah," Sunset said, sounding genuinely amused as she shifted her troops around again, filling in gaps on the board. "Zatemnennya is not a village fair. It is Wolf Night."

I didn't like the sound of this. I'd begged the *Beholder* to be here by the eclipse.

My mouth was dry. At my side, Aleksei wore a matching expression of confusion.

"What do you mean?" I asked.

"We celebrate Wolf Night with each lunar eclipse. They mostly come once or twice a year." Baba Yaga's smile was poison-bitter, knife-sharp. "On Wolf Night, nothing is prohibited. All laws of property and person are void. That to which you can lay claim, you may, and if it is yours come dawn, yours it shall stay."

Aleksei was tense beside me. Slowly, I took my hands from the board and put them in my lap.

When I'd disposed of the red claws and teeth I'd swiped from Sunset's *terytoriy*, I reached for Aleksei's hand and clenched it tightly. His face betrayed nothing. His fingers were shaking in mine.

I had invited the *Beholder* into a waking nightmare. I was going to be sick.

The tsarytsya caught another fish in the cluster that made up Australia. Then it was my turn again.

I moved into Yotunkheym, to the head of the wolf. I didn't

care if it was strategic; I moved twelve black armies into the red *terytoriya.*

I rolled twelve times. Sunset could only roll two. I took the head of the wolf, the heart of the Imperiya.

The little ash-girl from the backwater kingdom, daughter of the poisoned father, laid claim to Stupka-Zamok.

Sunset was baffled. But I felt no triumph. My stomach was churning, my mind racing.

Could I find my crew before the eclipse? Could I speak to the Rusalki—the mothers—or the Leshii, the Vodyanoi?

"And your soldiers allow this to happen?" I asked, a little breathless.

"My soldiers participate." Baba Yaga smiled. "One can only keep wolves at bay for so long, Zolushka. They must be allowed to sate their appetites once in a while."

Baba Yaga completed her conquest of Australia.

"Aha!" she declared, pleased, then sat back. "I am tired, and hungry. The game is ended." This habit of the tsarytsya's might have been jarring, had the game's end not brought such relief.

Meanwhile, Sunset sorted through the claws scattered over the board, counting territories under her breath and looking confused. She glanced up, thick brows drawn together. "You win, Selah. Congratulations." Then she rose, nodded efficiently, and strode from the room.

I stood, intending to do the same. "*Moy Rankovyy,*" I said, curtsying to Aleksei with no warmth on my face. "*Moya tsarytsya.*"

"Stop."

The tsarytsya's voice was hard. I turned back to her.

"Pockets," said Baba Yaga. I frowned, and turned them out, the ones in my shift and in my apron.

"Palms," she said. I blinked at her, and opened them.

Baba Yaga squinted, eyes raking over me. Then they lightened. "Your sleeves," she said, confident. "Unroll them."

My heart dropped. I didn't argue. I unrolled my sleeves slowly, one at a time.

Red teeth and claws spilled from the fabric as I loosened it, clattering to the stone floor.

I steeled myself for her anger. But Baba Yaga threw back her head and laughed.

"Well done, little ash-girl." She clapped her hands slowly. "What a delight you are."

My stomach turned over again. I was glad to live another hour. I loathed the sense of her approval.

"You cheated?" Aleksei asked, surprised.

"She bent the game to her will," the tsarytsya corrected. "As anyone who wants to win must sometimes do."

As Alessandra had. As the *freinnen* had.

A mere eight months ago, being caught cheating would have shamed me to death. I would have pleaded forgiveness, I would have apologized, I would have cast myself on her mercy.

Today, I tipped my head back and howled, ever so softly, at the ceiling. Then I sketched Baba Yaga a curtsy and left the room and left the pieces on the floor.

52

"I nearly pissed myself," Aleksei hissed as he and Torden entered the kitchens that night. "You, howling like a wolf? You're too good at it."

"*You* nearly wet yourself?" I demanded in a whisper. "I'm the one who had to figure out how to beat a military genius in a game of military strategy!"

"How did you manage it?" Anya asked idly, rubbing salve into her wrists. The pot of ointment had appeared before the oven a couple weeks before.

No one admitted to having left it. But Wash's eyes had darted back and forth from her cooking to the salve several times before I opened it, smelled it, and realized what it was. The skin around Anya's wrists, relieved that day of their shackles, had begun looking infected before; now her skin looked tender but healthy.

I would never be able to repay Wash for all the debts I owed her.

"I've become fairly light-fingered since we started working here," I said wryly. "Cleaning a fireplace quietly enough that Polunoshchna doesn't scream at you is quite the experience."

"She put them in her sleeves," Aleksei said dryly to Torden, miming cuffing his own. "Twenty or thirty claws, right off the board. Chattering nervously and distracting the tsarytsya and the general while she lifted them right off Sunset's *terytoriy* so she could take them more easily."

Torden stared, disbelieving, at me.

"I needed to win," I whispered.

"What were the stakes?" Anya asked, crossing her arms. "Who lost?"

"I think I did," Aleksei said, shrugging. "But without Polunoshchna at the table, I think the only price was my dignity. Which I had little enough of anyway."

Anya sniffed, unappeased.

"Enough," Cobie said. "Zatemnennya is in three weeks. I couldn't hear what Gretel told you. What's our plan?"

"Gretel and Baba Yaga called it a night of lawlessness," I admitted. "The Wolves can take what they will, and if they still possess it by morning, it's theirs."

We stared at one another for a long moment.

"Let's sit," Torden said. As the banked fire in the oven smoldered, he told us what he'd done.

He had come to Stupka-Zamok with about forty *drengs* in total, and they had seized a small fortress-house on the edge of town upon their arrival. "We didn't hurt anyone," he reassured me. "The owners will be restored full possession of their home when we've gotten you safely away."

I arched an eyebrow at him, and he blushed.

"I didn't like it, either," he mumbled. "But we had to have a base of operations."

Aleksei rolled his eyes and waved his hand. "Enough, get on with it."

"The doors to Stupka-Zamok will be unbarred that night," Torden continued hastily. "We have stolen an additional three Imperiya uniforms. After the three of you have changed into them, we will move from the castle to the house and pretend that we are claiming it. My *drengs* and I will defend the house until dawn, and we can escape the city."

"And that should work?" Anya asked, anxious.

Aleksei scratched at his nose. "It should. If the night is as chaotic as the tsarytsya described, we ought to pass unnoticed."

For all my bravado before the tsarytsya, my stomach clenched at the risk we ran.

Worst of all, I didn't want to flee. I didn't want to leave Wash and Vasylysa and every other innocent in this tower to Baba Yaga's mercies. I didn't want to abandon Yotunkheym's children to a life in the little *pestykk*. But without help from the resistance, I didn't know what we could do, and Gretel had—fairly enough—refused to help.

It was a beautiful dream. If the Leshii and the Vodyanoi and the Rusalki could take the city that night, would it, too, remain theirs come morning? Or would that be yet another of her own rules Baba Yaga would break?

"We'll have to stay together," Torden said fiercely. "I'll find arms for the three of you, and we'll make it to the house. It's barely a mile away."

"Twenty minutes." Cobie's gaze was fixed on the fire. "We'll find out if we can survive twenty minutes running with the wolves."

Torden stayed late again that night, hiding away with me in the laundry. I laid my head against his shoulder, basking in the warmth of the fire, in the warmth of him.

He was solid ground in a world of shadow and fog. In a world where I was an ash-girl, burned by fires I had not set.

"Are you worried?" he asked softly, running his fingers through my hair.

"I wish we were doing more," I confessed, meeting his eyes. "I wish I could help the resistance take this city, instead of running away from it. And I'm worried that the *Beholder*'s crew are walking in blind."

Torden hissed a breath through his teeth. "They don't know?"

"I couldn't raise Perrault. Unless he happened to be listening on the wire when I spoke to Fritz and Gretel and just couldn't respond because they were too far from a tower."

Torden studied his hands, as if trying to puzzle out a secret behind their freckles and scars. "Why not Captain Lang?" he finally asked. "Why have you been speaking to Perrault?"

I pursed my lips.

Because I don't want to be cut out of my own rescue for my safety.

Because somehow, plans with Lang always become a competition.

"Because Lang is complicated," I finally said.

Torden nodded, still staring down at his fingers. "Do you wish he were here instead?" he asked softly. "Am I the rescuer you wished for?"

I drew back, reaching for the ring in my hair and unbinding it from its braid.

"Ask me again," I said. My throat was tight.

I held the ring out to him, its blue stones glinting in the dim light of the fire.

"You want me to—"

"Ask. Me. Again," I said slowly.

Torden wet his lips and took the ring. He rolled it between his shaking fingers. "Selah, am I the one you wished for?" he whispered. "Will you marry me?"

I held out my left hand.

"Yes," I said.

Such a short word. It felt larger than my whole body.

"Yes," I said again, reveling in the power the word bore. Torden slid the ring onto my finger. I took his face between my hands and kissed him. "I will."

The next morning, after I prayed my Rosary, I began marking the days again. I stepped out of the closet and greeted Wash as she began to cover her hair and rinse her hands, took a burnt lump from the oven, and marked in black ash a row of tick marks on the oven's side, counting backward as best I could.

Midnight would mock the soot on my hands. I wondered if she would still call us *ash-girls* if we burned their world to the ground.

When I was done counting, I studied the line of scratches. We had been in the witch's house for sixteen days. We would remain twenty more.

My breath came heavy, angry, at the time that had been stolen from me. Time I could have spent with my father, with Torden, in Potomac.

Grandmother Wolf had taken it. I would give her no more.

Time felt shorter than ever. When we left the tsarytsya and her generals at breakfast, we raced upstairs.

Cobie shut Baba Yaga's bedroom door, facing it with her knife out, and began to count down from eight minutes. Anya tore around the room, refreshing linens with inhuman speed.

I strode instantly to the radio. Torden had given me a frequency to use.

"Hello?" I asked the silence.

Nothing.

"Hello?"

"What is our heart?" asked a voice in struggling English.

"Ash," I said, without hesitation.

Ash, he'd said, so very long ago. *It is Asgard's rune. All our blood wear this over their hearts.*

"And what is our journey?" asked the voice, as Torden had said it would.

"Reid," I answered.

And this—he'd pointed inside his left wrist—*is Reid. It*

means ride, *the work and the journey of our lives.*

"Very good. To whom am I speaking?"

"I'm Selah, seneschal-elect of Potomac. If Hermódr is at Flørli I need to speak to him immediately." Torden had told me his older brother spent many of his days at the fortress, keeping watch over the fjord and overseeing radio transmissions.

Seven minutes, Cobie mouthed to me.

I'd had no luck last time, failing to reach Perrault, rebuffed by Gretel. I hoped for better fortune today.

"Selah?" Hermódr burst out over the radio. My heart rose as I nudged the volume down.

"Softly, Hermódr," I cautioned him, even as I wanted to sing out with relief. Hermódr was Torden's steadiest brother, the wisest and most discerning son of Asgard, its best politician. I could rest easy with my message in his hands. "Look, I've only got a minute. I need you to listen carefully. Do you know where the *Beholder* has gone?"

"Yes," Hermódr answered immediately. "The *Beholder* sailed the day after you spoke to Perrault. Pappa declined to send aid, I'm sorry to say. Torden took as many of his *drengs* as would flout our father's orders just days before your people arrived, and he would transfer no more."

My heart raced. "But they sailed the next day?" I breathed. They could be here soon. If we could find them—but how? And what if they walked into Zatemnennya unawares?

Four minutes, Cobie mouthed, holding up as many fingers.

"That's probably for the best, anyway," I said quickly. "Hermódr, we suspect the tsarytsya is preparing to attack Asgard."

363

As simply as I could, I explained what we had found in Baba Yaga's office—the evidence she'd been gathering her *zuby* in the Upper Northern division of her ranks.

Hermódr sucked in a sharp breath. "Do you know when?"

"No," I admitted, pinching my lips shut. "The moon cycle," I said suddenly. "The lunar cycle is significant to the tsarytsya and her people, almost to a spiritual degree. She may attack the night of the lunar eclipse, or maybe the night of the next new moon or full moon."

"That makes sense." Hermódr's voice warmed. "Thank you, Selah. Thank you for warning us. You may have saved lives."

My voice turned wry. "Let your father know I'll be collecting on this debt."

Hermódr laughed. "Give her hell, Selah."

"Stay safe, brother."

I shut off the radio, returned the radio to its original frequency and volume, and turned to Cobie and Anya, heaving a sigh.

"And now," I said, "we watch, and we wait."

53

We spent the next twenty days pretending. We let Baba Yaga and her generals think us meek as lambs, gentle as doves.

Polunoshchna sneered at me and called me Zolushka and left me messes at the table to clean up. I kept my head down.

She and the rest thought they knew what was happening to us.

They thought they were grinding us down, as Sunset did when she led the *pestykk* into foreign lands, as Midnight did when she slipped through the night like a wraith and did the Imperiya's dirty work. As Baba Yaga did every time she ordered her Wolves to whet their claws.

They were not to know that we could not be ground down. We could not be broken. We would simply watch, and wait. And then we would loose our own claws.

* * *

Despite what Vechirnya had said, the day of the lunar eclipse dawned with a festival feeling on the air. We woke hours before dawn to begin cooking, to feed the tsarytsya and all her guests. We ferried food and alcohol up and down the stairs, avoiding the eyes of the courtiers and the hands of the soldiers as they grew progressively drunker and rowdier. Ivan was nearly falling down by eleven in the morning.

I stared out every window I passed, wide-eyed and waiting for any sign of the *Beholder*. I had heard nothing from Perrault, though I'd switched the radio on and listened feverishly every day.

Wash eyed us all with greater trepidation every time we left the cellar for the house upstairs.

Dinner, at twilight, was a raucous affair. Vechirnya and Polunoshchna and Aleksei, acting as Rankovyy, sat at Baba Yaga's left and right hands, at a long table of her soldiers. Tall bottles of vodka were passed up and down its length, the caustic-smelling alcohol sloshing into glasses and onto the floor. Sunset drank deeply; her breath was astringent. Butter and fat and meat and jam, more than anyone needed, were passed from serving dish to plate.

As I worked, Midnight bit into a greasy chicken wing and flung it at me. It batted lightly at my shoulder and I stepped back, confused.

"Eat up, Zolushka," she laughed. Her eyes were red and unfocused, wild and glassy with liquor.

"Thank you, my General Midnight." I bent to pick up the wasted food and put it onto my tray.

"What?" she screamed, her voice too loud even amid the

riot of the room. "Are you too good for my scraps now? You were glad enough to take them when they earned you a spot at the table."

I never wanted your place, you fool, I wanted to say.

I will smash the entire table and arm those you've hunted with all your teeth and claws.

But I was stronger than Polunoshchna.

"As you say, my General Midnight," I answered, almost mechanically. I kept my face pleasant.

Baba Yaga smiled into her glass.

A soldier grasped at Cobie's thigh as she walked past him, and she jerked away. The tsarytsya glanced out the window, brows arched. "Has night fallen already?"

"It has." Aleksei met my eyes, willed us toward the door.

Cobie glanced down at the soldier. "In that case—" She jerked her elbow in the direction of his nose. A sharp crack sounded, and blood poured down his face. "Go," Cobie ordered us as the soldier swore at her in Yotne, still trying to grab her. We dropped our trays and ran.

Baba Yaga laughed and howled with mirth.

"Run, run, little lambs," she called. "Run for the cellar and bar the door against the wolves."

The sound of her cackling chased us down the stairs to the kitchens. Wash locked the door behind us, chained it, and set the crossbar.

The kitchen was fuller that night than it had ever been after dark. Maids and cooks sat on piles of linens in the laundry, on top and in front of the oven. Some had babies with them. A few had even smuggled in small children. I wondered where the little *pestykk* were tonight, and how long these children could be kept from their ranks.

The women kept their voices low, kept their eyes open with glass after glass of tea from the samovar, and kept as far from the door as possible.

Cobie kept her knife out while we waited.

The knock came a little after midnight. A few of the maids started, but I rose and walked to the door.

"No!" Wash rushed to my side. "No, do not open it."

"Selah?" Torden called through the door. "Selah, it's only me."

"He's my friend," I said to Wash.

"No man is your friend on Zatemnennya." Her eyes were full of fear. "Those in this room you can trust. When you leave this place, you have left all promise of safety."

Her face was so earnest, her palm on my shoulder so insistent. Wash, a woman who barely knew me, desired to protect me more fervently than even my own stepmother had.

She was a good person, and I would not have been safe in this place without her. Tears filled my eyes, but I blinked them away.

"There's never any promise of safety," I said. "But I'm trying to have faith and be brave."

Wash took a short breath, a heavy one. "If I unlock this door, can you swear he will do no harm to the women inside?"

"On my mother's grave. By all the saints and angels," I swore.

She wet her lips and glanced between Anya, Cobie, and me. "I am going to unbar the door, and the three of you will go into the corridor."

We nodded.

"Inshallah, we will all live to see the dawn."

Inshallah. If Allah wills, it meant.

My throat grew tight. I had heard no sacred words these many weeks. Hers left me in awe of her bravery—to speak of her Muslim faith so boldly on a night like tonight. To look heavenward in an hour when men chose to become their lowest selves.

Wash bent and kissed my forehead. The maids drew back against the wall in horror as she lifted the bar.

"One—" I cast my eyes back to the kitchen and its women and thanked it for keeping me safe.

"Two—" Anya grabbed my hand and I took Cobie's.

"Three." Wash opened the door and pushed the cluster of us into the hallway.

The kitchen door slammed behind us, and the bar fell against it.

Torden waited in his gray uniform, holding three more. The chance we'd waited for was here.

But the relief I'd expected didn't come.

Soon, we'd be free. But though Torden stood before me, all I could hear was the clang of the crossbar behind us and the howl of the wolves outside.

54

"Put these on. Quickly." Torden shoved gray uniforms at us, then turned away, rifle lifted.

It felt like madness to uncover myself on a night like this. But I stripped out of my shift alongside Cobie and Anya and put on the loathsome gray uniform, tucking my hair under its cap, trying to ignore the bloodstain splashed across its ribs.

Cobie unwrapped the knife from her leg. Torden handed Anya a blade of her own and produced a small gun from his hip for me.

"Do you know how to use this?" he asked.

The metal of the gun felt hot under my fingers, as though it were cursed. More likely, it had recently been fired. I met his eyes but didn't speak.

"Point it. Shoot it." Torden pressed his forehead to mine, swallowing. "*Can* you do that?"

I would have you far, far from your enemies, he had told me once.

But my enemies—people who'd gladly kill my friends—were here. I couldn't use a knife the way Anya and Cobie could. But I could lift the gun. I could shoot it.

I didn't hesitate. "Yes. I can."

"Then let's go."

We followed Torden up the stairs and found the tower in chaos. Men and women—mainly men—ran up and down Baba Yaga's impractical stairs. On one of the landings, two soldiers fought with swords, laughing and bleeding, one wearing the tsarytsya's emerald-studded crown lopsidedly over his head. Another gray-uniformed guard burst through the front door with two guns under one arm and three burlap sacks stuffed under the other.

There were always sentries at the front door—always. But tonight, its guardians were the threat. The danger was inside and out and locks and keys made no matter.

Coins spilled against the floor and shots cracked against the walls. Blood spattered the stairs and the floor. The women in the basement would be scrubbing it from the stones tomorrow morning if they survived the night.

"Come on." Torden hurried us toward the door.

All was dark outside but for torches and the moon. Its pale face was a deep sunset red against the midnight sky.

It was every ill omen I'd ever feared.

Aleksei met us in the courtyard. "You took long enough," he said through gritted teeth.

"Then," Torden said, "we'd better run."

"Shadows keep us," Aleksei murmured, half a prayer, half

a curse. And then, we ran.

We raced through the streets of Stupka-Zamok, past private fortresses where fires burned against the night. On one side, men threw a battering ram against an iron-girded door. On another, a crowd of gray-clad soldiers lit a match and set a moat to blazing.

A trunk of gold and gems spilled in the street and a crowd descended upon it. When a young woman tried to snatch a precious stone from the pocket of the old woman beside her, the old woman struck her across the face and began to shove the gold and gems into her mouth, swallowing them whole. They would be hers come morning and hers thereafter—unless someone cut them from her insides before dawn.

Soldiers and citizens raced to and fro, stolen animals on leads behind them and stolen coins rattling in their pockets and stolen bottles of alcohol souring the night with their stench. We were far from the only ones running, seeking to hide their deeds and the things they had carried away.

All around us, howls rang up from men who had become animals. The moon burned low and threatening against the black sky, leering at the violence below.

On and on we ran. Sprinting down the dark street, we nearly slammed into them. Ivan and his friends, their gray uniforms and their hands smeared with sunset-red blood.

"Ivan!" he crowed at Torden, his face lit with unwearied delight at their shared name.

"Ivan!" Torden returned. His throat bobbed, tense and uncomfortable, beneath his smile. They exchanged a few words, slapping one another on the back, and Torden made to leave. But then Ivan spotted Anya.

"*Shcho vidbuvayet'sya?*" he asked. *What's going on?*

I'd heard the phrase often enough in the Mortar. But the expression on Ivan's boyish face, shifting from pleasure to confusion, was new.

Anya hesitated only a moment—the barest half second while she collected herself, arranged her features, pitched her voice just right. Then she darted forward, squeezing Ivan's arm, squealing something that hinted at marvelous games and secrets.

I knew Ivan wanted Anya. He'd flirted with her, favored her.

But I hadn't realized how far a captor's trifling fancy was from real kindness.

And Anya had been a second too late.

For the first time, Ivan saw behind her performance. Ugliness replaced the bafflement in his expression as he realized he'd been tricked.

It was the change that had come over the entire city playing out on one boy's face, Wolf Night in miniature.

Ivan wrenched Anya close by her arm, so hard and abrupt she stumbled. The other soldiers jeered as he kissed her, roughly, with no affection.

If Anya would not give herself to Ivan, he would steal her.

My stomach bottomed out.

I yanked the pistol from my hip and cocked it and pointed it at Ivan. "Stop." I hardly recognized my own voice.

373

Ivan blinked at me, as if he'd never noticed me before. It was entirely possible he hadn't.

A single shot hit him in the shoulder, and he staggered back, fresh blood blooming across his arm. Anya didn't flinch. She ran toward Torden, who was securing his gun back at his hip.

He'd spared me the shot. But my hands still shook.

Cobie took the gun from my trembling fingers and holstered it for me. "Come on," she urged, tugging me away. "We need to get off the street."

I followed her and didn't look back.

"Here!" Aleksei led us into a narrow, unlit alley, noisy with yowling cats and stinking of garbage. Panting, we slowed, creeping through the shadows, picking our way around bins and broken buildings, hoping the night would hide us. Minutes stretched out like hours.

My heart pounded and the dark was thick and my breaths were so loud that I didn't hear or see them until they were upon us.

The women were so quiet.

They must have followed us, waiting for our guard to slip. And after our brush with Ivan, it had.

Three or four dragged Torden aside. A crowd of them descended upon Aleksei.

I was sick at the prospect of even lifting my gun again. But I yanked it from its holster once more, my hands shaking. Sweat dripped down my back. Torden was very still in his captors' arms.

"*Stij*," barked one. She had a knife to Aleksei's throat. A woman, cast in red moonlight. More than a dozen of them. I recognized them at once.

They were the mothers. The Rusalki.

I shoved my pistol in my belt and threw my hands up. "Wait. Wait! He's a friend!" Torden began to speak to them in Yotne; Aleksei didn't risk talking with a blade so close to his neck.

"He is not a friend," spat the woman with the knife. She was young, dark-haired, and far too thin. "He is Rankovyy, Baba Yaga's cursed General Dawn, and he has stolen our children."

The parade ranks of little *pestykk*. The miniature gray uniforms. The choices and the childhood that had been ripped from them.

"Baba Yaga stole your children," I said, my hands still up, palms open. "Aleksei did not know what she would demand when he accepted his post."

The women murmured among themselves, restive. "Ignorance is no excuse," snarled their leader.

"No." I shook my head violently. "No, it's not. It's all despicable."

"Selah . . ." Aleksei's voice shook.

I shot him a glance. *Shut up.*

"But he's one of us now," I said. "We've been looking for you. We want to give you back your children. We want to help you take back your city—Aleksei, too."

"Lies," the Rusalka woman hissed.

The women's whispers grew louder. My pulse spiked.

"He is the *prins* of Norge and she is the *prinsessa* of Varsinais-Suomi, and we are prisoners!" I gestured wildly at my friends, my voice rising with my panic. "We hate this place! Please, please let us help you!"

"What?" The woman scowled. The mothers were confused, their brows furrowing.

I had tried to explain too much. I was losing them. My heart dropped.

And slowly, slowly, so did their weapons.

The women were distracted, exchanging baffled glances and whispered words, and Torden and Aleksei knew one another—knew how to speak without speaking, knew what the other would do in a match before he did it.

In a single burst, the boys broke away from the Rusalki and rushed to Anya and Cobie and me. "Please let us help you," I said to the women once more.

Safe at my side, Torden lifted his gun again, grimacing, but I doubted he would use it on these women, even to defend himself.

I knew he was wishing for Mjolnir tonight.

If I have to break another's body, I deserve at least to feel his suffering in my own arm, he had said. *I think the powerful would love less the fruits of violence if they had to deal it out by hand.*

Besides, these women were not the powerful. They were the broken. The suffering. They had lost too much already.

"We will *never* accept help from you. We will hate you forever," their spokeswoman raged, tears in her eyes. She nodded at Aleksei; a thin red cut ran across his neck, and blood dripped down his cheek from a row of jagged scratches. "Look at your scars and remember that."

Torden fired a shot at the stones well above their heads, and when the women ducked and scattered, we ran.

My heart was sick. I hated to leave the Rusalki behind in this city of death.

And yet—I'd tried and failed. What else could I do? Who was I to think I could aid them in this war they'd waged so fiercely for who knew how long? What place was it of mine to think I could help them find justice for all they'd lost?

On and on I ran after the others, my heart and my breathing growing ragged, until we came to a house near the edge of town. We raced inside and slammed the door behind us.

All was dark within, the only sounds our footsteps on stone and our breathing.

"Anya!" Fredrik broke from the shadows, his voice cracking, and caught his sister in his arms. I hugged them both, Torden and Aleksei and Cobie with us. We bound ourselves to their shaking embrace, a cluster of limbs and torsos and cheeks traced with tears.

As I clung to my friends, I tried not to think of how I had nearly lost each of them tonight.

I tried not to think about the gun at my hip and the way it had felt in my hands.

We listened to the howls and the screams for hours, waiting for dawn. Anya would not let go of Fredrik's hand, even when she fell asleep slumped against the wall. Cobie and I kept watch at a window at the back of the house with a few of Torden's *drengs*.

I tried not to let visions of the night play in my mind.

The cruelty and selfish lust on Ivan's face. The tears in the

Rusalka's eyes. I knew they would haunt me in dark moments for years to come.

Fires burned long into the night. The city quieted as the sky lightened, but only a little. When the shattering of glass and the report of bullets had slowed, Torden gathered us all in the front room and told his *drengs* how to proceed.

I reached beneath my cap and touched the ring hidden in my hair for luck. Soon, we could wear our secrets openly, and not fear they'd put us in danger.

"Walk like a soldier," Torden whispered to me, pressing his palms into my shoulders, anchoring me to the earth. "Don't speak to anyone."

He kissed me and let out a long, shaking breath as we drew apart. Then I followed him out the front door.

Ahead of us, the *drengs* carried away the house's treasures under their arms, crowing in Yotne like feasting wolves, like sated vultures. The skulls atop the nearby gates were every color of bone. Their eyes watched me, empty and lifeless.

A dilapidated little fortress blinded the last bend in the road. A dog was chained just outside its door, fur chafed away beneath its iron collar. The skinny mutt snapped at us as we passed. I paused, wishing I could unchain it.

"Come on, Selah." Aleksei tugged at my hand, pulling me forward. But the *drengs* had stopped short ahead of us. Confusion, and then horror, swept over me.

Dawn glowed on the horizon. But Midnight waited at the gates.

55

There was no fight to be fought. No battle to be won. Midnight's secret police descended upon us like thieves in the night, wrapped iron around our wrists and ankles.

We had been so close to the edge of town. So close to freedom.

Polunoshchna dragged us back to the city's center, Anya and Cobie to my right, Fredrik to my left. Torden was behind us, with more of his men. I had lost sight of Aleksei.

Midnight singled me out, drawing close to hiss in my ear. "Did you think *nasha tsarytsya's* radio was the only one in the house?"

I had. I had rejoiced in my own luck and cleverness. But I had failed to credit Polunoshchna's experience. I had forgotten that the tsarytsya's eyes were always watching.

"You made yourself so easy to track," Midnight whispered

to me, feeding darkness into my ears. "Yourself, and that ship of yours. The *Beholder*."

I tripped over my own feet, staggered by a fresh wave of terror. "No."

"Yes," Midnight said, cruelly sweet. "What's his name? Perrault? Yes, he told me all you've been up to."

Perrault, whom I had trusted. Perrault, who had never lied to me.

Perrault, whose priority had always been saving his own skin.

The *Beholder* had come to help me, and Polunoshchna had captured it, and Perrault had behaved the way I should have known he would.

"Sweet Zolushka." Midnight chucked me under the chin hard enough that I bit my tongue. I tasted blood. "Will you still believe I lack focus when I set to questioning you later?"

I didn't answer. Baba Yaga's house drew ever closer.

The Wolves howled around us, derision in their eyes.

The tsarytsya awaited us atop her tower, as she always did. She sat back on her throne, eyes alight with curiosity, Vechirnya at her side.

"Come you here of your own accord, or are you compelled?" she asked.

The question was a mockery of our shackles. Cobie spat at her feet. One of Midnight's soldiers hit her in the temple with the butt of his gun, and she crumpled.

"Get away from her," Anya snarled, lunging forward. Another of Midnight's men seized her by the arm and jerked her cruelly back. Anya's arm was already bruised where Ivan had gripped her; now there was blood on her lip and in the gold of her hair.

Aleksei wasn't among us. My stomach dropped another few feet.

"Last night was Wolf Night," I said, trying to stop the shake in my voice. I lifted my chin. "I attempted to steal my freedom. What of it?"

It was a gamble.

I prayed only that this one would not end as my misstep in Shvartsval'd had. Baba Yaga said nothing for a long moment.

Then, as she had the night before, she began to laugh.

"Oh, Selah. What a delight you are. So many boring people around me, and you never cease to amuse." She laughed and laughed, and when she stopped, she waved a hand at the guards. "Take off their chains."

"What?" Polunoshchna screamed.

"They took flight last night. What did you take, Polunoshchna?" the tsarytsya snapped.

Midnight said nothing. She was shaking with anger. Slow and uncertain, the guards began to unshackle us.

"So endlessly dull," Baba Yaga muttered, palming her forehead. "So predictable."

Torden flexed his wrists, drawing a little closer to my side.

Baba Yaga looked up in surprise at the movement. "Oh no," she said, shaking her head. "Not the men. Take the chains off the girls, send them back downstairs. Kill the men at once."

I bit back a cry. Midnight smiled broadly.

She trained her rifle on Torden's skull. I nearly blurted his name, but Anya seized my arm, her short nails leaving red half-moons in my skin.

It wouldn't have mattered.

"Now, which one," Sunset asked, speaking for the first time, "is he here to rescue?"

Anya drew in a sharp breath, and Vechirnya laughed, planting her lean-muscled arms on her hips. "As if we could fail to recognize the son of the Shield. It has not been so long since I've seen him, myself. We journeyed to Norge to pay our respects at the death of the Shield's youngest."

Baldr's funeral. Of course. The Imperiya had been represented.

Torden had endangered himself for us, and now he would pay the price.

My stomach clenched.

"Certainly, one of these two," Polunoshchna said, stepping over Cobie's prone form and wrapping her hands around my throat and around Anya's. She dug her thumb sharply into my windpipe. I tried not to give even a flicker of a response, tried to hold back anything that might put Torden in more danger, but I began to wheeze in her grip.

Over her shoulder, I saw Aleksei skid into the throne room. His gray uniform and white bands were spotless, as clean as the bandages at his throat and on his cheek. He took in the scene we made in one keen, curious glance.

"Polunoshchna. Enough," Baba Yaga barked. "If you cannot

discern the truth at a distance of two feet, it will not be any clearer with your hands wrapped around their throats. Kill the men and be done with it."

Midnight dropped her hands, and I clutched my throat, coughing.

Again, she raised her rifle.

"Wait!" I choked. The word was out of my mouth before I could think what I would say next.

The tsarytsya met my eyes, one silver brow arched in question. My thoughts had never run so quickly.

My Odysseus had come back to me, and he was still going to die if I couldn't change the game.

If you're one step ahead of them, they still haven't caught you.

If Torden was to live, I would have to wound him.

"Well played, *moya tsarytsya*," I rasped. It hurt to speak.

She cocked her head. "And what game are we playing now, little Zolushka?"

"The same one we were always playing." I coughed, tried to feign surprise. "The game for Potomac. I concede, *moya tsarytsya*, to a worthy victor. You shall grasp the phoenix by its feathers and soon take the whole bird."

My hands were shaking. I expected her to wave me off at any moment, for gunshots to sound and blood to spatter and for my gambit to fail. For my love to be lost forever.

She did wave a hand. It said, *Continue, please.*

Torden's jaw worked, his brown eyes fixed worriedly on my face. His concern for me—always for me, never himself—ached.

I focused on the tsarytsya. I couldn't watch Torden's face while I drove a knife into his heart. And it was only my knife that would save him from her claws.

"I will marry a courtier of your choosing," I said. "I will deliver Potomac into your hands, in exchange for easier terms for my people when you reach our shores, and for the lives of my men. These *drengs*, and the *Beholder* crew you've captured," I added.

"Selah!" Anya gasped.

Elskede. Beloved. That was what Torden had called me, and now I was betraying him.

So many lives to weigh and measure. So great a chance I would be found wanting.

The tsarytsya frowned. "Why should I give you easier terms?" she asked. "Why should I spare the lives of these men? I have them, already, in my hands."

Think. Think. Think.

"Because you understand the game." I smiled, trying to keep my voice loose and confident, though my throat still felt bruised from Midnight's grip. "You understand it's easier to reap your winnings when you don't overturn the board merely to spite the rest of the players." I cast a significant glance at Midnight, whose gun was still sighted between Torden's eyes. The raw hurt in them was palpable. I swallowed painfully and forced myself to look away. "I can give you Potomac cleanly, and lose you none of its pieces. You're not so petty that you'd cast away a useful resource."

I was mixing metaphors and madly insulting Polunoshchna

and I was desperately afraid I was about to piss myself with fear. But I schooled my face.

Behind the tsarytsya, Aleksei gave me a single sharp nod.

"I've seen how absolute your power is, *moya tsarytsya*." I took one, two steps through the cluster of guards, not watching Torden or Midnight but keeping that gun—the *gun*—in my periphery, watching it lower second by second in tandem with Polunoshchna's jaw. "I know you will eventually reach Arbor Hall, and I want to make sure those dear to me are safe."

I put a hand on Torden's shoulder. "*All* those dear to me."

"Ah." Victory lit the tsarytsya's eyes.

"He's a romantic. Even when his father ordered him to stay, he came anyway," I said quietly. "It was a grand but foolish gesture."

Torden bit his lip. The agony and betrayal on his face was enough to tear me apart.

This was the only way to protect him.

Think. *Think.*

I tried to recapture the feeling I'd carried the night I'd treated with Gretel, the stars above and a cadre of reckless, determined princesses at my back.

The uniform of the Imperiya was a far cry from the dress of black armor I'd worn, the cap slipping off my hair a long way from a tiara. Instead of kohl on my eyes, I had burns on my fingers and ashes on my face.

But I was still that girl.

I was Cobie's best friend and Anya's sister and friend to the Shvartsval'd *freinnen*. I was strong, and I was sharp, and I would do what I had to do for the ones I loved.

"You'll get no ransom from Alfödr for his return." I kept my voice as even as I could. "But if you spare his life, I'll marry someone of your choosing."

"Selah." Torden's voice cracked.

Elskede.

"I was never going to marry for love anyway, Grandmother Wolf," I told the tsarytsya with a shrug. "I might as well be the one doing the bargaining, instead of my stepmother."

A crowd was gathering around Baba Yaga, more of her courtiers and soldiers. I met Aleksei's eyes where he stood behind them.

"Please," Polunoshchna howled. "Please let me shoot her. Please let me shoot all of them."

Baba Yaga said nothing. I thought of the Rusalki I'd tried to persuade the night before, how I'd overexplained myself and lost their interest, and my panic spiked. "You need me if you're to take Potomac cleanly," I said, fearing even as I spoke that I was losing, had already lost, would lose them all. "You—"

"Don't hurt her," Aleksei burst out.

I lifted my eyes, and Baba Yaga turned. But not before I saw the abject delight on her face.

"Don't hurt her," Aleksei said again.

"Aleksei," she crooned. "*Moy Rankovyy.* What concern is she of yours?"

"None." But Aleksei stepped toward me, as if unaware he was moving.

Sunset rubbed tiredly at her eyes. "I saw them holding

hands the first time she played with us."

I fought a grim smile. *Thank you, Sunset.*

Torden's broad chest heaved. "Aleksei?" One more word, his voice still broken.

Suddenly, despite the tension in the air, Aleksei was easy, relaxed. "Vechirnya is correct, *moya tsarytsya.*" He took me in a thin, confident embrace, and I softened against him. "I loved Selah at Asgard, and I love her still."

It was an absurd falsehood. But I would gladly pretend to feel at home in Aleksei's arms. Because I cared more for Torden's life than for his feelings. I would sacrifice his heart and mine, and he would live.

I steeled myself, produced the ring from the knot of my hair. Aleksei slid it onto my right-hand ring finger and kissed my hand. His lips were cold, his black eyes lit with tentative affection, his gestures loose and assured.

"Very well," the tsarytsya said. She straightened and looked from me to Torden to Aleksei. "Seneschal-elect, the princeling's life shall be spared."

I knew I ought to feel relief. Torden and the *drengs* and the *Beholder* crew, wherever they were, would live. But all I felt were Aleksei's cold arms around my waist.

Polunoshchna screamed and threw her fist against the stone wall.

"And you, my Rankovyy, my Bright Dawn." Baba Yaga took Aleksei's hand, her eyes greedy. "Now that I know your heart, you shall marry our little ash-girl three days hence."

And she would own us forever.

56

Blood was everywhere. Blood and jewels and coins and broken stone.

I scrubbed it away with Midnight crowing over me. She went on and on about Perrault in her prisons, Perrault betraying me. She never mentioned any of the others.

Did they still live? Were Torden and his *drengs* suffering? I would push for their immediate release when it was time to serve the tsarytsya the next day; Baba Yaga was sleeping off her long, bloody night and was not to be disturbed.

Aleksei came to the kitchens that night as Anya and Cobie and I were scrubbing the blood off our hands and knees. "Well done," he said. I nodded, and sat before the oven.

The tsarytsya had no need to marry me to anyone; I'd known this. I had counted on amusing her by my brashness, and by insulting Midnight. I'd also counted on her believing she'd found a way to manipulate Aleksei.

I had thought carefully, and very, very quickly.

I had had three aims with my plea.

The first had been to tell the tsarytsya that I was ignorant. She would never reach Potomac's shores; Sunset's armies were spread impossibly thin as it was. But I'd indicated I didn't know that and given her an opportunity to preen in front of her people to boot.

The second had been to align myself with her selfishness—to show her I cared only for Potomac, as she cared only for Yotunkheym.

The third had been to allay her fears that Norge was involved. If Torden was here for me, without Konge Alfödr's permission, it meant he wasn't here to do reconnaissance; he represented no threat from the Shield.

I'd feared she would smell my deceit.

Still, the last piece of my plan had been the most essential. I was lucky Aleksei was such a talented liar. I'd known he was scheming alongside me as soon as he relaxed at my side.

Like the jade-green snake tattooed around his upper arm, he'd shed his skin again.

"You knew she wouldn't be able to resist, if she thought she'd found my weakness," Aleksei said, flopping down on the hearth. "You led her to think I loved you."

I shrugged dully. "I didn't have anything she wanted. I had to make her think marrying us would allow her to manipulate you."

I'd had nothing to bargain with. But I'd turned out my pockets and bought Torden's safety with what little I found.

"Thank God Gretel didn't send in the resistance," I said. "It would've just been more lives lost. More people captured."

Anya stared into the oven. "Do we know where she's keeping the boys?"

"She's trying to conscript them, for the moment," said Aleksei.

"The more fool she," Anya said bitterly. Cobie nodded.

Aleksei scratched the back of his neck. "You could try to contact Gretel now that Wolf Night's past," he suggested.

Cobie shook her head. "We'll never be allowed in her rooms again."

"And besides," I said, "Midnight's secret police have radios. They're listening in all the time. Midnight told me."

"Would've been smarter if she hadn't." Cobie rolled her eyes.

"I know," I agreed. "I might have tried again, but she wanted to get a dig in."

Midnight and her shortsightedness. She would sacrifice a lead without a second thought, all for a moment's gratification. She would never learn focus.

An idea began to buzz low and insistent in my veins.

"What we need," I said, "is someone capable of seeing past the end of their own nose. Someone who actually cares what happens to this city. Midnight is petty; that's her undoing."

Cobie frowned. "Selah, you're speaking in riddles."

I swallowed hard. "We need the Rusalki."

There was silence in the kitchen. Aleksei stared at me, looking tired enough to tip over.

Anya left the hearth and began to pace. "You heard what

they said. They will hate Aleksei and the rest of us forever. They will never work with us."

"They don't *care* about us. Not really. That's the thing." I shook my head.

I thought again of Momma. She'd been dogged, devoted. She'd taught me and disciplined me and loved me with everything she had.

The Rusalki wanted their children. If they had to pull the city down with their bare hands to take them, I believed they'd do it. Who they allied with was irrelevant as long as their children were safe when nothing was left of the Mortar but rubble.

"Did you not see the knife at Aleksei's throat?" Cobie demanded. "They'll kill him!"

"We can wait," Aleksei said urgently. "We can bide our time. Marry, watch, wait for a chance to get ourselves out."

I fought my cringe at the word *marry*. "Except Baba Yaga could change her mind at any time and kill all of us," I fired back. "Torden, the *drengs*, the *Beholder* crew."

Anya and Cobie both tensed.

It was cruel of me to press on their worries—for Skop, for Will. But we couldn't forget that their lives hung in the balance of our choices.

"We cannot trust her," I insisted. "She's a Wolf and she's made it clear that rules—hers and everyone else's—are made to be broken. How long is the tsarytsya going to wait, watching her armies dwindle, before she does something worse?"

Anya hesitated. "We don't know how to find them."

"But they know what they want," I said. "And one of us

managed to keep his hands clean last night." I fixed Aleksei with a stare.

He sat back, shaking his head. "I can't go to those women. I can't. They won't—"

"You have to," I bit out. "Aleksei, you're the only one of us left. If you don't, we will be married in three days and Cobie and Anya will be trapped here forever and Baba Yaga will get her claws into your home and mine."

Aleksei said nothing for a long time. Then he looked up at me, tears in his eyes. "The Rusalki won't speak to me. The tsarytsya stole their children. And I stole their childhood, because she told me to, and I was a coward."

"Tell them your plan," Anya said. "Tell them how you're going to help them get their children back. How if they and the Vodyanoi and the Leshii take Stupka-Zamok, they can take their sons and daughters home, to the wild or elsewhere in the city or wherever they want."

"Do we *have* a plan?" Cobie interjected.

"The wedding!" Anya said, decisive. "The maids have been talking. It's going to be a massive affair. People will be distracted and the city will be swarming again."

The wedding. *My* wedding.

I had set out in search of that day, had left my home and my father behind to quest for it, had marked the days in ink and ash as I waited for it to come. And now that it was near, I wished I could scrub it out of existence, like blood off stones.

Aleksei sat on the hearth and cried in silence. With his head bowed and his shoulders shaking, he looked little older than one of the children in his ranks.

When he was finished, he lifted his head, tears streaking his face. "I sold my soul," he said.

"So help these women." I put my hands on his shoulders. "And buy it back."

57

It took two days to clean the castle of Zatemnennya's filth. I was removed to my new rooms the next morning. The day before my wedding.

She was waiting for me when I arrived, standing over a trunk full of gray garments. A bridal trousseau the color of ashes, of a life burned to the ground. The tsarytsya spread her arms wide, showing me all her teeth in a smile. "What do you think?"

"I'd never seen myself in gray," I said as smoothly as I could. "Then again, I'd never seen my own claws for what they were."

To marry Torden, I would've worn green, or gold. But that day would never come.

I felt toothless. Clawless. My chest ached from the knife I'd driven into his heart.

Baba Yaga's smile only grew more ferocious. "Delightful."

"Will Aleksei be admitted to my chambers tonight?" I cast my eyes down, clasped my hands.

She arched her brows. "Do you wish him to be?"

With Anya and Cobie in the basement, so many floors away, I'd be glad of the company. "It might ease tensions tomorrow." I bit my lip, tried to look like a blushing bride.

The tsarytsya liked me blunt, forceful; I knew this girlish, timid version of me wouldn't impress her. But I wouldn't know how to feign confidence about a night alone with a boy—not even for Baba Yaga.

"As you will." The tsarytsya waved a hand, disinterested. Then she looked at me sidelong. "I wish to speak to you of other things."

The tsarytsya leaned near to me, whispering as though she had a secret. My stomach twisted. "I know that you despise my General Midnight, my Polunoshchna."

I smoothed my face. "I serve Polunoshchna as I serve Vechirnya, as I serve Rankovyy, as I serve you, *moya tsarytsya*."

She laughed wearily. "Oh, my little Zolushka. I may not be young anymore, but my eyes are still good. You are quite the pretender, but I see. I see."

The Baba Yaga of whispers and wild rumors was famed not for her eyes but for her nose, keen enough to scent out Bears and Wolves and Lambs alike. Could she smell me for the liar I was?

"I will marry you to my General Bright Dawn," she said softly. "And someday, after me, you will be tsarytsya."

The room rang with my silence. "Surely, *moya tsarytsya*," I finally said, "you jest."

But her face did not collapse into amusement. Grandmother Wolf waited, expectant.

"Why?" I demanded.

"Because I see myself in you." Baba Yaga bared her teeth in a smile. "I have not always felt like mistress of my own destiny. I took it, as you have taken yours."

I moved away from her slowly, backing against the fireplace. The ashes on the hearth were soft beneath my bare feet. "What do you mean?"

"I was captured once, as well." Baba Yaga's voice was low and sweet. "Held hostage for a week. Scared for my life. And I *did* escape. But that was long ago, before I even became headwoman." She paused. "Back when they called me Vasylysa."

I froze, then shook myself. No. She—

"You?" I breathed. "Your—your name is Vasylysa, too?"

It was a common name, I knew. Common as Ivan.

"*Too?* That's what they called me." She fingered the silver-gray thread on my wedding gown, smiling absently. "Vasylysa the Beautiful. Before they called me Grandmother Wolf."

"But you told me—that serving girl—" I broke off, unable to speak.

"The girl?" She frowned.

"The girl who was cleaning the fireplace." My voice grew shrill. "The girl I spoke up for. The reason you acknowledged me in the first place. You called her Vasylysa."

She waved a hand. "I don't remember her. I remember you lifting your chin in Midnight's face, speaking to her with no fear."

My mind reeled. I tried to focus, to remember everything the tsarytsya had said about Vasylysa's banishment, Vasylysa's testing.

"Selah!" The tsarytsya snapped. She was close to my face, her expression annoyed. "Forget about serving girls and fire-places. Forget about her. She is nobody. She is not like you and I."

Nobody.

I had called myself nobody when I first met Polunoshchna. But Baba Yaga had searched me out. She had even broken her own rule to lure me into the open, had told her generals to speak English, had seated me at her table to see what I would do if she gave me teeth and claws.

My mouth was dry. "And we're . . . ?" I asked.

"We are the stepdaughters. We are the girls who become wolves because no one will feed us like lambs. We are the girls in the stories, and the world is ours." The tsarytsya's papery-skinned hands clenched into fists. "We take what we will, and it belongs to us by right. We are wolves and queens and the moon, and our people love us. That is where the others belong in the stories: in the crowds, watching us from illuminated edges."

Baba Yaga had been pacing the room, chin lifted, eyes bright. Now she stopped, her gaze earnest on me. "That is why most of them should not read the stories, little Selah. The songs and the paintings and the stories make them think they are hero-ines and heroes. They put false visions into their minds."

It was brutal. Selfish. Hideous.

She had built herself a high, horrible tower, and she looked down on the world from above, and she believed herself greater than it all. "What happened to Vasylysa?" I asked, hardly able to breathe.

"I killed the captain who had captured me on the border in Medved," the tsarytsya said. "I rode back to my father's village and to my stepmother's garden and salted every square inch of the earth she tended more carefully than she had ever tended to me. And then I turned her and my stepsisters out and took back my house."

"And after that?" I choked out.

"I took my spoils to every impoverished home in our village. And then I took my revenge. On the Bear, and on everyone else who had been content to let us starve." Baba Yaga's brown eyes shone with terrible fire, lit aflame by the memory.

I pressed my lips together, terrified, desperate to stroke her ego and keep her calm. "And now you reign over all."

"And you will, after me. I want Rankovyy managed, and I want Polunoshchna to doubt herself at every turn. It makes her work harder." She winked at me.

Baba Yaga had escaped the monsters only to become a monster herself.

"I'm not like you," I whispered hoarsely. "I don't think I'm like you."

I did not want her favor, or her throne. The tsarytsya was wholly repulsive.

And yet, some part of me wished to know whether she saw a wolf or a lamb before her.

"You are the stepdaughter who was turned out, as I was," she said, fixing me with her gaze. "You are the prisoner who traveled barefoot across thrice-nine lands to come to the thrice-tenth kingdom, and arrived bleeding but upright on my doorstep. You are the girl who hung on by her fingernails, ash on her face as the world burned around her, and survived."

"No." I shook my head, ever so slightly. "I survived because I had friends to love and protect me."

"You survived because you had the *grit* to do so." Her tone was final. "And if you can survive, you can rule. If you will let me teach you, I will make you heir in the stead of the children I never wanted."

My heart was a block of ice. I was cold with horror at the glimpse I'd gotten inside her brutal mind.

I should have shut my mouth. I should have let her leave when she turned to go.

"*Moya tsarytsya,*" I called. She looked back at me. "What makes the girl Vasylysa any different from the girls in your cellar? If you escaped, and fought back, what makes you think someone else won't do the same?"

I posed the question as a rhetorical. As a fascinating thought game I wanted her to play with me. But I was telling her future. It was the same *verdammt* story, over and over again.

Alessandra. Vasylysa's stepmother. Baba Yaga herself. They were sisters in arms, guilty of hurting the Vasylysas of the world. Culpable for all the girls they had wounded and embittered.

Those girls would get their revenge. And the architects of their suffering would have only themselves to blame.

"Because there *are* none like me, and few enough like you," Baba Yaga said to me from the doorway. "We, little Zolushka, are the end of the story."

* * *

Aleksei came to me in the dark.

"Selah?" he whispered though the just-open door.

I tugged him inside. "Come in." Aleksei winked at the guard outside the door. I wrinkled my nose at him. "Oh, ew."

"You're right, I should've let him think we were plotting the demise of his empress and the end of the world as he knows it," Aleksei countered.

"Shut up." I pulled him toward the bed, sitting cross-legged on its edge. He bounced twice on the mattress before he settled, crossing his long, bony legs. Two candles flickered in sconces on the wall. "What happened today?"

Aleksei held up his index finger. "I found Torden, Fredrik, and the rest of the *drengs*." His mouth was a tight line. "They're alive."

I exhaled. Alive would have to be enough for now.

"And the *Beholder*'s crew?" I asked.

"Nothing." His voice was chagrined. My heart sank. "I searched high and low for them. Midnight's keeping her cards close to her chest. But I won't give up," Aleksei added quickly.

I bit my lip and nodded. "What else?"

Aleksei held up a second finger. "I found the mothers," he said. "The Rusalki."

"You did? How?" I exclaimed.

"They couldn't keep away," Aleksei said, smiling grimly. "Actually, I wouldn't have seen them at all, but a little girl started waving at nothing beyond the edge of the training ground, and my guards apprehended a few of them."

I leaned forward. "And?"

"And I recognized some of them. So when we were alone, I used the call sign from Shvartsval'd you taught me. I tried to reason with them, explained what we wanted to do." Aleksei paused. "And they spat in my face."

"They *what?*"

"They called me a thief. They called me a monster. A barbarian." Aleksei tried to smile. "It got very tiresome, mostly because they were entirely correct. But I tried, Selah. I tried to tell them."

"I know you did."

We are the girls in the stories, and the world is ours.

The tsarytsya was wrong.

This was not her world. Lands and worlds and stories belonged to everyone.

And Yotunkheym belonged to its mothers. Its children. Its cooks and its maids, its servants and its lambs, and the people who loved its wilds and its cities alike.

I hoped so badly not to leave it to the wolves.

"Can you remember anything about them?" I put a hand on his arm. "How many were they?"

He steepled his skinny fingers, thinking. "There were nine of them, not all Rusalki. Six women, three men, eight with Yotne accents. One with an English accent, actually."

"English?" I blinked at him. "Are you sure?"

"Absolutely. I couldn't forget a girl like that. Dark hair and pale skin." Aleksei smiled. "And it was the strangest thing. She had fistfuls of yellow flowers stuck in her pockets."

58

I had imagined my wedding day a hundred times. It was impossible not to, given the reason Alessandra had sent me abroad. I'd pictured it all so clearly—a gown, Daddy and Godmother Althea, a priest. Rings at Saint Christopher's, candles in Arbor Hall.

In Stupka-Zamok, my wedding day meant no family, none of the rites of my religion. It meant dressing alone in the gown Baba Yaga had supplied, with its sheer gunmetal chiffon layers, its silver embroidery. It was a dress for an ash-girl.

It meant waking to Aleksei, his thin frame curled up across a pile of pillows, his hair a shock of black against the sheets.

We had both come of our own accord, for our own reasons, and seen and done and learned hard things.

Aleksei had found that this place was not who he was. And I had learned that I could be sharp, and fierce, without betraying the person I wanted to be.

While Aleksei dressed, I prayed the Rosary. My fingers longed for the comfort of my old prayer beads or the knotted fabric of my makeshift version—abandoned now in the cellar closet—but even without them, I knew the sequence of prayers, etched into my mind by years of quiet meditation.

When I was done, I offered my own requests.

I prayed for Torden and the *Beholder* crew, locked away, that their guards would not harm them. I prayed that the Rusalki would forgive Aleksei for what he had done, and that we could restore their children to safety. And I prayed for the servants and the children and my friends and the other innocents inside this tower, that the end of the day would find them safe and whole, no matter what came to pass.

A knock sounded at our door. Aleksei opened it and greeted our guards.

They led us upstairs—up, up, up we climbed, to the very top floor, Aleksei's hand on my back—and beyond.

On the roof of Stupka-Zamok, fourteen floors above the ground, the tsarytsya waited for us. And below, all the city stood watch.

Men and women pushed and shoved for a better view on one side, and on another the little *pestykk* waited in their ranks. Their voices rose like a cold wave as I faced my groom.

I had pictured so many faces across from me, so many hands reaching for mine on this day.

Peter, with his bright laugh and his bright eyes and the gap between his teeth.

403

Bear, wry and smiling, a flower in his hands.

Torden, red-haired, red-bearded, steady and kind. His ring sat on my right hand, even now, but today I would swear on its rose-gold band to be faithful to someone else.

I'd never pictured facing Aleksei, gray-uniformed, his dark hair tied back with white. Kohl smudged around his eyes was the only nod to the occasion.

Aleksei. My sometime enemy, sometime ally, now friend. Would I have to kiss him at the ceremony's end? I tried to envision it, tried to imagine being his wife. It felt like visualizing myself beside King Constantine in England: impossible. My mind rejected it.

I looked around, hoping despite myself that the Rusalki were already here, waiting to fight. But besides Aleksei, I saw only enemies; we stood before Baba Yaga, with Sunset and Midnight at her sides. Polunoshchna was watching my face, trying to decide if I had won today or if she had.

"Bow, Zolushka," Baba Yaga said softly.

I bent, and the tsarytsya produced a crown from a cushion. Its arching sides and its base were crusted with diamonds, emeralds, and pearls, and it sat heavy on my head. A great murmur went up from the crowd.

"The Württemberg Crown," she said lightly. "It looks well on you." The tsarytsya's own crown was as grand as mine, gold and red velvet and decked with two-headed birds of prey.

Polunoshchna looked murderous at this. But I wasn't happy, either.

I was never born to wear a crown. And I did not want this

stolen piece of finery that told the world I was heir to Grandmother Wolf, empress of the mortar and pestle and her armies of devouring teeth.

"Come you here of your own accord, Seneschal-elect Selah of Potomac?" she asked, her voice bubbling like a cauldron.

They were not the vows I had dreamed of. They were the nursery rhyme I had feared since childhood.

I ransacked the crowd with my gaze, searching, my vision blurring, pleading with the faces I saw to be the ones I longed for. But there was no one.

"Selah," Aleksei whispered, reaching for my hands. He looked sorry, so sorry.

I had done my best to survive, had hoped to be rescued, had tried to escape. I had bargained to protect Torden, had schemed to deliver the city into the hands of those to whom it belonged.

Torden's life was enough. I would marry Aleksei, and be grateful his brother would live.

There was nothing to be done but do this.

"Yes," I answered Baba Yaga, certain as the stone beneath us.

"Rankovyy, come you here of your own accord?"

"Yes," Aleksei said simply.

The tsarytsya turned again to me. "Will you be wife to this man?"

I nodded. My throat was tight.

Again, again, my eyes again combed the crowd for the Rusalki. But they were nowhere to be seen. I was all that stood between the Wolves and Torden.

How I wished he were standing across from me today. How I wished I were holding his hands instead, broad and warm. Aleksei's fingers were cold as bones in mine.

The tsarytsya raised a stone-gray eyebrow. "The word, Seneschal-elect."

"Yes." I choked it out, trying to laugh, as if I were merely nervous and not on the brink of collapse. "Yes."

Aleksei echoed my vow when it was his turn.

Baba Yaga turned one last time on me. "As a Wolf of the Imperiya Yotne, will you honor the pack in all your doings, sparing not even your mate, should its hunger require he be sacrificed?"

I drew back ever so slightly. But I shouldn't have been surprised. This marriage wasn't about Aleksei and me. It was about the tsarytsya, like everything else in her world.

I didn't blame the Rusalki for not coming. I didn't blame the Leshii and the Vodyanoi for abandoning Aleksei and me to our destruction.

"Yes," I said for the third time, sealing my fate.

I stared down at the crowd, studied their curious faces, their squinting eyes.

I'd rolled the dice, played the tsarytsya for the city, and lost. I'd failed every one of these people.

Then, suddenly, at the edge of the gray slush of the crowd, I spotted a face. A face I knew.

I drew in a low, sharp breath.

Homer.

He wore a gray uniform but I would have recognized his

ruddy face and iron hair and iron eyes anywhere. His arms were crossed over his barrel chest.

I thought he'd been captured. But there he was. My knees threatened to buckle.

Perrault pressed in beside him, slipping from a nearby alley. His clothes were plain and his hair was cropped close to his skull, but he was a fox among Wolves, as sure as I lived.

He wasn't in prison.

And if he had not been captured, he hadn't betrayed me. Polunoshchna was a liar.

Perrault stood outside Baba Yaga's tower, waiting for it to turn and face him.

I didn't see Lang. But Yu stood at Perrault's side.

One face. Then another.

Bear. The prince of England, who had broken my heart by accident. His blue eyes were burned into my memory.

And another.

The girl—a girl whose name I did not know, but who had fought alongside Bear the day he defeated the Duke of Cornwall. Aleksei had just spoken with her.

Her breast pocket was stuffed with yellow cowslips.

My eyes raked the crowds, frantic. Dozens of women slowly drew near, forming rows close—so, so very close—behind the ranks of the little *pestykk*.

I turned to Aleksei, my eyes wide.

And then the explosions began.

59

I staggered and fell, my ears ringing, and Aleksei threw his narrow body over mine. When the earth stopped shaking, I raised my head.

The air was full of smoke. I choked on it, lungs aching. A few feet away, the tsarytsya lay prone, blood trickling from her temple. Midnight was out cold.

Aleksei hauled me up and pushed me toward the door in the roof that would take me downstairs. "Go." There was more strength in his skinny arms than I would have guessed.

I glanced back. Sunset was coughing, pushing herself to stand, bloody palms leaving red prints on her knees. "What are you going to do?"

Aleksei pushed me toward the door again. "Follow you."

We had to shove before it gave; the explosions had rocked the frame of the building. I stumbled through the door and raced down the stairs, gray uniforms jostling past, not seeing or caring who I was in their rush to get out. All around me people shouted, wailed, coughed in the smoke, pressing and pushing on the narrow iron stairs.

I had foreseen this. I had foreseen what a hellscape this tower would be, if Baba Yaga's enemies ever breached her gates.

I hadn't imagined that I'd be inside when it happened.

Two floors down, someone pushed a man over the railing. He fell the remaining ten stories and struck the flagstones with a sound that made me sick.

Somehow, Aleksei kept a level head through it all, pushing ahead of me and seizing my wrist with his skinny fingers. He threaded through the crowds like a needle through fabric, weaving and winding and dragging me along behind him. My head spun and the stairs creaked and I stumbled more than once, but Aleksei never let me go, never lost his cool.

Finally, we reached the bottom floor. Aleksei shoved me toward the front door as he raced toward the basement. "Go!" he screamed over his shoulder. "I'll find Cobie and Anya."

I watched his retreating back, frozen in place. And then the explosions began again.

A rumble, and a scrape, and a stone crashed from the ceiling. It smashed to the foyer floor and pinned a man beneath it.

My stomach lurched at all the blood. Smoke rose, thick and heady, around us.

The crowd swam, bodies pressing, nails scratching. Someone pushed me, and my knees hit stone; an elbow hit my back, and I lay flat on the floor. Heavy boots trampled my shoulder and arm.

I was going to die here, as surely as if the tsarytsya herself had ordered it. Blood flowed from my mouth, from my cheek, from my knees. A screaming pain wrenched through my ribs.

But when I looked up, there she was.

Dark hair spilled over Wash's shoulders, and blood poured from a cut on her forehead. "Selah! What are you doing here?" She tugged me close to the wall, out of the crowd.

"I fell." Tears stung my eyes.

"No. No! Do not cry! Stand!" Wash bent and helped me up; blood dripped from her wound.

I held as tight to her as I could, our backs against the stone wall, our shoulders pressed together. The foyer was a churning sea of bodies. The air stank of fear.

Wash prayed under her breath, and I did the same.

Please, God.

Her eyes were huge on the door and her hand was tight on mine. She said something in Yotne, then shook her head, searching for the word in English. But she glanced up at the ceiling, and I knew what she meant. We had to get out before the whole place came down around us.

Wash held up a hand, five fingers. Dragged in a long, shuddering breath.

Four fingers. She wiped the blood pooling at her temple with the back of her hand.

Another breath. The crash of rock not far away.

Three fingers, an arm around my waist.

Two. My arm around hers. *Please God please God please—*

One.

We pushed off the wall, heads down.

We drove toward the door, a two-woman battering ram. Wash's breath grated through her teeth, and I let out a guttural howl, more wolf than any Wolf in Baba Yaga's house.

We burst into the battle raging outside.

60

I had not known stone could burn. Chunks of it smoldered all over the courtyard.

Fire and brimstone and blood in the air and bodies on the ground. It felt like the end of the world.

Gray uniforms everywhere were stained with red. Knives and swords and guns sang violently in the smoke. Wash and I clung to each other, panting, unsure what to do.

The little *pestykk* were everywhere.

No, not little *pestykk*. They were children. Innocents, caught in the claws of a tyrant. Someone had to get them out.

I turned, searching for someone to tell, someone who could save them, there had to be someone—and nearly ran into her. The Sidhe girl with dark hair and a pocket full of yellow flowers.

"The children!" I shouted. I could hardly hear my own voice above the din.

She seized my shoulders and turned me toward a pack of women—the Rusalki, fighting for their children's lives. Their hair flew and their knives sliced through the air and they wept as they fought.

"The mothers are taking them!" she shouted to Wash and me, her voice straining, English accent just barely detectible above the furor. "The Rusalki are taking the children to the Leshii camp in the forest!"

The mothers pushed the children toward the edge of town, hurrying them toward the gates and beyond, and away they ran on little legs. *Go*, I saw one Rusalka woman say to another. She sheathed her knife, swung a small girl over one shoulder, hitched her pack onto the other, and sprinted for the wild beyond the wall.

Fur die Freiheit.

Fur die Wildnis.

I'd never seen such fierceness. I'd never seen warriors like them.

Not far behind, I saw Vasylysa—or, rather, the girl I'd known as Vasylysa. I didn't know her real name. She and a few other maids were running. Wash chewed her cuticle, staring after the backs of the women she'd protected.

I didn't know if they were headed to the Leshii camp or somewhere else. I bid the girl Godspeed in my heart and hoped she'd be safe, wherever she ran.

"Come on." The English girl took me by the elbow, dragging me away from the tower. I wanted to follow her—we had to get Wash out. But I twisted against her grip. "My friends,"

I shouted. "I need to find them!"

"Who are your friends?" she asked. "Who are you looking for?"

"Cobie!" I shouted. "Anya! Aleksei!"

Another explosion rang out, and I wheeled. Baba Yaga's spindly house was in flames, its dozens of eyes clouded with smoke.

But suddenly, I could see my friends all around me.

Torden and his *drengs* fought to one side of the courtyard. Bear and his knights—Veery and Kay and the rest—were nearby, swords humming and words flying between them.

Torden struck again and again, finally able to use Mjolnir in the open, the hammer like lightning in his grip. Sweat poured down his forehead as he fought, dealing out by hand the violence he took such pains to avoid.

The Rusalki were half gone, but others clad in green and gold and blue and white fought the soldiers in gray. And the *Beholder*'s crew were all around me. Still no sign of Lang, but— Yu and Homer. Skop. Vishnu. Basile. And Cobie and Anya.

The girls raced to my side, Anya clinging to Skop. "Wash needs care!" I shouted. Blood was still flowing freely from the cut on her head.

"Yu!" Skop bellowed into the mob, and the doctor raced over. He and Cobie helped Wash out of the courtyard, toward the gates. I cast a desperate glance at the battle, not wanting to join it but fearing for those I left behind. I saw more faces I knew every moment.

"Selah." Anya took me by the arm, turned me to face her.

"You're bleeding. You aren't a soldier. There's nothing you can do." She cupped my face. "Let's go home."

Home.

I began to shake.

I followed Anya past the ditch the rebels had dug as a firebreak at the edge of the city. Past Stupka-Zamok's walls. Past the empty-eyed skulls watching from the gates, their backs turned on the witch queen whose castle burned behind them.

I was going home.

61

I had seen a dozen rivers, a score of seas, a thousand miles of ocean since I had first set foot aboard the *Beholder*.

None of them had made my heart race like the sun on the river outside Stupka-Zamok's walls.

My blood stuttered. And despite the aching in my lungs, I began to run.

I raced downhill, the river surging close to me, the smoke starting to clear as I neared the water. And then I saw her through the haze of gray.

My ship. Her figurehead, beautiful and dangerous and persistent despite the wear of salt and time.

Polunoshchna had led me to believe the *Beholder* was taken. But she was waiting for me, arms wide and eyes full of light.

I stopped, hands on my knees, panting, as Skop and Yu helped Wash up the gangplank. Yu asked questions, eyes gentle, carefully assessing the gash on her head.

The crew emerged slowly, then rushed toward us. Andersen, Will, J.J., Yasumaro, Jeanne—everyone who hadn't joined the fray outside Baba Yaga's house, and those who had repaired to the ship's safety when the battle began. I embraced each of them in turn, my heart leaping every time a new old face appeared.

When Perrault ran out of the galley, I walked into his arms, and we clung to each other.

He wasn't a traitor. I cursed every doubt that had made me fear he was.

"You found the Sidhe?" I asked him when I could speak.

He nodded. "Constantine would not send fighters. But Prince Arthur came, and brought . . . an alternative."

I wet my lips. "And you were—never in prison?" I asked. Perhaps he had been captured—perhaps he'd simply escaped. Perrault did look different; he'd shed fine clothes for a gray uniform, his hair was cut short, and he looked soberer than I remembered.

"Prison?" A flash of the old Perrault appeared, scandalized. And despite everything, I gave a weary laugh.

"We should go farther downriver," Yu urged. "We need to get Selah out of here." But the thought of retreat rankled.

"She's back?" Lang's voice floated up the gangplank.

I whipped around, and there he was. Tanned face, ink-stained hands, dark eyes staring wildly around. Relief flooded his face like paper catching fire when he saw me, and he opened his arms as if to wrap me in them.

He stopped short at the look on my face.

"Where were you?" I asked.

Lang hadn't been in the courtyard outside Stupka-Zamok. I hadn't seen him anywhere. I hadn't realized until that moment how badly it hurt that everyone had been there but him.

"Organizing the Leshii camp. They were in chaos, the Vodyanoi, the Leshii, the Rusalki, the Sidhe, Bear's knights. We got the *drengs* out and were getting ready for the children." Lang's eyes were fixed on me, his voice distracted, as if he were only vaguely aware that he was speaking.

"I understand," I finally said. My voice cracked. "I've been trying to coordinate my own rescue from inside the tsary-tsya's house. So. I can imagine the administrative challenge you must've faced."

Slowly, he came closer. "You're angry." Lang's eyes were weary as they assessed my burns, my ripped wedding gown, the bruises blooming on my arms. Too late.

I swallowed painfully. This near, he smelled like salt and ink.

It was so good to see him. I was so angry at him. I hated that this moment had gone sour.

"No one else could've done it?" I whispered. "The camp? No one could've handled it but you?"

"The place was in chaos," Lang said again, sounding confused.

"I see."

He scrubbed a hand over his cheek and his temple. "I wanted it to go perfectly." His tone shifted, growing desperate. "No hitches. No surprises."

"And I wanted you to *be* there!" I burst out. "I wanted you in that courtyard while everything went to hell and I got married because I thought I had to bargain for your life!" Tears leaked from my eyes and I swiped at them, angry, impatient.

I watched his face, waiting for the moment I could see he understood. But it never came.

Lang dragged his hands over his face. "I want to know why you only get angry with me," he said, almost pleading. "I want to know why everyone gets a chance but me."

Defensive. Competitive. *Angry.* We stared each other down, breathing hard.

These questions, the accusations, the excuses—they were the last things that should be said between two people in love after so much time apart.

I am rash, Torden had once told me. *Impatient.*

By all accounts, he had charged in. Torden could have wrecked any number of careful plans when he'd come in to rescue me. Perhaps I should have wanted him to behave like Lang, who'd hung back and considered, again and again. In England, in Shvartsval'd, even today.

Lang had been doing important work in the Leshii camp. But I had wanted to see his face.

Perhaps that was selfish. But I couldn't be sacrificed again and again for the greater good, set aside for a succession of causes. No matter how urgent. No matter how noble.

"Because I cared for you—*care* for you," I said brokenly. "But I want the person I love to love me selfishly."

419

The river batted against the sides of the boat, and for a long time, both of us were quiet. The crew had moved away, none of them wishing to overhear this conversation.

Back in the city, the sounds of fighting seemed to have quieted, and the smoke had thinned. No explosions had shaken the ground for a while.

Every hour I waited in the Imperiya could have consequences for my father's life. For my own safety. For my position in Potomac. But I needed to see this through.

I walked down the gangplank and back toward the burning city, casting aside my own rescue.

"Get Wash and the ones who need to be protected to safety," I said over my shoulder. "Anyone who wants to see this witch burn should come with me."

62

The city had the abandoned sense of a ruin. But we could hear the crowds outside the tsarytsya's home from a mile away.

We hurried down a street lined with empty-looking little fortresses. I'd thought they looked familiar when I saw the dog I'd pitied the night of Zatemnennya, looking bone-thin, its fur covered in mud.

I didn't ask the others to pause for me as I climbed over the low fence to where he lay chained. The dog whimpered, but I came near slowly, crouching before him and letting him sniff my hand before I slipped the collar off his neck.

Once free, he scratched and wiggled, seeming almost to shiver with happiness. Then he sat up, tail thumping hopefully. I clicked at him, and he jumped the fence after me, trotting behind us as I caught up with the crew. And when we rounded the corner and came to face Baba Yaga's smoldering tower, we found that the battle was over.

A few gray-clad soldiers remained; but they sat in groups on the ground, their hands behind their heads, ringed by rebel guards. People all over the courtyard were stripping off their gray uniforms and clothes, pitching them into the fires still burning in the wreckage, changing into fresh clothes the resistance were passing out in shades of green and blue and white and gold. Some of the garments fit their wearers; some didn't; no one seemed to care.

The tsarytsya was nowhere to be seen. I wasn't surprised that more soldiers and civilians were surrendering than sticking to her side.

I promised myself that, someday, I would lead people loyal to me, or not at all. I would never govern the fearful. Because this was its end: fire, and a broken city, and people desperate for something new.

We moved through the courtyard, looking for our friends. One of the Rusalki began to sing.

The young woman was cuddling a tiny girl with soft cheeks; I supposed she hadn't gone to the Leshii camp. I supposed she wanted to stay. To see her choices through to the end, like I did.

Her song was a distraction for her daughter, a bright chant that repeated itself. The little girl laughed, and people around them began to stare, but a woman sitting beside them sang along. The dog I'd unchained trotted over to them. When the little girl patted him on the head, he settled beside her.

The song was simple, insistent, punctuated with claps and stomps. It grew slowly in the midst of the courtyard of spikes and stone, like a vine curling up a wall, insistent as a tree pressing up through soil. Others looked as if they wanted to join in, but weren't sure how.

It had been so long since music had sounded inside this city's gates.

Aleksei came to my side, looking like a starving man as he watched. His shirt was deep green and his trousers were undyed; the colors suited him.

"Teach them how to sing, Aleksei," I said, taking his hand. "This is how it begins."

He eyed the tower and nodded. "These are my people. And besides," he added, sounding grim. "It's high time we called down the witch."

Shed of his gray uniform, Baba Yaga's General Bright Dawn shed his title, and took up the song.

He clapped his hands, stomping his feet against the flagstones and making his way to the front door. Two men and a girl and the woman who'd started the song drew near his side.

"It's a song about a red berry," said a voice in my ear. "A red berry, and going to sleep beneath the pines."

It was a voice I would have known anywhere, even here, even at the burning end of the world.

I turned and flung my arms around Torden, and for a long moment, the fires of the revolution disappeared.

I was far from Baba Yaga's house. I was safe in Torden Asgard's arms.

He eyed my scrapes and bruises in dismay. But I shook my

head and nodded back to Aleksei and the others. "Who are they?"

"The leaders of the Leshii, the Rusalki, and the Vodyanoi. Marya, Ivan, Melek, and Ahmet." The Rusalka woman bounced her daughter on her hip as she walked and sang, the dog still trotting behind them.

"What a coincidence," I mused. "Isn't your name Ivan?"

Torden smiled, and I wanted to kiss him.

Aleksei and the resistance leaders sang on, weaving their way to the door. More and more of the crowd began to mimic them.

The former citizens of the Imperiya stood outside of Baba Yaga's house, singing and stomping and clapping, demanding she appear. They put me in mind of the children in the tale, standing outside the chicken-legged house in the woods.

Turn your back to the trees and your face to us, yzbushka! I wanted to scream up at her tower. *Come down and face us.*

Then, as if she had indeed been conjured, Baba Yaga appeared in the doorway, Polunoshchna at her back. Vechirnya was nowhere to be seen.

The tsarytsya eyed Aleksei, disappointed. I didn't understand her when she spoke.

Torden leaned down to me and translated.

"'You did not come of your own accord,' she's saying. 'You were compelled by your so-called father. The so-called Shield of the North.'" Torden scowled.

But he hadn't. Aleksei had come to her of his own accord.

And when he had seen the tsarytsya's claws and teeth for

what they were, of his own accord he had rebelled.

She was wrong, and the crowd knew it.

And then Baba Yaga's keen eyes sought me out. "This could all have been yours," she said in English. Around me, I heard whispers, murmured translations into Yotne and Deutsch and other tongues I didn't recognize.

I held her gaze, not flinching. "I never wanted it."

"The more fool you, Zolushka," she spat.

My anger rose. "No, you are the fool!" I shouted back at her. "These people aren't minor characters in a tale about *you*, or about me. Their stories are *theirs*. This is their country. It was always meant to be theirs."

I seized Torden's hand and Yu's nearby arm and nodded to Hermódr and Bragi and Bear. We crowded close behind Aleksei and the resistance leaders.

"Call me ash-girl, if you wish. But it's your house that's burned to the ground. And you lit the match yourself." I lowered my voice. "I did warn you."

Baba Yaga said nothing.

"We took what was ours," Midnight protested.

Always the taking with Polunoshchna, I thought. When she did manage to focus on one fact, she lost sight of the rest of the picture completely.

The night was ending and the sun was rising and she couldn't see it at all.

"No more," I said sharply. "No more."

I pointed at Aleksei, at the Vodyanoi and the Leshii in forest green and river blue, at the Rusalka woman with her daughter.

"These are the voices of the people you have wronged. And we"—I nodded at my friends standing behind them—"are the representatives of four sovereign governments, here to bear witness to these proceedings."

I cleared my throat. "Be assured, Baba Yaga, that we will not meddle. But be also assured that Yotunkheym will no more conquer. That its next leaders, whoever they may be, will no longer ignore the will of its people." I swallowed. "We will be watching. And so will the rest of the world."

Aleksei and the resistance leaders stepped forward. And I closed my mouth, and fell back, and let justice proceed.

63

YOTUNKHEYM, THE FORMER IMPERIYA YOTNE

Baba Yaga's empire had fallen.

Stupka-Zamok was taken, and her armies—her divisions in the east, west, south, and in the city—were scattered. But victory had not come without losses to our side.

The resistance had suffered blows. Many Vodyanoi and Leshii and Rusalki and Sidhe fighters had died, and many more were wounded; Veery, Bear's knight and friend, was among the injured. I passed by as he was carried into a tent for surgery, swearing and sweating, his lean, ropy limbs twisted in pain.

I stopped short, suddenly flattened by a wave of delayed fear and exhaustion and an overwhelming sense of our mortality.

Veery might live, but he might not. And he could have been Torden, or Cobie, or Anya, or Lang. I'd known this already—of course I had. But hearing the cries of one of Bear's best friends from inside the tent was different than just knowing the risk we'd faced.

There was news from Asgard, as well. The Upper Northern *pestykk* had attacked the Shield three days prior, the night of Zatemnennya, as I'd predicted. Torden and I stood over one of Baba Yaga's radios that afternoon, speaking with Hermódr.

"We subdued them, but we lost nearly eight hundred men," said Hermódr, voice so low it had the sound of a confession.

Torden paled. "I wish I could have been in both places."

I squeezed Torden's hand, feeling a surge of guilt. I'd wanted him to come for me.

He would not have chosen differently, but this was the cost: Torden, his heart torn in two.

But Hermódr was steady as ever. "The men knew you were fighting alongside them, on another front. And now the war is over. More lives have been saved."

Torden kissed my knuckles, jaw tense. "How is Pappa?"

"He's well. Minor injuries. Rihttá hasn't left his side."

"And Bragi?"

"Fine." But Hermódr hesitated. "And Vidarr and Váli are fine."

Torden stilled at this. I watched him taking inventory in silence. Fredrik and Aleksei were in Yotunkheym. Hermódr, Bragi, Vidarr, and Váli were fine. "Týr?"

He was the heir to Asgard, the one Alessandra had planned for me to court. He was a brute. But he was Torden's brother.

Hermódr said nothing for a long moment. "He fell, Torden."

Torden's mouth opened and closed, but he didn't speak. He sank into the desk chair, his hands planted on his knees, his brown eyes wide and dry with a grief too stunned for tears. "Did he suffer?" he finally asked, sounding strangled. "Was it a hard death?"

"We aren't sure," Hermódr said. "We found his body among others on the field. He died with his men."

The brothers were quiet together, mourning in silence with leagues between them.

Týr had died, and Torden had not. I was grateful. He was haunted.

Torden would feel the weight of the lives he couldn't save and the ones he'd taken. I knew him too well to believe otherwise.

High in Baba Yaga's tower, I wrapped my arms around him as tight as I could and did my best to hold him together, as he had done so many times for me.

64

It filled me with fierce pride to watch the dragon defeated, to know I had helped put swords in the right hands. To hear the Rusalki tell Baba Yaga that the little *pestykk* had been returned to their families and that her teeth and claws had been scattered to the wind.

For their crimes, the tsarytsya and Midnight were to be imprisoned, and not executed. Her people were weary of blood, and chose no more to be Wolves. Sunset was never seen again, presumably having fled into the lands she'd once been tasked with conquering.

Vechirnya was wise, and careful, and I doubted we'd catch her. But her escape would be its own punishment; she would be looking over her shoulder forever. Knowing that she had brought night to so many lands, and that the night might well fall on her someday.

But things in the capital were ended quickly.

Some in the city returned to the wild. Others remained within its walls. And there, Stupka-Zamok—the Mortar—was being transformed. The tramp of soldiers' boots and the city's ubiquitous gray were replaced with music and color; and as the sun sank down on the horizon and limned every stone with warmth, one of the Vodyanoi issued the call to prayer. A hundred men and women answered, Wash among them. And on Baba Yaga's house, others of the victorious rebels painted an icon above the door, the Madonna and Child larger than life and haloed with gold.

The city glowed with art and faith and defiance of the darkness they had shaken off, and it filled me with belief that all would be well—here in the place I left behind, and home, as I returned to right old wrongs.

The crowd remained in the courtyard into the night, eating and drinking and laughing and grieving for the lost. I sat with my friends against the tower wall, Torden nearly asleep against me, my crew and Bear and the Sidhe as easy and comfortable around our fire in Stupka-Zamok's remains as we ever were at court.

It was the Sidhe who had kept the *Beholder* from ruin, Perrault explained to me. "They knew what we did not, and they'd warned us not to risk Zatemnennya."

My protocol officer's face was drawn. He didn't look like a portrait, now, or a fox. He looked tired.

"I was supposed to guide you as you courted suitors. And instead, you end up in the middle of a war." Perrault hung his head. "I never meant for this to happen. I never intended to answer to a woman like Alessandra at all."

I thought of Aleksei trapped in Baba Yaga's service, and thought Perrault's might be a familiar tale. "Sometimes our plans get away from us," I offered.

Perrault *hmm*ed in agreement. "I wanted to join the Academy of New York. *The immortals*, they were called. I wanted to leave a mark, shape the language of New York with an eye to the future. And my mentor found me a place there." He took a long breath, eyes trained on the ground.

"But?" I prompted.

"But the cost was too great. I had to support his proposals unreservedly, curry favor at near nightly salons. Politics and etiquette became my life. Worst of all, if he needed someone to collect from his debtors, I was his man. The day he was found dead in his mistress's bed, I breathed freely for the first time in six years." Perrault went pink with shame. "And then his daughter, Alessandra, appeared on my doorstep."

I stilled.

"She told me that the debt I'd owed her father was now owed to her. When she left for Potomac, I prayed Alessandra would forget me. But we know how that story ended."

My nerves fired at the despair in his face.

Would everything return to the way it was before, when we faced Alessandra again? Would Perrault bend again to her will? Would I?

"No," I said, defiant. "We don't know how that story ends. It's not finished yet."

I had to believe we'd be different. Stronger. That even my

stepmother wasn't powerful enough to undo how much we had changed.

Perrault watched me, a little despairing, as though wishing it could be true.

I scanned the crowds around us. "Perrault, would you have believed this morning that tonight was possible?"

"No," he admitted.

"Me either." Torden's head drooped onto my shoulder. Across the circle, I caught Bear grinning at us, and I grinned back. "There's still a chance this story ends happily."

Torden reached for my hand in his doze, and Perrault eyed our linked fingers, curious. "Certainly, part of it will."

"And if some," I asked, putting all my heart into the words, "why not all?"

"Why not, indeed?" Perrault gave me a tired but genuine smile.

And when he returned to the *Beholder* to sleep and Torden finally roused himself to find some blankets, Bear took a seat next to me.

"Hello," he said tentatively, settling cross-legged on the ground.

"Hi," I said, almost like agreeing.

I couldn't believe how far he'd come to help us. I couldn't believe this was the heir to Saint George's England, the boy who had kissed me and lied to me. I had shouted at him on Winchester's doorstep, had left him behind in tears.

"So." He nodded after Torden's back, blue eyes wry. "Him."

I nodded, my smile going a little rueful. "It's that obvious?"

Bear bobbed his head slowly. "You're—easier together. Than you and I were." He cleared his throat, bowing his head. "But you used to look at me that way."

My heart gave a painful beat.

"I'm sorry," he blurted out. "My God, Selah, I'm so sorry for what we did. I've had so much time to think, and I know you must have been utterly humiliated, and it was just—"

"Bear," I interrupted him. "It's okay."

He winced. "Really?"

"Well, it was awful at the time," I admitted. He grimaced. "But I've had to make hard choices, myself, since I've left you. And after all the terrible things that have happened, it just doesn't make sense to fret over healed injuries."

"Well, that's a relief." Bear glanced across the circle at his knights, and I nodded meaningfully at the girl who had caught me earlier outside the tower.

"So," I said. "*Her.*"

"Gwyn, you mean." Bear blushed. "I saw her wearing cowslips not long after you left, and I started asking questions. And then Perrault radioed us, told us what had happened to you. My father said we wouldn't become involved. But I had to come." He pushed his rumpled hair off his forehead, grinning ruefully. "I think Gwyn was a little worried I'd show up here and fall at your feet and beg for your forgiveness and your hand."

My shoulders unclenched with relief at this. Because it meant he wouldn't.

I swallowed. "How's Veery?"

Bear sobered, heaving a long breath. "Lost all his charm and

434

a good deal of blood with that shot to the thigh he took. But the surgeons got to him in time. He's resting now."

"What a relief," I sighed.

He stared into the fire, looking pensive. "I don't know what I would do without him. We're supposed to be starting Oxford together in the spring, Veery and Gwyn and Kay and I."

"Oxford?" I brightened.

Bear nodded, his mood lightening a little, too. "We'll have missed the start of Michaelmas term so we'll go up in Hilary. Father's excited. And I find I am, too."

I didn't know what any of that meant, but I nodded happily, if a little enviously. *College.*

Then he shook himself, straightening, planting his tanned hands on his knees. "Right. I'm nattering on. What will you do next? Where are you off to now?"

Torden came and sat down next to me, and I nodded from him to Bear. "Torden, Bear. Prins of Norge. Prince of England." They shook hands, Torden serious, Bear amused. I linked my fingers through Torden's.

"We," I said, "are going home."

DAWN

By this the Northerne wagoner had set
His sevenfold teme behind the stedfast starre,
That was in Ocean waves yet never wet,
But firme is fixt, and sendeth light from farre
To all that in the wide deepe wandring are . . .
—*The Faerie Queene*

65

THE *BEHOLDER*

I hailed my godmother from the top of Baba Yaga's tower and told her all that had happened. She wept, but my eyes were dry as I looked out over the city the rebels had saved. And I had been allowed to help. To be part of a day so, so worth writing about.

I overheard Fritz and Gretel talking, too, that day. They didn't bother with code names, and they didn't seem to hear me, though I tried to speak to them.

Maximilian had been dispossessed, and Fritz was now the *hertsoh*. Leirauh went home to her sisters.

I hoped Katz Castle could come to life again, the way Fritz had dreamed of it. We saw it with every passing hour in Stupka-Zamok, the new city rising from the ashes of the tower the rebels had laid low with the powder and guns Gretel had sent them.

Bear and his knights, Aleksei, and Hermódr remained behind to continue supporting negotiations. I bid them good-bye beside the river, one after the other, embracing them each tightly as Torden and I moved down their line.

To Hermódr: "Come and see us soon." He pushed up his glasses and returned the offer.

To Aleksei: *Spasibo.*

He grinned at me, and it was a natural smile. Whole and unsullied by cynicism. "Farewell, Zolushka." He punched Torden gently. "We're going to have words over how you've stolen my bride, brother." Torden laughed, long and loud.

To Bear: "Safe travels home."

Bear held out his hand. "Friends?"

"Always," I said, pulling him into a hug. "And Potomac and England will always be, after this."

"Always," he agreed.

"Study hard at Oxford." I smiled, a little jealous.

Bear nodded.

Lang stood a little apart from the others. He hadn't been aboard yet.

I swallowed hard. "You got what you fought for." I looked around. "All this—this is what you worked for."

"I did," Lang said. "I got everything I wanted."

But his words were a lie, and his eyes told the truth.

He had lied to me, and I had undercut him. We had cared for one another, and we had competed with one another. We were lucky to be standing here, together, alive.

But the hollow sadness in his face haunted me like a story with no ending. I couldn't give Lang what he wanted, and there was nothing either of us could do about it.

"You aren't coming back with us," I finally said. Not a question.

Lang didn't deny it. "What for?"

My arms went tightest around him. I didn't know what to say. "You promised to keep me safe," I said. "You haven't delivered me back yet."

"You don't need me anymore to keep you safe." His dark eyes cut to Torden.

Torden wasn't what had changed in me. But if Lang had understood that, everything would have been different between us to begin with.

"It should be Yu, staying behind," Lang finally said, nodding at the doctor a few feet away. "He healed your cook. He got Zhōng Guó back on its feet. He'd be perfect to help get this place running again." He paused. "I'm just a smuggler."

I shook my head, vehement. "You're the zŏngtŏng's representative here, as much as Yu is."

Lang swallowed. "We both know why I can't go back, Selah. There was the job, and there was you. And now the job is done, and you . . ." Lang fell silent, and I lifted a hand to his shoulder.

Breath and wanting rose up in me, fierce and protective.

"Someday," I said, swallowing hard. "Someday, we'll find each other again. Someday when we can be friends, when all that is just an old story we tell people." I gritted my teeth a little.

"Maybe," Lang said dubiously.

"For sure," I insisted. I lifted my storybook, nodded at the radio we both knew was inside. "Keep an ear out."

I stuck out my hand, and Lang shook it.

"Here's to the next great adventure," he said.

And then we went our separate ways.

We climbed the gangplank of the ship, my feet keeping time with the pounding of my heart.

Home. Home. Home.

Up in the rigging, Cobie loosened the lines, and Basile and Vishnu raised the anchor, cheering as it came loose from the riverbed.

"Homeward!" Basile hollered, grin broad as the horizon.

I spun around in a circle, shouting along with them, and Anya caught my hand and twirled me around until I was dizzy.

Skop, our new captain, manned the helm as the current carried us downriver, sunset light filtering through the sails and the birches along the riverbank.

Home.

I skimmed my hands over the tops of my plants, feeling the health of their leaves, closing my eyes as I pushed into the galley. And when I opened my eyes I burst into a laugh.

Wash, whose real name had turned out to be Märyäm, was standing over the stove, trying to explain to Will how to pinch dumplings closed so they wouldn't leak. These weren't the pelmeni we'd made in Baba Yaga's kitchens; she called these chebureki.

Aleksei had helped us ask her yesterday if she wanted to stay in Yotunkheym, or if we could help her go somewhere else.

She told us her home—the place she'd been captured from twelve years before—was a peninsula downriver. She agreed to let us take her there.

I might not have been allowed to use the stove, but Märyäm had taken over without hesitating. She'd set Will to work rolling and chopping while she stuffed the chebureki with beef and onions and parsley and fried them in oil. The galley smelled like comfort, drenched in golden light from the lamps and Will's happy laughter as he tried to follow Märyäm's orders. Tears filled my eyes again.

Märyäm put her hands on her hips. "Do not cry," she insisted.

I shook my head, swallowing. "I'm happy," I insisted. "These are happy tears."

Märyäm passed me a handkerchief and I wiped my eyes. "Do not cry," she said again gently. Then she pointed at the sink, piled high with dirty flatware and plates and the rolling pin, and winked at me. "You. Wash."

We all ate together in the galley, huddling together beneath the lamps. Will had made stew to go with Märyäm's chebureki, and Perrault brought me a second bowl when I devoured my first in a few bites.

Torden ate three helpings of dinner and tried patiently again and again to tie the knot Vishnu demonstrated.

"No, like this," Vishnu said, nimbly untying the rope and showing him once more.

Beneath the galley lamps, I saw red was growing back in at the roots of Torden's hair.

I leaned against his shoulder and breathed him in, overwhelmed again that he was beside me.

He had asked Alfödr, and his father had agreed that he should go with me. Rihttá had given him her every blessing. Torden was coming to Potomac.

He would be at my back when I faced Alessandra again. When I defended my father. When I met my little brother or sister for the first time.

Cobie had told me I floated just fine on my own. But Torden was the one I wanted beside me as I soldiered forward.

No one balked when Torden took Skop's old bunk belowdecks; he fit in among the crew so naturally. Skop had moved into Lang's old quarters, and Anya stayed in my room. But that night, even with Anya curled up warm beside me, I couldn't sleep.

I climbed the stairs with my book. My godmother's voice was silent inside its binding, but I reveled in the smooth leather wrapped around words that I could drink as I pleased, that no one could take from me.

Out on deck, Basile and Jeanne were deep in conversation beneath the mainmast. Märyäm prayed softly, her head covered, her eyes turned east.

I climbed to the forecastle and met Homer at the helm. He rubbed one eye.

"Tired?"

"Eyes aren't what they were," he said a little gruffly.

"Want me to take over?" I asked.

Homer scowled a little, then nodded at the helm. "Go on. Ought to have taught you already, anyway."

The night grew deep as Homer and I pored over his star charts and nautical almanacs. I steered and he gestured at the map and at the sky, illuminating the constellations I already knew and those I didn't, teaching me how to find true north with Polaris.

"But all you have to do for now is follow the river." Homer crossed his hands over his chest, squinting out at the night. "Can you hold course?"

The way was clear before me. I was as awake as I'd ever been.

I nodded.

"I'll relieve you at dawn," he said.

Homer left me to the quiet of the water washing the ship and the stars wheeling overhead. But I was only alone for moment.

I knocked on one of the barrels beside the helm and gestured for him to sit, just as Lang had done so many months before. But Torden stood behind me instead, wrapping his arms around me and fitting his chin above my head.

"You weren't in your room," he said. "You're restless."

I swallowed. "I've done everything I set out to do."

Torden dipped his head, and I stole a glance sideways at him. "Selah."

His earnest gaze told me I couldn't hide from him. And I didn't want to.

I had held him together, and let him lean on my shoulder, and he would do the same for me.

"I'm afraid for my father," I said softly. "I'm afraid I've wasted too much time away from him. He would understand, but—"

But what if he's gone before I return? What if he can't speak, or doesn't know me?

I took a long breath, and Torden held me tighter. I thumbed the tattoo inside his wrist, and he reached with his other hand to angle my engagement ring toward the light of the moon.

It sparkled on my left-hand ring finger, where he had placed it for the third and final time the day Baba Yaga's house fell. It was exactly where it belonged.

"You took a risk," Torden said. "You chose to help people protect themselves. I did the same." He looked down at me. "You're becoming everything a leader should be. I'm so proud of you, *elskede*. And your father will be, as well."

Now all I had to do was follow the path of the river, like Homer had told me. The stars were so, so bright above, and the one I loved was warm and safe at my back.

I had come of my own accord. And now, of my own accord, I would go home.

[Der Jäger] trat er in die Stube,
und wie er vor das Bette kam,
so sah er, daß der Wolf darin lag.
"Finde ich dich hier, du alter Sünder," sagte er,
"ich habe dich lange gesucht."
—Rotkäppchen

So [the huntsman] went into the room,
and when he came to the bed,
he saw that the wolf was lying in it.
"Do I find you here, you old sinner!" said he.
"I have long sought you!"
—Little Red Cap

66

POTOMAC: ARBOR HALL

The sun rose, and the sun set, and the *Beholder* carried us downriver.

We took Märyäm to her home, a peninsula called Qirim, and Skop hired a horse and cart to take her to her village. She had sent letters there, and her sisters had responded in disbelief; they had feared the worst for Märyäm after she'd been captured more than a decade before.

Märyäm had cried as she read their replies. She hadn't stopped talking since about the nephews and nieces she'd be meeting for the first time, about how she couldn't wait to cook with her sisters again.

They were all home, waiting for her.

Märyäm had been a hearth for freezing women, a barred door against wolves. She was a good person, generous and kind and hospitable to strangers.

I hoped the fairy tales proved true. I hoped it came back to her a hundredfold.

"*Spasibo,*" I said into her shoulder as I hugged her goodbye.

Märyäm smiled at me, her chapped palm cupping my shoulder. "Safe travels, Selah."

We sailed on. I kept my radio close. My godmother said the Rosary every morning.

And seven weeks after we had left Yotunkheym, on a chill day in mid-November, I guided the *Beholder* into the mouth of the Potomac with Torden and Homer and Skop at my sides.

It was a gorgeous afternoon, clear, with a blue sky and a steady wind. Cobie clambered through the rigging; Jeanne and Basile and Vishnu worked the lines, and J.J. scampered across the deck, in everyone's way, giddy with excitement.

Movement on the banks caught my eye, and suddenly, there were cries on the air. I startled at the sound at first.

And then I heard their words. "She's home!" one of them hollered.

From an outpost on the banks of the Potomac, a runner began to sprint upriver, alongside the ship.

I'm home.

And they were waiting for me.

From one outpost to the next, the runners outstripped the *Beholder*, racing west toward the setting sun. Torden kept one hand on my shoulder, one around my waist.

The wind blew my hair into my eyes, and the river washed

over the hull of the ship, and my heart sang in chorus with it all as my city came into view.

Arbor Hall. My home.

I ceded my place at the helm, and Homer docked just as the sun began to dip toward the horizon. A massive, silent crowd awaited us on the pier.

My eyes searched them, scanning and discarding face after face that was not my father's.

"Selah!" A familiar voice called my name.

My heart stopped.

I raced down the gangplank and threw myself into my godmother's arms. She smelled like incense and the air smelled like earth and I was home, I was home, I was home.

I pulled away slightly, glancing around. "Where is he?"

Godmother put a hand on my shoulder. "He's at the house," she said, nodding in the direction of Arbor Hall. "I will explain everything. But you're tired, and I want you to rest, and not to worry. What matters is—"

"Godmother, tell me," I said more sharply than I meant to. "I'm sorry. But I—please."

She pursed her lips, clasped her hands as if in prayer. The world tipped sharply beneath my feet. "He's in bed, baby. The doctors don't know what to do."

67

Someone said something about getting horses or a carriage, but I hardly heard them. I felt irrational; I couldn't wait. I ran.

"Selah!" So many voices shouted my name, but I heeded none of them.

I had crossed oceans and rivers and mountains and plains, barefoot and bleeding and starving and terrified. I had survived all of that and made it home.

I had not done it so that my father could die poisoned on his bed.

Was it poison? Was it age? Were Daddy and I simply cursed?

For a moment, I heard only my own breathing, the ragged, terrified *in-out* of air in my lungs. And then I heard the heavy pounding of footsteps—of a pack running behind me. I whipped my head around, confused, but I should have known.

My friends were with me. Torden and Skop and Yu and

Anya, Vishnu and Cobie, even Perrault. I wasn't alone.

I thanked God that Konge Alfödr had raised a fast runner in his son.

My father was not going to die. He was not. I would stand between Daddy and Death himself and howl like a wolf with my pack at my side to fend off the reaper.

Sweat poured down my back, and my muscles burned as I chased the fading autumn light up and down hills, between buildings, through fields, sending birds and squirrels flying. I wanted to take it in, to run my hands over it all. But I didn't stop.

When the house appeared in the distance, though, I pushed myself faster, worry ringing through my body with every step. "The east wing, third floor!" I screamed to the others. They followed me, like birds flying in a V, each of us sharply aware of one another's presence. In my periphery, I saw Cobie and Skop and Anya and Torden had their knives at the ready, and Yu had a black bag in his hands.

In the door. Up the stairs. Guards waited outside my father's rooms, and they started as we approached. "Miss, you don't— Oh. Seneschal-elect."

I nodded at Cobie and the rest of my friends. "Weapons away."

"Seneschal-elect, your father is unwell," said the guard closest to the door. "I'm afraid you'll need to return later."

"What's your name?" I asked the guard, panting hard.

He frowned, uncertain. "Miller," he said. "Lieutenant Miller."

"Right." Sweat was pouring into my eyes; I wiped it away. "Lieutenant Miller, I'm sure you're following orders not to let anyone in my father's rooms. I'm countermanding those orders, which I'm able to do because I'm going to be seneschal of this country someday. Do you understand?"

"Yes, Miss—"

"Seneschal-elect," Cobie corrected him.

"Seneschal-elect," Miller said. "But the Esteemed Consort—"

"Does not outrank me," I said abruptly. "We're wasting time. Move, or I will remove you from your post."

The path to my father's room cleared before us.

We burst in and found Dr. Gold sitting at Daddy's side, nearly asleep in his chair. His head shot up when we entered, relief painting his every feature.

"Seneschal-elect, you've returned." Dr. Gold rose, bowing slightly. "I'm so pleased you're home." His light brown hair looked dirty, and his eyes were red-rimmed; but I trusted the gladness in his voice.

"And I'm pleased to see you watching over my father," I said. Something in my heart tugged at the picture of faithfulness he made; he wasn't actively tending Daddy, but he hadn't left him to suffer alone.

Dr. Gold looked over my shoulder. "Who is—"

I turned. Yu was bending over my father, a careful ear to his chest, listening to his heart and lungs, checking his pulse. "Dr. Gold, this is our ship's doctor, Dá Yu," I said. "He's from Zhōng Guó and very experienced."

I'd been afraid Dr. Gold would make some sort of display of wounded pride—that he'd protest his own competence, grow defensive or territorial. But again, at my words, he nearly sagged in relief. "Wonderful," he breathed, and the two of them began immediately to speak rapidly in a language full of medical terms I didn't understand.

Daddy was thin, so thin; his skin was papery and nearly gray. It held none of the glow of my childhood, the days when I'd followed him out to the fields and watched him work and sweat for his country.

I wished for something to do. I wished I understood what their words meant. Here, in this room, listening to his doctors, I wanted a translator more desperately than I had in Yotunkheym.

Dr. Gold stood to one side as Yu checked Daddy's pulse, listened to his heart, asked how long he'd been in his present state. It had been ten days. The number nearly drove me to my knees.

Presenting? Disorientation, insomnia, diminished vision, skin discoloration, melancholia. Diabetes? Alcoholism? No, no.

Torden held my hand amid the horror and did not let go.

Poison, Yu had said aboard the *Beholder* the day I'd pressed him for the truth, before I'd ordered our ship toward old Deutschland.

When Yu offered the word now, Gold put a hand to his heart, drawing back in horror. "Is that possible?"

"I have a hunch," Yu said. "Can you describe his course of treatment?"

"It's a therapy Pugh suggested, apparently a popular one in New York." Dr. Gold's hands twitched toward his breast pocket, retrieving a cigarette. Yu plucked it away, eyes wide.

"You can't smoke in here," he said, horrified. "Don't you know these cause hideous cancer in the lungs?"

Gold stilled. "You can't be serious."

"You can't tell how it makes you slower? Sicker?" Yu demanded. He snatched Gold's cigarette packet and brandished it at him. "These will kill you! And you certainly shouldn't smoke around patients."

"I . . . didn't know." The tips of Dr. Gold's ears turned red.

Yu softened. "I've got some books I want you to read. I'll have them fetched later. Most of them are in Zhōngwén, but some of them you'll be able to read. They're new. Modern medicine." He shook his head. "Now, regarding the patient?"

"Yes. Sorry," Gold said. "We embarked on a popular form of treatment—"

"So the runners spoke true," said a cold voice from the doorway. "You've come home, after all."

68

Standing in front of Dr. Pugh, my stepmother was slim again, delivered of her child, her eyes big and dramatic against her high cheekbones. She looked as if she hadn't been pregnant in years, though she'd only delivered in August. Godmother Althea had told me over the radio.

But I had been gone a long time. Alessandra looked different, and I *was* different.

I turned back to Daddy. "Dr. Gold, what were you saying?"

"Levi!" Dr. Pugh interjected sharply. "This is private. There are foreigners present and—and sailors. And the seneschal-elect—"

"Outranks everyone in this room," I said again.

Alessandra stepped forward. "I believe I made the conditions of your coming home very clear."

Torden moved to my side and took my hand—my left hand. His ring glittered on my finger.

My ring was exactly where it belonged, and so was Torden, and so was I.

"Are you wed?" she breathed.

"Interrupt the doctor again," I said quietly, "and see what happens."

I wanted the truth. And I wanted it immediately.

I put a hand on Dr. Gold's shoulder. "Please, continue."

"Blue Mass," he blurted. His words came quickly, as if to get them all out at once. "It's called Blue Mass, I mix it myself, it's rose oil, licorice, marshmallow plant, mercury, and glycerol. Pugh recommended it, he said it's a very common therapy in New York, he—"

Yu had stopped dead. If he'd had something in his hands, I was confident he would've dropped it.

"Mercury?" He dragged the word out, horror plain on his face.

Dr. Gold frowned. "Yes," he said. "I prepare it myself, very carefully."

Yu stared from Gold to Pugh, his handsome, solid face aghast. He said something in Zhōngwén and shook his head. "Not—mercury," he said. "Element Hg. Not that."

Yu waited, wanting to be told that he had misunderstood. But his ears hadn't betrayed him.

Alessandra and Dr. Pugh had betrayed my father.

He rounded on Dr. Pugh. "I might expect this from local expertise. That one wasn't even aware of the dangers of smoking. Potomac is removed—but if you have access to information anywhere, you have it in New York." Yu's jaw was set, so sharp

460

it could've cut glass. "If anyone would know this *medication* was dangerous, you would have."

I was shaking. "Tell me you didn't know," I said to Pugh, almost pleading. "Tell me you had a good reason to prescribe it."

"Blue Mass has its—risks," Pugh admitted. "But your father has been suffering from melancholia and its therapeutic qualities seemed to justify—"

"This man is dying. Any therapeutic benefits are clearly out-weighed by the fact that he's suffering aggressive nerve damage, which cannot have escaped your notice!" Yu exploded, jabbing a finger at Pugh. "I have read your oath, the one Hippocrates wrote. I took my own, from Sun Si-Miao. We're physicians. We have a high calling, and you've dishonored yours." Yu shook his head, disgusted.

Melancholia. The weight my father had carried in his bones for so long—the deep heaviness that had dragged at him, even after the sharp grief of my mother's death had passed—it had a name.

And rather than support him, my stepmother had taken advantage of his vulnerability. Because she was greedy and hungry, and because she could.

And even that name—*melancholia*, it tolled in my ears—was not so fearsome as the other word Yu has used.

Dying.

I squeezed Torden's hand tighter.

Dr. Gold was crouching, his head between his knees. "Do you mean to say—"

"Mercury is poison. We will discontinue this course of

461

treatment immediately." Yu held a hand out, and Dr. Gold stood. "We will set a course toward healing the seneschal at once."

I crouched at my father's side, looking at his closed eyes, watching the shallow rise and fall of his chest.

My fear was cold as ice. But my anger at Alessandra and Dr. Pugh burned furious and feverish in my stomach.

My father would not die.

I looked up at Yu and Gold. "I leave him to your charge. I'll be back in a few minutes." Yu acknowledged me with a nod.

When I stood, I felt ten feet tall. I felt myself grow, stretch, my shoulders squaring, like one of the giants from the stories in my godmother's book. I took one, two, three strides toward Alessandra.

She was taller than me, still. But I had put on muscle from eating well aboard ship, from gardening, from scrubbing dishes and sheets and stones in Baba Yaga's tower.

I towered before her.

"Step into the corridor, please." I glanced at Pugh. "Both of you."

My voice brooked no opposition. I was not surprised when both of them obeyed.

69

Torden and the crew followed me into the hallway, all but Yu. I shut the door behind me.

I had helped protect the innocents living in Baba Yaga's shadow. It was time to protect my own home.

I planted myself in front of the door and faced Alessandra. "You didn't have to do any of this," I said, staring her down. "Hurt him. Banish me. I would have been content to work in my fields and stay out of your way. But you wanted me gone, and you sacrificed my father to do it."

Alessandra smirked, eyes wide, thick lashes fluttering. "Sir Perrault, did you give her elocution lessons? She's grown so bold." Pugh sniggered. Perrault didn't respond. "You're a child," my stepmother said more evenly. "I arranged your courtship because your prospects at home were doomed."

I paused, considering her.

This would have wilted me once.

Alessandra had always professed to be powerful, just as the tsarytsya had. But so much of her power rested upon expectations and bluffs. Truth be told, she was much closer kin to Midnight than to Baba Yaga.

Something about my silence seemed to dampen her. "Selah?" Alessandra demanded, irritable. "Perrault? Have you forgotten our arrangement?"

I didn't even flinch. I knew Perrault better, this time.

"No." Perrault shook his head. "That debt's long paid. And it was never, ever Selah's to bear." He squeezed my shoulder, bracing me.

Perrault was different. Stronger. And so was I.

My stepmother glanced again at my ring and at Torden.

Once upon a time, I would have anxiously assured her that I'd gotten engaged, as she'd ordered, or explained with fear and trembling why I was not. I would have, at least, enjoyed her shock at seeing Torden. I would have played her game, terrified of what she could do to me if I did not.

Today, I just thought of Midnight flipping the Tooth and Claw board over in her tantrum, and smiled a little.

I crossed my arms. "You know, Alessandra, I met a lot of people on my trip. You remind me of a general I met. She was petty, and greedy, and in the end, everything she grasped at slipped through her fingers.

"I've been dragged in chains across Europe," I said slowly. "I have ventured out into Stupka-Zamok on Wolf Night and lived to tell the story. I have sat opposite Baba Yaga herself and played Tooth and Claw and *won*." I stepped closer to her. "You don't frighten me, or impress me, anymore."

Alessandra winced—just a little. Just enough. As the haughtiness on her face slipped, I saw there was nothing solider or stronger beneath it than selfishness.

"Tell me the truth," I said. "Now."

Alessandra drew farther back. But she ran into Cobie before she could get down the hallway. Skop and Vishnu backed her. The rest kept close to me.

"The builders of this place made room for the trees that grew beneath Arbor Hall's floors. They carved spaces out for tree trunks they should have just pulled up by the roots." Alessandra's voice wobbled. "Those builders made room for the trees as this house would never make room for me."

"That's not true." My voice was flat.

"I was never, ever allowed to forget who Violet Savannah Potomac was to this country," she breathed. "To you, or to Jeremiah."

I raised my eyebrows. "You wanted me to forget my mother?"

"There was nothing left for me!" Alessandra brayed. "I did my best to carve out a space of my own, to give Potomac's commoners something to aspire to." I gasped a weary, incredulous laugh; my stepmother ignored me.

"But you and your perfect dead mother took up all the air in the house. I realized eventually that I had to pull out by the roots those things that threatened to choke me." Alessandra's thin face grew hard and ugly. "How else would there ever be any room for my daughter?"

"Your—" I stopped short, startled. "Your daughter?"

Alessandra had had a child. Of course, I knew this. But to hear her speak of a girl, living in this house, my own flesh and blood—I reeled.

I needed a long moment to get my bearings.

Alessandra wiped her nose on her sleeve. "From the moment I knew I carried my Victoria, I vowed she would not live in anyone's shadow. She would not be an afterthought to a story already told."

"There is always breath for more than one story to be told," I said in a low voice. "My heart was never closed to you as yours was to me."

She had never loved me, had never wanted to make room for me. And it had never been my fault. The lack had never been mine.

"I would have been no trouble. Your mistake was sending me away. If my claws are sharper than yours now, it's your own fault."

Alessandra looked away from me, petulant. That night in the Roots, she had seemed so elegant, so grand and powerful; I had run from her crying, off-balance, terrified of everything that was about to change.

Here and now, I felt large. I felt broad and strong and grounded, flanked by my friends. I wasn't crazy or imagining things; she *had* hurt my father.

Backed against the corridor wall, Alessandra, queen of falsehoods and facades, was too small to scare me anymore.

"Skop, Vishnu, Cobie," I said, not looking away from her. "Restrain them, please. Anya and Perrault, please go get help."

They were not gone long. To my surprise, Captain Janesley—Peter's father—was one of several guards who answered my friends' summons.

"Selah?" He looked uncertain.

"You're not misunderstanding the situation, Captain," I said swiftly. "Please arrest my stepmother and the doctor. They've nearly killed my father—poison. Everyone here will attest to that, including Dr. Gold and my own doctor, who are tending to him now."

"It's a baseless charge. You have no proof," Dr. Pugh said. His eyes were darting wildly between the guards.

"Not yet." I kept my voice even. "But I've become a great believer in process, Dr. Pugh. In letting people speak, and letting the truth come out. I believe the same will happen here." I paused and glanced back at Peter's father. "Captain?"

Captain Janesley hesitated only a moment. Then he nodded efficiently at me. "Yes, Seneschal-elect."

Alessandra and Dr. Pugh were both speaking to me as they were borne away. Threats, apologies, protests. I wasn't quite sure what they said.

Words were powerful. In stories, in songs, in prayers, in promises.

But theirs had no power here anymore.

Скоро сказка сказывается,
да не скоро дело делается.

The tale is soon told,
but the deed isn't soon done.
—*Yotne saying*

70

If I had learned one thing from the stories, it was that work begat work, and tasks begat more tasks.

I had traveled the world, seen a witch removed from her throne, and rescued my father; but Potomac was not saved yet.

Yu and Dr. Gold were occupied those first few days with stabilizing my father—getting him well enough to travel, so he could receive more advanced treatment elsewhere.

I slept and paced at his bedside. Torden brought me my meals, so I didn't have to leave.

The night Daddy woke up, he asked to be taken to his bedroom balcony. I'd sat with him there as I had so, so many times as a child.

We had lost Momma. But we had one addition now.

I held Victoria, marveling at her pink toes, her funny little mouth that stretched and pinched like a rubber band. She had a full head of hair, soft and black as Alessandra's.

The first night I'd arrived, I had stood over her crib, afraid even to look at her. Afraid I would hate her, as her mother had hated me. What if Alessandra had been right to fear me? What if sending me away *was* the safest course for her daughter?

But I shouldn't have been afraid. I loved Victoria at once.

I'd looked at my sister down in her crib, clinging to a soft toy sheep, just three months old. And I knew that if anyone tried to hurt her, I would protect her. I would be a wolf so she could be a lamb.

My heart had swelled almost painfully in my chest as she burbled at me curiously, her green eyes so like mine and my father's. I'd slept that night on the floor in front of her crib.

She was a squishy bundle in the crook of my arm now, grabbing at the ends of my hair and sticking them in her mouth. I indulged her.

"We've got an owl back here in the woods we might hear in a minute," Daddy said, thumbing Victoria's little fingers. "Nest of robins on the edge of the tree line. Family of foxes a few hundred yards out. I know we need to flush them out, but those little kits are just too sweet to watch."

Yu thought, though nothing was certain, that Daddy would recover fully. Already, my father seemed less burdened, more engaged.

If I had gotten nothing else I wanted, I would still have called it a happy ending. Him and Victoria and me, here on the balcony. A family, whole and enough, despite it all.

"They hunted foxes in England," I said after a moment.

"I know they go after sheep and chickens, but I didn't like it much."

"I wouldn't have, either." Daddy shifted on his chaise, nudging me with his thin shoulder. His eyes were tired, but clear, and curious as I hadn't seen them in a long time. "Tell me how it went, baby girl." His brows arched. "You didn't come back alone, I noticed."

"Torden." I smoothed Victoria's hair again, my ring sparkling. "He's Prins Torden. From Norge."

"Was he the first one you met?"

"No," I said slowly. "Bear was the first. But I should start at the beginning."

Daddy took a bite of soup. It was pumpkin, made from the autumn's harvest. Winter would be well upon us soon, and we needed to be ready.

But for now—before Daddy left, for heaven knew how long—I wanted to tell him my story.

I told him about the four courts I had visited. The boys I'd courted. The kings and tyrants I'd faced.

The Imperiya I'd helped topple, and the idea I had for Potomac's future.

When I was done, Daddy squeezed my shoulder.

"I'm glad you're home, Selah. I'm sorry I didn't see sooner what she was doing." He swallowed and took one of my sister's tiny hands. "I was so wrong to let you go. I was afraid you'd hold it against Victoria, if I was fortunate enough to get you back."

"Never." I squeezed Victoria closer, as if to banish the

473

idea. "She's my family. And I'm glad to hear you say all that." I paused. "But I'm also glad I went."

"You are?" Daddy raised an eyebrow, surprised.

"I met and learned from people different from me. I fell in love, and I got to see a great wrong righted. And now I have a goal for our future." I shook my head. "And—I saw the world, Daddy. I wouldn't have missed any of it."

Especially because you're still here, I couldn't say aloud. *Everything is all right because you're still here.*

The owls began to hoot from the edge of the woods.

"Now," Daddy said, shifting again. "Tell me about this idea of yours."

Yu took Daddy to New York the next day. I went to Mass every single morning in his absence, lit every votive in the bank of candles in the church, prayed on my knees at Godmother Althea's side.

And I worked from sunup to sundown to ensure that when he returned, healthy and whole, Potomac would be, too. Our coffers were empty, our government in chaos, our people uncertain. I began the slow job of rebuilding what had crumbled and decayed while Alessandra manipulated us.

I read into the wee hours of the night. Not only my fairytale book, but law books Bear and Yu sent me from England and Zhōng Guó—as well as a few about looking after babies. Victoria had two nannies, but I moved her nursery across the hall from my room and spent my nights walking her across the floor as I studied.

And when the morning came and the sun rose, I wrote letters until my hands ached, to my mother's relatives in Savannah and to our neighbors, the Rappahannock tribe, to the *zŏngtŏng* and to England's king, and to the Shield of the North and to the new government of Yotunkheym. I refreshed relationships with our friends and neighbors. I gathered as much wisdom as I could.

We held elections. Proper elections, with public debates and town meetings, where the people asked questions and received answers. Secretary Gidcumb was the only member of the old Council innocent of corruption and collusion with Alessandra; he became our new secretary of state, on our new Council, which did actual work. There were to be no more hangers-on in government.

We seeded every public field. I oversaw it myself.

I met with Alessandra only once, the day our new state barrister interrogated her in advance of her trial. She charged my stepmother to explain her deeds from their beginning. Alessandra admitted to recklessness with Potomac's finances and to poisoning my father after blackmailing and manipulating Pugh (as she had Perrault).

"What about Peter?" I asked her suddenly, as Madam Turner, the barrister, finished her questions.

"What about him?" Alessandra's voice was tinged with the same disbelief that had colored it the day I'd confronted her, as if she couldn't truly believe she'd be met with consequences for what she'd done.

"Did you force him to decline my proposal?" I wasn't sure

why I asked; I had no reason to believe she'd give me a truthful answer.

Alessandra tipped her head back as if to think, exhaling through her nose. "I told the Janesleys I would audit their business if he accepted, and that something would be found. Does it matter?"

"Absolutely," muttered Madam Turner, retrieving her ledger to make an additional note. I fought off an unexpected laugh.

"No," I said. "Not really, it doesn't." I rose to go.

Alessandra clasped her hands, abruptly nervous. "Will you let me see Victoria?"

I frowned. "I love my sister. We won't keep her from you. You'll see her as often as the judge permits." Alessandra met my eyes. Her own were troubled.

She didn't trust me, or understand how I could love Victoria.

But her fear wasn't my problem.

I didn't see my stepmother again after that. I delivered my testimony in writing for her trial, and returned to work as they debated. I didn't want to sway the outcome with my presence, and I had a life to get on with living. Alessandra had claimed enough of it already.

The morning the trial began, I sat at my writing desk, staring at the piles of correspondence and legal texts and baby books.

It was overwhelming.

I had come so far. I was so grateful to my friends, to my

godmother, to Gidcumb—who I had learned was responsible for smuggling in my radio.

But I wanted—hoped—to do so much more.

I plunked my pen down, dipped my little finger in my pot of ink, and wrote my hopes down my left arm.

Happily
ever
after

We were so close to putting the past behind us, to the bright future that lay beyond all the fairy-tale endings.

A knock came at my door. "Come in," I called idly.

I didn't even have to turn. I knew his footsteps.

"Hi, sweetheart." I wiped the ink from my finger.

Torden tried to squeeze onto my chair beside me, then stole my seat and lifted me onto his lap when he didn't fit. "Art project, *elskede?*"

"Wishful thinking." I gave a rueful laugh, a little of the old doubt creeping in. "I'm excited about my plan, but our funds are still low. Are people going to say I'm overspending, like Alessandra did?"

"Selah." Torden turned my chin to face him. "You've done all you set out to do, and more. And this plan is going to take time. But it's a good plan, and it is nothing like Alessandra's wastefulness. Your Council approved it. After all you saw in the Imperiya, they see how important this is."

He kissed me, and my very bones seemed to still, to steady.

How I loved this boy.

As he had done in Norge so many months before, Torden dipped his finger in the ink on the desk. In his own more angular writing, he wrote on my right arm the words I hadn't been able to write myself.

> *And*
> *they*
> *all*
> *lived*

And we had.

71

In the first week of the New Year, my stepmother and Pugh were convicted and imprisoned for their crimes.

A week later, Anya came back from a long walk with Skop in the first winter snow, happy tears in her eyes and a garnet ring sparkling on her finger. Cobie and I squeezed her so tightly she pushed us away, laughing that we'd cracked her ribs.

In two more months, my father returned home from New York, pink-cheeked and thirty pounds heavier. Victoria had grown her first tooth. I turned nineteen.

And six weeks after that, we had a wedding in Arbor Hall.

I wrapped my arms around Anya's shoulders as she waited in the Roots, but she wriggled away from me. "You're going to wrinkle my dress, you oaf." I laughed and fluffed her skirt.

It wasn't new, since we were economizing. But Anya looked beautiful in the rose-gold gown I'd worn the night Torden had first proposed in Asgard. Cobie, for once, wore white—a silk dress that had been my mother's. It fit her like a sail, which was to say, it suited her perfectly.

I wore my green lace dress, the one I'd worn in England. I'd gotten my heart broken by a boy who'd admired me in it.

So what? Hearts healed. Stories twisted and turned for the better.

Besides, it was a great dress.

When the bow hit the *hardingfele*'s strings, it was time to go. Cobie started up the stairs, a crown of valerian woven into her hair. Anya took Alfödr's arm, and I followed Cobie up to the ballroom.

Anya wore a crown of yarrow and myrtle, for love. Bear would've been proud that I'd looked up the flowers' meanings.

"What's this?" Torden nodded at my wreath, leading me up the aisle behind Cobie and Hermódr.

I smiled up at him. "Wallflower."

"No more," he whispered, kissing the engagement ring on my hand.

It meant faithfulness in adversity. And we would be, come what may.

At the end of the aisle, Torden went to stand behind Anya, along with the rest of his brothers. Bragi. Hermódr. Fredrik. Aleksei. Hodr. Only Vidarr and Váli had remained at home to protect Asgard.

Cobie joined me behind Skop, along with the rest of the crew.

I smiled at Daddy. He wore a linen suit—no more black for him—and a bright smile.

"Hello, everyone!" he called out. "And happy Arbor Day!"

The congregation responded with words of its roots and stretching toward the sky above, and I felt it like wind in my hair.

When Skop and Anya had said their vows, we danced and celebrated, and I couldn't believe how different Arbor Hall felt from a year ago.

I laughed the whole night. I did not hide.

Peter was talking to his father beneath a holly tree when I finally saw him. He returned my wave, smiling brightly at Victoria and me where I stood near the buffet table, bouncing her on my hip and choosing a dessert.

I had wondered if I'd come back and find Peter smaller, diminished somehow in my eyes. But he wasn't.

I was the one who had changed. I had gone, and I had come back. And all was as it should be.

Peter crossed to my side, hands in his pockets, grinning. He looked happy and relaxed, his hair a little longer, his shoulders a little broader. "Glad to see you home again."

"Me too," I agreed. "A lot's changed." I smiled—a real smile. Not the brittle thing I'd tried on for him the morning I set sail on the *Beholder*, but something easy. Comfortable, as we always should have been, if I had asked the right things of us. If I had been content with our friendship as it was.

And I knew now what love really felt like. So I could be.

"It certainly has." Peter's shoulders rounded a bit, as they always did when he was thinking. "You seem so . . . content."

"I am," I said. "I wouldn't change a thing."

His smile broadened; I glimpsed the gap between his teeth. "That's wonderful."

"Peter!" Captain Janesley called to his son, gesturing at a circle of people around him.

"Yes, sir! Be just a moment." He glanced back at me, still grinning. "I'll see you at Mass later?"

I nodded, waving back at Captain Janesley. "Say hello to your mother for me."

As he walked away, Victoria began to wail; she had a second tooth coming in. I tried to shush her, but Daddy swooped in.

"All right, then." He scooped her out of my arms, cooing.

"But I—" I protested, stretching after my sister. I must have looked worried, because Daddy grinned.

"Who do you think walked with you at night? Do you think Victoria is my first baby girl?" Daddy smiled down into my eyes. "I'm back, Selah. I'm me again."

I swallowed, and found I believed him.

It was almost a physical relief. Weight seemed to slide off my shoulders.

He winked at me and walked away, the sound of his laughter echoing off the marble walls and through the trees. Godmother went to him, trying to coax the baby away; I wasn't sure who would win that battle. Probably all three of them.

As I watched, Torden took my hand and led me beneath a willow. We stood there together a long moment, taking in the party, his arms around me. Anya looked radiant.

"I want this," he said in my ear. "I want this day for us."

"I do, too." I leaned my head back against his chest and looked up at him. "But your brothers are going to need you."

Hodr had come home, and with Týr passed, it turned out neither Vidarr nor Váli wanted to take his place. Hermódr was the new heir to Asgard. He would someday be its Shield. He would need his brothers as he prepared for a role he'd never expected would be his.

As we watched, Torden's father walked through the trees, speaking to Daddy.

Alfödr's heart had changed toward me and toward Skop. I'd overheard the *konge* apologizing to our new captain the night before.

He'd said that he was wrong to lay hands on him, to dismiss his suit without consideration. That Skop's bravery at Stupka-Zamok had proven him as worthy an ally as a king could wish. That his love for Anya was all any father could hope for.

"Have you heard anything about—" Torden arched his eyebrows down at me. I produced a letter from the pocket of my gown, biting my lip.

What if Torden balked, after all? What if he didn't want to wait so long?

But his face lit up. "You were accepted?" I nodded, and

Torden swung me off my feet and spun me around. "I am so, so proud of you."

"You don't think it's too long to wait?" I asked when he set me down. The letter crinkled as my grip tightened anxiously.

Torden smoothed it out, tucking it back in my pocket. Then he led me out to the dance floor, to join his sister and his brothers and my crew, our friends and our family and the ones who counted as both.

"Take all the time you need, *elskede*. Chase all your hopes. You have so much possibility before you." Torden fitted his chin above my head, his hands around my waist. Beneath the music and the party, I heard the beating of his heart. "I already know where my journey ends. It leads me home, to you."

And they all lived
happily
ever
after.
—Traditional ending

Glory be to the Father, and to the Son,
and to the Holy Spirit,
As it was in the beginning,
is now,
and ever shall be:
world without end.
Amen.
—Gloria Patri

All shall be well,
And all shall be well,
And all manner of thing shall be well.
—Julian of Norwich

Itt a vége, fuss el véle!
This is the end; run away with it.
—Traditional ending, Magyar tale

Epilogue

POTOMAC: ARBOR HALL

I stood on the pier, Daddy's hands on my shoulders, God-mother's hand in mine, Victoria babbling in her arms. The breeze was still warm; summer wasn't over yet.

And my eyes were on the horizon again.

It felt like a morning exceptionally well suited to *happily ever after.*

I snapped out of my daze in time to see Skop pretending to pitch my bags of soil overboard. "Stop that, you miscreant!" I bellowed.

"Shouldn't that be Captain Miscreant?" Bear asked, inquisitive, and Gwyn laughed.

Vishnu and Will were debating with Jeanne and Basile over barrels of something on the deck. J.J. scrambled around the rigging after Cobie. Andersen, Yasumaro, and Homer had disappeared into Homer's office, bickering about our course.

Everyone was here. Well—almost everyone.

"Captain Miscreant it is!" I agreed.

Yu had returned to Zhōng Guó after Daddy had recovered, but we'd kept corresponding; and Perrault had gone back to New York.

"Come and stay sometime," my protocol officer had said with a smile. "Perhaps you can teach me a thing or two."

Lang was away somewhere, exactly where he wanted to be. And soon, I would be, too.

"He's only *your* captain for a little while," Anya said to me reasonably, leaning on Skop's arm. "It's not as though you're staying on."

"Exactly," Veery pronounced dramatically. "Once she gets to Oxford with us, she'll join our circus of mad academics, her god the Oxford Don, her prayer the pint at her lips and the pen in her hand."

Daddy looked alarmed. "He's joking," I assured him hastily. "Veery's still on—a lot of pain medication. From his injury."

"Am not," Veery called, swanning into the galley.

"Shut up," I called. I seized Daddy's hands. "I'm going to be fine," I said confidently. "Really."

I had been accepted to study—to *read*, I corrected myself—law and literature at Oxford.

I was thrilled.

I was going to university. And someday, we would build one in Potomac.

The tsarytsya had built her empire by keeping families

apart, by keeping music and books out of her people's hands. I was going to do the opposite for my home.

But I was going to have an adventure first.

Being at home with my father well and himself again had reminded me that I was still just nineteen. Though I ached to leave him and Victoria and my godmother again so soon, though I'd think of Potomac every day, I wanted a learn a little more before I set to work, and I wanted to be young for a bit before I had to be old.

Daddy laughed and looked down at our joined hands, nodding at my ring. "Are you going to miss him terribly?"

"Yes," I admitted. "But we're visiting Asgard before term starts, so Anya can see her parents, and I'll see him then. And he'll come down to visit sometimes. And when I've finished school . . ."

When you've finished school, Torden had promised me the night before he left for Norge, *I'll come to you.*

When your stepmother has had some years to heal, I had agreed with him. *When Hodr doesn't need you so. When Hermódr feels ready.*

When you've done your duty to your family and your country, you will come to me.

Some rumors said I was stalling—that I had agreed to marry Torden because Alessandra had forced me, and now I wanted to back out.

But no one was forcing me to do anything. And I didn't care about what anyone thought of me anymore.

But for now, we would give ourselves time.

"Selah!" Cobie called. "Tide's going out. Time to go."

I kissed my father and my baby sister, wiping tears from my eyes. I let Godmother Althea say the prayer for travelers over me, and I boarded the ship with my friends. Bound for the old world. Bound for a new world. Bound across the sea, the sun bright before us.

For now, there was the adventure at hand.

Appendix

The following are tales, songs, and religious writings referenced in *The Beholder* and *The Boundless*. Their creators and translators are noted, where available.

THE BEHOLDER

Beowulf
translated by Lesslie Hall

"Cinderella; or, The Little Glass Slipper" (*Cendrillon; ou, La Petite Pantoufle de Verre*)
Charles Perrault, translation from *The Temple Classics for Young People* edition

"The Fairy of the Dell"
from *Welsh Fairy-Tales and Other Stories*, edited by P. H. Emerson

"Little Snow-White" (*Schneewittchen*)
Jacob and Wilhelm Grimm, translated by Logan Marshall

The Odyssey
Homer, translated by A. T. Murray

Sir Gawain and the Green Knight
translated by Rev. Ernest J. B. Kirtlan

"The Three Little Men in the Wood" (*Die drei Männlein im Walde*)
Jacob and Wilhelm Grimm, translated by Margaret Hunt

THE BOUNDLESS

The Faerie Queene
Edmund Spenser

Gloria Patri

The Lady of Alba's Lament for King Charles
John O'Tuomy, translated by Edward Walsh

"Little Red Cap" (*Rotkäppchen*)
Jacob and Wilhelm Grimm, translated by Edgar Taylor and
Marian Edwardes

"The Parting Glass"
Scottish traditional folk song

Revelations of Divine Love
Julian of Norwich

Acknowledgments

Stephanie Stein: Everyone talks about how hard the second book is to write; I was still more or less blindsided. Thank you for sticking with me through this year. Thank you for asking me the right questions and pushing me, all while being such a gentle cheerleader. This book is just about what I hoped it would be, and so much of that is down to you. Thank you, thank you, thank you.

Elana Roth Parker: You respond to every panicked text, every minutiae-laden email. I appreciate you more than I can say. Thank you for coaching me through debut year. Here's to many more wonderful years of working together.

Laura Dail Literary Agency, especially Laura Dail and Samantha Fabien: You guys are champs. Absolute pros. I'm so grateful to have you all looking out for me.

Team *Beholder/Boundless* at HarperCollins, including the tireless Louisa Currigan, Jon Howard, Gwen Morton, Erica

Ferguson, Kimberly Stella, Vanessa Nuttry, Kadeen Griffiths, Kris Kam, Caitlin Garing, Michael D'Angelo, Jane Lee, and Tyler Breitfeller: Thank you. Thank you. Thank you for fixing the details of this book that escaped me. YOU are the reason I can relax when I start panicking in the middle of the night. Thank you for telling readers about this story that means so much to me and writing copy for its cover. Thank you for arranging events and taking photographs and making audiobooks happen. You guys made my dreams come true. I am so thankful.

Chris Kwon, Alison Donalty, and the folks at Vault49: Your talent is such a gift and it absolutely astounds me. Thank you for making *The Boundless* look as magical and beautiful as it feels in my heart.

Natalia Morozova: Спасибо for answering my endless Russian and Ukrainian language questions and for your translation of the proverb. You have saved me so much frustration, and I am deeply grateful. Tom Thomson and Dr. Seamus Reilly: Many, many thanks for your aid with Irish Gaelic. Sally Anderson, for answering my French language questions: *Merci*, darling. As always, any errors are entirely my own.

Sasha, Sabrina Egan, and the rest of the Compass Georgetown staff: Thank you for the coffee and daily kind welcomes as I wrote this book. I appreciate you so much.

Brigid Kemmerer: Thank you for talking me out of every panic attack that had me knocking at your door. You are a good friend and a good person, and I'm so thankful to have you for a friend. Lizzy Mason, Katy Loutzenhiser, Sara Faring: It's been a joy to be a human life raft with you guys. I'm so proud of us. Katie Blair: I didn't expect the year to bring me you. But I'm so, so grateful it did. I love you, friend.

Anna and Sally, my Jelly Babies; Lei'La' Bryant, my Soulsie; #TeamElana (and especially Lily Meade, for your endless cheerleading and graphics wizardry); Abbey and Erin; and Eileen, Lelia, Rebecca, Rosie, Amanda, Lauren, Trish, Sally, Taylor, Amber, and Jeremiah, my One More Page family: Thank you for all your support and friendship and for helping me survive this year. I wouldn't have made it without you.

Grace Downtown's Georgetown CG: Thank you for being home to me. I love you all so much.

Stephinephrine, Laura, Jensy, Joanna, and Hannah, my Pod: I never feel alone, knowing you guys are there. You are my small, constant joy. I love you all.

Dormineys, Shafers, Gardners, Sernas, Andersons, Simkinses, Burkhalters, Stiglishes, Hayeses, Bischoffs: I am unimaginably lucky to have you, especially my Mamaw, Grandmother and Granddaddy (Washing Machine), Momma and Daddy, Zack, Chelsie, Cohen, and Callan. Y'all are every good thing in my life. Thank you.

Wade: Thank you for never letting go. Thank you for being with me through every magical day, every meltdown, every disappointment and adventure and hard slog. You're the person I want to do it all with. I love you.

To my Father: All glory to you. As it was in the beginning, is now, and ever shall be, world without end, amen, alleluia.